The Glassfire Serpent: *Ashes*

Also By James Fahy

The Changeling series:

Isle of Winds *(book 1)*
The Drowned Tomb *(book 2)*
Chains of Gaia *(book 3)*
The Glassfire Serpent: Embers *(book 4)*

Phoebe Harkness series:

Hell's Teeth *(book 1)*
Crescent Moon *(book 2)*
Paper Children *(book 3)*

The GLASSfiRE SERPENT
Ashes

JAMES FAHY

LUME BOOKS

LUME BOOKS

First published in 2021 by Lume Books
30 Great Guildford Street,
Borough, SE1 0HS

ISBN 978-1-83901-425-3

Typeset using Atomik ePublisher from Easypress Technologies

www.lumebooks.co.uk

For my mum

Who jumped out from behind doors to scare me when I was seven,
And who still jumps out from behind doors to scare me in her seventies.
The person who taught me to play all my life long and never get old.
And who never showed anything but support
in my choices and my paths chosen.
I wouldn't have the fantasy in me to write these books if it wasn't for you.

Tucker

1

High Places and Hidden Paths

By the time dawn had broken, and the sky filled with salmon-pink clear light, the four companions had finally cleared the tree line. The land had climbed, becoming increasingly vertical over the last few miles, rockier and bare, and the trees thinner. Although they were tired, none of them thought it prudent to stop and rest until the dark and misty clutches of One Horn Forest were far behind them. Karya assured them that the unicorns would not follow beyond the borders of the forest. They were creatures of darkness and shadow, and the rising sun would drive them back down to the fog and the shaded damp hollows of the swamps. Onward and upwards, into light and fresh air was the clearest route to safety.

By morning, there could be no doubt that the companions had reached the mountains beyond the forest. High and rocky hills of brown and grey stone reared up before and around them, revealing more majestic splendour as the mist burned away. Looking back, Robin was surprised to see how far they had come already. The forest lay spread out below them, a sprawl of trees glimpsed in a great valley of creeping mist. It was larger than he'd imagined. From here in the hills he could not see where they had entered from the River Dish. Only treetops stretched away, a great tangled flow casting shadows beneath it, home to things best suited for the darkness.

"If we're not coming *down* mountains, we're going *up* them," Woad noted. His head had finally cleared in the last hour or so of walking, and he was back to his old self, seemingly none the worse for his encounter with the hungry bog hag. The others had questioned him about his Skyfire as they trekked onwards, but the faun could only shrug. He didn't feel any different, he told them. And he had stopped giving off little random sparks and fits of flickering electricity some time ago. He assured them that he felt fit as a fiddle, which led to a thoughtful discussion on why that particular instrument was traditionally considered so particularly hale and hearty.

"These mountains don't seem anything like the Floreo near Titania's Tears," Robin mused as they climbed onwards. "That was like a picture postcard of the Alps. This is a lot more …"

"Deadly?" Woad nodded in serious agreement. "Rocks and cliffs and bits to drop off and fall from and such. Proper mountainy mountains these ones. The kind that want you dead and don't pretend otherwise. No messing about."

"I believe we are in the Caeners," Karya suggested, looking thoughtfully up at the pale jagged peaks looming intimidatingly out of the mist. Beyond the foothills, vast shadowy shapes promised high and broken peaks ahead. "Quite a distinctive range. They pass down from the north-east, skirt the One Horn Forest and continue south, all the way down to the very northern tip of the Elderhart, I believe."

"The Corners?" Henry sounded more than a little breathless. He had snapped off a thick twig earlier, before they had left the treeline below. It was almost as tall as him and he was using it as a walking stick as they made their way up the increasingly steep and rocky ground. "Weird name for some mountains, if you ask me. But hey, as long as all we have to deal with up here are rocks and cliffs and places to fall off, like Woad says, I'm happy." He glanced over his shoulder at the forest, now far below them. "Seriously. Two minutes in the Netherworlde. Two! And I'm surrounded by cannibal swamp monsters and chased by a pack of slobbering hell-beasts. Why is it never twinkly imps? Eh? That's what I want to know. Just *once* can we not have twinkly imps?"

"What *I* want to know," Woad said, leaping deftly on top of an outcropping of stone, "is why your hair has turned to snow, boss." He hadn't been able to take his eyes off Karya since he had shaken off his sleepiness. "You look like a grandma. Did you leave your colours back in the human world?"

Karya shot him a look. "Hilarious," she said, swatting at him as she passed the rock he perched upon. "I feel like Hestia's photocopier. The one that's always running out of ink. Still can't believe she accepted that particular Christmas present from Mr Drover, but honestly, I've never seen a woman work a machine further into the ground. How many magazine recipes does one person *need* to organise into ring binders?"

"She copies and collects the agony aunt pages too," Henry noted.

"Well, anyway," Karya shrugged. "That's how I feel. Overworked and out of ink, and full of carefully organised agony, that's what. Every time I do … anything." She tucked a stray strand of white hair behind her ear. "It's as though there's less of me left."

"Stop *doing* things then," Robin suggested. "At least for now. Until we can get you … sorted."

She scowled at him.

"That printer of Hestia's has got it in for my dad," Henry observed, oblivious to the bickering. "It's always buggering up. And it's bad tempered too, like you, Karya. Only works when it wants to. She's always got him fiddling with it. Half the time the computer can't find it. Drives my dad mental." He shook his head in wonder, adopting a rather good impression of Mr Drover's voice. "Whatever that blasted well means, Henry, my lad!" he grumbled. "I mean, it's right there, on the desk! It's not like it's hard to find! Damn it all, why doesn't anyone just write letters anymore? Harrumph harrumph!" He shrugged, resuming his normal voice. "Anyway, whenever it's playing up, he just turns it off and on again."

Robin shook his head at Henry's prattling as they scrambled upwards through the rocks. "Are you suggesting that we help Karya get better by switching her off and on again? Rebooting?"

"That sounds most unpleasant," Karya smirked, peering at them both. "I'll be the one giving a booting if there's one to be given. Booting you lot off this charming mountainside. Besides, we have concerns other than my impeccable sense of style, namely what we are going to do about saving Jack,"

"*And* Ffoulkes," Henry bristled slightly, kicking a small loose stone that rolled away down the rugged hillside. "He got captured too, remember."

Robin coughed a little in the rather tense silence that ensued. "We're doing this to save the both of them," he said, thickly, after a moment. "We need a way into Dis, and our only lead requires us to find this missing noble lady, clues for which are scattered up here, according to my mystery source."

Karya, ignoring Henry with determined aplomb, nodded her head at the steeper land ahead. "So that's the plan, to climb way up here? Only, if this mist doesn't clear up soon, it's going to be harder going. It's getting seriously craggy around here. The Caeners are not the most forgiving of ranges. Did you know that this is where the Isle of Aeolius came from?"

"The Isle of Winds?" Woad perked up. "Ahh, that brings back memories. Remember when we rescued you there, Henryboy?" He jogged Henry in the ribs. "Back when you were kidnapped, for the first time I mean, not the second, and we only had two Grimms in the world to worry about?"

"*You* were the one who needed rescuing this time," Henry spluttered. "And not for the first time, I might add. When you're not being cooked by Shrek's uglier brother, you're drowning in a lake or being dragged off through the snow to be Mr Ker's pet!"

"Yes, *that* isle," Karya said loudly, deliberately drowning out their bickering. "It was a mountain-top town here, once. The satyrs, scholars and masters of the Tower of Wind, they moved the whole thing far out to sea. Didn't leave much behind, I don't think."

"Except for *maybe* a library," Robin chimed in. "And that's the plan, for what it's worth." He filled them all in as they climbed higher through the morning, into the rocks and mist, dawn light burning away at the landscape around them, golden and sparkling mist glowing in every dip and hollow. Told them of events in the Sorrows, his odd visions and memories, and the confusing hex message in the woods.

Seek swift wings at the library. Karya thought carefully about this. "I don't see how that helps us, but if the satyrs *did* leave anything behind, they've certainly kept it very quiet and very secret." She looked upwards. More of the mountains had come into view as the haze burned slowly away. They stood tall sentinels against the sky, sharp and cruel, a ragged and sublime serration, burning in the sunlight. On the very highest peaks, white snow glimmered and blew from the pinnacles like sugar caught in the high winds, trailing out and making wedding veils for the procession of peaks.

"Secret from us might mean secret from Eris too," Robin mused. "There might be something we can learn. Maybe 'swift wings' means they have some kind of flying contraption? Something that could carry us from here all the way to Dis. We know things like that exist here in the Netherworlde."

"Or maybe they have a phoenix," Henry suggested. He shrugged as the others looked at him doubtfully. "Maybe they're not all extinct. I know legend holds that this noble Fire family owned the last one and that Eris already confiscated it, but you never know. We found one feather, right? Maybe we could find another. Maybe *that's* what Strigoi is after, too."

"Strigoi and the Grimm are after Lady Tinda Calescent, if I'm any judge." Karya shook her head. "Or something she possesses or has hidden, at least. I bet that pawnbroker's shop isn't the only place the forces of Eris have turned upside down in their quest for lost treasure. I wonder what could be so important to them? To Nyx, in particular?"

"What I want to know," Woad said, his tone thoughtful, "perhaps the greatest mystery of all, is why no-one has bothered to tell this faun about the existence of a photocopier at Erlking before now."

Everyone eyed the boy carefully.

Henry spoke for all of them. "Because, Woad, none of us want bleary black and white photocopied faun butt-cheeks sliding under our doors at night."

"Or every portrait in the gallery on the fourth floor replaced with them," Karya nodded seriously.

"Or faun butt-cheek leaflets being fly-tipped all over Barrowood village, getting us all in trouble."

The faun made a disgruntled face. "None of you are any fun!" he sulked.

They all continued walking, leaving the peeved blue creature behind; Woad tapping his foot with the particular frustration of a prankster foiled. When it became apparent that they were not waiting for him, he kicked a stone grumpily off a cliff and scurried after them.

"It's not like I don't do squats!"

As the day wore on and everyone's energy wore down, they kept any further theories about their current mysteries – and thoughts on how to tell Hestia the news that her prized photocopier was no longer secret and safe – to themselves. They saved their breath for the climb.

The grass had long since given out to bare, loose scree, and by the time the sun was directly overhead, the wind practically whistled around them. At this altitude, they had begun to see the first signs of frost and ice, turning the barren landscape around them both beautiful and treacherous.

Occasionally, Robin would stop, consult his compass, and redirect them up one trail or another, along one particularly precipitous ledge or through a narrow canyon between ever more towering rocks. One Horn Forest was now little more than a smudge in the haze.

The wide vista of the Netherworlde, with its rolling empty spaces and distant glittering rivers threading through the hills below, was laid out beneath them like a spread blanket.

It was strange for Robin to see such a vast scope of wild and untamed wilderness. Back in the human world, even from the highest mountain he knew of in Britain, there were always *some* signs of civilisation. The distant fields were often patchworks of hedgerows or dry-stone walls. Or the hills and dales – even on the highest moors – were divided by a lace-work of black tarmac motorways. And the sky always held the tell-tale threads of aeroplane trails, reminding them that they were never too far from others.

But here, the world was wide and unapologetically lacking the stamp of human touch. No fingerprint of humanity marred the wilderness laid out beneath them.

They could well have been the only four people in the world.

The higher in the mountains they travelled, the colder it became, despite the clear blue bowl of the spring sky above them, marred with only the occasional wispy cirrus. Henry soon began to grumble about leaving his winter coat somewhere back down in the woods, and Karya wrapped her coat of animal skins tighter around her. Of all the companions, she looked most exhausted. Robin had seen the girl hike halfway across the Netherworlde before now without ever breaking a sweat or raising a word of complaint. Now ... although she said nothing, it was evident that she was struggling.

The chill wind cut through Robin's clothes too, making him shiver, and he couldn't help but think about every documentary he had ever watched about people getting stranded on mountainsides and dying of exposure. That would just be typical, he thought. To survive Strigoi and shadow spiders, falling from the highest waterfall in the world, bog hags and unicorns, only to die from not wrapping up warm. Gran would meet him in the afterlife with a smug "I told you so" look on her face.

The only one of them who didn't seem remotely bothered by the increasing cold, as they picked their way higher into the spiky towering rocks and frosty valleys, was Woad, who had never yet met a weather he didn't like. It was Woad who came up with a solution to their chilly predicament as the afternoon wore on, and, shivering in the relentless and increasingly violent wind, they tried to find a sheltered spot to rest.

They eventually found a place between three large boulders, which served to keep out much of the wind. Less essential, but a definite boon, was the fact it also afforded them wide views back down the mountainside to the distant landscape below, a window onto the Netherworlde. Woad, after much prolonged persuasion, convinced Henry to give up his beloved walking stick for the greater good. Henry grumbled to himself with chattering teeth as the faun set about snapping the wood into several pieces over his knee.

Robin suspected that Henry's reluctance to part with his walking stick was less to do with it affording him any stability and assistance in the climb, and much more to do with the fact that he had been secretly pretending to be a wandering wizard with a staff for much of the day.

When they had a roughly circular heap of sticks, Woad stood back, hands on his hips with pride at the makeshift campfire. He looked expectantly at Robin.

"What?" Robin realised that the others were also looking at him. Karya had her arms folded against the cold, her coat whipping about her legs.

"Tower of Fire, Rob," Henry prompted him. "Come on, you did it during the eclipse. Ffoulkes might well be a fraud about being all lah-di-dah, but even if he is as common born as I am, and not lord of the manor like he pretends, he did still teach you fire magic, right? We all saw it." He rubbed his hands together, shaking in the wind and stamping on the cold ground. "Get one going, we need to warm up before the sun goes down or bits of me are going to start dropping off."

"It's late afternoon," Robin gestured at the sky. "We're stopping for dinner, not for the night."

"Night falls fast in the mountains," Karya observed. "Much faster than in any lowlands. Something that has caught out countless explorers in high places before now. We probably only have another hour until the light fails completely, and it only gets more treacherous ahead. We don't want to be caught out in the open in shadowy twilight. The last thing I need is a Scion snapping his ankle or sliding down some loose scree off a cliff edge into oblivion."

Woad had dropped to all fours and was rummaging through Robin's pack eagerly.

"There's some sausages in here," his voice came, rather muffled and echoey as his head was entirely within the knapsack. "Old lady Hestia packed enough for a month."

Robin swallowed and looked at the pile of twigs made from Henry's staff. The pyramid of wood seemed to look back at him expectantly.

Okay, he thought, *I can do this.* He shook himself mentally. He was the Scion, after all. He had used the Towers of Air, Earth and Water to tremendous effect in the last couple of days. What was Fire, except another string to his bow? He had to stop doubting and second guessing himself and trust in his own capabilities.

Holding out a hand in the direction of the sticks, he clutched his mana stone with his free hand.

"Fire is a symphony," he muttered under his breath. He closed his eyes and concentrated, trying to block out the biting chill and noise of the wind and to ignore the expectant stares of his friends. *Focus on your mana*, he told himself. *Try to find the music within.*

He tapped into his mana and threw it invisibly out across the air towards the sticks, with a grunt of effort and determination.

There was a deafening boom and an enormous fireball erupted upwards, knocking all four of them backwards with a blast of light and heat. The fireball climbed swiftly into the air, a mini mushroom cloud of roaring flames. The twigs were incinerated, blasted to charcoal smithereens in an instant and sent careening in all directions like meteoric shrapnel.

The great fireball dissipated above them in the air with a sucking roar, leaving behind it a cloud of thick black smoke which was whipped away on the wind almost instantly, and smeared across the mountain.

Robin stood frozen; arm still outstretched. His fingers were smoking slightly, like candles just blown out. His hand was black and sooty. The others were struggling back to their feet, having each been knocked back against the rocks, coughing and spluttering.

"A symphony, eh?" Henry wheezed; his voice hoarse. His tangle of brown hair had been blown straight back from his face, which was now ringed with soot.

"That was a very loud note, Pinky," Woad giggled. He wiggled his fingers in his ears, having been slightly deafened by the explosion.

"Sorry," Robin said in a very small and shocked voice. He was still staring at the spot where the campfire had been, which was now merely a blasted patch of black rock, still scorched and smoking. There was a small crater melted into the rock, hissing.

"I think it's clear that the issue here is certainly not a lack of *mana*," Karya brushed smouldering embers from her snowy hair. "But rather a lack of *control*, yes?"

"I … I didn't expect …"

"I've got another idea." The girl waved at him dismissively, as though people almost incinerated their friends on a regular basis. She retrieved Robin's satchel from where it had been thrown in the blast and rummaged through it until she drew out a large red jewel, half the size of her fist.

"Remember this?" She shook it lightly in the air, showing it to the others. "Ffoulkes gave it to you for Christmas, Robin."

"The cubey corny boblia." Woad nodded, wisely.

"Cubic cornucopia," Karya corrected. "It's a way to carry an element, if you remember. Your gift from Ffoulkes."

She passed it to Robin carefully while Woad and Henry went off in search of more sticks. There were no trees this high in the mountains, but the occasional scrubby bush clung to the steep slopes. They had passed plenty of these during their ascent. Tangled and wiry things, like fixed tumbleweed. Woad and Henry were gone a while, and the sky had indeed begun to glow with the anticipation of evening. Robin inspected the gemstone, turning it this way and that, watching it catch the light in its crimson facets, while Karya sat leaning against a rock with her cloak pulled tight around her to keep out the wind.

Robin was fairly certain she fell asleep, bundled up in her fur cocoon. He didn't mention it. She clearly needed rest. Woad and Henry hadn't suggested she come with them to look for firewood. Robin hadn't wanted to leave her alone.

She was awake when the two boys returned, clearly pretending she had never passed out in the first place, and once a small but bushy new tepee had been laid with the meagre twigs and branches they had managed to forage nearby, Karya swept her hand at it.

"I just … throw it?" Robin sounded doubtful.

"Ffoulkes told you it was already loaded," Karya nodded. "Hopefully not with very *much*, but give it a go, before it really does start to get dark."

Robin lightly tossed the red gem into the sticks, its facets glinting in the sunset as it tumbled through the air. It landed with a flash and the wood and twigs were instantly alight with a soft *whoomp*.

The fire grew and crackled merrily as though it had been burning and well fed for an hour at least.

"Well, that's handy," Robin admitted with raised eyebrows. He was impressed. "Like having a campfire in your pocket at all times."

"And when you're done, you just fish it back out." Woad approached the happy campfire with a string of sausages draped around his neck like a pearl necklace. "It will suck up the flames, and keep them safe inside for next time."

"And hopefully avoid any further explosions that could have caused a huge avalanche and killed us all," Henry said cheerfully. "Honestly, my pyromaniac Fae, if I had any eyebrows left, I'd be frowning at you right now."

By the time they had cooked and eaten the sausages and had drunk from the fresh water bottles they found neatly packed in Robin's bottomless bag, the light truly had faded from the sky. It could not have been late, but so tall were the mountains that they blocked out the sun as soon as it dipped behind their ragged peaks, sending long dark shadows stretching out to the hills and valleys below. The sky slowly turned to gold, and then to blood, as Karya and Woad bickered back and forth about whether to heat some of the water to make a herb tea and warm them all some more.

Woad was all for it, determined that his recent obsession with herb-lore made him an expert, and that the berries of these scrubby bushes high in the Caeners mountains would provide for them a brew both delicious and restorative. Karya argued against this, pointing out that she was fairly certain they were lichberries, which could potentially be wonderfully tasty, but also have the slight downside of poisoning them all to a swift and foaming-at-the-mouth-in-agony death.

Robin munched on their meal quietly and thoughtfully, watching Henry poke at the flames with a skinny stick, and looking out over the red sky which, after being clear all day, was now beginning to thread with long clouds, ethereal fingers reaching across the heavens above them all. As night deepened, the landscape below them was still bright, painted in that particular thick golden light that is only ever seen when the sun spills sideways in the evening. Fox-wedding weather, Gran had always called it – dark skies and bright grounds – though he had no idea why.

Robin was thinking about Jackalope and Ffoulkes. It had already been too long since they were taken. Days and nights spent on the river and in the forest, back and forth between worlds, and now another day spent climbing into these mountains. Night now approached again, a relentless march of time, running away from them. Pyrenight, he knew, was drawing closer, and his friends' lives hung in the balance while they dallied here in the frosty hills having a barbeque.

Night fell, peppering the sky with more stars than he had ever seen, and plunging the breath-taking views they had enjoyed all day into deep, yawning darkness.

Rested and warmed, they packed away their things as they finished the last of their supplies. Wiping the grease from his face with the back of his hand, Robin was just about to interrupt the others' quiet conversation to suggest they try and press on, rather than stay here a moment longer, when a light in the hills below them suddenly caught his eye.

Peering down the slope, at first he thought he had imagined it. The moon and stars were the only light, appearing intermittently between the now black fingers of long cloud. But this had not been a cold light.

Searching the darkness from their camp at the lip of the cliff, he saw another … and then another. They were some way off, back towards the forest they had been travelling from all day, but the more Robin stared, the clearer he could see them. A procession of yellow pinpricks moving in a rough and weaving line between the rocks below.

"What is that?" he said, getting to his feet and edging carefully further towards the lip of the slope their campfire perched atop, wary of missing his footing in the darkness and stumbling off the edge. "There's something … a lot of somethings, moving down there. Not far back the way we came."

Henry was at his side, still clutching half a burnt sausage. "Fret-olas," he muttered dramatically, chewing. "What do your elf-eyes see?"

"There are people, following us from the direction of the forest," Robin realised. He had a sudden chill that had little to do with the wind or the night air. In the spilled ink of the craggy foothills below them, it looked like a procession of lanterns or flaming torches. Weaving their way through the hills and gullies.

"Those are not *people*." Karya and Woad had joined them, and the four of them stood with the fire at their back, looking warily as one down the slopes.

"Peacekeepers!" Woad hissed. Robin glanced at him in concern, then stared back down. They were too far away to make out, but the shadowy shapes with their bobbing lights were picking their way upwards and onwards. A centipede procession.

"Are you sure?" he whispered, not quite sure why he was keeping his voice low. There was no way anyone could have heard him from that far away.

The faun nodded. "I can smell them from here," he said, sniffing for emphasis. "Dark mana of Mr Ker. Puppet-boys must have been tracking us ever since we went over the waterfall, Pinky. Must have followed us all the way through the woods here while we were distracted getting to know the locals."

"Is Strigoi with them?" Robin wanted to know. He had a sudden mental image of coming face to face with the Wolf of Eris, up here in the mountains. They had the advantage of the high ground here. He imagined using the Tower of Earth to send a landslide down, crushing the loathsome man once and for all.

"No," Woad shook his head. "No wolf-demon here, can always sense him more than smell him anyway. My bet is that he's gone off to Dis with his prisoners, wagging his tail to lick the back of Eris' hand and be given a doggy-treat." His voice was filled with unusual scorn.

"Grimm one is here, though."

"Mr Knight?" Robin still couldn't make out a single figure below. He was, however, acutely aware that their merry little campfire here in the heights would be eminently visible to anyone looking up at the mountain, even from miles away. "Mr Nyx, I mean."

"Spider-hands is coming," Woad confirmed. "I reckon he's been sent to collect the rest of the Erlking pack. Worth more as a full set, aren't we?" He raised his little blue hands. "Well, they're in for a surprise, 'cause they don't know there's a faun here, with Skyfire now!"

A single, rather small and pathetic crackle of lightning flickered from one of his thumbs to his forefinger, like a small white moth. It fluttered out with a sad *ptht* noise.

Woad grinned bashfully and hid his hands behind his back. "Well, I haven't quite figured it out yet, but …"

Karya cut him off. "It would be very unwise to meet a Grimm out here in the wilds, especially in the dark. Any of them. Nyx is as bad as Strife himself. Worse, maybe. At least Strife usually fights fair. He's upfront about being a stone-cold bogeyman. Nyx is like poison laced with sugar. He can get inside people's heads with those spiders of his. Tells people what they want to hear, offers them what he knows they desire most and bends them to his will. Leaves them hollowed out husks." She shivered a little in distaste.

"You've met this lovely chap before?" Henry asked, squinting at the distant and silent procession of peacekeepers. "It sounds like it."

Karya's face was unreadable. "All of the Grimms have their … *areas of interest*," she sneered. "Strife loves power, Peryl craves attention, Ker is simply a fan of violence for violence's sake. But this one?" She was watching the distant line of lights creeping upwards into the hills, her eyes narrowed. "Nyx is known as the alchemist." She hugged herself. "He likes to … *meddle* with things. Tamper with nature. It was he who turned the dryads into the swarm. It was his hand that corrupted the centaurs, made them the mad beasts they are today. He doesn't see people as people, he sees them as experiments. I knew him in Dis … I think." She shook her head, as though to loosen her thoughts. "My memory is jumbled. But there was a pool. And a circle … somewhere high … and *he* was always there. The taskmaster of Eris, twisting the world a piece at a time to fit her dark vision."

Something in her words jogged a memory in Robin. The journal they had found in his office in London. There had been something like a pool and trees sketched there, too. He remembered making a joke about the book's owner being a keen landscape gardener.

And when he had touched the fossilised phoenix feather, in his jumble of visions, hadn't he glimpsed a pool with trees all around, sickly and filled with spiderwebs? Spiders like those Nyx commanded.

"He and I have history somewhere …" Karya was frowning so much she looked pained. "I can feel it, like a wound, but I can't *see* it." She snorted down her nose, frustrated. "My memories are like shattered glass. I only know I hate him more than any other Grimm. I feel that in every aching bone in my body."

"Wait until Aunt Irene finds out who he really is," Robin said. "Nyx is Knight, pretending to be human. She'll sort him out then." He shook his head in confusion. "Thought what the Grimms are doing running around with human-world companies in the first place, I just don't understand. Sire Holdings? Why on earth does the Empress of the Netherworlde care about the mortal realm at all?"

"It's a reflection," Henry said suddenly, coming to a realisation. The others looked at him, questioning. He still held his stub of sausage, which quivered in his fingertips as he stared out over the landscape with a face lit up by epiphany.

"The worlds," the boy explained, rolling his hands. "Two worlds, reflecting each other, we already know this, right? Karya, you said it once, like two sides of one coin. Sire Holdings is the same. It's a reflection!"

Robin shook his head. "What are you on about?"

Henry shook his half-eaten sausage at his friend. "What's *Sire* backwards, numbskull?"

"Eris," Woad whispered with wonder.

"So, the empress seeks to extend her influence to both worlds, not just the Netherworlde," Karya mused. "Vying with us to gather the Shards of the Arcania, racing us to find this lost book that's going to show us all the secret of Titania and Oberon's last mystery. She's not content with destroying just one world. She means to spread chaos to both."

The thought was a worrying one. Robin tried to imagine the Grimms controlling the human world from the shadows of powerful business, from government, from every corner of society. It didn't seem impossible.

"Whatever Strigoi and the Grimm were searching for in the Sorrows, whatever Lady Calescent has that's so valuable …" Robin said, shaking his head. "Eris obviously thinks it will help with her plans."

"*Half a heart*," Henry said, looking at Karya. "That's what you said, back at Christmas when you had your funny turn after your romantic stroll with Jackalope."

The girl looked flabbergasted. "It wasn't a romantic stroll, you ninny.

He was upset and missing his brother. It consumes him. Just because he doesn't talk to any of you about it …"

"But he confided in you?" Robin asked.

Karya looked a little uncomfortable. "I think we're similar," she said. "Both outsiders, both spent time under Eris' thumb. We both carry a lot of regret. That's all it is."

Henry looked as though he had more to say but decided against it, instead tossing away his remaining bite of sausage from the cliff, as though his appetite had fled.

"Half a heart is a strange thing to say," Robin said, steering them back to Karya's vision.

"I say a lot of strange things though, don't I?" she admitted. The girl looked as clueless as anyone else. "Maybe I really do need rebooting."

Standing around spitballing about Eris' grand plans was all well and good, however it wasn't helping their current situation.

Karya watched the silent line of unseen peacekeepers weaving ever closer to their camp, then looked up at her companions. "Whatever the case, we absolutely cannot meet Nyx here," she insisted. "My mana is on the fritz, Robin's is … powerful but unpredictable, and you two …" She looked to Woad and Henry, who both smiled back at her.

"Well …" She seemed uncharacteristically diplomatic. "You're just full of untapped potential, I'm sure, but if four more spider cocoons head back to Dis, there'll be no one left to save Jack and Ffoulkes. We can't risk a confrontation here."

There was the sharp snap of a twig behind them, from the deep shadows of the boulders beyond the fire. All four jumped and turned.

"Then all of you would do well to get off the mountainside," a voice said from beyond the flames. A figure stepped forward into the light. It must have been watching them for some time.

For a second, Robin's heart leapt with recognition. He was sure it was Phorbas, his old tutor, somehow freed from the enchanted blade he haunted and stepping forward into the light. But an instant later, when the figure approached the fire, he saw he was mistaken.

The newcomer was indeed a satyr – half man, half goat – but the fur of his legs and hooves was darker than Phorbas' had been. His skin was lighter and his beard, pointed and neat, was heavily streaked with grey. He looked old. Milky eyes sat in a weathered and deeply-lined face.

The aged satyr wore a thick fur cape slung around his shoulders and he was leaning on a tall staff. His hooves glinted in the firelight as he regarded the visitors suspiciously.

"Four children, or something like them," he said, his attention roaming over each of the companions one at a time with wary interest. "Making enough light, noise and racket on my mountain to draw even the hordes of Eris to us, it would seem. The empress does not wander in these high rocks. We are safe and hidden up here, left in peace – although it seems you four have led trouble to the door."

"You're a satyr!" Henry pointed at the stranger. "Where the bloody hell did you pop up from?"

"Observant, this one," the satyr replied. His eyes settled on Robin, singling him out as the rogue pyromaniac of the group. "My people have lived here in secret and peace since the war began," he said. "That is, we did until *someone* set off a large fireball a short while back, large enough that we saw it even from our home above." He glanced back at the sheer and shadowy mountain behind them, and then down past the children at the peacekeeper procession, which was still some way off but moving closer with a kind of lazy inevitability. "And we are not the only ones who saw it, it would seem. Hardly subtle of you."

Robin stepped forward. "Are you from the library?" he asked, oddly already certain it was true. "You are, aren't you? The town of the satyrs, it isn't *all* gone, is it? Not all sent off to sea with the Isle of Winds. Some of you really did stay here."

The satyr seemed to be studying them carefully, weighing up if they were a threat or a nuisance. He reached up and scratched absently at the short nubbin horns which lay nestled in his curls of greying hair.

"Should I decide to leave you here …" He considered. "Those cursed scarecrows will take you and leave." It was clear to all that this was an outcome the satyr considered acceptable. "If I *don't* leave you here, who knows what will happen?" He seemed thoughtful, as though weighing his options lightly, as if deciding what to have for lunch perhaps.

"We don't mean to bring danger to your doorstep," Karya said, very formally. "But you are right. If we stay out here on the mountain, we're in trouble. If you can help us … is it far to your home?" She looked up at the steep darkness. Above them, the landscape became impossibly sheer. It was doubtful anything other than a mountain goat, or a satyr, could climb much further. Definitely not in the dark. "Is it possible to get up the mountain, even? In the dark, I mean. Without killing ourselves?"

The satyr shook his head. "*Up* the mountain? Of course not, don't be absurd. It's sheer cliffs and pinnacles above us." He gestured behind himself with his staff. "*Into* the mountain – now that's a different matter." His eyes flashed in the firelight. "There are tunnels. Hidden well, perhaps even well enough to be missed by the empty eye sockets of peacekeepers."

"I was told to come here," Robin said, hoping to win the trust of this stranger. If he could help them get off the mountain before Nyx and the peacekeepers arrived …

"Yes, yes, all things are foretold," the satyr replied, sounding a little weary at the thought. "It's all written down somewhere, no doubt."

"I was told to seek swift wings at the library," Robin said, trying not to sound too urgent but acutely aware that every second they stood here chatting, their pursuers were getting closer.

The satyr blinked at him, looking extremely thoughtful. "Swift wings, eh? Told to seek? That's interesting. By whom?"

"We're not really sure," Henry said, with what he hoped was a winning smile.

The satyr blew air down his nose, as though the four of them were a nuisance. He took one last, rather unconcerned look down the mountain, then turned away. A moment later he raised a hand, beckoning for them to follow him.

"Well, whoever it was who sent you searching, you have found what you are looking for," he said. "I am Celerialae. Follow me. The tunnels will take us to my home, though my sight says they may bring others, too."

None of them needed asking twice. Woad reached into the fire as the others hastily picked up their things, swiping the cubic cornucopia gem, immediately extinguishing it with a whoosh. As Robin stowed it away in his pack in the sudden darkness, he glanced at Karya.

"I don't get it," he whispered. "Can we trust this guy? What have we found?"

Karya nodded. "You can trust a satyr more than you can trust a Grimm," she said. "And either way, it's a moot point. We need to get off this mountain face. But his name, Scion. Celerialae is high tongue. In the

23

common tongue it means 'swift wings'. Clearly, this is the person you were directed to seek out."

Robin peered after the receding satyr, disappearing into the gloom between the huge boulders, little more than a rough shadow wrapped in a fur cape.

"Why would a half-man, half-goat be called 'Swiftwings?'" he wondered. "It's not as though he's covered in feathers."

Karya looked at him with withering weariness. "And I suppose every human girl named Rose or Lily is covered in petals, are they?"

She had a point, Robin supposed.

The satyr led them swiftly away from the edge of the slope and through a field of rocks, his hooves clacking sharply on the loose earth. He didn't look back once to check if the children were following him and, after a short walk, they reached a sheer patch of stone covered with scrubby brushes. The bushes concealed an entrance, a crack in the rock, which was so narrow that even Woad had to turn sideways as they passed inside. Within, as the bushes fell back into place, hiding them away from the evening world without, they found themselves in a passageway stretching away into blackness. Soon this opened up and widened, spilling them into a long tunnel which sloped up steeply through the dark rock. As they followed their strange guide into the depths of the mountain in single file, Robin reached out and ran a hand along the wall. The rock was cool and dry – carved seamlessly, as far as he could tell. This was no simple mine shaft, crudely hacked into the mountainside. This was strange and unusual craftsmanship. There were tall steps cut neatly into the floor at regular intervals at places where the constant upward slope through the smooth tunnel became too steep. The shadows in here were deep and cold, but they were not left in blackness as they burrowed upwards through the mountain.

"What are these things?" Henry asked, breaking the silence as they passed a softly glowing clump of crystals. They were embedded in the wall at roughly head height, spiky outgrowths that emitted a soft glow, which seemed to cycle back and forth from blue to green as they watched.

"Celestite crystals, I believe." Karya peered at them, the light reflecting on her face like moonlight through water. "Though not any type I've seen before. This isn't natural luminosity, it's an enchantment – and a pretty ancient one at that."

The entire tunnel was lit at regular intervals by these glowing, unearthly crystals, each set back in a recess carved into the dark stone. It soon became apparent that they were not natural formations. They had been set deliberately, or grown, in place, in order to illuminate the absolute darkness within the rock. The lights stretched away endlessly ahead of them in a procession, as the tunnel through the mountains carried them swiftly up and onwards. Their feet scuffled and echoed in the silence as the satyr led them through the smooth tunnels, ever upwards in the wavering celestial light. Robin imagined he could feel the entire weight of the mountain around them. Though the passage was tall and airy above their heads, it felt claustrophobic, knowing the immensity of weight and solid rock pressing in on them from all sides. Robin took what comfort he could from the flawlessly and seamlessly inlaid stones, which clearly hadn't shifted in millennia, and were unlikely to decide today was the day to collapse.

"Where does this lead?" Robin asked, directing his question to the satyr's back as they followed him. His voice echoed strangely along their silent path.

"Oh, these mountains are riddled with tunnels, like honeycomb, little Fae boy," his cracked old voice floated back out of the darkness as they shuffled on. "Some believe redcaps burrowed here, long ago, in the time before my people came to the mountains." He shook his shaggy head. "But I doubt that. The stone here is too hard for them. Industrious little devils like lower ground and softer soil to steal through." He tapped one of the glowing crystals with the tip of his walking staff as they passed it, making it emit a low thrum like a tuning fork. "Stick to the lighted paths within the hidden ways, however, and all is well. These are the pathways my people use. They will lead us up. Up and out. To the sky of the world."

They seemed to walk for a long time. Occasionally, other tunnels split off from the one they climbed, curving away, or sloping down into shadow and silence, unlit by any markers.

"As for these other roads, who knows." The satyr shrugged. He did not sound overly concerned. "They were here before us. They'll be here after us. Some might lead all the way down to the great Nethercity itself, if such a legendary place even exists at all. Satyrs don't delve in the deeps when we can avoid it. We are a people of light, of sky and air."

"Why did you stay here?" Karya wanted to know, her voice coming from the darkness behind Robin. "We all know that the Air-Masters moved the town of the satyrs…the whole top of the mountain…and they hid it away in the clouds as the floating Isle of Aeolius. We've actually been there ourselves. It was empty. Abandoned."

The satyr grunted, as though it were all the same to him whether his self-exiled people were flourishing or vanished. "Worse things happen at sea," he said. "Revenants, no doubt. You always get revenants in places far from help. They're drawn to them."

The tunnel threaded onwards, becoming wider and more decorative as they progressed. It was broad enough now for them to walk two abreast, and better lit. There were now steps more often than not, and strange, stylised carvings began to appear between the glowing crystals, threading thickly on the walls. "The town went up in the sky, yes," their guide told them. "But the Precipitous Library? It would not be moved. It wished to remain here, that much was made clear to us. The items it houses, safeguards you might say, are more ancient and powerful than any might imagine, and they exert their own will on things."

"What items?" Robin wondered. "Books you mean?"

"You'll see what," Swiftwings replied. "It's clearly what you've come for."

He still hadn't looked back at any of them, even once, his hooves clacking smartly on each step, supremely confident that they were following obediently – or perhaps simply unconcerned that any one of them might have wandered off down one of the unlit branching tunnels into darkness and mystery.

"The point is, the library remained. It was here when we first settled our home. We built the town around it, in the days long gone. It is not a place made by satyrs, though my people have become its custodians. When our home was lifted away, the library had no intention of joining it. And so, a number of us remained as well. Guardians. To hold the ancient knowledge. To try to keep it safe. Someone must."

Robin couldn't imagine a library with a mind of its own, though the satyr's story made him wonder who built it, if not them.

"Safe from Eris, you mean," Karya said. "She controls everything, even the history books. When she came to power, she erased so much of the past. That's how you control people. You limit what they know, or what they knew. You fiddle with facts and rewrite history to suit yourself."

The old man grunted with humour. "There is much that dark one doesn't know," he said. "She doesn't even know where she came from, where *any* of us came from. Might as well ask her where the Elementals went. We are all in the dark as sure as if every lantern here went out, barely anyone in the Netherworlde knows the real truths."

The tunnel took another twist, still climbing steeply up through the rock. Robin's ears had popped, and his legs were burning from the endless climb. Occasionally, he glanced behind them, back into the shifting cool glow and shadows. He was sure it was only his suspicions, but he couldn't help but feel they were being followed still. Had Mr Nyx and his army of peacekeepers discovered the hidden entrance to the mountain's interior? Sniffed them out? The thought of that man creeping along behind them in the darkness, an envoy of shadowy spiders moving at his feet – a thriving black carpet – as he smiled his wide and friendly smile down there in the darkness, made Robin's skin crawl. He forced himself to look forward again, berating himself for getting the heebie-jeebies. It was just the unearthly surroundings setting him on edge. The ghostly light, the silence and the stillness – that was all.

"Of course, even if the all the lights of truth go out, we can, with questing hands, still find our way, step by step through the darkness," the satyr said. "So long as we do not tire, and sit, exhausted in the shadows, giving ourselves over to lies and the helpless comfort of being lost, there is always light eventually."

He stopped, and for the first time turned to face them all as they came to a shuffling halt behind him. His face flickered in the pale light, beard and horns making him appear more than a little devilish, but his wrinkled and milky eyes, Robin noted, looked kindly on them. "Always," he repeated. "See?"

A door now stood before them; large and carved from the dark stone of the mountain and filled with more odd geometric patterns. They had reached the end of their path. From somewhere within his bulky fur cape, the satyr fished a large iron ring of keys, flicking through them industriously and slotting the selected one into the lock.

The door swung inwards, flooding them with fresh air. A strong, chill wind ruffled their hair and clothes.

"Brisk night on the mountain-top," the satyr declared smartly, beckoning the travellers to follow him.

The door emptied them out of a shallow cave onto a wide, flat plateau of rock, open to the sky. It was huge and so unreally smooth it might have been steamrolled. It reminded Robin of Table Mountain back in the human world, as though the crown of the peak had been sliced neatly off. The rock beneath their feet seemed oddly iridescent in its smoothness and full of slow rippling light, the same soft blue-green as the crystals. Glowing from below their feet like shining waves through deep ice.

"It looks like the northern lights are caught in the mountain rock," Henry breathed, shivering in the wind.

The air up here cut through them. Above this large and empty plateau, there were no more towering mountains, only sky, fully dark now, the deep blue-black void littered with stars winking behind shredded clouds.

"Yeah … umm, that's all very breath-taking and all," Woad said, looking off behind him. "But you're kind of missing the headliner here, Henryboy."

He took Henry by the shoulders and turned him around, the others following his gaze. Across the flat and shimmering stage of the mountain, the companions gaped as one.

"Welcome to the Precipitous Library." Swiftwings the satyr pointed proudly across the great empty expanse of rock with his staff, his cloak whipping out behind him in the mountain air.

To Robin, the singular feature on this otherwise flat mountain top could not have looked less like a building if it tried. At first glance, he had thought it was an enormous mass of crystal, a natural formation dwarfing the mountain top around them, some goliath cousin to the tiny lights within the mountain's veins.

But as he craned his neck to follow the softly glowing, sword-like spikes piercing the veil of night, he noticed the great growths and fingers of crystal were hewn – countless whittled windows glowed rich and bright in the night, carved into the surface of the gargantuan crystalline mass. High buttresses linked one great spur to the next, looking as inconsequential as delicate spiderwebs between the branches of some vast tree. The whole structure was clearly hollow, and lit from within by the same shifting boreal light as the rest of the mountain top.

Henry stared. "When you said 'library', Rob, I was imagining something a bit more municipal. You know, maybe a clock tower, some columns, a lady at the desk with glasses on a chain shushing people, that kind of thing? I wasn't expecting …" He trailed off.

"Superman's Fortress of Solitude glowing with magic ghost light?" Robin finished the sentence for him, shaking his head in wonder. "No. Me neither, if I'm absolutely honest."

It was immediately obvious how the alien structure had got its name. The enormous organic building was positioned right on the very lip of the rock. Only a relatively small portion of the crystalline mass actually touched the flat mountain top at all. The vast majority of its spiked and faceted bulk hung out over the cliff edge of it, leaping off into space, a frozen ice sculpture of knives, anchored to the rock below with only a few spurs of crystal.

"It looks like it's about to fall off the mountain," Woad said, as they followed their guide across the wide shimmering expanse of rock, curtains of wavering light moving under their steps through the stone. The shadows of whales, deep beneath icebergs.

"It looks like someone dropped it and it landed on the lip of the cliff," Henry agreed. "Or like some alien meteor that fell out of space. One good cough and it would be off that edge. Is that … I mean, is it safe?"

"No library is safe," the satyr shrugged, hurrying along beneath the arcing sky, clearly keen to be inside the structure and out of the biting wind. "All contain secrets that can change the world."

"But not all are literally hanging off the edge of a mountain by the skin of their teeth," Robin pointed out, staring at the huge gothic daydream of glowing diamond as it drew closer.

"The human boy is not far wrong when he says the library looks as though it was dropped," Swiftwings acknowledged. "It was."

He raised his staff, sweeping it ahead of them like a tour guide. "Our whole town, the mountain top, up and up into the sky. Shook like the end of the world it did, library came back down, like a great stubborn elephant. Landed right on the edge of oblivion and dug its heels in. We house things here, you see. As I've mentioned. Things that quite clearly wished to remain. You can manipulate the Towers of the Arcania, oh yes. But the relics of the Elementals?" He shook his head, with something between frustration and pride. "Well, *they* have a mind of their own. They only go where *they* want to go. Though if anyone can fathom their reasoning, it certainly isn't me."

"Relics of the Elementals?" Karya asked. "This is a place built by the Elementals themselves, isn't it? It pre-dates the Panthea – and the Fae."

The satyr glanced back warily at the cave, across the smooth expanse, his eyes narrowed as though he had heard or sensed something. After a moment, he shook himself and faced the library once more.

"Come," he said. "We will talk more inside, out of the wind and the night. There's more darkness than usual out here in the open, and it's warmer within the library's walls."

2

Pasts and Futures

The entrance to the great library was reached by a wide flow of steps, cut directly into the glowing crystal close to the edge of the mountain. In the darkness beyond their high flat vista, Robin could see other dark peaks, circling below them like sentinels. Huge and solid shadows in the night, and a great yawning emptiness between them. There were clouds and mist threading below the drop, rivers suspended in the sky, glowing in the rising moonlight.

The doors of the great library opened of their own accord as they reached them, and closed swiftly and silently once they passed beneath the tall archway, cutting off the dark night-time outside, leaving them all in soft warmth and undulating light.

"Now *this* is what I call a library," Karya said, peering up and around the large room they found themselves in. "It makes the one at Erlking look like a village book store."

The interior of the library was massive. Everything was carved from the same glass-like material, each surface dancing with a dreaming inner light. It made Robin think of jade – the same beautiful lustre of iridescence – of ancient artefacts he had seen in museums, where skilled craftsmen had carved whole scenes into a tiny nub of blue-green stone. Only here, all was writ large, an interior to dwarf Notre Dame, all hollowed and whittled by the hands of ancient giants, it seemed. The floor stretched away, a polished mirror, with countless crystalline stalactites punctuating the open space, making it into a glimmering maze. Each spire was whittled and carved into shelves packed with countless tightly-wrapped scrolls and books. The vast walls of the great hall were similarly loaded.

31

Nooks and crannies covering every inch of space and climbing to heights which were both dizzying and completely impractical, punctuated only by leaping archways and windows parading away ahead of them, their transparency making it difficult to tell the true shape of the room. It was like a hall of mirrors, bouncing light softly back and forth, ghosts in the ever-moving air.

"I can't believe people live here," Henry said, craning his neck to take in the shimmering majesty of the crystal palace's interior. "It's like ice ... only ... like *haunted* ice."

"How practical are these sky-scraping bookcases though?' Robin wondered. "How do you even get up there? Jetpacks?" He felt dizzy just looking off into the angular, spiralling heights. However, as their eyes adjusted to the light within, they began to notice near invisible walkways and slender bridges, translucent leaping arcs of crystal leaping in the heights from case to case.

"Not a place for the vertiginous," Karya observed, looking around. "How hard is this crystal? None of those death-defying bridges look like they could take our weight."

"I could run up one, if you like?" Woad offered, grinning up into the complicated puzzle overhead like a child in a candy store. "Test the bearing points? You know, for science!"

"No!" everyone whisper-yelled at once. Swiftwings frowned at them in the manner of all librarians everywhere when confronted with noisy children.

"Deadly drops, infinite mystical knowledge, glowing spikes of carved magnificence ..." Karya said. "An ancient and hallowed space." Her voice was reverent.

Henry clapped his hands together, giving them a rub. He smiled around at his friends. "Nice and warm in here too, that's the main thing," he added, clearly grateful to no longer be shivering under the heavens at high altitude. "Toasty!"

Robin agreed. It was lovely to be out of the elements. The walls of the Precipitous Library muted the high winds outside. He could hear them only faintly as they caught and were funnelled around the gargantuan spikes and spires, twisted into faint but constant song outside.

The ceilings high above – how far it was almost impossible to see with the refracting and confusing angles and transparency – was strung with no lights, no chandeliers. No added illumination was needed when the very fabric of the building itself glowed like marsh mist.

"This is the main hall," Swiftwings told them, looking pleased, in a proprietorial way, that they seemed so impressed. "There are many rooms in the library." He nodded towards the various deep archways. "Further in. There is much to know here. We have added our own knowledge to this repository of course, during our time as custodians, but much was always here. Too much to ever read in one lifetime, even for a satyr."

He looked at them curiously. "There is something more you should know about the library," he told them. "For those who spend much time here, the knowledge of the world ... it seeps into us." He waved a hand thoughtfully in the air, as if trying to find the right words to explain himself. "There's some strange resonance here ... we do not fully understand it ourselves. But there is a power here, a deep and old power, and prolonged exposure to it seems to echo in our minds. We know things of the world when we are here. Echoes of things. We *see* things we might not *know*."

"Like radiation from spending too much time near a nuclear reactor?" Henry offered.

"Like a breeze making ripples on water," the satyr countered. "Knowledge, it would seem, is contagious."

Karya regarded the old man with a keen new interest. "You're telling us you're a seer?"

Swiftwings shrugged. "Only when I'm in here. Things don't ... echo ... as much outside these walls. But now we are within ..." He eyed each of them with interest. "I hear all of your echoes."

"What are they saying?" Robin wondered aloud, but the old man didn't reply. He just scratched at his horn nubbins absently, as if listening to something other than the conversation.

"There's more than books and scrolls here, little wanderers. History itself." He nodded at the upper levels. "Up there. Follow me, get warm. I will find us a place to talk where we won't disturb the others of my order. Libraries may seem like quiet places, but for those of us here, there is always noise and whispers, and it is our duty and our art to listen to them."

* * *

They made their way through the interior of the library, room by glittering room. The way the light moved across everything reminded Robin of sunlight on water, reflected back up on the roofs of sea caves. Sliding lattices of hypnotic light.

There were other satyrs here in the interior rooms, walking softly between the stacks, their hooves clicking cleanly on the floors, each carrying armloads of scrolls or stacks of bound books. Most wore either capes, like Swiftwings, or, more often, hooded cowls. They seemed like monks quietly moving through their monastery – only instead of Gregorian chants, the music of the wind played around the crystals like whale song. Robin wondered if any of those they passed had known Phorbas, if indeed his tutor had originally come from here. From this order of arcane custodians, the guardians of ancient ways.

They were led up another wide staircase, and along a curved balcony, transparent and shimmering. Stepping out onto it at these heights, with nothing beneath their feet but seemingly thin glass, made Robin's legs feel a little watery. With a moment of queasy trepidation, he shuffled along after their guide, hugging close to the wall as the satyr led them deeper and higher into the Elemental edifice.

"What do you all do here?" Henry asked, his voice filled with curiosity. "Besides listening to whispers from the walls, I mean. I know Robin here is a bookworm – this must be like Disneyland for him – but you guys are just living on a mountain up here all alone, with all this …" He stroked a hand along the rows of scrolls as they passed.

"All this knowledge," the satyr replied. "Yes. And what we do, human boy, is keep it. Keep the knowledge from being corrupted."

The corridor they followed ended in a twisting spiral staircase, glassy steps curling upwards. Karya eyed the stairs, whether with distrust or simply tiredness it was hard to tell, but she followed upwards with the others.

"The past, you see, is not a fixed truth," Swiftwings explained, his voice grim. "What happened at any given point in history obviously happened. But *how* did it happen, and *why*, and *to whom*?" He grunted. "That very much depends on who remains standing to tell the tale. History is written by the winners, you see. When the Empress Eris rose to power, she left no stone unturned in moulding the Netherworlde to her liking. Including its history."

34

"But you can't change the past," Henry frowned. "What's done is done, right?"

They had reached the top of the tight spiral of steps, now high in one of the towering spears of the great library sculpture, far out over the abyss beyond the mountain, and their guide once again fiddled with his large ring of keys. He made a derisive noise. "Eris rules not only the *lands* of the Netherworlde, little ones. She rules the *minds* of its people. Many of them, at any rate. That is how one commands. How one keeps power. One of the first things she did on taking the throne was burn, discard and destroy as much information as she could of the time before her reign. The Panthea who fill this world, their own past ... is lost in rumour and memory. All that remains is the official story. Eris' own penned fairy tale."

The lock clicked loudly. "The Fae, a terrible and cruel oppressor, standing on the backs of the enslaved Panthea, were freed by the glorious rebellion!" Swiftwings recited dramatically. "They rightly took the lands for themselves and their wicked masters, dangerous and lower than wild beasts, were relocated for re-education! The mercy of the empress! In her infinite grace, she was moved not to crush her enemy, but only to thin their overwhelming numbers, to stop the unchecked pestilence of their race from overrunning the world. And those conserved she looked kindly on, and sent them to unlearn their savage ways, fed and housed them while they worked their penance for their crimes."

"Slaughtered, you mean," Robin replied. "Or thrown into death camps. That's what you mean by 'conservation', by 're-education'. That's what Eris means. But that history isn't true, is it? The Fae were here *first*. This was *their* land, and they welcomed the Panthea when they arrived. The two races lived in peace together before Eris betrayed the Fae."

The satyr looked back over his shoulder, giving Robin a thoughtful look in the shadows of the corridor. "You have learned a different history than most in the Netherworlde, I see," he said. "And where does the truth lie? In your Fae version? Or in Eris' Panthea version?"

"As you say, history is written by the victor," Karya said darkly. "Whether we like it or not, we are living in Eris' reality now. The Fae side of the story was well and truly destroyed when the Arcania shattered. When the king and queen fell, and Erlking became a ruin."

"Who the *victor* is remains to be seen," Robin said firmly. "This war isn't over, not until there's not one member of the rebellion left standing."

Swiftwings smiled with one side of his mouth, though his expression seemed to contain very little humour. "Spoken like a true revolutionary," he said. "You sound like her."

"Like whom?" Robin frowned.

"Like Eris." The satyr turned away and pushed open the door, filling the stairs with brighter light.

He beckoned them to follow him into the room beyond.

"Here, we do not deal in which side of the story is true," he said. "Nor which is noble or right. Here, we simply guard what knowledge is left. With neither approval nor condemnation. We preserve what we can from being lost forever."

He had led them into a large domed room. They must be up by the tip of the spike somewhere here, as the ceiling was a large sheet of curved glass. Sheer, like a softly glowing aquarium against the black night sky outside. The prismatic walls were filled with shelves and stacks like everywhere else in the huge building, but in the empty space in the very centre of the room stood a circular set of seven waist-high plinths, arranged roughly like a Janus Station. Atop some of these there was an item, all carefully displayed like artefacts in a museum. Three plinths lay empty. In the very centre of this circle was another plinth, also empty.

"What is this place?" Robin asked as they entered, and the satyr closed and locked the door behind them.

"This place is the past," the satyr told them with levity. "The very *distant* past, or all that remains of it, at least. These relics here before you are all that remain of stories told in song, a time before any wrote in scrolls or books." He flicked his eyes over them all.

"I wonder who sent you to me. I can almost hear the echo of them," he mused, although he didn't seem to expect any response, for which Robin was secretly glad. He didn't think he would inspire much confidence in their scholar-guide if he revealed they had been led here by a random unknown stranger writing them cryptic messages in blood. The old man's eyes roved over them each in turn. "I see you all for what you are,' he said, not unkindly. "I have devoted my life to truth. We all have, here. It is a talent and a curse. And never once have I turned my face away from it, no matter how beautiful or ugly it has been. In the end, it is the best we have."

"This one," he walked slowly past Woad, peering at the blue faun, "has only just become himself. Anyone can see that. Though he doesn't know what that means yet, or how it will end for him."

"I have Skyfire," Woad grinned proudly. "An old bog hag unlocked my fabulous innate faunness for me." He frowned. "I mean, not out of the goodness of its heart or anything. It did it so that I'd be tastier ... But hey, I'm not complaining! It all worked out in the end."

The satyr's eyes were deep and thoughtful in the candlelight. "A hungry bog hag," he mused, shaking his head softly in wonder. "From such a small action ... toppling dominoes. Empires can rise and fall, little one."

He flicked his eyes to Henry, narrowing them slightly. "And this one?" he muttered to himself, assessing the boy. His head was tilted to one side as though listening to the echoes he had mentioned, though none of them could hear anything but the distant song of the wind. Henry shuffled his feet, uncomfortable with the scrutiny.

"Me?" he smirked in his lopsided way. "No big mysteries here, I'm afraid. I'm nothing special. No Skyfire or anything. Just a regular human lad, well out of his depth, but – ah, well." He thrust his hands into his pockets. "I'm used to treading water by now, hanging around with this lot."

The satyr shook his head, reaching out a gnarled hand, tapping Henry on the chest. "No," he said simply, shaking his head. "Rivers roar and foam, yes. And lightning is full of flash and bang, this is true also. But mountains are still and quiet. And far stronger than they know." He spread his long fingers, tapping them against the boy's shirt. "Little brown mouse with the roaring heart of a lion," he concluded. "You'll give your right eye to save your friends, without a moment's hesitation. Such loyalty is rare in either world and is not to be diminished."

Henry sniffed, not looking at any of the others. "Well, course," he said, withering under praise. "Anyone would. That's what friends do. We look after each other."

"Something that many *claim*." The satyr removed his hand. "But few *believe*. Fewer still are those who stand by their bold words." He looked sharply to Robin. "Trust this one's judgement," he instructed. "He sees clearer than the rest of you put together. Your minds are clouded with storms and busy squalls, but this human boy ..." He wagged a finger back in Henry's direction. "This one is a clear summer sky."

Leaning on his staff, the satyr turned to Karya, who was standing with her arms folded, looking rather defensive.

"Are you going to do me next?" she asked. "Is that what we're here for? An evaluation? So that the satyrs of the mountains can judge the truth of us?"

The satyr stroked his beard, and to Robin's judgement, he looked a little sad.

"Would that I could," he said to her. "But there *is* no truth to you, girl. I think you suspect this already."

Karya blinked back at him, refusing to break eye contact. Her lips were set in a defiant line.

"You are one who should not be here," Swiftwings muttered. "One who has no place. Born from darkness, greed, and the worst of motives. Your very presence is a curse, an affront to truth."

"Hey, hang on," Robin said hotly, but Karya held up a hand to silence him.

"However, from darkness, such light can be born." The satyr tilted his head, inspecting Karya closely. "You came from villainous purpose, but your choices …" He nodded. "Your path, and your conscience, can turn a curse into a blessing. You never should have been, but the Empress Eris, in her infinite vanity, has never before had one of her own turn and bite her hand. In you, her arrogant ambition may have set in motion a tool of her own downfall."

Karya's eyes were shimmering, and Robin wasn't sure if it was from the flickering light that filled the library.

"I'm not a tool," she said. "I'm a *person*. Eris would have me a tool. Would you have me a tool against her?"

The old man shook his head. "Not I," he smiled at her, conveying that he meant her no harm or insult. He pointed briefly at Robin. "But that one may."

Robin opened his mouth to argue his innocence, but Karya cut in.

"I know that already," she said. "I made my choices a long time ago. When I fled Dis and went to him. I went where I was *needed*, not where I was disposable."

"It is a shame," the satyr nodded, accepting this. "That now, at this juncture, you are barely *anywhere* at all." He indicated her white hair and her dark and dull mana stone bracelet. "You are fading from this world, are you not? One who should not be. The world is trying to erase your anomaly."

"Karya was wounded," Henry said, folding his arms. "She got ill, that's all. We're finding a way to make her better."

"And you may," the old man nodded carelessly. "You may yet. Is that what you are here for? To search the library for a cure for this one?"

"We'll search the whole Netherworlde if we need to," Henry said. "It's one thing you going on about me and Woad being powerful and brave and empire-toppling, but don't think we will stand here while you insult our friend. She's not a curse or an anomaly or an abomination."

Karya reached out and took Henry's hand, giving it a brief squeeze and startling him into silence. "Henry, it's okay," she assured him. "He wasn't insulting me." She looked back to the satyr, who was still watching them all with his unfathomable milky eyes. "He was only describing me."

"And what about me?" Robin stepped forward, feeling offended at the suggestion that he might use his friends as tools in the war. "Don't I get to hear your echoes too? Might as well, seeing as we are all being evaluated here like we're on trial?"

"You?" Swiftwings waved his hand dismissively. "You are the Scion of the Arcania. What could I tell you *that you would wish to hear* about yourself?"

Robin had no ready reply. Their host sighed down his nose. "Would it comfort you if I tell you of the darkness ahead? Or the choices you are going to have to make? Would it change a thing? You will do what you *must*, Scion of the Arcania." His grey eyebrows knitted. "You will do what you must; because that is what it means to *be* the Scion of the Arcania. And it will doom us all or it will save us all. Nothing I can say will change that."

"You talk as though everything's fated and written down," Robin said. "The future isn't fixed. Maybe people's interpretation of the past is multiple choice like you've said, but I believe we write the future ourselves."

"A game of chess has only so many moves, Scion," the satyr said. "And one who has studied chess all their life can see many moves ahead. Perhaps not all the moves, but many." He looked upwards, gazing distantly out of the crystal ceiling to the blackness of space above them.

"I see the move where you try to take the knight and in doing so, sacrifice a pawn. I see the move, right there in your eyes, where allegiances shift like water." He stepped closer, looking directly at the boy. "And I see the move where you destroy the heart of one who loves you – for duty."

Robin stepped backwards. "I would never do that."

"But you *will*." The satyr looked terribly sad, listening to the whispers of the Elemental bastion of future shadows. "Because they will make you. You asked to know. Do such truths comfort you, Scion? No. Your path is hard. Better to walk it blindly, concentrate on the next step, than look ahead to what awaits you on your horizon. If you look too far ahead and see what you must face, how will you ever make your legs move?"

"What *is* the next step ahead?" Karya, having dropped Henry's hand, stepped forward, putting herself protectively between Robin and the satyr. "If, that is, we've finished scaring the Scion with all the horrible things looming in his future, of course?" Her eyes were murderous.

Swiftwings laughed – as though this had all been a fun distraction and nothing more.

"Fair enough, fair enough!" he nodded. "The truth is not so welcome to everyone. You must forgive me. A satyr of the Precipitous Library indeed. We deal only in truths; our lives are spent hardening ourselves to face them. We forget at times that those outside these walls are bruised so easily by it at times." He bowed a little to them in apology.

"Come!" he said, turning away. "This is what the library tells me you are here to meet! Do you know what these are?" He led them into the centre of the room, to where the circle of plinths stood reverently. "They are the first truths," he continued, not waiting for a reply. "The highest valued. Before the Panthea, there were the Fae. And before the Fae?" He turned to them, eyebrows raised like a teacher throwing the question open to his class.

"The Elementals," Karya answered. "Even without any written history, everyone knows the old stories."

"Do enlighten us all," the satyr said, resting his walking staff gently against one of the plinths.

Karya held her hands up, shrugging. "Very well; if you're testing my knowledge of mythology." She began, glancing at the others. "When the Netherworlde was young, there were seven beings. Eternal, powerful, close to being gods of a primal kind, I suppose. They were the Elementals. Earth, Air, Fire, Water, Darkness, Light and Spirit. They made the Netherworlde. They sculpted the mountains, they filled the seas, they raised the skies.

40

And when the Fae filled the land, the Elementals taught them magic. They gifted the Netherworlde to them. They lived amongst them for a time, guiding, teaching. But eventually they left. They gave the Arcania to Oberon and Titania, a gift of power and magic encapsulating all of their gifts, a facet from each of them, all woven together in one source. They gave the King and Queen of the Fae the Arcania with which to rule and govern the Netherworlde."

"So far so good," Swiftwings conceded, graciously.

"And then they were gone from the world. Forever. They never came back. And the Netherworlde from then on belonged to the Fae. For aeons and aeons, until the Panthea arrived."

"At which point, as we have covered, history becomes rather muddy." The satyr raised a finger. "And all kinds of knots and kinks and dropped stitches and frayed edges appear in the tapestry of history." He sighed ruefully. "But yes. That is the story of the Elementals. But as well as the great gift of the Arcania, on their departure, each Elemental also left behind a gift, a tool for the Fae to utilise in their governance of the Netherworlde. Some of these ancient relics are lost in time and memory, but those that we know of, those that remain …" He bowed his head in deference, "are what you see laid out here before you."

He raised a hand to the first plinth, which cradled a long spear of shining and highly polished silver. "The Spear of Light," he said with pride.

"You have real relics of the Elementals?" Woad practically cooed, wide-eyed, scampering forwards to get a closer look. "All here together?"

"The Mirror of Shadows." Swiftwings moved to the next plinth, atop which a small and ornate hand mirror of darkest jet lay on a cushioned pillow, its glass dark and polished to a high shine. "Over here, the Cloak of the Waves." Robin saw a neatly folded item of clothing atop the next plinth in the circle. It looked gossamer thin and was shining, spun from something as light as spiderwebs.

"And finally, the Arrow of the Flames." He passed a plinth where a slender arrow, white and nocked with crimson fletching, was suspended.

"Wait, why are some of them empty?" Woad exclaimed. "It's not a full collection without them all."

"Some are still lost, out in the world," the satyr said. "These relics here are the heart of the library. They are the reason the library remains here alone on the mainland. They did not wish to leave."

"Why not, I wonder?" Karya said.

"I believe they are waiting to be claimed," the satyr said. "We librarians do not own them. As with the library itself and all contained within, we are merely custodians."

"We've met one of them," Robin told him. "One of the other relics, I mean." This made the satyr's eyes widen with surprise. "The Mask of Gaia. That was the relic of the Elemental of Earth, right? I've actually used it myself. I know where it is. It's with the dryad queen of Rowandeepling now, in the Elderhart. It had been hidden at Erlking for who knows how long before that?"

The satyr nodded at this, looking very thoughtful. "Many things lie hidden at Erlking, there's no doubting that. It is good to hear the Mask of Gaia is in safe hands. Had I the judgement to choose safe hands for the rest of these, I assure you, we would not need them here in the library. But that decision is not up to us satyrs."

"You have the relics here from the Water Elemental, the Fire Elemental, the Light and the Dark." Karya walked around the circle, looking at them with great interest. "We know where the Earth relic is already." She nodded her head towards the two empty plinths. "But you do not have the Air relic, or the Spirit relic. Are they lost?"

Their guide held up his hands. "Hidden, perhaps?" he suggested. "Even with all of our research, even working here in the library with all its whispers and ambient knowledge, still we barely know even what they are. We have here a mirror, a cloak, a spear and an arrow. We know now of a mask. As for the remaining two …" He shrugged a little helplessly and sighed with the weariness of a devoted collector whose treasures are incomplete. "All written accounts, even with the resources of the great Precipitous Library, tells us little. The oldest recorded songs sing only fragments of the time before the Fae. Many of our order believe the relic of Air to be a shield, though others think it is a bird, perhaps a statue of some kind. And the relic of Spirit?" His hands dropped. "A jewel perhaps, some precious stone. We may never complete this collection."

"Do they all have powers?" Henry asked. He was walking around the circle, staring at everything with interest. The objects exuded energy like a low vibration or a heat haze. His fingers hovered over the suspended arrow, peering at it curiously. "Like the mask we found, I mean. The Mask of Gaia lets you see true things, right?"

The satyr peered at him carefully. "Oh yes," he said, clearly enjoying their enthusiasm. "Each of the Elemental relics has a singular purpose, and like the Elementals themselves, they possess the ability to exist in both worlds. To make a path between them, regardless of Janus Stations. If the worlds are separate pages of a book, then these relics are the spine that binds the book together." He waved a hand in the air. "The Mirror of the Dark here reflects doorways. The Cloak of the Waves appears to have tremendous healing powers. Arrow and Spear alike have their uses too. Of course, we do not know of *all* their gifts. We are custodians only. Satyrs do not presume to temper the ancient magics." His eyes flicked between Robin and Henry. "*That* task falls to others."

"This feels like it's vibrating," Henry said, his fingers hovering over the arrow. It was pure white wood, fletched with feathers of red and gold. "I can feel its energy from here. Not the other things as much." He frowned around the circle of artefacts. "But this one I could feel as soon as we stepped in here, from right across the room."

"I don't feel anything from it," Robin confessed. He looked to Karya and Woad, his face an open question. Karya shook her head. Woad simply shrugged.

"This one sings only to you, human boy," Swiftwings gave him a curious look. "All things in the right place at the right time. I said before, you have the heart of a lion." He looked upwards, thoughtfully, at the dark night sky high beyond the crystal above. "Though you have yet to give it to another who will take it from you."

Robin was at the centre of the circle, surrounded by the relics. He rested his hand on the empty display space. The central plinth.

"And what should be *here*?" he asked. "You have a space for all seven elements. Seven Towers, just like the Shards of the Arcania. But what's this space in the middle for? Something else you don't have?"

"Why a *book*, of course," their guide said. "This is a library, after all."

"What book?" Henry frowned. "'Ancient Elemental artefacts and how to use them, a beginner's guide'?"

"The most important book," the satyr told them. His face flickered in shadow and light from the ever-moving glow of the walls around them. "A most calamitous book."

Above them, the night sky outside had begun to fill with green and red curtains of light, wide and silent. Flickering in and out of existence in

43

slow waves like the skirts of ghosts as they rippled across the darkness of the heavens. Robin had seen the northern lights before, but never from so high in the Netherworlde mountains. They were otherworldly, pouring down their strange and alien sheets of illumination on the library below, shimmering in through the glass and making the static shadows of the circle of relics leap and undulate.

The satyr gave little heed to the lights above. Clearly working and living here, they were a common enough sight for him. He walked over to Robin and patted the empty space on the plinth. "A book that belonged to King Oberon himself, and in which is entwined the history of our peoples, yours and mine, young Fae. A book which is very lost, and very powerful. One that could undo the world – or make it anew."

Robin stared up at the man, whose ghostly eyes were unreadable in the dark.

"What book is it?" he asked, the hairs on the back of his neck standing up.

The satyr stepped away. "No one knows." He smirked ruefully. "Rumours again! Legends! Whispers and hearsay!" He shook his fist in the air in a comical show of scholarly frustration. "All enemies of the valued truth. It matters only that it is lost, and that without it, we may *never* know the truth and meaning of the Netherworlde. Not even if all seven relics of the Elementals were reunited. Not even if all the shattered Shards of the Arcania were found, and the Arcania itself made whole again."

He turned to look at them all. "Only King Oberon and Queen Titania themselves knew what was contained in the book, and they are gone, far beyond us all."

Robin knew, deep inside, without any shadow of doubt, that this was the same book, the one all at Erlking were searching for. The one even Eris herself was seeking – both here in the Netherworlde and in the human world, through her organisation, Sire Holdings. This elusive book, which the king and queen had gone to such trouble to hide, splitting clues between their Sidhe-Nobilitas, leaving no shreds of evidence other than a crumpled human-world library card, was the answer to everything.

"These greater mysteries of the Netherworlde are important to everyone; right now what we need is to find *someone*," Robin said. "That's why we were sent here, I think. To find a way to them, or to get something we need."

"And what is it you think you need?"

"A way into Dis." He pointed at Karya. "To save our friend. There are answers there, to what's wrong with her, we know it. If we don't get into Dis soon, two of our other friends are going to be put onto bonfires or enslaved, and this one here …" He trailed off, looking helplessly at Karya.

"Printer not found," she said, flatly.

"There is no way into Dis without an invitation," the satyr told them. "Not for anyone. The walls of the city are impenetrable and closely watched at all times. And I can assure you, invitations to Eris' private celebrations are not extended to the satyrs of the Precipitous Library. I don't know who sent you here, or what they expected you to find, but if it's a ticket to Pyrenight, you are very far off course."

"Only the nobles have access to Dis," Karya said. "High-ruling Panthea fanatically loyal to Eris, and we happen to be looking for one of them. Admittedly one that was declared dead, but still, it's our only lead."

"And we're not the only ones looking for her," Robin explained. "Strigoi and the Grimms seem to be after the same person, though whether for the same reason, I have no clue. Can you tell us anything about the Calescent siblings? I think that's what we've been sent here to find information on. This is a storehouse of knowledge, after all, isn't it. They are, or they were, a noble house of Fire Panthea."

Their guide nodded. "Noble once, yes. The old Lord Calescent was a dear supporter of King Oberon and Queen Titania. Although this was long ago." He shook his head, leaving the children waiting in the circle of the elements while he walked off towards the nearby shelves. "His wife died in childbirth, bringing twins into the world. A boy and a girl." His voice floated back to them from somewhere in the shelves. "Old Lord Calescent raised them both himself. They were his legacy, his future. When the war came, the rise of Eris, and those who supported her, the Netherworlde descended into chaos." His gnarled fingers ran along a shelf, searching the books. "War tears apart more than bodies, Scion of the Arcania. It tears apart families, too." He had reappeared, having selected a book, large and bound in black leather, drawing it slowly from the shelf and giving it a gentle blow and pat.

"The uprising was fierce," Swiftwings told them. "Eris demanded loyalty, called on *every* Panthea to renounce their ties or allegiances with the Fae.

45

You were either with her or you were against her. And if you were against her, may the fates help you."

He shook his head sadly. "Old Lord Calescent was executed. Shortly after Eris' victory. A traitor to the cause, to the new world order. He never renounced the Fae. He remained loyal to the King and Queen even unto his death, and he was punished for it."

He walked back towards them, his hooves and walking stick both clacking on the floor, as the aurora borealis above sent its shifting light down onto them, refracted and reflected in every shining surface.

"Rumour holds, though nothing is written," the satyr said, in conspiratorial tones, "that he was working on something with the Fae, you see. A secret project? Something to aid the resistance against Eris? Something to help the remaining Fae survive or escape?" He shrugged. "No one knows of course. The rumours may have been false, nothing was ever proved. But rumour, and the testimony of his own bloodline, was enough to condemn him to death. His children, Lord Flint and Lady Tinda, both full grown by this point, well, they inherited the lands and titles of Calescent after his death. Holding sway over the Black Hills."

The satyr placed the book in his hands, letting it fall open and shaking his head as he began to flip through the pages. "They were not cut from the same cloth as their father, those two. Not in the least." There was concern in his voice. "Young Lord Flint was – and still is – fanatically loyal to Eris. Utterly devoted to the cause. He considered his own father weak. A shame and a traitor to the Panthea, his own people. Lord Flint thoroughly embraced the rebellion, he swallowed every morsel of propaganda that Eris and her cause fed him. He is a true believer in the empress and her hard new Netherworlde."

Robin frowned with disgust. "How could the man side with Eris when she had his own father put to death?"

The satyr glanced up from his book. "Ambition," he said simply. "All that was his father's passed to the children on his death. The power, the wealth, the status. And of course, anyone vocally in support and the good graces of the empress is considerably *safer* than anyone not so."

"Greed," Karya said. "Greed and cowardice. That's what it usually comes down to. He sounds like a less than lovely person."

The satyr chuckled a little, nodding his head as he leafed through the pages. "Greed and ambition, oh yes. No doubt of that. A lord who would

46

sell his father for silver and gold. And as you can imagine, for one inclined to seize power with such bald hunger, he was not likely to be inclined to share it – not with anyone."

"You believe Lord Flint killed his sister?" Karya questioned. "We know her death was announced not long after they came into their inheritance. After the victory of Eris, less than a year. But any details of her passing are scarce. An illness, that's all the official line said, wasn't it? Tragic and unavoidable."

Robin looked at his friend. "Renouncing your father for power and to keep yourself safe and rich, that's vile and unforgivable already," he said. "But to also kill your own twin, just so you don't have to share your new-found station? I can't even imagine someone being capable of that."

"Well, that is what everyone thinks, and of course, what nobody says," the satyr pointed out. "Flapping tongues and noses poked where they are not wanted can land you in very hot water in our current world, young ones. There was little investigation into the death of Lady Tinda. The funeral was swift and private, and Lord Flint spent more and more time in Dis, where Eris found use for him as an assistant to one of her dark-hearted Grimms."

"Wait," Woad said. "So, this horrible lord worked with the Grimms? In what way?"

"At Heaven's Lens in Dis," their guide explained. "Are you familiar with what goes on in that dark place?"

They shook their heads, though Karya pursed her lips. "Nothing good, that's for sure," she said. "Never was a place more inappropriately named."

"Experiments," the satyr said. He shrugged. "That's what we hear, anyway. Mr Nyx, the Alchemist of Eris, locked away in his high tower, tinkering with the fabric of the universe, though who knows what, or why." He indicated for them to come closer and laid out the page of the book he had found for them all to see as they gathered round. "Lord Flint was eager to cement his place at Eris court. To ensure his ongoing favour, one supposes. He gave all resources of the Calescent estate to Nyx. He eagerly assisted him in his workshop for years, though only he could tell you at what they toiled."

He tapped the book. It seemed to be a genealogy of some kind. The page contained a sketch, a portrait of a haughty looking young man, handsome in a sharp way with a high clear brow, aquiline nose and strong jaw. He had long, unbound hair falling down behind his ears, hair as red as blood, and he was dressed in fine and highly decorated robes. The clothing looked similar to what Ffoulkes had worn during his first lesson back at Erlking, Robin thought.

"Lord Flint is handsome," Woad observed. "He hardly looks like a moral-free monster to me."

"Few monsters do," Karya said. "But anyone who could work for Eris, work with Nyx, anyone who could denounce their father and kill their sister to save their own skin and fortune – there is no light behind his eyes for anything other than power and gold."

"You said he put everything the Calescents had at Nyx's disposal?" Robin prompted. "For these … experiments or whatever. What did he have that Eris' people wanted so badly?"

The satyr smirked. "At last, you begin to ask the right questions," he said, approval in his papery voice. "It is said – and as with all information about this family, it is a rumour only – that the Fire Panthea of the Black Hills once possessed the world's last phoenix. Still living at the time. That seems to me something Eris would be interested in possessing."

The old man seemed ambivalent.

Robin tapped the book in the satyr's hand. "Nyx must have had Lord Flint's phoenix at one point, that's for sure. When Jack and I investigated his office in London, we found his journal. Though it was full of snakes, not birds, it had a naked quill, a used feather, tucked in the pages. A phoenix feather."

"If the feather was dead, then so is the bird," the satyr announced. "Phoenix feathers do not burn up until the creature itself has passed for good. Clearly, Nyx used up that resource in his dark experiments, whatever they were. It is a sad thing that phoenixes are now gone utterly from the world."

"Lady Tinda is not dead," Karya said firmly. "Whatever the official story says. We think she ran away, escaped her brother somehow. Maybe she knew he was planning to kill her and had the common sense to get out of harm's way before he could." She glanced from the old satyr to her friends and back. "We think Nyx is looking for her, or for something that she has. Whatever that might be, it's not a phoenix feather, that's clear now. It must be something else."

"Half a heart," Woad murmured to himself.

"Lord Flint let the world believe his sister was dead, but it's not true," Karya continued "She's on the run, or in hiding, and all the forces of Eris are desperately searching for her."

"That's very interesting information, if it's true," the librarian mused. "What could Nyx and Eris want from the Calescents that they haven't already taken?

"Robin went all the way to Titania's Tears to try and learn where this woman might be, and gained nothing," the girl said. "And now we've been led here, but we're still no closer to knowing where she might be."

The old satyr turned the page. Amidst the looping and blotted pen scratched that covered the rest of the page, there was a second sketch. The other Calescent twin.

Robin stared at the drawing of Lady Tinda resting beneath the satyr's fingers. She was shorter than her brother, with a round, smooth face and large eyes. Her hair had been sketched in the colour of flame, and it fell around her shoulders in a wild frizz.

Henry gave his friend a strange look. Robin was staring at the drawing with such intensity, it was unnerving.

"Rob?" he prompted. "It's just a portrait of some little noble woman with exciting hair, mate. You look like you've seen a ghost."

For several seconds, Robin couldn't find words. He shook his head as though to clear it, staring down at the drawing of the short woman peering enigmatically out of the page at him.

"Scion," Karya leaned over at his side, watching him study the sketch. "What is it?"

"Lady Tinda …" Robin managed eventually, unable to tear his eyes away from the portrait. "I've seen her before." It seemed so outlandish. What he was thinking couldn't be true. "The soothsayer, Luna, she *told* me I'd already met her. I thought she must be wrong – I mean, I would have remembered any Panthea or Fae I've met, surely. But she was right. I have. I know her."

He dragged his eyes up and away from the page, staring wide eyed at his confused friends. "I know where she is! She was right under our noses!"

The softly glowing chamber had grown darker around them, little by little, as they explored the book. Unlike Henry and Karya, who were both staring at Robin with undisguised confusion, Woad tilted his head back and looked up at the huge dark pane of translucent rock above them. His brow knotted in worry.

"Umm, guys?" he began in a small voice.

"Under our noses?" Karya ignored the blue boy, still staring at Robin. "What are you talking about? Strigoi and Nyx are hunting her to the end of the world, but you think you've just stumbled across her, easy as you like? When have you met her?"

"Guys, I think …" Woad tugged at Karya's sleeve.

Robin looked at the satyr as Swiftwings snapped the book closed. "Not *just* me," Robin said, still sounding shocked at his own realisation. "Woad has met her too – and Peryl."

"*Peryl?*" Henry rubbed his temples. "I think this is giving me a migraine now. What has that nutcase got to do with anything? And at what point did you and Woad go on a picnic with a bloody Grimm and a missing noblewoman? Was I off sick that day or something, because you'd think we'd all remember a big event like that?"

Robin shook his head. "No, that's just it," he said, still gathering his thoughts. "It *wasn't* a big event – it was nothing. And Woad, well he wasn't exactly Woad at the time. And Peryl wasn't Peryl, either."

"You are making absolutely no sense, Scion." Karya sounded impatient and worried. "Are you sure you didn't hurt your head more than you realised back in the forest?"

"GUYS!" Woad yelled, finally getting all of their attention. He pointed upwards urgently as his companions stared at him. "Where did the sky go?"

Robin and the others looked upwards. The northern lights were indeed gone. They had faded away while they had been talking and had been so engrossed that none of them had noticed it getting darker and darker. But up there, beyond the glass, there were no stars. There were no clouds. There wasn't even any distance. There was only a deep blackness, as though someone had thrown a dark blanket over the roof of the library chamber. And the blackness was moving.

"What … what is that?" Henry said quietly, a tone of foreboding in his voice as he craned his neck to look upwards. The solid blackness outside was moving, undulating and squirming, a solid mass of shadow that writhed ceaselessly and silently, just on the other side of the great pane.

The satyr took a step backwards, looking up in worry, his large book clutched protectively against his chest. From below them, along the unseen corridors and halls of the library, they could all hear distant and muffled noises.

Robin stared up again. His mana stone was tingling, a cold and worried heartbeat on top of his own.

"It's a shadow," he whispered. "No, *lots* of shadows …"

"It's spiders!" Woad suddenly yelped at his side, his yellow eyes like circular lamps.

Karya stepped into the centre of the circle of relics, glaring up, her pale face set and her white hair trailing down her back like mist.

"It's Nyx," she said in a thick voice. "So, he's found us."

Swiftwings, like the others, was staring up at the crystal roof of the chamber of relics, his head inclined to one side as he listened to the echoes of knowledge that vibrated through the Precipitous Library; noises only he could hear.

"The Grimm is here, yes," he confirmed. "Tracked through the tunnels, tracked through the forests, tracked through the waters. He has come for you, and he will find you. He will leave here with prizes, but whether that is you four, or the relics of the Elementals, I cannot foresee."

"He can't take either!" Karya said.

"One is worth more than the other, I suppose." The old satyr stroked his beard. Below and all around, they could hear distant commotion, echoing strangely around the faceted building. Sounds of struggle back and forth, far below them.

The door to the relic chamber burst open with a whoosh of air, making them all jump with alarm.

Robin knew that Swiftwings had locked it as they entered. This was a featherbreath cantrip, expertly wielded to throw the door open wide.

A young satyr in plain robes stood in the doorway, looking desperate and afraid. "The library!" he gasped, staring at the old man across the room. "We're under attack! They have us surrounded." He shook his shaggy head, a mass of sandy curls, looking terrified. "Peacekeepers are here. Here in our sanctuary! A hundred of them, at least! They have breached the doors, Celerialae! What do we do?"

From behind him, down the shimmering spiral staircase they had earlier climbed, they could all hear raised voices and loud crashes, clearer now that the door was open. It sounded like bookshelves being toppled, shattering and crashing as tables were overturned.

"It's our fault." Robin stared at their host, overcome with guilt. "I'm so sorry! They followed us here. I didn't imagine they would find your tunnels. Nyx has been tracking us since the Tears."

He could hear the distant shouts and cries of the book-guardians of the Precipitous Library, the tumult of struggle and chaos that had been led into this place of quiet and reflection. Nyx and his peacekeepers were down there in the main body of the great carved crystal, this monument wrought by the Elementals themselves in the early days of the Netherworlde. Like thugs they were tearing the place apart, righteous in the name of Eris – all because of him.

"We've brought them to your door." He felt helpless. This bastion of knowledge, this secret place, had been hidden away for so long, was now besieged and violated. He had brought death to the satyrs.

Swiftwings looked Robin clearly in the eye, laying a hand on his shoulder. "I brought you to our door, Scion of the Arcania," he told him. "And I did not have to. It was my choice, my judgement. And the consequences …" He looked upwards again, at the shivering mass of ever-moving darkness beyond the dome. "The consequences are mine to bear, not yours."

The sea of spiders above them, writhing against the ancient barrier, was making it creak and crack under their amassed weight. Swiftwings ignored them. He pointed his staff at the satyr, who was still standing, shell-shocked. "Offer no resistance," he instructed. "I am aware we are satyrs, masters of the Air and not unable to defend ourselves, but in this … offer no resistance, do you hear? We are all loyal subjects of the Netherworlde here. We have committed no crime. These brave and loyal soldiers of Eris who have come humbly to our door believe we harbour war criminals. That is why they are here,"

"But master," the younger satyr, clearly confused, indicated the ragtag band of four children. "We do! They're right there!"

"And you and the others must keep the peacekeepers away until they are *not*!" Swiftwings snapped. "Go! For the love of the fates! Delay them, distract them, offer them every possible assistance in searching

52

the library for these dangerous fugitives! Everywhere but *here*, while I think!"

The satyr at the door looked shocked, though he nodded and left without hesitation, closing the door again behind him. They heard his hooves descend noisily down the spiral steps beyond. The librarian swiftly crossed the room and locked it once more with his great ring of keys.

"They'll destroy your library," Robin said desperately. "They'll never believe you weren't helping us, not in a million years. We have to surrender, or all of your satyrs will be killed. It's our fault. You can't sacrifice yourselves for us."

"Listen well to me, Scion." The old man crossed back to him and took Robin by both shoulders. "For there is little time."

"That lock won't hold a Grimm," Karya said quietly to Woad and Henry. She shook her wrist, but her bracelet was dark and dead, useless.

"The path you tread, Robin Fellows, is littered with sacrifices," the satyr told Robin. "And not all of them are yours. You came here to find a lost woman and you have. You were drawn here because the relics of the Elementals called out to your group, and you found them. You must go to her, this woman you seek, who holds the key to saving your friends. If you surrender yourselves now, even with the most noble intentions of saving myself and my brothers here, your mission will have been for nothing."

"We can fight!" Henry said desperately. "There's no way out of this room anyway. We don't have to surrender!"

Woad was nodding in furious agreement. "We might go down, but we won't go down without a fight!"

There was a horrible noise above them, a squeaking crack. They glanced upwards. Several splinters had appeared in the ancient roof above them, frozen lightning against the blackness of the shadow spiders.

"You *must* flee," the satyr said, turning to Henry. "All of you. Take what you came here for, human boy. There is always a way out."

He crossed to the circle of relics, trailing the others with them.

"What does he mean? Take what?" Woad asked Henry. The faun's puzzled expression was lost on his friend. Henry's face was uncharacteristically serious and he reached out and reverently took the shining arrow from the plinth. The relic of the Elemental of Fire. The one he had felt vibrate beneath his hands. He looked at his friends and their questioning faces.

"It's mine," he said simply, seeming unsure how to explain himself. "I don't know why. I just know it is. I knew as soon as I saw it. It was waiting for me." He glanced down at the white shaft, tipped with silver, and the red and golden feathers. "It feels like it belongs in my hand." He blinked, frowning at the simple but elegant creation. "I've never been more sure of anything."

Robin expected the satyr to argue. It didn't seem reasonable for them to simply take one of the greatest treasures of the library, an ancient gift from the Elementals themselves, as though it was a seaside souvenir. But to his surprise, the old man nodded at Henry in approval, leaning with both hands on his staff. "You'll find your role, boy. The fire burns in your heart. Your skill is spreading that to others," he told him with approval.

Swiftwings himself snatched up the small hand-mirror. "The Mirror of Shadows is your exit," he told Robin and the others, speaking quickly now as more tortured creaks and weighty groans came from the darkened crystal above them. The whole chamber was creaking now, like an old wooden ship in a gale. The peaceful and reverent sanctum of the library crushed by the dark mana of Mr Nyx. From beyond the closed door, there was the sound of an argument close by, on the very staircase now. Raised voices and a scuffle.

"I told you all before, the relics are the spine between the pages. They can move between the worlds," Swiftwings explained. "Some of these artefacts ..." He looked at the arrow held reverently but firmly in Henry's hands. "We do not truly know what they do, or how they work. But others ..." he held the hand mirror up, its polished ebony surface catching the light. "Others we do. It can take you anywhere. In this world or the next. Through the shadows and out the other side. But only somewhere you *know*."

He regarded the mirror himself, looking distant. "Listen well. In order to cast a reflection of where you have already been. You need to concentrate on where you desire, where you remember. A clear picture, reflected in your mind. Do you understand?"

Robin didn't but he nodded urgently. More sounds of struggle on the staircase beyond the locked door, and the cracks above them were now raining down a thin sparkling snow of ground dust, fine and weightless.

Swiftwings held the mirror up to the glow of light flowing from the floor, tilting the glass with care and precision, so that its reflective surface caught the light and threw a large oval on the distant angular wall away from the door, in a bare space between the bookcases. In the constant movement of shadow and light, the wavering disc was as tall and bright as a doorway.

"Go now," he insisted. He grabbed Robin firmly by the wrist with his free hand. "And concentrate. You *must* concentrate. You have been schooled in no part of the Tower of Shadow. It allows for no fools, no shred of uncertainty. To make sense of shadows, you must be firm and resolute and *sure*. Know who you are and where you are going, otherwise you will be lost in the darkness."

Robin nodded. "I know who I am," he said with absolute certainty, the shadow of the bog hag's words evaporating from his mind as he stared at the impossibly bright reflection cast by the mirror onto the diamond shine of the wall. He thought of the sketch of Lady Tinda in the old book. "I'm Robin and I'm the Puck. I'm two halves of a whole. And I know exactly where I'm going."

The old man nodded in approval – and at that moment, several things happened. With a crash, three large sections of the roof high above them shattered, raining down shards around the room like deadly hail, shattering deafeningly on the floor and tables. Through the holes, countless spiders immediately began to pour, descending down into the great space in their thousands on endless streamers of web, their legs twitching. They fell like smoke, writhing in great clouds, emitting a low chitinous hiss.

The door across the room from them exploded, bursting inwards in a thousand splinters, scattering across the floor musically. In the doorway, his enormous bulk filling the frame, in his crisp pale suit, stood Mr Nyx.

There were peacekeepers behind him, blocking the stairwell. Robin noticed immediately that several of their patchwork bodies seemed to be spotted with blood, although the Grimm himself appeared pristine. Peacekeepers didn't bleed. It wasn't theirs.

The man surveyed the room quickly, taking in the scene with his small, merry eyes. His mouth curled into a wide smile, and he smoothed back his shock of yellow hair as he stepped, with some degree of pomp and theatre, into the room. The Grimm raised a ghastly white hand towards his horde of spiders above as they tumbled downwards into the space, falling shrouds of twitching darkness, welcoming them fondly.

"Little horn-spawn," he called out in greeting, the same jolly voice as ever. "Where, oh where, to find a bookish boy?" he asked himself aloud. "Why, at a library, of course!" He laughed a little, as though this was all terribly good fun. Spiders pooled at his feet, smoky forms darkening the glowing floors wherever they landed and dimming the room second by second. They were still streaming down from above, hanging in mid-air like thick vines of twitching darkness. "And *what* a library it is!"

"You've no business here, alchemist," the satyr said defiantly. "Go back to your tower and your twisting of the world into lies and deceits. You stand in a place of light and truth."

The smile dropped from the Grimm's face abruptly. "Oh shut up, you old goat, before I have you skinned and curried for my dinner. I'm not here to bother you hermit-scribes, scribbling in your scrolls, scared of the world outside, with your little nub-tails twitching with fear. Keep your ruins and scrabble in the scraps of the old gods.' He pointed across the room playfully.

"I only want those treats there. Especially the skinny blond one. He's a prize for the empress and no mistake. Hand them over and I'll be on my way."

His smile reappeared, wide and oily, as he looked sidelong at the old satyr. "They are nothing to you, anyway. You never met any of them before tonight. What care is it of yours what happens to four foolish wanderers on a mountain-top at night? Your thoughts should be on higher things. Consider it carefully, goat. I might even leave the place standing, I'm in a good mood."

The satyr ignored the Grimm. The air was filled with the sound and movement of spiders. He still clutched the mirror, holding the bright reflection on the far wall behind the Erlkingers, although his hand was shaking, making the image shimmer and shiver like heat-haze.

He looked at Robin. "Find her, this woman," he said quietly. "Find her before this Grimm does. You know where she is?"

Robin nodded. He grabbed Karya's hand, who wordlessly grabbed Henry's and he Woad's in turn.

"Do not lose yourself in shadow," the satyr warned again. "Your reflection must be clear."

Robin *felt* clear. He knew exactly who he was and where he needed to go. He didn't feel helpless, wandering or lost. He wanted to stay, to help the satyr fight the Grimm, and his army of spiders and peacekeepers. But the old man had told him to run. If the relics in the library fell to Eris, it was a sacrifice, and his path was littered with them. He understood why the old man was telling them to go. They were not running away. They were running towards.

Across the room, Mr Nyx had taken several steps into the room, the spiders gathered at his feet, parting before him like a black sea, but as his eyes alighted on the children, he suddenly faltered, coming to an abrupt halt and staring.

His eyes were trained on Karya, whom he seemed to have noticed for the first time, in all the chaos.

"So … you *are* alive," he called over to her. His eyes, once he regained his composure at seeing the girl, glittered greedily.

Although Robin held her firmly, Karya looked back across the room at the large, smiling ghoul, and Robin thought she looked scared. Truly afraid. It was not an expression he was used to seeing on his friend's face.

"I find you in very strange company. You don't look well, child," Nyx said. His eyes roved over her, taking in her white hair and pale face. "Not well at all. How interesting." He tilted his head at her. "You should come home. Let me try to fix you up."

"That place," Karya said, a slight tremor in her voice betraying her, "is nothing but a nightmare in my memories. You don't know the meaning of the word home. You're a monster."

My Nyx did not seem offended by her words. In fact, one corner of his mouth turned up into a half smile. "Your sisters miss you, I'm sure." he said. "Alas … all such tragic failures, to a one. But none of them so rebellious as you. I must say, though you caused me no end of inconvenience, I do admire your spirit."

"Karya, we have to go. *Now*," Robin hissed. From the corners of his eyes he could see spiders pushing in through the broken shining roof, some as large as mice, others like cats. Silent as they crawled in, pushing their fat glossy bodies across the underside of the glass while Nyx kept them talking.

"I don't know you." Karya was staring at the Grimm across the debris of the room, more of his animated mana descending between them, filling the air with movement. The will of Mr Nyx made solid belied his warm smile. They made dark mockeries of the northern lights. "But I know I *did* know you," she continued. "In my bones, I know it. You feel like every bad thing in the world, twisting in my stomach."

The Grimm raised a finger, admonishing a naughty child.

"Now, now," he admonished her. "Manners and decorum, please. Is that any way to talk to your father?"

Karya bared her teeth, allowing herself to be dragged into motion towards the shining reflection of light on the wall by Henry and Robin tugging on an arm each.

"You are *not* my father!" she growled.

Nyx looked thoughtful, frowning at her, and the others, clearly lost in his own meandering thoughts. But then he started to attention, seeming to realise for the first time that something was going on. That perhaps he didn't have his quarry as comfortably cornered as he had imagined. His eyes shot to the satyr holding the mirror, then back at the oval of light on the wall.

"Drop that mirror!" he snapped. Swiftwings ignored him, staring at the children.

"Go!" the Satyr commanded them.

Without Nyx's stare fixing them in place, it was as though a spell had been broken, and they could move again. Robin, Woad, Henry and Karya all turned and bolted towards the patch of bright wall. Robin heard the Grimm yell a command to either the peacekeepers or his spiders to stop them. The hordes of dark and shadowy bodies seemed to turn as one in a huge wave, surging across the floor and walls towards them, a dark tide. Rolling after them.

Fuelled by panic, a treacherous thought entered Robin's mind as they hurtled towards the wall. That the spiders were faster, they would swarm over them, ahead of them. They would cover the walls and block out the oval of light from the shadow mirror, engulfing them all in darkness. He pushed the thought roughly out of his mind.

There was no room for uncertainty. No leisure for it.

It is a very difficult thing to run full speed straight at a solid wall. No matter how hard you try, part of you braces for impact, survival instinct wants to throw your hands up at the last second before you hit, protecting yourself from impact. Robin did neither. He threw himself, body and soul, into the glow cast on the wall from the mirror. Without doubt and without hesitation, he held tightly to his friends as he led them beyond the shadows and out of the world.

3

Broken Heart

Robin hit the ground still running hard, tripping over something and tumbling head over heels. The wind was knocked out of him as Karya, Henry and Woad crashed behind him and followed suit, ending up in an ungainly pile of confusion on top of one another. Brightness stung his eyes and a chill slapped at his skin.

There was a shimmer behind him at the corner of his vision, the Elemental portal through which they had just passed closing, no doubt. As the others rolled off him with a series of ungainly grunts, groans and complaints, he pushed himself up to his knees, a shaking hand raised as he blinked against the unexpected bright light.

"Were we followed?" he asked in a shaking, rather breathless voice.

Passing through the light cast from the shadow mirror had felt nothing like a Janus station. The experience had been something quite distinctly other.

For a second that had felt like an eternity, he had been engulfed in a darkness so vast and smothering, he may as well have been cast adrift in the depths of a cold and starless space. A void so remote and lonely that even hope seemed infinitely too distant. He had struggled to focus his mind on his destination, holding the image like a bright talisman against the icy nothingness dwarfing him. He knew that to waver in that deep and empty place, even for a moment, would mean becoming trapped there eternally. Even now, back in brightness, surrounded by blessedly solid things and wonderfully cold moving air, he still felt he was shaking off numbness and shadows.

He heard a nauseating crunch behind him as Woad stamped heavily on something.

"Just one shadow spider," the faun declared. "Squished now. Horrible icky thing."

Robin peered around. They were all standing on the pavement beside a narrow, cobbled road, which was currently deserted. Rows of small stone houses and shops lined both sides, and a few parked cars stood silent, each encased in a glistening shell of frost. It was bitterly cold, and shallow drifts of dirty grey slush were piled up against the kerbsides. The cold air made a latticework of ice where its fingers traced between the cobbles of the empty road.

The sky above them was clear and bright pink, threaded with only a few pale clouds.

"Where are we? I think I'm going to vomit," Henry asked, swaying a little with disorientation as he got to his feet. "Ow, I've ripped my jeans at the knee there, bugger it."

It must be early morning, Robin thought, and was quietly relieved for that small blessing. There was only that hushed sleepy feeling that falls over quiet places just after dawn. The only sounds a few shrill and distant bird calls from somewhere beyond the street.

"The human world?" Karya asked, still looking terribly shaken up after her confrontation with Mr Nyx.

"Barrowood village." Robin stood up too, brushing himself off and unable to stop himself turning to check behind them. There was nothing there of course, just the dark and shuttered front of a closed barber's shop, but a small part of him still half expected to see Mr Nyx descending on them, with his aggravatingly cheery smile and a wave of disgusting spiders. His skin was still crawling.

"Barrowood?" Karya asked, looking around. She was pulling herself together already, in her usual manner. "We're back at Erlking, you mean?"

Barrowood, the small village that lay at the base of Erlking's hill, was little more than a hamlet. A small and sleepy place with only one high street, a smattering of cottages and a very modest train station where, a lifetime ago it seemed, Robin had first arrived.

"We should get off the road before someone comes along," Robin decided. "I'm dressed like a Netherworlde peasant, and Karya and Woad, with white hair and blue skin, are hardly inconspicuous."

"And I've got a magic arrow. *And* a bloody knee," Henry added, pointing at it emphatically. "But why have we come home, Rob?"

Robin glanced across the street at the shops opposite, all still closed so early in the day. Directly opposite them, sandwiched between a tiny chemist and a rather barren-looking florist, was a narrow shop whose windows were filled with wind chimes, tiny gaudy fairy statuettes, and all the trappings of new age paraphernalia.

"Because Lady Tinda has been hiding here all this time," he replied, setting off across the empty street. The cobbles were slick with frost beneath his feet. "Hiding right in Erlking's shadow."

The others followed, ducking beneath the awning of the rather tatty-looking shop just as a motorised street-sweeper turned a distant corner into the street, clearing away the slush and lumbering along in their direction like an industrious beetle.

"I recognise this place," Woad frowned.

"I don't think it's open yet," Henry peered through the glass panel of the door, hands cupped to either side of his face to shut out the light. "Looks dark inside."

Robin waved a hand over the lock, throwing a casual featherbreath inside to play with the tumblers. There was a swift series of clicks and the door popped open, swinging inwards with a quiet creak and a ding as it hit a door-mounted bell above.

"Oh yeah," Henry mumbled. "Forgot that."

"This is breaking and entering," Karya pointed out as they filed into the gloom of the shop. She didn't sound overly concerned about this, merely stating a fact to be sure they were all on the same page.

Robin closed the door behind them once they were all inside, peering back out through the glass to check no-one had seen them enter from the street. The coast looked clear. "Didn't break anything," he muttered absently. "So it's just 'entering' really. No one ever got arrested for entering a shop."

It was hard to argue with that, so no one did.

The air inside smelled strongly of cheap incense, pungent and rather musty, and he peered around at the rows of old vinyl records stacked here and there, the tottering jumbles of second-hand paperback books and dark wooden shelves full of tarot cards and crystal balls.

"What is this place?" Karya asked.

"Morgana's Sundries," Robin told her, as he made his way towards the glass counter and its silent, shadowy till. "I came here at Christmas. Not *this* Christmas, before then. Woad, you were with me, under a glamour to look human, remember? And we met ... Penny."

"You mean Miss Peryl?" Henry sneered. "Mental psychopath and Grimm. You guys did a bit of Christmas shopping together, did you?"

Robin bristled at Henry's tone. "We didn't *know* she was a Grimm then," he said. "She seemed human."

"Ah yes! That's why this place seemed familiar. I remember now," Woad said. "You were all goggle-eyed and tongue-tied and making a massive idiot of yourself, and she was really annoying."

"No, I wasn't!" Robin snapped, a little louder than he'd intended. "And no, she wasn't," he finished, much quieter.

Karya rolled her eyes as Woad wiggled his eyebrows suggestively at her and Henry in the gloom, clearly indicating that his memory of the encounter was quite different from Robin's.

"She recognised Morgana, even back then," Robin said. "Penny ... Peryl, I mean. I remember her saying that she looked familiar, like the two of them had met before, sometime in the past. I wonder why she didn't go back and tell Eris she'd found her?"

"Who can fathom why Miss Peryl does anything?" Karya reasoned. "Recognised who, Scion?"

Robin slammed his hand down on the old fashioned 'ring-for-attention' bell several times, sending a loud and shrill ringing through the shop. It seemed obscenely loud in the silence of the early morning.

"Morgana!" he called loudly. He rang the bell again.

"Pinky and I got your bow from here, Henryboy," Woad said in conversational tones over the din. "And the purple girl bought him some silly little keychain with a cat on it. He still has it in his sock drawer – not that I root around in there, or anything."

For a few seconds, nothing happened, and then, tentatively, the heavy multi-coloured bead curtain which led into the back of the shop rustled and was drawn aside, and a woman peeped out, managing to look both suspicious and half asleep at the same time.

"I ... we're not open yet," she said groggily. "Dinging me right out of bed. How'd you get in here?"

"I need to talk to you," Robin said. "We're not here to buy anything."

The woman emerged fully from beyond the rustling beads. She was wrapped in a bulky pleated maroon dressing gown and wore large fluffy slippers. Her hair was a sleepy tangle of flame red around her head, and she was blinking at them worriedly through large horn-rimmed glasses that distorted her eyes, making them appear large and owlish.

"Why *are* you here then?" she asked cautiously, her eyes taking them all in. If she was startled by the outlandish sight of any of them, she certainly didn't show it. She was clearly not as shocked at the sight of a blue child or a white-haired girl in furs as one might expect the average independent retailer of Northern England to be.

Robin leaned on the counter. "You know who I am," he told her. "You knew who I was when I came in here ages ago. And you knew who I was with at the time too." He was looking at her earnestly, as she clutched her dressing gown tight around herself at the throat.

"And now I know who *you* are too ... Lady Tinda," he finished.

The short woman froze for several seconds. She appeared to be considering things carefully. Eventually, she pushed her winged glasses further up her nose and approached the counter, her slippers shuffling on the shop floorboards. She spread her hands on the surface and her fingernails, painted a deep purple despite being bitten to the quick, rapped on the glass top a few times.

"Well," she sniffed at length, regarding Robin with narrowed eyes. "Suppose it was only a matter of time until *someone* found me, wasn't it?"

Robin had recognised her as soon as he saw her portrait in the book in the Precipitous Library. The hair of the woman facing him across the counter was a little frizzier perhaps than in the old sketch, the round face hidden now behind ridiculous glasses, but there could be no mistaking it.

"It's better us find you than the other side," Robin said to her. "Morgana ... Lady Tinda. Everyone in the Netherworlde is looking for you, it seems. Strigoi, peacekeepers, the Grimms."

"Wait, wait, wait." Henry raised his hands. "Hold on. Back it up a second, Rob. *This* is Lady Tinda?" He pointed to the woman, looking incredulously at Robin. "It's just ... well, no offence, but ... she doesn't look very ... well, *noble*."

"It's her, I'm sure," Robin still looked at the woman, not sparing Henry a glance. "Lady Tinda, I'm Robin Fellows. I'm the Scion of the Arcania. A friend."

The woman hmphed, sounding unconvinced. She resumed drumming her nails on the counter. "Well, at least two of those things are true, I suppose," she conceded. "Remains to be seen about the last one. I know who you are, I'm not bloody blind." She peered at Henry over the top of her glasses. "And what exactly does this one think he knows about what a noble Panthea looks like anyway?" she asked frostily.

"Oh, ignore Henryboy," Woad said. "We all thought Ffoulkes was noble, and turns out he used to scrub bedpans for the posh folk. Anyone can see you're in disguise, right? Trying to look as un-noble as you can. You deliberately look like that."

The woman pursed her lips a little defensively, patting her frizz of hair. "Erm ... yes, quite so."

"It's a wonderful disguise," the faun said, enthusiasm beaming on his face.

"Yes, *thank you*." The woman glared at him.

"Almost impenetrable," Woad continued.

The shopkeeper turned her attention to Robin, clearly having decided to pretend the faun wasn't there.

"I have been hiding for years in the human world." She frowned at him. "How in the name of the fates did you find me?" She swept her arms around the shop. "This place is deliberately invisible. No-one ever comes in here, and I hardly ever leave it."

"A book in a library, a vision of a memory on top of a waterfall ... it's a long story." Robin waved his hands. "I'll tell you, but not here, it isn't safe anymore," he insisted. "If *we* can find you, *they* can find you. We should leave the village as soon as possible. Come up to Erlking."

Lady Calescent's eyebrows shot up. "*Erlking*," she practically spluttered. "The House of the Fae? Are you absolutely having a laugh? I'm sure I don't need to remind you, but I'm noble, knee-deep-in-Eris, Panthea. I'm hardly welcome there."

"Are you with Eris or against her?" Karya asked the woman, blunt and simple.

"Oh, most assuredly against," the little woman told her, her lip curling. She hadn't hesitated in answering, for even a second. "Unlike my 'loyal' brother. I can assure you, there is no love for that golden witch in my heart. Eris took my home and my family from me. She took everything. That's what Eris does."

"Then you're welcome at Erlking," Robin told her. "Fae, Panthea, all are welcome. It's my house, and I welcome you there. I can offer you sanctuary. Real sanctuary, not hiding in dust and shadows here."

He glanced back through the shop at the street outside. "We really do need to hurry, though," he insisted. "If the Grimm following us is as good a tracker as his elder Strife, they won't be too far behind. I don't want us to be here when they arrive, or worse, when Strigoi blasts the door in. Erlking is safe."

The woman folded her arms, the fluffy cuffs of her voluminous dressing gown sliding down to her pale elbows. "Hah! There's nothing safe about Erlking, that's for sure," she declared.

She looked around the jumbled shop and out of the windows into the morning light, her eyes darting back and forth behind her glasses. After a few moments, she blew air down her nose. "But you're right, it seems. Here isn't safe anymore either, is it? Not if you've found me. Game's up."

She turned away and headed back off towards the beaded curtain. "Give me a moment to get dressed and gather my things. Erlking Hall itself, eh? A frying pan is as safe as a fire it seems."

It was an odd feeling, returning at last to Erlking Hall, especially with the elusive, but quite definitely alive, Lady Tinda Calescent in tow. They passed through the tall iron gates and made their way up the long winding avenue of trees to the top of the hill, quiet in the early morning snow. The trees were bare of leaves and made a skeletal canopy above them, feeding them through a latticework of shadow and light as they ascended the hill, and the hall itself finally came into sight.

Robin knew Aunt Irene and Calypso were currently away from the hall and he was secretly glad of the fact. Having to explain why they were returning from what had originally been a simple expedition, without Ffoulkes or Jackalope, with Karya looking frail and snow-haired, and accompanied by an errant Panthea woman, would not be a quick or simple conversation.

Mr Drover, however, *was* at the door of Erlking when they reached it, halfway up a ladder and snipping away at brittle grey creeper vines as he worked his way through his groundkeeper chores. He almost fell from the top step in surprise at the sight of the four children approaching across the gravel with a strange red-haired woman in tow.

Lady Tinda, formerly Morgana of Morgana's Sundries, Barrowood, had changed from her flannel robe into clothes and a long white coat of what appeared to be soft deerskin, its wide hood lined with white fur. Against the shock of her red hair, the little woman stood out from the muted winter colours of the trees and grounds as clearly as a hunting blaze painted on a forest tree.

"Henry, my lad!" Drover called, scrabbling his considerable bulk down the ladders. His bristly moustache was quivering. "Where in the blazes have you been? You and Karya up and disappear in the middle of the night! Old Hestia pitched a fit. Wanted to fetch Lady Irene back here right away, she did!"

"Sorry, Dad," Henry said sheepishly. He flicked a thumb at Robin. "We had to go and rescue this one and the faun. Spot of bother with a bog hag, you know how it is." He looked rueful. "It's not like I didn't leave you a note."

"A note!" Mr Drover spluttered, shaking his head in disbelief. "A ruddy note!" He looked very much as though he wanted to hug his son and give him a sound clip around the ear. Quite possibly, both at once. He scowled at Henry's bloodied knee. "What's this?"

"Don't fuss, dad. It's just a scrape. It's not like my leg's hanging off."

"And here's the lord of the manor himself," Mr Drover looked to Robin as their group reached the steps. "Good to know you're in one piece! Though you brought a ghost home with you?" He nodded at Karya, who bit back a retort.

"I'm not a ghost, I'm just … very tired," she said, looking it.

Mr Drover shook his head as though this was just the kind of bothersome pranks any parent had to put up with. Children going off to other worlds willy-nilly, coming back days later with grey hair and ripped jeans and covered in scratches from fleeing through forests and bogs and mountains. He dismissed them all with a tut and rested his eyes on the strange woman accompanying them.

"And this is?"

"This is Lady Tinda Calescent of the Black Hills," Robin introduced them. Tinda bowed formally, and Mr Drover snatched his cap off his head.

"We found her, thought it took a lot and cost a lot," Robin said. He turned to the Panthea. "Come inside. We can talk in the lounge."

* * *

Mr Drover showed them inside without any further questions, although Robin heard him muttering something to Henry about ruining a perfectly good pair of jeans again. Erlking Hall was wonderfully warm and welcoming, and Robin wished they were back to stay, but of course, that couldn't be the case. Pyrenight was racing towards them in the Netherworlde, and Jack and Ffoulkes' fate hung in the balance. It was time to finally find out why this missing Panthea woman was so important to Eris' forces, and a way to save their friends before it was too late.

But first, he decided, Henry would get some ointment from Hestia for his knee, Woad and Karya would have a hot drink, and Robin himself would change out of the ragged Netherworlde clothes which had once belonged to a bog hag's previous meal.

"Well, this is all rather grand," Lady Tinda said. She was sitting in a high-wingback chair in a softly lit room. Above the panels of blue-painted wood which ran tastefully all around the lower half of the room, tapestries hung from the walls, covering every inch of the bare plaster above, and depicting the wild hunt in colourful and detailed embroidery. Dogs and rabbits, stag and doe, and riders on horseback flowed around the room in procession, frozen in stitches. There were even a couple of unicorns depicted in the detailed decoration, although they were decidedly more noble and ethereal than the predatory beasts they had met in reality.

A merry fire was crackling in the large stone fireplace, sending hisses and pops into the room. It chased the morning chill from the air and its flickering light seemed to make the embroidered figures all along the walls shiver and dance, as though the wild hunt was in motion all around them in an endless circle.

Lady Tinda, of noble birth herself – despite all appearances – seemed to feel much at home.

Mr Drover had disappeared into the depths of Erlking, gruffly mumbling something about going off to find Hestia to arrange some refreshments for their guest. Henry had taken himself off upstairs to his rooms, saying only that he had to fetch something for the journey ahead. And so it was Karya, Robin and Woad who found themselves sat side by side on a firm and delicate sofa, across from the Fire Panthea who was nestled in her chair, her feet barely touching the floor as her eyes took in Erlking.

"I'm sure you're used to grander," Karya said. "Nobility of the Black Hills, after all. Makes one wonder, really, why someone would fake their death and run away from a life of such luxury."

"I didn't *fake my death*," Tinda said smartly.

All three of them looked at her expectantly. "Flint did that. My worm of a brother." She sighed, realising they were waiting for an explanation for the rumours surrounding her alleged untimely demise. "After I'd gone, I mean. After I fled my home." She narrowed her eyes behind her glasses. "Too much of an embarrassment for him, you see? To let it be known that I'd slipped away, out of his grasp. That wouldn't do at all. People at court would talk! No, better to say I had died. Saves face. Keeps his position. And that always was more important to him than anything else. Position and power."

"Your own brother would rather pretend you were dead than risk losing face in noble society?" Robin found this difficult to believe.

The little woman curled a lip, the reflected flames of the fire flashing in her spectacles. "My brother condemned our own father to death. For power. For wealth and blind ambition. So yes, it's not so hard to believe. Flint dubbed our father a traitor and betrayed our family, all to keep his position. A little thing like faking his sister's death is peanuts after that."

She drew her coat tighter around her, despite the warmth of the fire.

"You said others were looking for me still? Eris' goon squad?" She apparently wished to change the subject.

"Mr Nyx, yes," Robin said. "He's one of the Grimms …"

"I know who he is," she sneered. "Dark meddler, perverter of nature, that one. Oh, I am more familiar with Mr Nyx that I would like to say. He sank his teeth into my brother. Flint spent a deeply unhealthy amount of time at Nyx's workshop, Heaven's Lens. Assisting in … fates-know-what kind of … abominations." She shook her head. "Flint has always had a dark heart, even before the war and what happened to Father. My brother has always been attracted to the darkness behind the flame. But the alchemist? That Grimm butcher? Well, he has a talent for finding a person's weakness, their deepest fears or most ardent desires. He puts his shadow spiders into their heads." She looked as though she would like to spit into the fire. "Nyx twisted him further than ever."

She looked up at the three of them, pursing her lips. "It's why I had to flee, you see?" she insisted. "That's what you want to know, isn't it? I wasn't *safe* there anymore. With Father gone. Flint wanted all the power. I was in his way. Nothing works without the two of us, that's something Father always made sure of. Half Flint, half me."

She leaned forward and tapped the small coffee table between them for emphasis. "But I'm no fool. Never was. I can tell when there's trouble coming. I knew it was only a matter of time until …"

She sat back, a little slumped in the chair. "Well, until either I got accused of being a Fae sympathiser, same as Father, and ended up in one of the camps, rotting away in the Hills of Blood and Bone, or worse … waking up one day to find my throat's been cut in my sleep."

"I don't think you wake up if your throat's cut," Woad raised a hand, as though offering an insight in a schoolroom.

The woman seemed just as scattered as she had the last time Robin had met her, back in her store when buying presents. "So, you fled the Netherworlde, and came to hide here, in the human world," he prompted. "You became …" He gestured as politely as he could at her rather dishevelled and eclectic appearance, "*this*, and then you just kept your head down? Hoped your brother and his Grimm cronies would never track you down?"

"You don't know what it's like, living in constant fear for your life," she sniffed. "Knowing there are enemies out there, hunting you all the time, waiting to drag you back to Eris."

"Robin knows exactly what that's like," Karya pointed out, her tone rather sharp. "He's the Scion of the Arcania, remember? Even *less* popular with Eris than a deserter noble, I imagine."

"Ah. Yes." Tinda rubbed the bridge of her nose between her glasses a little absently. "Well, I suppose you do know how it feels, after all." She sniffed, glancing at the fire, and the tapestries, her eyes flitting around the room like a distracted bird before settling back on her audience. "To answer your question, yes. I came to the human world. Moved around a lot, went by a lot of names. Disappeared every time I thought I saw a shadow jump." She sighed, smoothing her deerskin coat affectionately and seeming a little wistful. "I've been batty Morgana for a couple of years now. It's been nice and quiet, to be honest. For a while I actually thought I'd found somewhere out of the way enough to get a little peace." She raised a hand and pointed across the table at Robin.

"Right up until the day *you* came strolling in my shop like bally-o, trailing one of the bloody Grimms themselves along with you, bold as brass and twice as shiny, that is."

She puffed her cheeks out. "Put the cat amongst my pigeons that day did, I don't mind telling you."

"But you didn't flee," Robin said to her. "You still stayed in Barrowood, even after you'd met me, after you *knew* a Grimm had found you. Why not run again?"

Tinda considered this for a moment, looking off away from the children and staring unfathomably into the flames. The light of the fire played across her face, her expression unreadable.

"It's not easy to put into words," she said eventually, sounding irritable. "When you came in the store, I just felt ..." she shrugged, "like it was meant to be. That it was no accident that I was there, and you were there, and that everything was in the right place at the right time." She laughed humourlessly. "Funny old thing. I'm not a huge believer in destiny but listen to how I speak. I sound like the Oracle herself!" She flicked her thumbnail. "You seemed the right place to hide it."

Robin was confused. The three children perched on the sofa before the fidgeting woman exchanged looks. "Hide what?" he asked

The Fire Panthea didn't respond or look back to them. She was inspecting her thumbnail with great scrutiny.

"There's more to why you ran away from your home, isn't there?" Karya pressed, ever perceptive. "It wasn't just that you thought your brother might be trying to do away with you. You strike me as the kind of resourceful woman who could defend herself if it came to that."

"Nyx and Strigoi," Karya said. "Both of them are searching for you, but I doubt it's simply to ask after your health, am I correct?" She nodded towards Robin. "This one says he saw them in the Sorrows, harassing some poor pawnbroker, seemed to suspect you might have fenced something through him, or hidden something at his shop."

The woman didn't reply. She glanced intently into the flames, looking withdrawn and rather sulky.

"I get the impression," Karya fished, "that they have been doing the same all over the Netherworlde. You have something of great value. Something you fled the Black Hills with – and they want it back, don't they? And you feel they mustn't have it. That's why you really ran away."

Tinda turned to look the girl over, seeming rather thoughtful. "Not much gets past you, does it?" she said. "You look like you're at death's door, girl. But you're practically a sleuth. I'm still deciding what to tell you."

"Decide quickly." Robin couldn't keep the impatience out of his voice. "Our friends' lives depend on it, and we don't have time to dance around like this."

"Half a heart," Woad chirped, repeating his earlier suggestion. Karya and Robin looked at him, waiting for further elaboration. The faun grinned and jogged Karya's elbow.

"That's what you said, boss. When you were all trance-like at Christmas. Secret sister." He indicated the Panthea noble with a display spread of his hands. "She's got half a heart."

Robin remembered the family crest of the illuminated pages of Mr Nyx's journal. Twin snakes, one light, one dark, rising up and twining around each other, the notes on either side reading *brother* and *sister*. They had been crowned in the crest with something resembling a large jewel, cracked in half down the centre.

"I've never pawned my treasures," Tinda snorted. "Though that's just the sort of irresponsible thing I would expect Flint to imagine I would do." She looked back to them from the fire. "No. My burden has travelled with me, and has been kept well away from my brother and his venomous spider superior at all costs."

The door to the tapestried study opened, surprising them all, and Hestia shuffled in carrying a tea tray laden with cups, milk jugs and sandwiches for all, and looking most terribly put out at having to serve the children as well as their guest. She busied herself laying the refreshments on the small table between them, then Henry came in, almost colliding with the housekeeper on her way out.

"Sorry all," he said. "Did I miss much? Took me ages to find it. Think *someone's* been tidying my room while we were away." He said this last sentence in a loud and disapproving tone, clearly meant to be heard by the retreating Hestia, who muttered something back to him that Robin dared not repeat.

"Find what?" Karya wanted to know as Henry closed the door behind him, shutting the nosy housekeeper out. The girl sounded clearly irritated. It was hard enough to get a straight answer out of Lady Tinda without interruptions.

Henry held aloft his bow. The white wood pale in the firelight, the three red gems set along its length catching the flames and flashing impressively. He grinned. "We were in such a rush last time to come and save dear old Woad from becoming an *amuse-bouche* for a bog hag, I didn't think to bring it. But if we're headed back into the Netherworlde to save Karya's boyfriend and the old man, I thought I'd be better off armed."

"You're more likely to have someone's eye out with that thing than be of any use with it," Karya complained. "And he is *not* my boyfriend, you absolute pedant."

Henry shrugged. "Well, I'm bringing this anyway, especially since I got that arrow from the library. Arrow's no good without a bow, right?"

"Henry, sit down and be quiet," Karya told him. "Lady Tinda was *just about* to tell us why she's been in hiding and why Eris' people are hunting her." She gave the red-headed woman a pointed look. "*Weren't you?*" she added in a firm voice.

Robin shuffled up on the sofa, moving his satchel and placing it across his lap to make room for Henry, who slouched bonelessly down beside him. He was in agreement with Karya. This woman was cagey to a fault, and they needed straight answers – quickly. His mind kept straying back to the library, wondering what had become of the satyrs there. What had become of the other Elemental relics still held in its crystal chambers. Had everything fallen to Nyx now? To Eris?

Tinda looked curiously at the tray of small fancies which Hestia had brought in. She daintily selected a small caramel wafer and sat back in her chair. The fire had begun to die down a little.

"My kind need flames for a good story," she said, half to herself. "Then I can *show* you the past."

"You're a Fire Panthea," Woad noted. "Can't you just *whoosh* it?" He waggled his fingers emphatically.

She shook her head. "I have no mana stone."

"Why not?" Karya looked confused. Every free Fae and Panthea had a mana stone with which to focus and direct their magic. They had only ever met Jackalope without one, and that was because his had been taken forcibly from him in the prison camps of Eris, along with his horns.

Tinda looked amused in a bittersweet way. "I gave it away," she said. Before further questions could follow, she flicked a hand at Robin. "You, however, have fire in your little handbag, I can feel it from here. Pass me that."

"It's a *satchel*," Robin grumbled, but he fumbled inside it until his fingers found the fire-gem. The cubic cornucopia still felt oddly warm in his hands, last used to light and extinguish their campfire in the mountains of the Netherworlde. He passed it carefully into her outstretched hand, and she immediately turned and cast it casually into the grate.

The fire leapt with a rush and a roar as it landed amongst the logs, brightening the room and sending long tongues of flame up the dark chimney.

In the flickering glow, the room seemed to grow darker around them, as though it were evening beyond the windows, not the crisp cold air of morning. The tapestries fluttered in the firelight and shadows, creatures of the wild hunt rearing and shivering, and the Lady Tinda stared fixedly into the flames.

Robin and the others followed her eyes, watching the flames dance hypnotically as she began to speak.

"My brother was right about one thing," she began. "My father *was* a traitor to Eris." There was pride in her voice. "Although that's twisting history of course. Eris was the real traitor. My father, like *all* Panthea before her rebellion, served loyally the King and Queen of the Fae."

She shrugged. "When the war came, it tore apart not only the Fae and the Panthea, but tore the Panthea from one another as well. Eris was brutal, unbending. You were with her or you were against her. Anyone still loyal to the king and queen, anyone who refused to betray them, people like my father, were branded traitor by the traitors." She laughed; a little snort of derision.

"War," she said. "Makes sane men mad, and fools of us all. But my father never wavered. When the long war began, he remained loyal to the Fae. This was before we were born, Flint and I."

Robin, staring into the fire as he listened to the woman, fancied he could see figures moving, dancing back and forth in the leaping flickers.

"My family ruled the Black Hills," Tinda said. "And we were skilled in many ways useful to the cause. I learned much later that, when the uprising first began, King Oberon and Queen Titania set my father a secret task. The construction of a device. A great and powerful thing. I didn't learn much of what it was until I was an adult myself. But it was a tool for the Fae to use."

In the flames, a figure seemed to stand, with a taller figure flanking either side of him, both crowned with tall antlers. Lord Calescent with the King and Queen of the Fae.

"The rulers of the Netherworlde were shrewd and wise, you see," Tinda told them. "They knew ahead of time what was going to happen, even in those early days, with all the long and bloody years of the war ahead of them. They knew they were going to disappear, that Eris was eventually going to win, and that their remaining people would be doomed without them. They laid groundwork, they made plans to save their people when that moment came. To take the leaderless Fae away, far beyond Eris' reach. Their people would be driven underground, quite literally. Hiding beneath the Netherworlde avoiding persecution."

"And this secret tool your father was told to make, that was supposed to help the Fae with hiding and surviving after the shattering of the Arcania?" Robin asked.

"It was. It was to help them reach where they needed to go," the Fire Panthea confirmed. "The Nethercity. Have you heard of it?"

"Everyone in the Netherworlde has heard of the Nethercity," Karya said. "It's a myth, most believe. The last fully standing city built by the Elementals themselves, before the Fae even came into being." She looked to Robin. "Fairy tales, like your world's Atlantis, only not beneath any ocean. The Nethercity is supposed to be deep underground somewhere, buried beneath layers of impenetrable rock, and sealed away for eternity."

"A good place for your people to hide when everything inevitably went badly for them," Tinda said. "A good place to live, protected, and to eventually plan a rebellion and to overthrow the one who would crown herself empress."

"But even if it was a real place and it could be found," Karya argued. "We're talking deep, old magic. What part of 'layers of impenetrable rock' is unclear here? The fabled city is said to have been deep in the earth, beneath the hardest bedrock. No drill, no pickaxe could reach it. Even an absolute master of the Tower of Earth could not make a crack to break through the crust of the underworld into that place."

"If it even existed," Woad added helpfully.

"That's true. Not without the right *tools* at least," the lady agreed, allowing a nod. "And so my father was, in secret, commissioned to construct a way of travelling beneath the world. A burrowing marvel, unmatched by any before it and utterly unstoppable. After the fall of Oberon and Titania, at the shattering of the Arcania, this was to be brought to the Sidhe-Nobilitas. A gift for those noble knights, a transport by which they might ferry their lost people to deep and silent safety, far from the fury of Eris above."

"But … that didn't happen, did it?" Henry pointed out, looking confused by the story. "I mean, we all know what happened when Eris won. There was no mass exodus of the Fae to safety. Most of the Sidhe-Nobilitas, Robin's parents and the others, they were hunted down and outright killed by Strigoi and the Grimms. The few of the old knights who were lucky enough to get away went into hiding, like Hawthorn."

He looked at Robin apologetically. "And most of the rest of the Fae people were captured and killed, or dragged off to camps in the following years. There was no great rescue. No exodus to any secret safe haven."

In the flames, the images of the king and queen flickered, and they were lost, leaving only the solitary figure wavering alone.

"No, it did *not* happen," the Panthea said, looking a little haunted. "This device, my father's last and greatest work, an ark to carry the Fae people to salvation, never saw any use." She swallowed, seeming to gather herself. "My father's skills, all his hard work and devotion, and all the mighty magic and power of the king and queen themselves … all of it wasted, all plans ruined, and all … because of me."

She looked over to Robin, facing the only Fae she had seen since the war, and there was an unbearable unspoken apology in her eyes. "All ruined – because myself and my brother were born."

The fire crackled and hissed. Shadows played across her face a moment before she continued.

"The power of the device, you see, this salvation ark of the Fae. The magic that animated it, made it burn through the earth, unstoppable, unimpeded by *any* wall of rock – even the great shell of the Nethercity. That fuel, that all-important powering source, was something the king and queen did not give to my father until after the war was lost. *After* they disappeared."

"So they had him construct a great toy," Woad whispered. "But only gave him the batteries afterwards?"

Lady Tinda nodded, glancing away from the fire and up at the watchful beasts hanging in cloth from the walls all around.

"Eris had won. The Arcania shattered, the rulers gone. It was a chaotic time. The Netherworld was in turmoil, uncertain. The factions of Eris sweeping through the land, cementing their new-found sovereignty.

"A messenger of the Fae, Hammerhand himself, arrived one night at our mansion in the Black Hills. My father at the time was still mourning the loss of the King and Queen. His wife, my mother, was heavily pregnant, ready to bring new life into the world, now a dangerous place of uncertainty and upheaval.

"Hammerhand brought something with him, as he had been instructed. The predestined heart of my father's subterranean ark. A great ruby it was, large as a baby's head, and filled with such power." She sighed, looking back at the four Erlkingers. "Such power," she repeated. "Hammerhand had brought my father a shard of the shattered Arcania. The Shard of Fire."

Everyone exchanged looks. So, the Fire Shard had lain with the House of Calescent all this time.

"They had to wait," Karya realised. "King Oberon and Queen Titania knew their fate. They knew what was going to happen to the Arcania. And that afterwards, one of the shards could power this contraption they had commissioned. From their own destruction they forged a way to save their people.

"Quite so," Tinda said. "Sounds noble on paper, doesn't it? The trouble is, though, that the Fae rulers, in their typical whimsy, did *not* bequeath the Shard to my father. They wished to ensure that the true loyalty of the Panthea to the Fae would continue, would follow in subsequent generations. Hammerhand told my father that the Shard, this great and potent source of magic, was promised to his unborn child. Only when the child was born would the Shard come into ownership, and the device would be ready to sail away, taking the lost Fae through the darkness. New life would be the catalyst to their own death. A new Panthea birth would signal the birth of a new way of life for the Fae. Deep in the shadows and safety of the great, lost Nethercity."

In the flames of the grate, Robin saw, there were two figures now flickering in and out, and one seemed to lean their head on the shoulder of the other. Lovers, comforting one another. Above their heads, a flicker of flame seemed to shimmer, like a suspended jewel. Lord and Lady Calescent and the Shard of Fire, their legacy gift from the Fae to whom they were so loyal.

"What went wrong with this plan?" Robin asked.

"We did," Tinda sighed. "Flint and I, twins. How ... unexpected." She looked down at her hands in her lap. "Our mother died bringing into the world not the one child they were expecting, but *two*. Following our birth and her death, our father was left to raise us alone. And the Shard, the heart of the great device, which had never been intended for more than one person, but promised by the rules of the old magic to the offspring of the Lord ..."

"It split." Robin saw the flickering jewel in the fire. It seemed to divide, cracked and separated down the middle, as one of the two flame figures faded away, leaving one bright silhouette standing alone holding twin bundles, twin babies.

"That's what happened, isn't it?" he realised. "The Shard of Fire, faced with not *one* owner as expected, but two souls in its charge, it broke into two halves."

"Half a heart," Woad whispered, nodding and looking pleased with himself.

Tinda nodded, taking a poker and stirring up the fire, displacing the imagined figures Robin had been looking at. The agitated fire in the grate seemed to writhe like snakes.

"We should have been one," she said. "Our double birth, our very existence, rendered both halves useless. The great work to which my father had dedicated his life could never be used. It sat in secret beneath our halls, huge and still and silent, gathering dust, useless and dead."

She looked from the fire to Robin, and her eyes seemed to shine. "And so the Fae died," she whispered. "Because *we* were born there was no ark to save them, to carry them to the Nethercity. Because *we* were born, they burned on bonfires in countless numbers, and the Hills of Blood and Bone piled high with sawn-off horns. Because *we* were born, what remained of the Sidhe-Nobilitas had nowhere to lead their people, nowhere ... except into the wilds, to hide and scavenge like animals.

And Eris hunted them down, one by one … like bothersome foxes."

Her eyes slid to her lap. "Because we were born, your parents are dead, and your people are slaves or worse, with no place of safety."

No one seemed to know what to say. Woad, Karya and Henry seemed to be avoiding each other's eyes.

"That burden can't be placed on you," Robin said to the woman eventually. "You were just babies. The plan failed, that's all. It's tragic … but it isn't your fault."

"We grew up …" the Panthea told them. "Flint and I, in the greatest luxury. It was the new age of the Panthea, and we were a noble and powerful family, full of wealth and opportunity. The world belonged to Eris, the Fae were almost all gone. Captured, killed or tucked away out of sight of decent normal people." She shook her head. "We feasted while what remained of your people starved. We danced at balls and dined at parties while the last remnants of your people scrounged and starved in the woods and the wild places. We had stolen their salvation, and we didn't even know it."

Lady Calescent reached down and casually poured herself a cup of tea from the pot Hestia had brought in. Her face was calm, difficult to read, though her hand shook a little as she raised the cup to her lips and took a sip. It occurred to Robin that the woman had been running and hiding from many and complex things, not just her brother.

"When I was grown," she nodded to Robin, "and my kind grow much faster than yours, my father finally took us both beneath the mansion. He was old and ill by then. I believe his guilt at failing to carry out his mission ate away at his life more than time and age ever could. In the caverns below, he showed the device to us. He told us that the two Shards we each owned, our mana stones as far as we understood, were meant to be whole. He told us the purpose of the vast device." She set down her cup with a click.

"Well! Flint was in a rage." Her voice quavered slightly. "He had been raised on Eris' propaganda, we all had. The Fae were monsters. The Fae were the enemy, tyrannical overlords we had righteously cast down. He was fanatical and loyal to Eris. Many Panthea are … or at least many of them make a show of being, to save their own necks from the block, I imagine. More than you'd think." She pursed her lips. "Not Flint, though. He was a *true believer*."

"And you weren't?" Henry asked.

"I loved my father," she said simply. "I trusted my father. Flint loved nothing but power and wealth and influence. And he trusted no one."

"Your brother saw an opportunity to seize all the power of the Black Hills for himself," Robin guessed. "He betrayed his own father, exposed his past … his allegiance with the Fae, and his plans for this device to save the sworn enemy of Eris."

"Exactly," Tinda confirmed. "Father had wanted the two of us to find a way to make the burrowing ark work. There were still Fae out there, he told us. He had contacts, and he had heard encouraging whispers. There were rumours of an underground rebellion forming, led by a few surviving members of the Sidhe-Nobilitas. Instead, Flint delivered our own father into Eris' hands. Father was executed, of course."

She paused a moment, and sipped her tea, slurping it loudly.

"And the power and standing of the Calescents passed to the two of us. Flint went … downhill, after that. Perhaps the enormity of what he had done began to gnaw away at him, the fact that he had killed his own father." Her eyes narrowed behind her glasses.

"I like to think so, but in truth, he was *always* greedy and unbalanced. He began to spend more and more time away from our home. Months at a time in Dis, moving in the very highest circles of Eris' court. Taken under the dark wings of the Grimms themselves. He became an assistant to Nyx. Which was the worst thing that could have happened to him."

The tea seemed to have left a bitter taste in her mouth, as she had a sour expression as she set it down in its saucer on the table. "The Grimms came to our home several times. Strife and Moros, the terrible twins. That sharp-tongued young girl and the great flame-haired brute, Peryl and Ker. I hated *all* of them, but none more than Nyx. The alchemist had his claws in my brother, his spiders whispering in his mind, twisting his thoughts, and the two of them spent countless hours together, either at the Grimm's foul workshop in Dis, or hidden away beneath our mansion, trying to coax even the slightest bit of life from my father's ark."

She tilted her head to one side. "Understandable of course. I mean, think about it. What a treasure to find! What a boon that would be for Eris! Imagine it in her hands. A siege weapon which could breach the defences of *any* castle, *any* keep. A burrowing battering ram that would leave no door unbroken for her." She looked around the room at the fluttering tapestries of the lounge. "Even Erlking, perhaps." Her voice was quiet and thoughtful.

"They couldn't make it work though, could they, your brother and his new master?" Karya guessed. "Despite how much honour and reward such a gift would bestow upon them from the empress. Not with the Shard of Fire broken in half, and unable to power it."

"Now I understand why you ran away," Robin realised. "You knew it was only a matter of time until …"

"Until my brother decided to take my Shard from me, yes." Lady Tinda confirmed, her face dark. "Of course, it had occurred to me, too. The Shard had always been meant for one, and the chance of our birth had torn it in two. But if one twin was dead … could the Shard be re-forged? Made whole again? And my father's great work completed? It occurred to me, so I knew it *must* have occurred to Flint."

"So this is what Strigoi was looking for at the Sorrows, at that pawn-broker's, and everywhere else." Robin stared at her. "He suspects you might have hidden your half of the Shard somewhere. Squirrelled it away, so that even if *you* were found and captured, they still couldn't take *it*."

"You said you gave it away," Karya said, sounding very concerned at the thought of this. "Where is it now? Who did you give it to?"

Lady Tinda laced her fingers together and gave them all a long look, as though she had finally decided that none of them were very bright.

Eventually she nodded to Robin. "Why, I gave it to him, of course."

Robin's eyes were wide. "What? To me?" His voice was incredulous. The woman was talking nonsense. "I think I'd remember something like that!"

"I already told you," she insisted. "That day, when you came into my shop. I knew who you were, and I knew where you were from. Here was a Fae at last, right in front of me, after all these years. And I knew you lived in the great house on the hill, and what this place really was. What safer place to hide something valuable from Eris than at Erlking itself? I would *finally* be able to stop running."

The others were staring at Robin, clearly as confused as he was.

"Don't look at me," he said, defensive. "You really think I'd pocket half a Shard of the Arcania and just not bother to tell any of you about it?"

"It's rather reassuring to me that none of you have ever even known you have it. More likely to keep it out of Eris' hands." Lady Tinda pointed to

Henry. "My brother still holds his Shard-piece, I imagine. But *my* half a heart is right there … in that human boy's hands."

Everyone turned to look at Henry, who looked back like a deer caught in headlights. Slowly he looked down to his hands, at the white bow he held, the one Robin had bought as a gift for him, long ago from Morgana's shop down in the village. His eyes rested on the three red jewels set glittering along its length.

"The two little ones are paste. Just fake for decoration, camouflage," the woman by the fire explained. "But *that* one …"

Henry's fingers lightly stroked the large angular jewel set at the centre of the bow, carefully inlaid into the pale wood.

"*That* is the broken Shard of Fire."

4

Hills of Silver and Scarlet

Several things happened immediately after Lady Tinda's declaration.

Robin reached out tentatively to touch the Fire Shard, frowning in confusion as he felt nothing. No power emanating from it, no echo of the resonant hum he had felt with each of those he had encountered in the past. The Fire Panthea watched him with caution, her eyes hidden behind a flare of reflected flame flashing on the lenses of her glasses. Behind her, the fire in the grate suddenly roared, surging and growing in strength and heat until the mouth of the fireplace looked more like the open maw of a steam engine's molten belly. A tornado of flame shot up the chimney like a howling beast as the tongues of fire pushed and pressed against the stones of the grate. Light blazed in the room, making the embroidered walls glow orange, the beasts seeming to leap and arch their stitched spines, as though trapped not in an illustrated forest but some molten inferno.

Beside Robin, her ghostly hair glowing in the sudden light like a halo, Karya, looking woozy, leaned unsteadily forward on the sofa until she was doubled over and with no great ceremony, threw up noisily on the hearth rug.

"What on earth was that?" Henry asked. He was pacing the floor of Karya's bedroom, back and forth like a twitchy drill sergeant, as Robin and Woad tried to encourage the shaky girl to lie down atop the bedsheets. In the doorway of the room, Hestia stood, wringing her hands looking frantic. Beside her, the small form of Lady Tinda, with her arms folded and a thoughtful look on her face, regarded the girl with her purple-painted lips pursed.

"I'm okay," Karya insisted, her voice hoarse. "Stop fussing me. It was just a dizzy spell. I don't need to lie down!"

They had brought her directly to her room following her sudden sickness downstairs. Lady Tinda had extinguished the fire immediately, trapping the sudden and powerful inferno within the cubic cornucopia before handing it back to Robin, as Henry and Woad had steadied the swaying girl. Hestia had been summoned immediately and there had been a fair few minutes of frantic flapping.

Robin now crossed to the window of Karya's bedroom and opened it, letting the cold winter air into the room. He thought Karya looked terrible. She was sweating and shaking. He was no medic, but Gran had always sworn by the restorative powers of 'a bit of fresh air'.

Looking back to the bed, he regarded his friend. Stripped of her bulky animal skin coat, which always made her appear larger than she was, she now seemed frail and small as a bird. Her eyes were dark and sunken, and her skin as white as paper. She was getting worse by the minute.

"You're not okay," he insisted, for what felt like the tenth time. Karya was a terrible and uncooperative patient. "There was blood in your … when you …"

"Barfed," Woad added, helpfully but quietly, from where he perched, a ball of anxious shadow at the foot of her bed.

"What was that?" Henry asked, alarmed. He was still pacing, with his bow slung over his shoulder. "Ever since the lake during the eclipse, when your hair turned grey," he said. "And then when you tore us through to that village to meet up with Robin to save Woad …" He ran his fingers through his hair, at a loss. "No, before *that* even, when you collapsed at Christmas, you've been getting worse and worse, but it's faster now, we need to *do* something."

"What we need to do is save Jack and Ffoulkes," Karya snapped, shooing Robin away as he approached the bed, and sitting up despite everyone's wishes.

Henry shot her a look which seemed both exasperated and hurt. She caught it and looked away, fuming.

"Oh, we'll save your bloody boyfriend, don't worry about that," the dark-haired boy snapped, his cheeks and neck red.

"Henry …" Robin tried to interject.

"But what's the use of bringing him back if by the time we do, you've ..." Henry flapped his hands, unable to make himself finish his sentence.

"Shuffled off the mortal coil? For the last time. He's not my boyfriend, you absolute ... insufferable ... git!" Karya said darkly, through gritted teeth. Henry scoffed, looking fraught, which didn't improve things.

"No?"

"No!"

"Then why the hell did you kiss him? Eh?" Henry blurted out. His eyes were wide and shocked, as though he had surprised himself. Robin felt that his friend looked as though he wanted to clap his hands over his mouth, to stop himself saying anything else he didn't intend to. Instead, Henry settled for gripping the bed frame tightly with both hands, knuckles white.

"Because I'm *dying*!" Karya yelled.

The room fell into silence. Nobody seemed able to look at anyone else. Robin found himself peering fixedly at a spot on the wall just behind Karya's head, feeling sick to his stomach. Woad looked down. Henry was glaring at his own knuckles, the red flushes in his face drained to pale.

"You're not ..."

"Yes!" she cut him off. "Yes, I am. I'm dying, okay? And I know it. We *all* know it. And not that I owe an explanation to you of all people, or to anyone for that matter, but as you simply must know, I kissed him because I was scared!"

Her voice cracked a little, hoarse, and she coughed, her throat still raspy from throwing up downstairs. When she continued, her voice was quieter. "I was scared, and I was sad, and it didn't seem fair. And it was wet and dark, and the moon was on fire, and he was there, and he was pretty. And it seemed like a good idea at the time." She sighed, leaning back against her pillows.

"I didn't feel I had time left to *waste* ... on anything I wanted to do. Anything I wanted to see or be or experience." She passed a hand over her eyes, looking extremely tired. "I feel I have even less time, now."

"You're not going to die, boss." Woad's voice was as quiet and subdued as Robin had ever heard it. His hushed tone was almost superstitious, as though to speak it any louder would be inviting the world to challenge his words. "We won't let that happen to you."

Karya dropped her hand from her eyes, staring up at the ceiling. Robin reached out and took it in his own. Instinctively, she tried to pull her fingers away, but he closed his hand over hers, and begrudgingly, she allowed herself to be held.

"Woad's right. We won't," he said to her. "I promise. You, Ffoulkes, Jack …" He trailed off.

I'll save you all, he said in his head, but found himself suddenly unable to speak the words out loud. He felt all at once very young indeed, a child trying to play the part of an adult, and being rather useless at it. Seeing Karya so tired and scared, Henry and Woad so afraid, his words dried up in his throat. Hardly the saviour of an entire race. Robin found himself wishing Aunt Irene was here, feeling sure she would know what to do for the best. She always knew what to say, what to do, to make things better. It was comforting. And he felt immediately angry at himself for wishing it.

Karya seemed to read his face. "Scion of the Arcania," she said with a wan yet affectionate smile. "Always determined to save everyone in the world, as usual. All on your own."

"He's *not* on his own," Henry said. His voice was quiet and contrite, clearly feeling terrible about his outburst. They looked over at him. His eyes flicked to Karya. "I'm … you know … sorry," he mumbled. "About…"

"Being an ass?" She raised her eyebrows. And then, softer: "I know. It's okay."

"None of us are on our own," Woad nodded encouragingly. "Team Erlking, right? We're the good guys. The good guys always win."

"What we are looking at here is an unravelling." It was Lady Tinda who had spoken, still observing them all from the doorway in her thoughtful way. "This girl … or whatever she is. She is falling apart." She nodded decisively, as if she had gotten to the heart of the matter. "Unravelling."

She looked around at the rest of them gathered around her. "But all of you lot, for all your fretting and hand-wringing and histrionics, you're the opposite. Together, pulling tighter. That means there's hope yet. Often you can find it in the most absolutely unlikely of places."

"Dis," Karya asserted. The Fire Panthea nodded at her.

"Heaven's Lens," Tinda agreed. "It's the belly of the beast, so to speak, and the workshop and laboratory of dear old foul Mr Nyx. Not the most likely place you'd ever think to go for help, but I'd warrant that if anything can put this mess of a girl back together before she falls apart completely then, loathsome as it is to consider, it will be found there." She fiddled a little with the buttons on her coat as they all looked at her. "Fates, my brother spent enough time there with the fat old creeper, so I've overheard what sorts of things go on in Nyx's playhouse. He was always banging on about bringing things back to being whole, improving this, tampering with that. Fiddling with the way things and people are put together, or taken apart for that matter. Took our last phoenix, they did. Flint killed it and Nyx used up the feathers. Shudder to think for what."

Karya looked to Robin. "I can't stay here in bed," she told him. "I really can't. If I lie down again, I won't get up." Tired as she looked, Robin knew her well enough to recognise the steely determination in her eyes. "I have to go to Dis. I have to go home."

"Not without us, you don't," Henry assured her.

Hestia, who seemed utterly overwhelmed by these events, fluttered her hands to her chest, shooting a very disapproving look at the noble lady by her side for encouraging an expedition to Eris' city. "Foolish, foolish children," she quavered. "This is all such silly talk! Even if you did want to go to that awful place, there is no way in, not for your kind. Pyrenight is not the kind of celebration one can crash. Oh no." She shook her head with certainty, biting her lips so they became a thin and worried line. "No way through the gates. No way over the walls, always watched, they are. No way under them, either. Hilly Dis is built on solid rock. No way to go knocking on Eris' door."

"There is *one* way," Robin looked up from Karya's bedside towards Lady Tinda. This was why their contact in Dis, the elusive hex messenger desperate to escape the city, had sent them on a quest to find the Calescents. Whoever they were, they knew about the failed underground ark. "A device that can breach *any* wall or any rock beneath it."

Henry shrugged his bow from his shoulder, brandishing it. "And we have half the means to power the bloody thing already." The inlaid gem shone in the sunlight from the window.

Robin held Lady Tinda's gaze, imploringly. She looked at their faces, at Robin holding the hand of his doomed friend.

"You said that all these sufferings befell my people, the Fae, just because you and your brother were born," he said to her. "I know you wish you could go back and somehow save all those lost, but there's a Fae right in front of you who needs help right now. We can't go back and change the past, but we can stop running and hiding from the future. We can save

Karya. We can complete your father's work and get into Dis. There are Fae and Panthea alike who will die if we don't."

Lady Tinda narrowed her eyes at him. "I wasn't aware, Scion, that one of the Towers in which you were skilled was manipulation." She blew air down her nose, resigned. 'It would seem," the woman in the doorway said with a kind of grim finality, "that my own time of running and hiding is done. You, girl, are apparently not the *only* one who must return home."

"Will you take us to the Black Hills?" Robin asked her. His voice was level, but it was a plea. "I think it is time we faced your brother, and we claimed back your inheritance, don't you?"

Once decided, there was no more time to waste. Despite Hestia's beseeching that they should wait and rest a little, consider their foolhardy notions, perhaps try to contact Irene and Calypso, Robin knew there simply wasn't time. Karya needed answers quickly. She was deteriorating fast and Jackalope and Ffoulkes needed help now. Pyrenight loomed. They had half a shard and half a plan. It would have to do.

They gathered less than an hour later at the red door on the third floor, Erlking's Janus Station. Karya was on her feet, doing her very best to look well. She had tied her brittle white hair back harshly into a ponytail, which only served to make her look even more hollow-cheeked and drawn. She was determinedly shaking off Woad's well-meaning attempts to keep her upright. Robin had repacked his bag, bringing along the moral compass and the cubic cornucopia, and Henry resolutely refused to step foot in the Netherworlde again unarmed. His bow, carrying Lady Tinda's half of the Fire Shard, was slung across his back with a fresh and full quiver of arrows, the relic of the Elemental nestled amongst them. He had also changed his jeans for a new pair with less of a bloody hole in the knee.

Lady Tinda herself seemed to have made no more preparation for their journey than buttoning her coat and finishing off the tray of finger sandwiches Hestia had prepared for them earlier in the parlour, despite the fact they had by now become a little dry and curled at the edges. She muttered a little about who would look after the shop down in the village, but she had pushed her winged glasses firmly up on her nose and her mouth was a thin defiant purple line. It was clear to everyone that returning home after all this time was absolutely the last thing she wanted to do, but Robin could see a flicker of wary and guarded hope in her. Hope that a faint chance to put right the injustices against her father, and against the Fae whom her family had failed, was perhaps finally in reach.

"If we're going to go, we should go now," Henry said, urgency creeping around the edges of his voice. "Before old Hestia gets back here with my dad. I know she's scurried off to tattle on us and he's only down in the gardens. If he gets back before we scarper, that'll be it. There's no way he's going to let us go off gallivanting in the Netherworlde again. Not if he can stop us." He was practically hopping from one foot to another, like a naughty schoolboy planning to skip lessons.

Robin shrugged his pack onto his back and looked to the little Fire Panthea. "Are you sure this will work?" he asked. "I mean, you're really able to get us all the way to the Black Hills from here? It's such a long way, almost all the way to Dis."

The woman gave a rather careless shrug. "Don't hold me to it," she said. "I can't begin to imagine how Janus Stations work. But I do know this. The Shard of Fire doesn't want to be two halves. It wants to be whole, to be together. It's probably why Flint and I were so close back when we were children. Inseparable, we were." She looked sad. "Probably why it took me so long to leave. I kept hoping I could claw him back to reason somehow. For far too long I fooled myself. Even when that Grimm had scrambled his mind, drowned any loyalty my brother had to me. It wasn't until I ran and started getting further and further away, that the pull became manageable."

She patted at her red and frizzy hair. "Even so, from a world away, my whole life I've felt the pull back home, during all my running and hiding. It's a tug, like toothache." She nodded to Henry's bow and its glittering central gemstone. "The shard half I own wants to be with the other. I believe it will use Janus, take us to the Black Hills. If there's skill in navigation between here and there, well, it falls to the Arcania, not to me."

Karya's hand was on the door handle. "This would be a lot simpler," she muttered murderously. "If I could just tear between worlds like I usually do. Honestly, you don't know what you've got until it's gone. I could flip us over there, then a few good flips across the distance, leaps through space and reality, and bang, mission accomplished."

"Yeah boss, but your hair might all fall out," Woad said. "Or one of your legs fall off, so let's not wish for falling stars and get a meteor in the face, eh?"

Lady Tinda started to say something about having never met anyone with the skill to pass back and forth between the two worlds without using a Janus Station, but Robin barely heard because Karya threw the door open wide, the misty light distracting them. Henry led the way carrying his bow with the embedded Shard held out before him like a dowsing rod as they had planned. They passed out of Erlking Hall, smelling faintly of beeswax polish and caramel wafers, and plunged into a darkness beyond that sent a warm breeze into their faces, tinged with an odd peppery smell like gunpowder. Lady Tinda brought up the rear, the door slamming behind her with a crack and cutting off the human world with a sharp finality.

Robin found himself absently wishing, as the ringing in his ears subsided, and the lurching, dizzying tumble of crossing between worlds receded, that just once, he could experience a flip to the Netherworlde that *didn't* leave him feeling as though he had been briefly turned inside out.

It would be nice to arrive in style, he thought, as the darkness receded and he found himself once more face-down on a hard surface, smarting and winded. Rather than arriving as a failed pancake flip that had ended up on the floor.

Blinking away shadows as the world righted itself around him like a lurching ship at sea, he pushed himself up off the floor. His shaky hands were gripping what felt like moist soil between his fingers.

He felt hands grip his shoulders as he blinked away the fuzzy vision, helping him up.

"Rough landing, Rob?" Henry, sounding a little nauseous himself.

"Well, our theory was right," he heard Karya say in a hoarse voice nearby. "Lady Calescent's half of the Fire Shard does indeed have homing instincts. It seems to have done the trick,"

"We're in the right place, boss?" Woad's voice came.

"Oh yes. This is definitely the Black Hills. We've travelled a tremendous distance. Just think, Henry, if you'd ever bothered to bring your bow through a Janus Station in the past, it would have dragged us all the way here, and we would have no idea why."

"Congratulations, Pinky." Woad said. "You're clocking up your Netherworlde frequent flyer miles now, that's for sure."

Robin hadn't given a huge amount of thought to what he expected from the Black Hills. All he knew about the region was that it was far to the south and east of the Netherworlde, somewhere close to the city of Dis. That it was the home of many Fire Panthea. He supposed in his mind's eye he had been picturing bare and barren hills of dry, dead rock. A blasted, charred and lifeless wasteland, craggy landscapes of unwelcoming darkness, fitting for a place so near to the empress and her dark city. All shadows and ash.

As he wiped away dizzy tears and finally looked around, taking in their new surroundings, he discovered he could not have been more wrong.

They were standing on a hill, a large and gently sloping valley nestled amongst many others. Shallow and peaceful hills undulated away from them in all directions. They were swathed in long, whispering grass, which to Robin's surprise was not green, as one might expect, but as black as liquorice. The landscape shimmered in a light spring breeze. It was beautiful and surreal. Like being in the rolling south downs of England, only in negative. The glossy black fields, shimmering away on all sides, were not the most surprising sight, however.

Scattered everywhere he looked, the tame rolling hills and gentle hollows of the valleys were carpeted with blood red flowers. An ocean of them, spread out on the dark landscape like splashes of thrown paint. The bright flowers grew in wide clumps in their thousands and they swayed and bobbed in the breeze, an undulating sea of floral fire.

Blinking in surprise at the beauty of it, Robin ran a hand across the top of the long grass, feeling it whisper softly under his fingertips. He reached down to touch one of the countless crimson flowers. The petals were soft and oddly warm. They looked something like roses but smaller, with pointed star-shaped leaves. The breeze carried the scent of them over the landscape, petals on distant hills caught by the wind spiralling up into the air like clouds of scarlet confetti.

"Good job none of us has hay fever, eh?" Henry said lightly as the group found their balance after moving between worlds. He too was gazing around with wonder at the abundant and wild sweep of blooms bobbing around them, countless pinpoints of ruby jewels sparkling in the soft black grass.

The flowers were not the only feature they could see from where they stood. Nestled here, there and everywhere between the hills and breaking up the ocean of fauna, were occasional groups of trees, small copses and spinneys, like groups of neighbours gathered together in the countryside to gossip. The trees had squat and twisted trunks, seeming to spiral around themselves like massively overgrown bonsai.

There could be no doubt that it was spring, as each and every tree they could see was topped with a crown of vibrant white and pink blossoms. The wind rolling around them caught gusts of petals, dreamily carrying them from the trees like drifting spirits.

"It's absolutely beautiful here," Robin observed with surprise, sliding his pack back onto his shoulders. He turned his face heavenwards. The sky rolling over them was dark and filled with moody and grumbling clouds, the sunlight breaking through their shadowy skirts here and there and falling to earth in slender pale shafts, stitching together the darkness above and darkness below. The sunbeams rolled silently across the hills like fingers gently tracing the braille of the landscape.

"What did you expect from my homeland?" Lady Tinda asked, shrugging out of her winter coat in the spring warmth of the Netherworlde. She dropped it carelessly to the ground amidst the tall black grass, clearly intending to leave it there. Woad tutted, scooping it up behind her with a frown.

"Dunno. Mordor, I guess," Henry shrugged. "You know, big scary volcanoes, choking smoke and fumes, lava and cracked up ground, your usual run-of-the-mill hellscape."

Lady Tinda gave him a wry look. "Shame we don't have more time, or I'd give you a tour of my lands, you little human bugger." She swept a heavily-bangled arm at the landscape. "This whole area, all of the Black Hills, is volcanic. It's why the salamander flowers grow so well – good soil. Nice and warm underneath, too." She raised her eyebrows at him. "So, no choking fumes, but there is plenty of lava though, yes. You'll do well to watch your step in the Black Hills. We have plenty of geysers here, hidden away in the grasses."

"Geysers? Water spouts?" Robin asked. "Like Old Faithful, you mean?"

Karya, Woad and the Fire Panthea all returned blank stares. Clearly, none of them were familiar with the natural wonders of the human world.

"Not water," the woman said. "Fire. Molten."

Robin considered this, looking around again. Stunning flower-filled hills dotted with ethereal blossom trees ... and the occasional geyser rocketing deadly molten magma hundreds of feet in the air without a moment's notice. It sounded about right for the Netherworlde, as far as he was concerned. He had always found it a place as likely to kill you as charm you. Often both, at the same time. That odd juxtaposition of beauty and danger had always been part of its appeal to him.

"We're not afraid of the fire of the earth here," Lady Tinda told them, adjusting her many bracelets fussily and peering around at the hills, trying to get her bearings. "Many grand houses, mine included, have decorative lava pools, the same way your world has fountains."

"We should be fine as long as we stick to the roads and don't wander off into the wilds," Karya said. "How far are we from your home? Your half of the Shard clearly hasn't dropped us on your old doorstep, but do you recognise where we are?"

Lady Tinda was peering over the rippling black grass of the hills thoughtfully, watching the countless red flowers bob their heads in their ceaseless dance. "Oh yes," she said. "Like I've never been away. I know this place. Flint and I played here often as children." She pointed to a mass of trees, black and pink and snowing blossom, which lay in a hollow perhaps half a mile across the rolling meadows.

"Beyond there," she told them. "Through those trees, there's a small dell. There's a stream, a glade where we used to go fishing. With makeshift poles, whenever we could sneak away from the manor for an hour or two while Father was busy. We used to go hunting for frogs, fireworms, and at night, the darkness in the trees all along the river was alive with pyreflies. They used to reflect in the running water, sparking like Christmas lights."

She sighed a little, the corners of her mouth turned down as though disappointed. "If only we could remain children, eh? Catching pyreflies and chasing shadows with an open heart and no knowledge of the darkness in the world. Wishful thinking that, though. Life rolls on, for all of us. If you're not careful, it rolls right over you." The woman looked distant for a moment, far away and unbearably sad. She stood hugging her arms at the elbow, her red hair tossed around her shoulders by the breeze, and the flowers bobbing, tears of blood, around her knees.

Robin looked away. It seemed an intrusion to view such defence-less misery.

There was a brief glow between two distant hills, a bloom like a silent beacon in the darkness. He watched it fade, wondering if it was one of the many magma geysers.

Gathering herself, Lady Tinda peered at all of them. "So, you lot should take heed, young whippersnappers. Don't let it. Don't let life roll over you too and crush your nights of pyreflies … the simple freedom of youth."

"None of us here have much leisure time to chase pyreflies," Robin observed.

The woman brushed a strand of red hair, caught by the wind, back behind her ear and blew out her cheeks. "Yes. That's the truth alright," she said. "Heavy is the head that wears the crown, eh, little Fae lord? In many ways, your innocent youth has been snatched away from you as surely as my home was from me. You shouldn't be out here, fighting evil. You should be at home playing XBox and doing your Duke of Edinburgh awards at school. It's not fair. Any of it."

Woad was squatting in the grass and sniffing interestedly at the large red flowers. "We're all very sad that your dad died and your brother went crazy and over to the dark side, and you had to run away from home and hide your whole life so he didn't cut your head off and everything," the faun said in a quick lilt. "But the past?" He looked up. "It's never something to long for or want to go back to. The past is gone and done." He smiled at his own, rather blunt statement and looked over at the distant trees where the lady was gazing. "Your pyreflies and frogs aren't over there, not anymore." He tapped the side of his head. "They're just in here now. But that's not a bad thing, is it? You carry them forward with you every day. Happy memories, bad ones. Scars and jewels alike. You decorate yourself with them. Make it your armour and strength." He shook his head, looking uncharacteristically thoughtful as he stood from the long grasses, stretching with his arms above his head like a carefree cat. "Really strong armour, like … dragon-proof."

"Pyrenight is tomorrow," Karya reminded everyone. "Notwithstanding the poetic wisdom of fauns, our friends are due to die very soon. I'd like to save them before I die myself, if that's alright with everyone else here? We need to move."

Robin considered that Lady Tinda had been moving for far too long. Despite her nonchalant and somewhat fidgety manner, the woman looked tired. Running and hiding, constantly looking over your shoulder for many years, will do that to a person. And then at the end of it all, to be coming home … to find all that running had turned out simply to be a big circle after all, bringing you back to face what you had spent your life fleeing from. Was it any wonder she was nostalgic for a simpler time, and fearful of the present?

"Karya's right. Come on," he said to all of them. "It feels like it's already afternoon here, time is running out. We can have pyreflies in the future, when all's said and done. All of us." He nodded to Lady Tinda. "You too."

She walked off through the grass, towards a thin strip of clear ground that wound through the landscape like a dark river. The road, no doubt, though from here it looked little more than a narrow footpath. She beckoned them to follow, giving Robin a rather cautious look over her shoulder. "We'll see about that, my optimistic little Fae," she said. "It's likely that for the Shard of Fire to be re-forged, it may mean the end of my brother, or myself … perhaps both. I'll take you to what was once my home, just like I promised. But I'm not walking towards pyreflies."

They fell into step behind her, a small hiking line through the flowers and glossy grass, beating a path beneath the dark and sun-torn skies.

"I'll walk to ensure pyreflies for *others.*"

The track through the great flower fields took a long and undulating path, leading them up, over and around the gentle hills. Occasionally, as they followed it through the afternoon, they passed stands of trees, tiny woods full of dark boles and crowns of blossom which rained down silently on them. Red and pink and white. Snow that did not melt but settled instead in their hair and landed in the black grass to lie like countless stars. The sky ahead remained troubled and low, dark as a bruise and filled with roiling motion, with only occasional breaks allowing the sun to peep through silent searchlights across the world.

Woad and Henry had fallen silently and naturally into step to either side of Karya, who walked behind their Fire Panthea guide. Neither of them dared to offer an arm to the girl, to aid in her stumbling steps. Both of them knew better and that any such assistance would likely be slapped away. Even fading and shaky – unravelling, Tinda had called it – Karya was still fiercely independent and proud. But they were clearly positioned to catch her if she fell. Robin, bringing up the rear, watched the shine and glimmer of the Shard of Fire in Henry's bow as it bobbed across the boy's back with every step.

Slinging his pack from his shoulder, he fished out the heavy moral compass, pondering the gift. It had led them truthfully so far, warning him, though he hadn't figured it out at the time, that Strigoi was at Titania's Tears. It had guided them into One Horn Forest, showing him the way to the library and the satyr who had revealed the gifts of the Elementals. Might he now turn to it for reassurance? He glanced down at it cradled in his hands and mentally asked if Ffoulkes and Jackalope could be saved. If it was really possible to break into Dis and get them both safely out, swiping them right from under Eris' nose?

The needle span gleefully, finally coming to rest straight ahead, the direction they were walking. The tiny face which gilded the edge was almost unreadable, the carved expression, rendered in polished brass, was blank and expressionless, staring back at Robin. It didn't even seem to have any eyes.

Well, that wasn't much help.

Rummaging again in his pack, he found his crumpled hex message sheet.

As the others walked onwards, Robin stopped and dropped to a knee, balancing the sheet of parchment against his own thigh he wrote.

We're coming. Are you still there?

He was directing all his thoughts to the unknown stranger. The one he knew was waiting in Dis, who had promised to help him get inside in exchange for Robin's promise that he would get *them* out. Robin may not know whom he was speaking with but, as infuriatingly vague and cagey as they were, they had led him to his goals so far. They seemed trustworthy.

His companions walked on, unaware that he had paused behind to send the message, and he waited impatiently for a reply. Perhaps his odd conspirator couldn't answer right now. They had said that they were often watched. It might not be a safe time.

But after a moment, words flowed into being on the yellowed sheet in a spiky red handwriting that had become familiar to him by now.

Was it there? At the library? Did you get it?

Robin blinked down at the words as they faded. It was obvious that the sender was talking about the half-Shard of Fire. Lady Tinda's legacy. Had they expected it to be hidden away there? Made their own deductions, perhaps knowing the satyrs of the Precipitous Library were keepers of great and powerful artefacts?

No, he wrote back. *Lady Tinda's Shard wasn't at the library. But a path to her was. I have what I need to get inside Dis. Almost. Just wait a little longer.*

He nibbled the end of his pen thoughtfully as these words sank into the parchment, fading, before adding more.

I have to save my friends. The ones captured. But I need to get into Heaven's Lens. The Grimm's laboratory. Do you know where it is in Dis?

The reply came quickly and simply

Up

Robin wrote back again. *And how will I find you, once we're inside the city?*

The reply was very spiky handwriting, as though the writer were irritable or extremely impatient

Down!

More words bloomed on the page. Robin glanced up. The others were some way ahead now. He needed to be quick.

Be careful, he was warned. *If you bring it here, he will try to take it from you.*

He? Robin thought.

Strigoi? he asked hastily. *I know he's been looking everywhere for it. Him and the Grimm, Nyx. I don't care.* He thought about adding *I can handle them* but considering that all he had ever done was flee when faced with either of them, it didn't ring true.

Don't worry, he wrote instead. *I'll be careful. Strigoi won't get the Shard for his empress.*

Don't be naïve, the reply came immediately. *He doesn't want it for her. He needs it for himself. Be careful and hurry. Don't contact me again until you're here.*

"Pinky?"

Robin looked up, distracted, as the words, now read, evaporated. Their little troupe had stopped ahead at a bend in the winding road, and all of them were looking back at him.

"No time to write to your penfriend, Pinky," Woad called out. 'Barbeque time soon! Send them a postcard later." He made urgent flapping motions with his hands, beckoning Robin to keep up.

"Yes, sorry," Robin pushed the hex paper and the compass back into his satchel and hurried down the slope to join the others. The mild and shadowy afternoon was growing darker. The sunbeams, when they broke the cloud cover ahead, were now golden and slanting in from the side as the great orb of the sun moved down invisibly toward the horizon. This time tomorrow when it set, he thought, bonfires would be lit and the dark skies would be filled not with pyreflies, but with smouldering embers.

The Black Hills rolled on as they walked, stopping more often than any of them would have liked in order to let Karya rest. Nobody mentioned it out loud, but Robin was alarmed at the speed in which she seemed to be growing weaker. Her skin became paler with every passing country mile, until in the fading twilight, she began to look like a ghost, dark eyes sunken and heavy. It was a bitter mercy when evening closed in and amongst the dark landscape it became difficult to see one another clearly.

A sunset unseen, hidden behind the thick clouds as it fell, led not to blazing fire in the sky, but a more insidious leaching of colour from the blossoms and roses all around, a soft layering of shadows, slowly dropping night upon the hiking company in a hushed and muffled way.

Soon, the world around them seemed to exist in black and white. The lavish flowers covering the hills became fields of dropped hailstones. The soft and frequent sunbeams which had traced shadow and light across the landscape all afternoon were replaced with questing fingers of moonlight, pale and cool, shifting wraith-like in the air above the shivering long grasses, now even more surreal than its sable daytime incarnation. In the scattered moonlight, the black grass shone like celluloid.

The only colours they saw were the occasional magma pools of golden-red, far off in the deep hills, glowing like sunken cauldrons and making the air above them shimmer; or amongst the huddled groups of trees they passed, the soft yellow-green of pyreflies, dancing their silent mirage.

Henry asked several times how much further it was, until Lady Tinda told him quite tartly that every time he asked, her home got a little further away so he would be better served by staying quiet.

Once, at Karya's insistence, they ducked off the road and made their way some distance into the long, dark grass, all stumbling a little as they rustled through the flowers in the dark. Nobody could see any reason for this, but Karya insisted they hunker down, stop questioning her and keep quiet. A moment or two later, the distant sound of hoof beats could be heard, carried across the hills, and a few minutes following that, a troop of horses appeared, their riders clad in ragged patchwork clothes, the silhouettes of their heads like great sack-cloth porcupines.

The troop of patrolling peacekeepers thundered by along the road they had walked only moments earlier, heading west in the night, riding their steeds hard. The flanks of the dark beasts were glossy with sweat, and not a word was exchanged between the riders as they flew past, fleet shadows in the night. Robin wasn't even sure if peacekeepers *could* speak. But he and his companions went unnoticed, silent and hidden in the grasses, as still as mice sensing an owl circling overhead in the night.

"Windbags of Ker," Woad spat, once they were long gone and the dust was settling between the flowers once more. He blew an insolent raspberry. "Well spotted, boss. Even I didn't hear them coming and no one has sharper ears than a faun."

"I didn't hear them," Karya replied, brushing off petals as they all got back to their feet. "I felt them through the ground. Hoof beats like drums in my ribs." Her eyes may have looked tired, but they were still glowing golden in the dark. "The Tower of Earth still serves me," she sniffed defiantly. "At least a little. I'm not completely useless yet."

"Peacekeeper patrols are common in many places," Lady Tinda told them as they re-joined the road and continued their winding way. "But I never used to see them this far south. This close to home. They were always further from Dis, controlling the outlying frontiers of the empire. Eris never needed much muscle here in the Black Hills."

"They're probably looking for us," Henry suggested. He looked to Robin. "Do you think Strigoi is expecting us to do something amazingly stupid, like try to make our way inside Dis?"

Robin nodded. "Oh, I think he's absolutely counting on it," he said. "He knows we won't leave Ffoulkes and Jack to burn or be enslaved. He doesn't consider them traitors to be put down. If he did, Strigoi and Nyx would have ended them there and then, on the spot, back in the Sorrows."

Karya nodded in agreement with this. "Robin's right. They're bait," she said. "Dangled in front of us. What better way to lure a fly into the spider's parlour?"

Woad sounded frustrated. "I wonder how much time he spends polishing all that armour? Preening his feather cloak? Blowhard! I'd like to drop a few scorpions down the back of his neckplate and watch him dance."

"Wish I'd brought a can opener now," Henry said. "We could open him up like the tin of sardines he is, see what's actually inside. What do we reckon? Lizard man? Werewolf? Dragon with one eye in the middle of its scaly forehead? Three raccoons standing on each other's shoulders?"

Robin's face was set, still looking after the peacekeepers' trail. "I already know what's under the Wolf of Eris' armour," he said. "A murderer. My parents are dead because of him. He led the Grimms to the hideout of the Sidhe-Nobilitas. Had them all slaughtered. My mother, my father, so many others. Why do you think Hawthorn hates him so much? He wasn't there at the time, it's the only reason he and a few others are still alive, because they were scattered when the attack went down." He considered a moment, remembering the visions of the past he had been shown in Luna's hut at the Sorrows. The Sidhe-Nobilitas trying to organise themselves after the disappearance of the king and queen, seeing himself being delivered safely on the moors by one of their number into the arms of Mr Drover. The ark waiting to take the Fae people away to safety. All that desperation, all those plans, destroyed because of Strigoi and the Grimms. "And they're still scattered. And the Wolf is still hunting them down like rabbits, even now." His face was a mask of distaste.

"Well if that's the case, he mustn't be hunting them very successfully, at any rate," Lady Tinda said blandly from the front of their troupe. "The *surviving* Sidhe-Nobilitas are all still rumoured to be at large. Slippery folk, you Fae are. Not a one of them who escaped the initial decimation has since been caught. It's not the sort of event that the empress would keep quiet. I think if Eris gets hold of an openly rebellious and defiant Fae she would …"

"Throw a big celebration and execute them publicly on a bonfire?" Woad suggested. "Yep, we know. That's why we've got to get Jack back. Silvertop lost one family to Eris already. He isn't going to lose another."

The night was deep before they stopped again. The hills had grown taller and wilder as they travelled, climbing the landscape. The hollows they passed became more thickly dotted with blossoming trees, and more and more often the surface of the hills was pitted with deep craters filled with liquid fire, always far off and glowing like calm nightlights.

Only once did they see one of the many geysers of the Black Hills erupt, a sudden low and surprisingly gentle rumble underfoot preceding a sudden thrust from their left, and all stopped to watch in awe as the ground no more than a hundred paces away suddenly spewed a column of shimmering orange lava straight into the air – fifty, maybe sixty, feet high.

It hung in the air a moment, a thick glowing fountain, monumental in its rage, casting a bright light on the dark grasses around it. They watched it shed thick ropes of flame, liquid snakes flung out into the night, before it collapsed as quickly as it had appeared, leaving behind nothing but a plume of hissing steam and smoke hanging steady in the air behind it.

"Wouldn't want to be jumping over one of these little pools when *that* goes off," Henry observed wisely, as they blinked away glowing after-images. "Get you more than a suntanned backside."

Tiny golden dots had risen, glowing, from the dark flowers and grass all around them. They floated upwards from under every leaf and flower in their thousands, lighting up the night like countless tiny stars, as they drifted towards where the geyser had blown.

"Pyreflies," Tinda explained, their faces alight with the twinkling reflected light thrown by the countless tiny insects passing between them. "They're drawn from the darkness by the light."

"Yes, we know," Robin breathed, surrounded by the spectacle. "We saw the same thing during the eclipse, back at Erlking, at the lake."

"I didn't really see it," Woad pointed out. "I was drowning at the time."

"The eclipse?" Tinda's forehead furrowed into a frown.

"You wouldn't have seen it from down in the village of Barrowood," Karya explained to her. "It only happened over Erlking's grounds, and here in the Netherworlde too, I presume."

The woman shook her head. "You presume quite wrongly," she insisted. "The seasons may differ from one world to the next, but so, evidently, do other events. The solar eclipse in the Netherworlde has not come yet. It is tomorrow. What you saw in the human world must have been out of step. You saw a future sky."

She glanced at their confused faces. "*Pyrenight.* You're not familiar with it?"

"We know what we learned at Erlking," Robin frowned back at her, unsure what she was saying. "That the celebrations are to be held in Dis tomorrow night."

Lady Tinda shook her head once more. "Oh no, not at all," she said. "Pyrenight does not begin at night. The eclipse will happen here in the Netherworlde tomorrow at noon. That's when Pyrenight begins. That is when the fires will be lit. Not at dusk, but in the darkness of midday, under the shadowed sun."

Robin was aghast. Midday? "That means we have even less time than we thought!" he said. "We thought we had all tonight and all day tomorrow to get to them. We didn't know the eclipse was as out of step with the other world as the weather." He panicked a little. This cut their time so short. "You didn't think to mention this before to us?"

"I assumed you knew," she replied with a tart shrug.

"Everything's out of sync," Woad sighed. "Unravelling like a jumper come apart at the seams." He looked very put out, as though he were taking this very personally. "And unravelling unevenly and unpredictably."

"I know the feeling," Karya sympathised.

Robin quickened his pace along the road, the clouds of pyreflies scattering before him. "It's already well into the night," he said. "We don't have any time to stand around, not if our timeframe just got a lot shorter. How much further did you say it was to this place of yours?"

They had hurried after him, cresting a rise in the hills and passing between two tall and twisted trees which grew like pillars either side of the path.

"Not far at all," Tinda told him. "We're here."

Beyond the two trees, a shallow valley dipped away, threaded with bushes and blossoms, and a solitary house stood. A large structure, triangular peaked roofs stark and sharp-edged against the night sky. The house on the hill was large – a mansion, even – and surrounded by a dark and decorative wall. Their path weaved up to a wide arch, and dark gates. To Robin, Lady Tinda's home looked like a cross between a haunted house and some old Greek temple, with porticos and fluted columns interspersed with random turrets and impossibly delicate balconies. Except that, rather than the white marble you might expect from a temple, or the old, weathered wood of a haunted house, this place was pitch black and shiny, carved from smooth obsidian. Every plane and angle of the mansion seemed to have been polished and the dark sheen caught the light of the moon above in soft, diffused glow.

A single light burned in one of the many slim windows of the upper floor, golden in the stark night, leaving the rest of the manor in deepest blackness against the sky.

"The ancestral home of the family Calescent," Lady Tinda announced. "The resting place of my father's most precious device and the lair of my most dangerous enemy. Welcome to Glassfire Manor."

5

Blind Ambition

They approached the house with caution. Both Robin and Henry made suggestions that they scout around the back of the great encircling wall, maybe find a quiet place to sneak in. There was always the chance after all that the charming Lord Flint might be deep asleep and his half of the Shard could be taken without too much trouble, but Lady Tinda would not hear of it.

"I've hidden in shadows for too many years already," she insisted, biting her bottom lip and looking determined. "I've had enough of it. I won't come to my father's house like some kind of guilty thief in the night. I will enter with my head held high – for as long as I am able to keep it attached to my neck, at least."

And so they made their way boldly along the path, watching the pointed rooftops and columned walls loom above them in stark and spiky grandeur, a shining black silhouette against the moonlit skies, until they reached the heavy doors barring the archway in the courtyard wall.

"The gates are locked," she told them.

"Are we going to knock?" Henry asked, eyebrows raised and sounding a little unsure of himself. He looked at the others, sheepishly. "Sorry, I'm not really sure what the correct protocol is for when you're visiting an evil brother who wants you dead in the middle of the night."

Robin saw the set expression on Lady Tinda's face, finding herself barred from her own ancestral home.

"No," he said, his own face firm. "We're at the house of our enemy, here. The lackey of Nyx and Eris. Betrayer of the both the Fae and Panthea alike. We're not travelling salesmen. We are the Scion of the Arcania, the rightful Heir of Calescent, and the rebellion of Erlking." He smiled darkly. "We don't knock."

He placed a hand in the dead centre of the heavy stone gates, feeling how cold and smooth they felt beneath his fingers and as his seraphinite stone flashed on his chest, he thrust his mana outward from the palm of his hand in a blast.

The great doors shuddered and then exploded inwards, breaking apart and sending large chunks of stone flying into the courtyard beyond as though catapulted from a trebuchet. The shockwave tore down not only the gates, but half of the archway with it, and blocks of masonry as large as Woad skipped and rolled across the inner courtyard bastion of Glassfire Manor like tossed pebbles, scoring great troughs in the gravel within and crashing like thrown dice.

"Avon calling," Henry whispered, coughing slightly in the settling dust as Robin lowered his arm, his mana stone flickering like a strobe light on his chest. They made their way inside, following Lady Tinda, who strode confidently into the ornate inner gardens, looking pleased to be making a grand entrance but wily enough to look warily around.

"Be on your guard," she told them, as the dust settled. "My brother is a dangerous man, and when I left this place it was full of peacekeepers – and worse – most days."

"Well, I imagine he definitely knows we're here," Karya pointed out, looking sidelong at Robin with a smirk. "That would have woken the dead."

Woad shivered. "Hope it didn't," he muttered to Henry, who had unslung his bow. "I hate revenants."

Robin looked around the large courtyard suspiciously. The main doors to the great house stood opposite, across a span of combed gravel, now littered with debris, at the top of a wide span of steps leading under a column-flanked portico. The doors were closed.

Here and there around the rather stark courtyard were silent watchful statues and huge decorative urns, filled with ferns and twisting plants. All the plants were dead and black. Withered in their pots. They clearly hadn't been tended for some time. The place looked severely unloved. A desperate fall from grace. He had expected lights to come on all over the house after the cacophony of their entrance. Guards, peacekeepers or other staff of the manor to come running out of the building to confront them.

But the house stood largely dark and still. It was silent.

The only light in the courtyard came from a wide central pool, flanked with decorative stones. It seemed like a well, and its depths were brimming with liquid fire, a deep and sullen red. Robin had no idea how deep this wide well was, but it was filled and bubbling almost to the brim, and its glowing light shone back from the polished obsidian façade of the house. The walls, windows and doors, all black as jet, seemed to shimmer in the molten glow. The reflection of the lava pool gave the illusion that flames rolled and moved beneath the surface of the walls deep inside, behind their shining surfaces. It was easy to see why the place had been named Glassfire.

"Where is everyone?" he asked. "It's too quiet."

The Fire Panthea was turning on her heel in a circle. Her face suspicious as she peered around. "We had a staff of forty here," she said. "Before I left. Butlers, chambermaids, footmen, cooks, valets. Many of them would still be up and working at this hour. It seems … deserted. Abandoned."

"Not completely." Karya nodded to the upper floors, where a dim light flickered. Somewhere deep in the house, a light was burning. They had seen it from afar.

"No peacekeepers here now," Woad assured them. "This close, you can always smell them. If you're a faun, that is. Funny smell there is around this place though – but whatever it is, it's not straw men."

It seemed Glassfire Manor was not the hive of activity it once had been.

They made their way boldly across the courtyard, skirting the large deep fire-well. It seemed an odd feature to Robin, but for Fire Panthea it was no more unusual than a turning circle or a statue-filled fountain would have been back in the human world. There was no such thing as health and safety in the Netherworlde, he had long known that.

Tinda led them up the wide steps and into the shadows beneath the grand porch.

"My brother is – or was – a noble lord," she said. "Haughty and vain. I can't for a moment imagine him surviving without a full retinue of staff to wait on and serve him. Flint has never made a bed or built a fire in his entire life. I doubt he'd even know how to boil an egg if left to his own devices. There *must* be others here."

"I suppose you learned how to look after yourself," Karya said as Lady Tinda, finding the double doors of the manor unlocked, pushed them open slowly and carefully. "When you left and hid, I mean."

Tinda snorted down her nose. "My eggs are terrible," she muttered. "I live on takeaway food. I do love a good kebab."

The interior of the mansion was, or at least had been, opulent. The doors spilled them into a grand hall dominated by a sweeping double staircase. Inside, the walls and floor were dark marble, but they did not shine. A thick layer of dust hung over everything, muting and muffling the glamour of a once grand house. It was very dark inside. The huge chandelier above them, hanging from above the open stairs, stood unlit, and candle stubs melted down to the wick hung in alcoves along the walls, silent in their cold shadows.

"Looks like things have gone downhill a little," Woad observed, looking up into the heights. His voice echoed faintly in the utter silence. "Look at all these massive cobwebs everywhere. How long have you been gone again?"

"Not long enough for this," Tinda replied, quiet worry in her voice. There were indeed thick cobwebs everywhere. Up in the roof space, floating in the updraught like ghosts, threaded between the silent and still columns of the interior hall like threadbare curtains, draped shroud-like over delicate and expensive-looking tables. On the carved stone bannister of the great staircase they filled the space between each rise, grey and thick, and covered themselves with undisturbed dust.

"This is Nyx," she said. "His dark spiders follow him everywhere. He must have spent a lot of time here with Flint, after I fled. They have desecrated my home. They have made my father's house into a tomb."

Robin wondered if the unsettling Mr Nyx might be in here with them, even now watching them silently from some deep shadow, of which there was no shortage. Lurking silently behind the cobwebs, with his immaculate hair and bright friendly smile, spiders of smoke and focussed will falling from his hands like blood droplets to land softly at his feet. But he didn't feel anything. No watchful eyes. Glassfire Manor felt…dead.

A soft creak somewhere above them drew all of their attention to the upper floors. They could see no movement in the shadows of the balcony above them, running the perimeter of the entrance hall.

"Someone's up there," Karya whispered.

There was another creak, muffled footsteps perhaps. A strange, very heavy shuffling noise, and then a thud. Something stumbling in the dark.

"And whatever walked there …" Henry said quietly, "walked clumsily."

"What?" Karya looked at him in confusion.

"Sorry, just misquoting a book," Henry shrugged. "I guess we're going up? To investigate the strange noise in the dark of the world's most haunted house? Of course we are. You do realise we just became the biggest horror cliché?"

"Stay close, and be careful." Robin headed for the staircase, brushing aside cobwebs in the dark. The feel of them, delicate, dusty, and slightly sticky on his fingertips, made his skin crawl. He was halfway up the wide stairs when he heard a gasp behind. Looking back, he saw that Karya had stumbled on the steps behind him, grabbing the handrail for support. Henry was clinging to her arm.

"Are you okay?" he asked, knowing from the sight of her that the answer was clearly no. She looked exhausted, her white hair the brightest thing in the darkness, her face hollow and pale. Karya looked on the verge of collapse.

"I'm fine…" she insisted. "Just…dizzy…out of breath…I just need a minute."

Henry looked up the stairs a little helplessly to Robin. "We've walked all afternoon and night to get here," he said. "She needs to rest."

"Don't tell me what I need, Henry James Drover." Karya snapped, but the irritation in her voice was somewhat diminished by her ragged breathing. "We don't have time to rest."

"*You* do," Robin decided. "Just … wait here. Get your strength back. Henry, stay with her. Keep an eye out."

Karya sank down shakily onto the stairs, leaning her head back against the banister railing with her eyes closed as though she had the world's worst migraine. "Perhaps … just for a moment then," she conceded gracelessly. "Only to get my breath back, that's all."

Henry had squatted down on the stairs beside her, taking her hand and nodding in agreement. He looked worried to death. Karya must have really been exhausted, Robin thought, as she didn't shake Henry's hand away.

No, it's not that, he told himself. It's not because she's tired. It's because she's scared of what's happening to her. She would never show it, of course, but she is. And when we're afraid, whether we choose to acknowledge it or not, we all want someone to hold our hand in the darkness.

"Don't worry," Robin heard Karya say to her worried companion as he, Woad and Lady Tinda continued upwards towards the upper storey. "I'll protect you from any ghosts, Henry."

The upper floors of the mansion were even more consumed with cobwebs, hanging in thick ropes and strands across the galleried landings. They choked the dim and abandoned corridors, leading away into darkness.

"Something smells *bad* here, Pinky," Woad said in a whisper, glancing back the way they had come. There was a tiny crackle of electricity in his hair, which startled them both. Woad was clearly concerned about Karya and Henry, about leaving them behind. "Something's with us, and it's not a fascist and murderous lord of the manor. Or not *just* a fascist and murderous lord of the manor, at least."

As they made their way stealthily along the hallways, following Lady Tinda as she picked through the sepulchral gloom and aiming towards the front of the house, Robin was inclined to agree. Everything about the manor felt wrong. It didn't feel like a house. More like the ghost of a house. If Lord Flint was still here, in residence, he certainly wasn't holding glamorous galas and opulent candlelight suppers in the empress' honour. The place felt more like the lair of some dangerous beast.

"I know," Robin replied, scanning the dusty shadows. "I feel it too, Woad." He glanced at Lady Tinda, a pale shadow in front of them. "Is this the life of luxury Eris rewards all her most loyal subjects with, do you think?"

Tinda snorted her usual derisive noise. "The empress doesn't even see them as *people*," she said. "She sees *tools* to be used. When you are in her favour, it's said to be like basking in bright sunlight on a warm day. But once you no longer serve a purpose … well, then you're a burden, a discarded toy. Or worse, an irritation to be dealt with."

She ran her hands along the dusty, empty surface of a long table in the upper hallway as they passed. "Everything has gone," she mused. "There used to be a clock here, antique, worth an absolute fortune. And at the top of the stairs, my priceless chalpie collection … priceless," she mourned. "The forces of Eris have hollowed out my home. Taking anything of worth for their own, for the 'war effort', no doubt. Scavengers and magpies."

Distaste dripped from her voice. "My brother was charmed by Nyx, hook, line and sinker. Such a loyal assistant to the high alchemist. Promised all the glory of my father for himself, his deepest wishes dangled right before his face. Nyx knows what makes people tick. He sees into the secret places in people's hearts, then places one of his squirming spiders there." She brushed aside a thick and papery wall of webs as they proceeded. "A rising star in the shimmering circles of high Dis society, just what fanatical Flint desired. That's what they do. Just like spiders. Lured into the parlour ..." She glanced around at what was once her home, now stripped bare of anything of use or worth. "Then sucked dry and hollowed out, until you're just a husk."

"Do you think your brother has abandoned the family home?" Robin wondered, as they left the hallways and made their quiet way through open doors and into what might once have been a grand space for entertaining. Their ghostly reflections keeping step with them in the many tall mirrors set deep all along one wall. "Perhaps he's gone to live in Dis permanently, to enjoy the spoils of Eris' favour?" Surely no one could still live here, he reasoned. The place wasn't fit for habitation.

Lady Tinda disagreed. "It wouldn't make sense," she reasoned as they creaked across the old floorboards. "Not to leave permanently, with Father's device still here. There's no way Nyx and his forces could have managed to move it anywhere, even if they wanted too. It will never move without the Shard of Fire. It *can't* move forward until the Shard is re-forged." She brushed a trail of dust from one of the large ghostly mirrors. "None of us can."

At the far end of the cobwebbed room, a further set of doors lay closed and all three of them stopped to see a thin band of light emanating from beneath.

Someone, or something, was in the room beyond.

At either side of the doors, Robin noticed, there hung portraits. Lady Tinda, dressed in fine dark silk, adorned with glittering necklaces of ruby and jet, her red hair in elaborate curls and a haughty look on her painted face. He looked at the little woman at his side, with her thick glasses, frizzy and untended hair and chipped and bitten-down nails – she was barely recognisable as this distant lady of the manor.

The portrait on the opposite side of the doors was clearly her brother. The same proud, clear eyes, long hair combed neatly and falling down his back in a shining wave. Clear skin and high cheekbones. He was dressed in what Robin would guess was some form of Netherworlde military dress, very formal and tasselled and trim.

To see these visions of the past, lit only by moonlight and covered with Nyx's spiderwebs like a funeral veil, sent a helpless sadness running through Robin.

"Be wary," Tinda counselled, as Robin put his hand on the ornate doorknob. "My brother is a skilled swordsman and has plenty of aptitude in the Tower of Fire. He can be a formidable opponent, should it come to violence – which I imagine it will. He believes in Eris. To him, I'm just a cowardly traitor to my own kind, and you, well … you are Fae. Unclean."

Robin remembered how he had twisted the fury of the waterfall at Titania's Tears to save himself and Woad in a bubble of mana. How he had trapped the carnivorous bog hag in a prison of wood dragged from the earth with sheer willpower, and how he had spirited his friends from the clutches of pursuing unicorns on racing dragons fuelled only by his own determination. He nodded seriously to her. He could handle Lord Flint. His horns might be invisible, but more and more constantly Robin had been able to feel them, sense the air passing around them, as an amputee still feels the phantom form of their lost limb.

"I won't let him hurt you," he said, glancing at Tinda and Woad.

Woad's response was a sudden small crackle of electricity, bright in the shadows. It leapt from one of his hands to the next, a small static lightning bolt, swiftly followed by another, which crackled from his elbow to his nose, making him sneeze.

The faun seemed as surprised as his companions by this and gave them a sheepish grin. Lady Tinda blinked at him.

"Skyfire … um …" he explained, self-consciously tugging at an earlobe.

Robin opened the door and moved into the room beyond, braced for battle if it came to that, with the lord of Glassfire Manor.

The scene brought them all up short.

The room was, or had been at some point, a study. Bookcases lined the walls, desks and worktops – although it looked as though it had been ransacked, and some time ago at that. Great drifts of books lay strewn across the floor, their spines broken and their open pages mouldering like rotting autumn leaves. A swathe of loose parchment littered the desks and floors, everywhere, each sheet covered in unintelligible scribble. Some had been pinned to the walls in a seemingly haphazard pattern. Odd diagrams, strange ramblings in a cramped and incoherent hand. There were platters and plates here and there in the chaos of the room, covered in half eaten and long forgotten food, much of it rotting or near-fossilised. Clearly the remains of countless abandoned meals.

Robin took a hesitant step forward and something crunched beneath his foot. A broken glass. There were toppled bottles and beakers laying discarded on tabletops and in the corners of the room, all the strange paraphernalia of Netherworlde science. The drifts of apparatus suggested that some discarded experiments had been swept to the floor in a fit of rage. The layers of dust covering everything indicated this had happened some time ago.

And the *webs*. The webs were everywhere in the chaos, tying one scene of discarded destruction to the next like mouldering silver puppet strings.

"This looks more like a nest than a study," Woad whispered.

Near to the centre of the room, amidst the fetid detritus of the ravaged study, something slumped in tattered rags, looking for all the world like a misshapen sack of potatoes dropped on the floor.

Lady Tinda took a shaking and horrified step into the room, surveying the cell, lit by its single, guttering candle stub by the distant window. The candlelight made the shadows of the countless spiderwebs dance fitfully on the walls and ceiling.

"What ... what is this? It's like a wild boar got in here." Her foot accidentally kicked a platter on the floor, sending it skittering and dislodging mouldy crusts of bread as hard as rock. "Like something has been *kept* here."

A horrible, creeping sense of foreboding flowed through Robin. From the corner of his vision, he felt, rather than saw something move in the room behind them, the empty, mirrored space they had just left. Large and shadowy. But when he turned to see, there was nothing back there but dust and cobwebs, moonlight reflecting from the walls.

When he turned back, it was to a gasp from Lady Tinda, and Woad had taken a step back in alarm. What they had taken for a crumpled sack in the centre of the chaotic and messy study was moving, getting unsteadily to its feet. It was a person, facing away from them in the room, slump-shouldered and barely visible in the guttering light.

"Who ... who is it?" a whisper came from the shadows, sounding dry and sepulchral. The cracked voice of a throat long-unused. "Who's there? What do they want?"

Lady Tinda's hand was at her mouth.

"Flint?" she whispered, eyes wide with shock at the ragged figure swaying unsteadily before them. It looked like something that had dragged itself from its own grave.

"Is it Nyx?" the rasping voice came again, sounding more than a little feverish, wheedling and almost hopeful. "It is? It's been a long time. He never comes back. Not for a long time. Said he would … said to keep trying … but the sun sets and the sun rises, again and again and again, and nothing. I keep trying, and he doesn't come back. Never checks."

If this pitiful-sounding creature was Lord Flint, he was not what Robin had been expecting. From behind, it seemed they looked at some emaciated and wizened old man. A stick-thin beggar, swaying unsteadily on his feet.

What he had taken to be rags were in fact finery and robes, but they had become so threadbare, unwashed and thick with dirt and neglect, they were barely recognisable. What had once been a mane of straight and shining hair, proud and manicured in the portrait of the parlour, was now a greyish, tangled mess. It hung loose and matted around his shoulders, unwashed, clumped and stringy. Piebald in places.

"He is angry at me …" the figure said to himself, holding out thin and shaky arms before him. His wrists were terribly thin, hands filthy and stained with ink, as he slowly turned around, shuffling. He seemed unsteady, stumbling in the darkness, shaking fingers brushing the webs all around him as though lost. "He is cross. Nyx is cross. I know he is," he babbled to himself, muttered words coming from a face hidden beneath the ragged hair. "I cannot make it work. The infernal, hateful, device! Not without the other half. It makes him so cross. I've failed him. I cannot find her."

The man made a low noise of keening dissatisfaction. He steadied himself against a table, sending a drift of loose notes and books toppling unheeded to the floor.

"He will see. I *will* make it work! I will! I'll prove my worth. and then …" A low and cracked chuckle escaped the man, filled with such an unexpected manic glee, almost childlike, that it chilled them all. "Then he will be *proud*. Then I can leave here, go back to Dis and hold my head up high. He promised. *Promised*. If I can only make it work … then I won't need *her* watching me all the time. Always bloody watching." He spat this last sentence.

He had turned to face them completely now. His face was still hidden almost completely by the hair. They could see only his mouth and chin, sunken and hollow cheekbones. He looked like something freshly unearthed. A ruined figure

"Flint, what's happened to you?" Tinda breathed, her shaking voice barely audible, but making the sensitive strands of web criss-crossing the room vibrate, nonetheless. "What happened here?"

Flint took a wavering step forward, stumbling unsteadily and almost falling, thrusting out a hand at the last moment to grab at a dusty bookshelf and steady himself. Several beakers and bottles tumbled from the surface, falling to the ground, where some shattered, and others rolled away noisily into the detritus of the corners of the room. He paid them no heed at all. Robin wasn't convinced the man knew where he was. He seemed broken. Scrambled.

"No ... not Nyx," he muttered, clearly talking to himself. "It isn't Nyx. Has he abandoned me? Why is he so cross? It's his failure too! Leaving only *her* to guard me? 'With you in spirit!' That's what he said when he left! Hah to that!" He laughed bitterly. "I'll show him though. He's wrong. I can make it work ... I can make it all on my own, I don't need him ... then they'll all see. Come back and lift me back up, where I belong!"

"He can't see," Woad said quietly.

"Lord Flint Calescent?" Robin said, making every effort to keep his voice steady and calm. The man froze, and his hidden face tilted up to Robin from across the space, like a rabbit sensing a twig snapping in the forest.

"Do you know where you are?" Robin asked carefully.

The man grinned, looking manic. His teeth looked too large. His gums had receded, likely malnutrition, but then his lips shivered, and the grin fell away into something like despair, before he dropped his head, hiding his face in the shadows.

"Home ... home ... my greatest work ... my proof to Eris. I am in my prison," he whispered to himself, hissing in the dark. "My prison."

"What's wrong with him?" Tinda asked, looking to Robin and Woad in horror. The blood had drained from her face. Robin could see that she was struggling to reconcile the broken creature squatting in this dilapidated ruin with her memories of a feared and despised brother.

"Prison, prison, prison ..." Flint was muttering to himself. "Spiders in the mind, see? That's how it happens...Whispering legs, riches, wealth, heart's desire … all lies." He raised a shaking hand as though to block out the moonlight filtering in through the leaded window, and Robin saw he only had two fingers and a thumb. The other fingers were gone. There were no wounds, no sign of injury. They were just … missing.

"Has he always only had …?" Robin began to ask Tinda, but she was already moving away from him, ignoring his question. Pushing the cobwebs aside as she made her way through the mess, kicking aside broken glass, filth-splattered plates and torn and sodden books to reach her long-reviled brother.

Her hands shaking, she took him by the shoulders and the two boys saw her visibly flinch, her shaking hands feeling how horribly emaciated the man's frame was beneath the ragged clothes.

"It's not Nyx," she told him firmly. "Flint. Brother. It's me. Tinda. What has happened to your hand? What has happened to *you*?"

"Ohh … feeding …" Flint explained dismissively, as though that was a boring or obvious question. He was still looking down and swaying on his feet deliriously. Lady Tinda was practically holding him upright. He seemed to hear their questions, but not to realise who she was. As though he truly thought he was talking to himself. Robin got the impression that Lord Flint had been alone here for a while – alone in this dead place. Talking to himself for a long time now. The man held up his shaking half-hand. "She always needs feeding. Nyx told me that … when he left her with me …"

He gripped Tinda's shoulders for balance, almost falling, and for a moment in the shadows the two twins who had been at war since the death of their father looked to Robin like nothing more than a brother and sister, trying to hold one another up in the darkness. "She keeps me safe, that's what he said… He left her here with me to keep me safe, to encourage me …" He laughed his unstable giggle again. It sounded like hysteria or panic trying to bubble up from somewhere deep down. "She's to see that I don't try to leave. I … I have to keep trying … to make it work … Father's stupid serpent … even only with my half of the Shard. With me in spirit. That's Nyx's little joke."

He shook his greasy head. "She gets hungry though, and there's nothing else to feed her… She doesn't take much. Only a little at a time."

Flint finally looked up at them, his long hair falling back from around his face. Robin flinched backwards in shock, bumping into a bookcase in the dark, sending volumes tumbling noisily to the floor all around him.

"Where are his eyes?" Woad gasped.

Lord Flint was blind. Like his missing fingers, there were no wounds on his face at all. No signs that there had ever been eyes there at all. Only a patch of blank skin above his nose and shaking, grinning mouth.

"She takes a little of me at a time," the man explained as they stared at him in horror. "Body and soul, see? Eris was not happy. No, not at all." He turned his blind and surreally-empty face to where Robin stood. "My sister, you see, she disappeared with her half … her half of our heart. I can't make it work without. Nyx says it must be done. It *must*! That Eris must have the serpent. Father's work." He nodded to himself urgently, as though giving himself a good telling off. "It falls to me. To make it work. Somehow. But she … that dark thing here." His voice became low and resentful. "She gets hungry and I must let her take a little of me. It's what Nyx does. He consumes."

Tinda looked across the room to Robin and Woad and her face was white, her expression conflicted. In her arms she held the broken frame of the man she hated. The brother who had condemned their father to death for wealth and power. She held him like a helpless baby.

"See here? This is punishment," she spat at them. "This is the wages of loyalty to Eris. The price of failure, even for her favourites. This is how the great Empress of the Netherworlde rewards her subjects. Because I fled with my half of the Shard, he could not make the device work for her, not without it. I can imagine her rage."

"We tried …" Flint said eagerly, insistently, furrowing his horribly blank brow up at her. "Nyx and I, we experimented! We worked so hard! And for so, so long! After *his* failure up at Heaven's Lens! The scrying pool, the sisters. The empress was so incensed, when one of them … the only success … was lost." He shook his head fearfully. "She was so incensed to lose that prize, that power that should have been hers." He leaned close to his sister, as though whispering salacious court gossip. "Nyx told me … he valued me, trusted me … if we could make *this* work, if we could power the serpent, find the Shard of Fire, make it all worthwhile, then she would forgive him. Forgive us all."

Robin wasn't sure what the man was babbling about. He seemed far beyond reason.

"But we couldn't," the man lamented. "My teacher and me. We couldn't. Not with only half a heart. I mean, no-one ever achieved anything great half-heartedly, did they?" Flint giggled helplessly.

"We tried everything. Every cantrip, every spell. We tore Father's library apart, searched his books ... nothing! Blood magic didn't work! Nyx's shadow mana could not move it! Months, *months* we laboured. And all the while Nyx grew more and more furious. He had already lost favour ... one of his greatest successes escaped him, brought him to shame in Eris' eyes. This, the great serpent, this was to be his redemption. And *my* glory!"

"But you couldn't make it work," Robin said. "Your father made it to save the Fae, and you betrayed both them *and* him. His work is far beyond your reach, isn't it, Lord Flint? Without both halves of the Shard."

"If only she hadn't disappeared!" the mad lord spat, suddenly spiteful. "The brat! The traitor! No loyalty to Eris. She was a deviant just like Father. Deviant! Stealing away into the night! Taking our heart with her. Both halves should have been mine. It's her fault! All her fault!"

"He doesn't know who you are," Woad said to Tinda. "He doesn't know who any of us are. Whatever took his eyes and fingers took his sanity as well."

"Why did they leave you here, Flint?" Tinda asked him. "You say they left, but you stayed?"

"The Wolf came," Flint sounded apprehensive. He whipped around suddenly, scanning the dark and ruined room with his blind eyes. "He's not here now? Is he here?" He sounded frightened, like a child.

"No, no," Tinda soothed. "Strigoi is not here."

"Wolf came," Flint repeated, sullen. He turned his blind face to the window, moonlight falling across his strange visage. "Blunt fist of Eris! Hateful demon-man! He told Nyx. Told him I was a failure. That we would never make it work. Not without the other half of the heart. Wolf told Nyx that the empress was tired of waiting. Tired of our lack of progress. She wanted the heart. Find the girl, find the missing half. Then ..." He waved a finger in the air knowingly. "Aha! Then it would work, and only then."

His face fell. "They went away... to hunt ... to search the world for her, for it. I wanted to help. I was Lord Flint! I was important and loyal! I was a good and diligent student. But Nyx said no. He told me I'm helpless ... useless." His voice cracked a little. "Left his pupil ... cast aside. Told me my duty was to stay... to persevere! Keep trying... Keep trying. Redeem my honour. He was laughing." The man shivered. "But he left *her* to guard me ... made sure I did stay. And that I kept trying."

"They abandoned you, Lord Flint," Robin told him. This was what came of turning your face to the darkness. Their father had been loyal to the king and queen, had devoted his life to creating something that could save their people, that could take them away from the coming war. His work, his will, had been based on light and love, compassion and selflessness. His son, the great and ambitious Lord Flint, had wagered all of that against his own petty ambition. His thirst for power, for a high place in the new world, riches, influence ... And what had it bought him? He was cast aside in this tomb, broken in body and mind. Forgotten.

"You couldn't give Eris what she wanted. You sold your father, betrayed your sister, and for this." Robin looked around the decrepitude of the ruined room, the hollow and lifeless manor house.

Flint shook his head fervently. "No, no, no," he insisted, sounding desperate. "I can ... I can still make it work. I can still ... climb." He had crumpled to his knees in the ruin of the study, clattering on plates and the broken paraphernalia of countless, ever more desperate experiments. "I *will* be the glory of Dis! I will sit at Eris' right hand! Nyx will reward me. His greatest pupil. You will see!"

He made a strange, hawking noise deep in his throat that could have been an anguished sob. "I will be the shining jewel of the Netherworlde, and none shall sit higher than me at court." He flung out a shaking hand, in the direction of his handsome portrait hanging in the adjacent room, his remaining fingers shaking uncontrollably. "The most beautiful ... most noble! Most highly regarded ..."

He was grinning up at them, chin shaking, the blind, blank mask of his face under his greasy ropes of hair. Something about his rant was almost pleading. Robin knew he should have felt revulsion, disgust, that the creature kneeling in his own ruin here deserved this. To have fallen so far, to have reaped exactly what he sowed.

But he felt only pity. A cold, horrible and helpless pity.

He watched Lady Tinda, who had hated and feared her brother for so many years. A woman who had never forgiven him and never could. She held him still. This loathsome ghost of a man, eaten away by his own deeds, consumed by his ambitions and crimes. She clung to him, her face set in a hard mask. After everything, all she could do for her twin was offer comfort. No tears fell. Robin wasn't sure that the woman was even capable of shedding a tear for him, but her eyes shimmered in the cold moonlight.

"My stupid, heartless broken brother," she whispered. "Who did he leave with you? Who … *what* … have you been feeding your thin little soul to, piece by piece?"

"His pet." The man sounded distant and distracted. He had crumpled utterly into her arms, as exhausted as Robin had ever seen a person. How long had it been since someone had last spoken to him, offered him the simple comfort of touch, whether he deserved it or not? "One of his greatest," Lord Flint chuckled, quietly, and there was a nervous horror under his voice. "He has a dark soul, that Grimm. Dark and hungry! So hungry. He will have a new assistant now. Done with me. I know that. She is … a good companion for me."

Woad softly touched Robin's forearm. "Pinky," he whispered. "Something's out there."

Robin glanced once again back into the large shadowy parlour they had crossed to get to Flint's cell. He thought he saw a shadow move, but it could merely have been the moonlight passing behind clouds outside, reflecting off the mirrors. He was wishing fervently that they hadn't left Henry and Karya alone downstairs.

"Brother," Tinda said firmly to the collapsed man in her arms as they sat on the floor. He seemed to have slumped, as though all the fight had gone out of him. "Where is it? Where is your half of our Shard?"

It seemed a shaft of lucidity passed through the splintered mind of Lord Flint, a sunbeam breaking softly, if only momentarily, through deep and rolling storm clouds. His mind appeared to clear, and blind or not, to understand who he was, and who she was, and to comprehend what was happening.

"You. You're really here. You came back," he whispered.

"Yes," she said, and a hand hovering above his head, uncertain as she wrestled with herself, descended and stroked his matted hair. "I came back, to stop you."

"You knew I would kill you, if you came back," Flint said helplessly. His bottom lip wobbled. "I need … to redeem … I need not to fail … I need the Shard."

"I know," she told him. "The halves of the heart must be reunited."

There was a moment of horrible silence in the darkness of Glassfire Manor, the only sounds were the soft wind outside the window, the only movement was the slow dance of the moonlit cobwebs of the room, swaying ceaselessly like seaweed underwater. And then Lord Flint spoke again, still cradled in his twin's arms.

"I think I am dying," he said flatly, whispering as though sharing a great secret.

She nodded, sniffing. "I think so, too," she said, still stroking his matted hair.

"I'm not sorry," he muttered. "I'm not ... I'm not. If I was sorry ... that would mean that everything I did ..." He took a deep shuddering breath of horror. "I'm not sorry. I can't be. I have to be right ... or ..."

She took a deep breath, shushing him, as though calming a child who had woken from a nightmare. "I know you're not," she said quietly. "Brother. Give me your Shard. Let me finish the work. Let me complete what Father started. Choose to help me right a terrible wrong. I can't do it without you." She smiled with the sarcastic half-smile of all siblings everywhere when teasing their kin. "You know we've only got one heart between us."

Lord Flint, with great effort, sat up, shaking all over. He balanced himself carefully with hands outstretched on the floor, until the siblings were kneeling facing one another. Even with his disfigurement, Robin could see they were twins. Two halves in and of themselves. The man reached into his tattered, filthy robes, and with shaking fumbling hands, removed a pendant he was wearing around his neck. They saw a jewel flash, red as blood, in the dim light.

"I'm ... so ... tired," he whispered, rattling.

"Give it to me, Flint," Tinda held out her hand between them. It seemed to Robin that Flint had been close to death long before they had arrived at the manor, only holding on to life from sheer, deranged determination, a mad compulsion to complete his dreams. His terrible, exhausting dreams. Now someone was here before him. Someone who could take it all from him, the terrible burden of his ambition.

To the blind and ruined Panthea, the woman kneeling opposite him symbolised not forgiveness, but release.

"Give it to me ... and rest," Tinda said.

Lord Flint grinned in the darkness, looking terribly sad and oddly mischievous. "She won't let you leave with it," he said. "She knows you're here, which means Nyx knows you're here. He'll be coming now. Coming to claim the glory. She'll keep you here until he does. Like she keeps me."

He reached out a hand and stroked his sister's face, very tentatively. It wasn't an act of tenderness or affection. It was more from a fear that he might reach for her and find her only a hallucination. That perhaps he was still alone here in the darkness and ruin, and no one had come to help him. Blind and alone with himself.

"But I know a way to leave," he smiled weakly. "A path that she can't follow."

He pressed the jewelled pendant into his sister's hands, and closed her fingers over it. "Complete the work, my hateful sister," he whispered. "For the glory …"

Robin fully expected him to say, 'for the glory of the empress.' Loyal to his misguided cause until his last breath.

"For the glory of our father," Flint breathed.

As Tinda held the jewel, her brother slumped forward, landing softly in her lap, a broken shell. In the cobwebbed shadows he moved no more.

Lady Tinda's face was calm and collected, her eyes dry and hard, but she sat there for several seconds. Lord Flint's body was a shapeless shadow in the darkness, and she turned her face away from Robin and Woad, looking instead out of the window at the moonlit night. She looked out to the dark hills of blossom and flowers beyond this horror, to where long ago and far away, children might have played in a creek beneath blossoms, and there had always been pyreflies in the night.

6

Darkness and Light

Robin took a step forward, unsure what to say, or even if there *was* anything to say. Anything that came to mind seemed redundant, empty words.

But before he could open his mouth to speak, there was a crash from the adjoining parlour, a clattering and splintering noise, as though one of the dust-covered tables had been toppled, sending candlesticks bouncing across the floor. Both boys jumped, and Lady Tinda's head whipped around, eyes wide behind her glasses.

"It's her," she whispered urgently. "Whatever that vile jailer Nyx left."

Robin and Woad motioned for the Fire Panthea to stay put, out of harm's way, and they rushed out of the cluttered study. Robin's heart was pounding, and a small part of him was wishing desperately that the sound had been caused by nothing more sinister than Henry and Karya having made their way upstairs clumsily in the dark and knocking into furniture.

But what awaited them in the long-mirrored room beyond was no bumbling friend. Squatting in the darkness, suspended from one corner of the ceiling and shrouded in webs, was a shadowy and writhing mass, a vast blob of darkness that was stirring, long legs unfurling, awakening at the death of Lord Flint. It was a spider, braced in the high corner of the ceiling. Larger than a horse, its grotesquely bulbous body shimmering and hazy with black, coiling smoke.

They must have passed right beneath it on their way into Lord Flint's cell, without even realising it was there. But now, at Flint's demise, the giant spider had awoken. Both boys froze in the doorway as it reached out its many legs, spreading across the walls and ceiling with obscene grace and leisure. Robin felt rooted to the floorboards. Fixed in place with a primal fear, unable to take his eyes off the monster unfolding in the rafters.

It dropped suddenly from its perch, landing with a heavy muffled thud that made the floorboards shake and sent up clouds of dust. The mirrors along the wall wobbled with the impact, making the moonlight dance and jitter in the room.

Robin had seen Nyx's mana spiders before, but nothing this large. The Grimm had left a watcher to torment and guard Flint. This dark and twisted creature had kept him prisoner here in his own ruined home. Had driven him mad and fed on his body and soul, one morsel at a time. *With him in spirit*, Nyx had joked with the blackest of humour, and Nyx's spirit was dark indeed.

"Pinky?" Woad's voice was a little more high-pitched than usual as he looked urgently to Robin for direction. Robin, unable to take his eyes off the shadowy monstrosity now crouching at the other end of the dusty room, saw a flicker from the corner of his eye, as a crackle of blue-white lightning danced across the faun's skin through sheer nerves.

"Stay behind me," Robin instructed, holding out an arm to shield both Woad and the room behind them containing Lady Tinda and the two halves of the jewel. Whatever happened, Nyx must not get his hands on the Shard of the Arcania.

The spider reared up slowly on its powerful long back legs, multiple eyes glittering like fist-sized beads of jet. Its body shook, making a chittering hiss that Robin could feel in his ribcage, as its forelegs wavered in the air, twitching at him.

"It wants the Shard," he said, his other hand closing over his mana stone, feeling the reassuring weight of the seraphinite. *My Fire Shard*, he added in his head. *Not yours, Nyx. Just try and take it.*

If Nyx had left a large portion of his mana here in the form of this vile and demonic thing, then that meant he *knew*. That the two halves of the Shard were now here. Nyx would be coming to the manor – and fast.

Without warning, the spider lunged, moving across the moonlit room with hideous speed, legs thumping into the ground with tremendous noise, scattering dusty and threadbare furniture before it like matchsticks. Woad yelped and jumped away, and Robin threw himself to the side, dodging the shadowy mass while instinctively throwing out a galestrike.

The invisible javelin of air sliced through the cobwebs in the room and slashed the beast across its face like a whip.

As Robin scrambled back to his feet. The great spider was already turning. A hazy mass of rolling shadow. It had barely been knocked off balance, even with Robin's strongest cantrip. The thing was strong.

Focussing and breathing hard, Robin threw out both hands before him and reached for the Tower of Earth, lifting his hands sharply from floor to ceiling like a one-man Mexican wave. Under his will, the old floorboards between him and the creature shattered, flying upwards in large, splintered shafts, pikes suspended in mid-air. Directing his will, Robin sent the deadly missiles with their jagged edges flying at the spider, whooshing through the air. Lightning quick, the hissing beast batted them away, its hideous legs weaving and waving. Only one spear of broken wood found its mark, piercing the thick and shiny hide of the spider and passing straight through it to land deeply embedded in the wall behind. Robin watched, panting from the effort, as the hole in the creature closed up immediately, no more substantial than smoke.

Rallying quickly, he cast a waterwhip, dragging damp from the walls and condensation from the windows with determination. Lashing out with a lasso of thin but strong liquid, glittering in the dark. It tangled around two of the monstrous spider's huge legs as it came for him again, skirting around the new hole in the floor to get to him. Robin pulled with all his might, his mana stone blazing as he dragged it forward.

Unbalanced, legs tangled in the watery mana, the spider stumbled into the hole, flailing as it fell gracelessly into the gaping hole, the weight of its bloated body dragging it helplessly downward through the ragged tear in the floorboards to the floor below.

Away from the Shard, good, thought Robin. But Karya and Henry were down there somewhere too, which was bad. Very bad.

Before he could lose his nerve, Robin leapt into the hole after the spider, following it down to the hallway below. The creature had landed heavily enough to crack the marble of the great empty entrance hall below, falling on its back with all eight of its huge legs flailing around as it shrieked. It recovered quickly, flipping itself over, more agile that its huge bulk would suggest. It scuttled away, legs pounding as Robin dropped out of the darkness behind it. He cast a featherbreath beneath him as he fell feet-first, softening his own landing with a cushion of directed air.

Looking around desperately in the gloom, Robin could hear Woad on the upper floors, running along the corridor back towards the staircase, fighting his way through cobwebs. He could hear Lady Tinda shouting. His eyes fell on Karya and Henry, still halfway up the stairs, their faces frozen with shock at the sudden intrusion of the great shadowy mana creature, rearing up and heading straight for them. Hissing as it barrelled towards the staircase, homing in on their surprised cries. Drawn in arachnid fury by the vibrations and movements through the room's many webs.

To his credit, Henry had already stood and had an arrow nocked, letting it fly straight for the creature's underbelly as it reared up against them. Much as with Robin's attack with the splintered floorboards up above, the loosed shafts of Henry's arrows all hit their mark, but passed directly through the spider's fat body with a series of whistling hisses. They made it stagger but it recovered almost immediately, the small and insignificant holes punched through in their passing already closing up harmlessly like a gap in dark clouds.

Behind Nyx's vile guardian, the tormentor of Lord Flint, Robin backed away towards the main doors of the manor. It was no good. They were fighting smoke. He had to get this thing out in the open. Away from the others. He yelled and waved his hands, throwing galestrikes at the back of the beast in quick and precise succession.

Even with all his force, he might as well have been peppering it with thrown spitballs. The spider hissed and chittered more with angry irritation than pain, spinning around and fixing its many alien eyes on the boy at the doors. Abandoning Henry and Karya, the beast moved, making for Robin quickly, dashing across the great darkness of the hall with terrifying speed. Heavy thuds that shook the cobwebs above.

Behind it, Robin saw Woad running down the staircase to Karya and Henry, a small blue blur of motion – and then the beast was upon him, crashing into him like a battering ram and throwing him against the outer doors, bursting open in a shower of new splinters.

Robin and the shadow-spider rolled over and over, tangled together, down the wide sweep of steps and into the open courtyard, the boy's arms held up instinctively to shield his face from snapping and gnashing mandibles. The creature wrapped around him, heavy and suffocating, feeling both crushingly heavy and yet insubstantial at the same time. Its smoky and blurred edges of shadow wavering. The stink of it filled his nose as they struggled together, like car exhaust and brimstone. It had substance and a terrible weight, but it felt to Robin like trying to grip shifting tar through thick smoke. The bulk of it was crushing him, driving the air from his lungs.

They had stopped rolling, grinding to a halt with Robin pinned beneath the beast. Its wide angry bulk filled his vision, a smothering nightmare, and somewhere, what felt like miles away, he could distantly hear the panicked cries of his friends.

Gravel was digging into Robin's spine and the back of his neck, scraping at his skin, and a source of great heat from somewhere nearby seemed to singe at his hair. An orange light illuminated Nyx's oily monster as it shifted its great weight off him, pinning his arms agonisingly to the floor with two of its legs as its huge body reared upwards.

We must be near the fire pool, Robin found himself thinking in a distant, almost detached way. The large circular well of molten fire that decoratively centred the courtyard of Glassfire Manor.

He struggled to free his hands, to cast a cantrip, *anything* that would get the demon-thing from on top of him. But to his horror, the spider was draping him in webs, swiftly and firmly, covering his hands, laying strand upon heavy strand across his chest like wet and heavy rope. The weight of it crushed his ribs, muffling his mana stone.

Closing his eyes, Robin forced himself to focus, against the rising, suffocating panic and the desperate hammering of his own heart. He pictured Ffoulkes, back at Erlking, in the necessarium, spinning columns of fire around his body like a ribbon dancer.

Unable to move, with the weight of his opponent's webbing crushing and suffocating down atop him, Robin threw out his mana, directing it not through his hands, but out of his mind alone, a sheer force of will, towards where he felt the orange light glowed. He plunged his consciousness into the deep well of fire and pulled. *Make it dance*, he thought desperately, over the deafening hiss and insane chatter of the huge spider inches from his face. *Make it sing.*

Nyx's mana spider shrieked in pain and alarm as jets of flame shot out from the courtyard well. Molten ropes of lava and flame leaping up like snakes to slap at its many legs and slash across its bloated stomach in bright, stinging whips.

It reared up and backwards, the creature of shadow shrinking back from the light and heat as the flame tongues struck again and again. Robin, trapped immobile beneath the webs, pinned to the floor by their weight, was gasping with the sheer effort of holding the fire aloft and directing its movements left and right, back and forth, in a dance of striking violence. His heart felt about to burst and he felt a tickle on his top lip as his nose began to bleed.

The mana felt so heavy. He had drawn from Air, Water, Earth, and now Fire, and his mana stone, crushed and muffled beneath the sticky half cocoon of webbing which held him pinned to the floor, was spent.

Scion or not, he felt his strength reach a limit, and though he saw that he had beaten Nyx's spider back, and that the magma snakes and whips, those tongues of molten fury, had left glowing lashes across the beast, he knew it wasn't enough. The creature was too dark, too angry, too fuelled by gorging on the vainglorious ambition of Lord Flint. And Robin, finally, had nothing left to give. As his power blurred and the bright streaks of lava fell from the air, splashing unformed onto the gravel and hissing as he lost control of their shaping, the spider was already bracing itself. Shaking off the pain, pulling its great darkness back around itself, and preparing to lunge. To bite the head from its pinned prey.

A flash of light suddenly tore through the courtyard, so bright that it blinded him. Brilliant as burning magnesium and tinged with blue, making Robin's exhausted eyes fly wide with shock. A crashing rumble tore all around the manor. *Thunder.* It was everywhere, shaking the very stones of the glossy outer walls, vibrating powerfully through the ground beneath him, making the gravel dance and leap.

Robin, still pinned, saw arcs of lightning tearing across the walls like questing fingers, blowing out the glass from window after window in their wake. A series of gunshot explosions. The spider, silhouetted against the sudden blinding brightness, was lifted off the ground, as helpless as a toy, cradled in a net of arcing electrical light.

Every hair on Robin's head stood on end as the air in the courtyard was charged, and in the belly of this sudden and unearthly thunderstorm, he saw Woad from the corner of his eye, standing framed in the shattered doors to the manor, his arms aloft. The boy's eyes were white and shining from corner to corner, his face bared in a feral grimace, and the lightning roared and poured from him, filling the courtyard with light and noise, chasing every shadow away and bringing harsh and burning light in thrusts and spikes to every corner. Urns and statues exploded under the questing strikes.

Bolt after bolt of lightning tore through and around the beast, tossing it around, and beneath the roar and constant rumble of thunder, Robin could just hear its anguished squeals and shrieks of pain and shock. The beast flew over his head, legs spasming as the current passed through them, and with a grand gesture Woad threw the noxious beast down, casting it into the pit of fire. From his position on the steps, he directed the lashing cradle of light and power, plunging Nyx's dark spider down it into the glowing, molten well of light. Thick fingers of white electricity followed it down, stabbing into the magma – where its screams were silenced, lost in the thunder.

Electricity coursed like writhing snakes all along the courtyard floor, making the webbing of Robin's half-finished cocoon snap and jump. It crackled inside his head, a series of bright flashes, as a ringing noise built in his ears over the endless din. As Robin's vision disappeared down a long black tunnel, his last view was of Woad, still shining like a blue burning flame, arms outstretched as the lightning danced around him, suspended a foot off the floor, his feet dangling, a vengeful spirit of fury.

7

The Glassfire Serpent

Robin came back to his senses groggily, feeling every part of his body ache, and aware that someone was leaning over him, jogging his limbs roughly. His mouth felt dry as sandpaper and he wished very much that they would go away and leave him alone.

Blinking open his eyes he saw it was Henry, crouched over him under a sky that was now clear and quiet, dotted with icy stars. The boy was hacking and tearing at the remaining strands of webbing. He could see Karya standing just behind him, a pale ghost in the night.

"There you are, mate," Henry grunted in a friendly manner, his voice only slightly betraying deep relief. "Left us a for a second there, you big delicate fainting thing. Lie still. Have you free in a second … ugh, this stuff is vile."

Robin struggled against the sticky, heavy strands of the spider's spewed prison as Henry pulled at them, but with the death of the beast, they were already disintegrating on their own, falling away like grey burned paper and crumbling into nothing.

"Woad?" he sat up, blearily grabbing Henry's hand and allowing himself to be hoisted forward.

Woad was hurrying over. He looked a little dizzy, as though he had just stepped off a fast merry-go-round, but otherwise unremarkable. Gone were the shining eyes and glowing electric skin, gone was the sense of sheer power funnelled through his tiny form to draw the fury of the sky down into the dark courtyard of Glassfire Manor. He was once again his small self, a willowy blue boy with an impish grin spread all over his face. His hair could have been smoking slightly, but

Robin might have imagined it, still coming to his senses.

"I'm fine, Pinky," he said, noting Robin's concern. He flexed his fingers, staring down at his hands as though he had never seen them before. "Guess I've figured out my Skyfire then, eh?"

"That's an understatement," Karya said, hoarse but happy. "This is why people are wary of fauns, you know. They say every storm is a faun showing off somewhere. That was quite the light show."

Robin got unsteadily to his feet, acutely aware that his hair was standing straight up from his head. He smoothed it flat with his hands, and then on impulse, drew Woad into a bone-crushing hug.

"Oi! Gerroff! Don't be soft!" the faun mumbled, but he didn't struggle too much to get away. Henry and even, to Robin's surprise, Karya, joined in, so that the four of them stood unsteadily, a tight circle of relief beside the glowing central firewell of the courtyard.

"Thought you were done for, see?" Woad said, as they broke apart, blushing a little bluer. "That big smoky critter was wrapping you up faster than its baby brothers and sisters did with Jack and Ffoulkes back at the Sorrows. But I wasn't for letting it take you anywhere. No-one messes with my Pinky!" He shook his head, slowly regaining his balance after expending so much mana. "I mean, you were doing some serious Scion-level combat in there, pretty impressive, but I could see you were tapped out. Ugly incy-wincy was getting ready to bite your head off."

"A Scion without a head is no use to any of us," Karya noted, patting Woad on the back proudly.

"That's what I thought too," Woad said. He grinned again at Robin, looking a little self-conscious and absently scratching behind his own ear. "Good old Marrowstride, eh? Turning the right keys after all. Almost makes it worth nearly getting made into a bog hag's buffet brunch for."

He blew out his cheeks, looking around at the many shattered windows. The courtyard was covered in glass. The walls and floor scarred by many still-smoking scorch marks. "It might be a while before I do that again though, I don't mind telling you."

Robin turned and looked down into the fiery well. "That's a large chunk of mana that Nyx won't be getting back, anyway," he said.

"Good." Karya's voice was harsh. "I hope he felt every *second* of it, wherever he is."

"He's likely to be high-tailing it here, isn't he?" Henry pointed out. They all tore their eyes from the well – the grave of the spider monster – and looked back to the mansion. "We shouldn't be wasting time celebrating not being killed to death." Henry reasoned. "It's hardly like it's a novel experience is it, let's be honest. *Something* tries to kill us roughly every ten minutes." He slung his quiver off his shoulder. "Wasted all my good arrows on that foul thing," he muttered. "For all the good it did. Look, I've only got that one from the library of the satyrs left." He pouted a little.

Karya gave him a tired smirk, rolling her eyes. "I've never heard anyone sulk over having possession of one of the hallowed gifts of the Elementals before, Henry." she said. "At least you didn't waste it on that vile eight-legged freak."

She looked to Robin and Woad. "What happened up there? Did you find and defeat Lord Flint?"

"He defeated himself," Robin glanced up at the dark windows, shivering despite the warm spring night. "Flint is gone."

"And his half of the Shard?"

"Inside, with Lady Tinda." Robin motioned for them to move. "Henry's right. Nyx, or worse, will be descending on Glassfire Manor any second now, and I'm with Woad. I won't be casting any combat cantrips for a while either. With me and him exhausted, Henry with one arrow and you barely able to walk without passing out, we will be sitting ducks. Let's get what we came here for, and go."

Lady Tinda was waiting for them inside the ruined hallway, standing at the foot of the staircase and staring up at the ragged hole in the ceiling through which the spider had fallen from the room above.

"It's dead, then?" she asked, her voice only faintly curious as the four children made their way inside. "Then all the evil that has plagued my home is gone, at last."

She was holding a red jewel in her open palm, having pried it from the pendant her brother pressed into her hands, and she held her other hand out expectantly to Henry, who unslung the bow from his shoulder and passed it to her.

"And this is now, finally and wholly, mine," the woman said. The red gem along the length of Henry's bow fell from its indentation – almost eagerly, as if it wanted to – and after passing the bow back to the boy, the Fire Panthea examined the two halves of the Shard, quiet and dim rubies, one in each hand, in the shadows of the hall.

She smiled in a bittersweet but – Robin thought – quite pragmatic way. "Twins separated by death and stones now reunited. My brother and I, two halves of a whole, are forever apart, and the Shard of Fire, separate for the span of our lives, is now one. Poetic, eh?"

She pressed her hands together and, as she closed her eyes behind her glasses, there was a soft, muted flash, red as blood and deep as an ocean. It flooded the room, flickering out through her laced fingers, and a blast of warmth, like the hot sun on a summer's day, rolled through the empty hall, blowing every disintegrating cobweb away. All around them, in every sconce, candles that had long stood dark, puffed into flame, and the chandelier above them, hanging crooked beside the hole in the high ceiling, blazed into light.

When the woman opened her hands again, the two jewels had become one, and also more than twice their previous size, having fused into a fist of shimmering faceted rock. The Shard of Fire.

Blood red and lit from within with a rolling and dancing light, orange and yellow, swirling and churning silently, it pulled their focus like gravity. It was hard to look at anything else.

Power hummed from it, flowing out into the newly lit room in waves that raised goose bumps along Robin's arms. The energy from the Shard seemed to chase away all of his exhaustion and aches, renewing him. He felt his own mana stone vibrate with absorbed energy, as though it were soaking up the heat and light of the sun.

"The fourth Shard of the Arcania," he breathed. They all stared, its light playing softly across their faces.

"Given by the king and queen to my father," Lady Tinda said. "To give to me. And now …" She held it out, nodding, as though raising a toast with a champagne glass, "I give it to you."

Robin crossed the hall and took the Shard from her. The jewel was heavy and warm, making his fingers tingle and vibrate. He could feel the power in it, just waiting to be commanded.

"Always have to show off with the horns, don't you?" Henry said, making Robin frown with confusion, but then he caught sight of himself in a long mirror set into one of the freshly candlelit recesses of the hall.

His Fae horns, usually invisible and intangible, were visibly crowning his head, formed of soft and silent blue flame, tall antlers of fire flickering in and out of existence.

"Are you going to … you know … Puck out?" Henry asked curiously. "Here and now, I mean?"

Robin couldn't help but smile. "I don't *become* the Puck anymore, Henry," he said, feeling the rightness of the Shard in his hands. "I'm always the Puck."

He looked back to Lady Tinda. "Where is this device of your father's? It'll be light soon. Pyrenight. We have to hurry."

She nodded. "Follow me, all of you. I'll take you to the Glassfire Serpent."

None of them had known what to expect when first told of the Calescent's device back at Erlking. Only that it was a secret project commissioned by King Oberon and Queen Titania, a vehicle to spirit away the Fae people in the coming war, to take them to a place of safety in the legendary and impenetrable Nethercity far below the Netherworlde's surface. As Lady Tinda led them through a set of large hidden doors in the shadows behind the grand staircase, and down a set of steep and spiralling stairs deep into the ground below, their apprehension grew.

The staircase was tight and functional. Here, there was none of the faded grandeur and opulence of the mansion above. No marble, no carved wood, no shiny jet walls. The staircase was bare rock and it burrowed far beneath the roots of Glassfire Manor, into the secret workshop of a Panthea noble loyal to the pre-war Fae. When the flight of stairs eventually ended, it emptied them into a vast subterranean cavern, hung with stalactites around which the fluttering of bats could be heard.

The echoing space was lit only by the soft reddish-gold streaks of veins that ran everywhere through the rock, light glinting from the strange ore like frozen streams of lava. The floor of the cavern had long ago been flattened and tiled over with worn stone. Their footsteps echoed back and forth in the glowing shadows and still, stale air as they made their way across and away from the surface world. At both ends of the long cavern were large black caves, hewn tunnels leading away in either direction, and sitting between them in a deep recessed trench, there was a long, shining object, massive and still. It looked for all the world to Robin like a huge train. In fact, the entire place resembled a rudimentary underground train station. He might have been on the London Underground, except for the glowing stalactites, and the rather notable fact that this particular long shining bullet of a train was no crude affair hammered together from metal and glass. It was a masterpiece of carved obsidian, a parade of enormous, jagged scales laid neatly over one another along its length, shining and reflecting the infernal glow of the cavern.

It does look like a serpent, Robin thought to himself, looking over the glossy bulk of the long craft, sleeping and still, as long as a freight train and as solid as diamond.

"My father's great work," Tinda said, her voice, though hushed, echoing around them, whispering back to them from the walls. "His ark. The salvation of your people that never came. Deprived of its engine." She glanced at the Shard of Fire, still cradled carefully in Robin's hands and throwing its light back up onto his face, lending him an eldritch air. "Nyx and my brother … all the time they spent down here, trying to fathom its depths. Fruitless and frustrated. I'd say it's enough to drive a man mad, but we've already seen that's the case. They never even figured out a way to open it up."

She looked from the glowing Shard to the great long bulk of the jagged train. "Ironic really. Here we are at last … too late to help the Fae. We've just come to use it."

"Not too late to help *us*," Henry said as they walked over to the huge volcanic glass train. Its immense flank towered over them. He ran a hand gently across the intricately carved surface, eliciting a low vibration – felt, but unheard. "It can help us save our friends. The ones already in Dis." He glanced at Karya. "And the ones who need to get in there."

"I've seen this before," Robin realised, seeing his own dark and distorted reflection in the softly shining sides of the serpent. "Back in Nyx's journal. There were lots of hints about you and your brother, all your family crests, the maps where he had been searching for you. But there was this, too. A sketch of a great snake, burrowing along beneath roughly drawn mountains."

He turned to look at the Fire Panthea.

"I'm sorry it took your brother," he said. "I really am."

She sniffed and shook her head. "Eris took my brother years ago. It isn't just my father's death on Flint's hands, it's the death and imprisonment of all those Fae who could have – should have – been saved here." She smiled at the great serpent, the vast underground train of black rock, though it was the saddest smile Robin had ever seen. "No … he wasn't killed by this machine. Flint was dead a long time ago. It just took this long for him to realise it."

She glanced at them all. "You four … you really do mean to go to Dis, don't you? You know how dangerous Eris is. You've seen with your own eyes what horrors wait for those who seek her out. You've seen what loving Eris does to you, upstairs." She shook her head in resigned bewilderment, clearly thinking them all mad.

"We do and we have," Woad nodded. "And that's why we have to go, of course. Our friends are waiting for us. All three of them."

Henry gave the faun a sidelong look. "Three?" he asked. "You mean two? Jack and Ffoulkes, right?"

The faun shook his head. "Don't forget Phorbas," he said. He looked to Lady Tinda, explaining. "He's a magic knife, but he used to be a person. Silvertop has him. He's an Erlkinger too, even if he is just silverware."

Lady Tinda stared back at the little blue boy's happy face, unsure how to process this.

"Okay then," she settled on, deeply confused. She looked at Karya. "This one here looks as brittle as paper now," she said flatly. "If you think going home to Nyx's lair will save her, you had best do it quickly."

"I'm not dead yet," Karya argued, frowning, though she looked hollow, as though the slightest breeze might knock her down. "Might feel that way though. I don't know if answers wait for me there, or simply the end, but …" She shrugged, seeming both resolute and a little helpless. "At this point, I have nowhere else left to go."

"How does it work?" Robin asked. He reached past Henry and touched the great sides of the long contraption. He couldn't help thinking of it as the serpent train. At his touch, the Shard of Fire flickered in his hand, growing brighter, and a section of the scaled side silently folded back, opening up like the petals of a flower to reveal a dark and cool interior.

"Like that … I suppose," she replied.

The four children tentatively stepped inside, peering around. It was indeed like being on a train, only with no seats or windows, and yet somehow, from within, they could see out through the walls, like peering through clear but fractured crystal.

135

"Tinted windows," Henry observed. "Very swish for a big magic drill."

Lady Tinda remained on what they couldn't help thinking of as the platform, the little woman's arms folded as she regarded them carefully through her glasses.

"You shouldn't stay here," Robin turned back to her. "Nyx will be coming after us. This place will be swarming with peacekeepers soon, maybe centaurs, maybe worse. It isn't safe for you."

She nodded. "Well, I'm not stupid enough to go to Dis," she said. "I will see to my brother's body. And then … don't worry about me." She smiled lopsidedly. "I'm good at disappearing. I've been doing it for a long time. There's nothing left for me here anyway. No point hanging around in dusty old memories."

"You're welcome at Erlking," he told her, and the others nodded emphatically. "Make your way to the hall if you wish. It's safe there." He considered this. "Well, safer than here," he amended.

She took a step backwards as the scales that had formed an opening in the Glassfire Serpent slowly began to close in again around them, shutting the children inside. "Erlking, little Scion, is absolutely the least safe place I can think of. But thanks for the offer. I'll see you again, I'm sure."

As the train sealed the Erlkingers within, as surely as if they had been swallowed, Robin saw Lady Tinda hugging her own arms and looking thoughtfully up at the high roof of the cavern, towards the distant mansion she had once called home, silent and ruined. High above them through the glowing rock. She might have looked like something lost, buried beneath the horrors of her past weighing above her in stone and shadow, except she was smiling faintly, and looked lighter than when they had first met her. When she left, there would be no more ghosts at Glassfire Manor.

None of them had any clue how to make the Glassfire Serpent move – it was hardly as though Old Lord Calescent had left a handy guidebook. But they all agreed, if any answers were to be gained, the front of the odd and otherworldly train would be a good place to start.

Walking the length of the serpent's interior was a curious experience. The crystal tube, angled and scaled on all sides, was impenetrable from outside, but from within, they could clearly see out to the cavern beyond, albeit in a fractured and angular way. It was like looking out of a kaleido-scope or through the multi-faceted eyes of a fly. The hugely long vehicle was not broken into distinct sections, as a human world train was divided into carriages. Instead, the whole cylinder seemed somehow more organic, although at regular intervals, as they walked their way to the front, the pattern and density of the angular scales making up the body frequently changed their formation. Henry suggested these ribbed sections might act in the same bendy way that those rubber concertina-like sections between long buses or trams did, allowing the serpent to angle, move and sidle in any direction, much like a real burrowing snake.

"There are no tracks," Karya observed, looking down through the glassy floor. And as they reached the front end of the long tube, carved into the funnel-like shape of a serpent, close mouthed, with the sculpted layers of stone scales rotating outwards from the nose-cone in an elabo-rate spiral, they also noted that in front of them was no kind of tunnel. The cave into which the serpent pointed was shallow and ended in bare rock.

Nor were there, to their surprise, any operational levers, dials, or indeed any other kind of mechanism that one might expect to find, to guide the thing forward. Just a deep semi-circular recess, right in the middle of the serpent's nose, shaped like a depression made by a large egg. Robin discovered that the glowing Shard of Fire, pulsing with waves of quiet power, slotted perfectly into this – as neatly as Cinderella's shoe fitted onto her foot.

"How are we supposed to make this thing burrow through the rock all the way to Dis?" Henry asked. "It's not like we have a map or even a compass. Does anyone actually know which way Dis is? Or how far from the Black Hills?" He scratched his head absently. "Or even which direction we're facing right now? Because to be honest, I'm stumped."

Woad looked thoughtful. "Well, speaking of stumps … I heard that in the forests, moss always grows on the north side of a tree," he offered knowledgeably. The others all looked at him, their faces blank as he blinked happily in the dim light of the serpent's interior. "Does anyone have a mossy stick on them … maybe?" He finished with a shrug.

"We did not come all this way just to navigate our way to Eris' capital using dowsing rods, Woad," Karya said. She had slumped down to sit on the floor, looking too exhausted to do much else.

"Although, to be honest," she admitted, "I have no better idea, really. I'm just so terribly tired. I could just lay down on the cosy and comfortable floor of this subterranean magical crystal snake train and get some decent shut eye." She looked thoughtful for a moment. "That's not a sentence I would have imagined myself ever having said before now."

"I don't think it's a good idea for you to drop off," Henry said. He seemed to want to add more, but stopped himself. Karya gave him a knowing look.

"In case I drop *all* the way off, you mean?" she finished for him. "Stop panicking, will you? If I'm due to kick the bucket in the immediate future, please rest assured I have no intention of doing so quietly and peacefully in my sleep."

Woad squatted on the floor next to her, looking concerned, but smiling, nonetheless. "Boss has always said that we should all aim to go out of this world the same way we came into it."

"What?" Henry frowned. "Naked, confused and bald?"

"Kicking and screaming and covered in blood," Karya corrected him with a dry laugh that turned into a deep and racking cough. "Preferably that of your enemies."

Henry grinned back at her. "You're still the scariest person I know," he said with admiration.

While they talked, Robin was running his hands over the small indentation where he had neatly slotted the Shard of Fire. There was a blank space either side of the cradle, just wide enough for him to place a hand on each.

"I think I know how this thing works," he said. The other three looked up at him.

He shrugged. "By magic, of course. This *is* the Netherworlde, after all." He nodded to Woad, "And actually, your dowsing idea isn't half bad."

"We don't have any magical mossy compass sticks though, Pinky," the faun pointed out. "There's a little hole in your plan right there."

Robin rummaged through his backpack, fishing out the heavy, circular moral compass. "No, but we do have this." He propped it up in front of him on the minimalist control panel, balancing it above the embedded Shard. "It points to things. It's guided me a few times …" He gave an uncertain, one-shoulder shrug. "More or less. It knows *where* I need to be, and right now, that's Dis."

They watched as the needle on the compass span this way and that, eventually coming to rest at an angle which, were it a clock, would have been around eleven. Robin leaned forward to inspect the tiny carved face with which it had aligned. Like all the symbols, it was a rudimentary face, though this one surprised him.

"What is it?" Karya asked from the floor, stifling another worrying cough.

"It looks like a face made from leaves," Robin said. "Tree branches. I don't know what that's got to do with Dis, or Nyx, or Heaven's Lens?"

Something itched at his mind, however. A sketch in Nyx's notes had indeed been a circle of what looked like trees, arranged around a pond or pool. Now that Robin thought about it, peering at the tiny brass face of leaves on the rim of their guiding compass, he *had* seen a ring of trees again. When he touched the denuded phoenix quill and was given his confusing vision. A circle of trees in a garden around a pool – only their branches had been threaded, overwhelmed in fact, with webs and spiders. It hadn't made much sense at the time, but in the past few days, Robin had come to associate spiders and webs with one particular person, very strongly.

"Lord Flint told us that Nyx had failed in some kind of great experiment at his laboratory, at Heaven's Lens," he told the others. "That's why he was trying to earn back Lady Eris' favour by trying to get this serpent to work. I don't know what he was doing up there in his workshop at Dis, but I think it was bad." He glanced at Karya. "I think you were involved somehow. And I think that's where in Dis we need to go, to get answers."

Nyx had been tampering with things that should not be tampered with. Robin knew it, as surely as he knew his own name. He felt it with the certainty of the quiet and commanding voice of the Puck in his mind.

Resolutely, he placed a hand either side of the glowing Fire Shard, allowing his mana to leach out into the smooth crystal.

"If we keep this needle pointed to noon, it will take us where we need to go," he said with certainty. He smiled back at his friends. "If you can find anything to hold onto, do it. I have the strongest feeling that this thing moves *fast*."

He pushed his mana out into the world, through his hands and into the cradled Shard. With his eyes closed, he could feel the entire length of the train around him, above and below and stretching out far behind like a tail in the darkness. It was immense. It could have carried a thousand passengers. Refugee Fae in their multitudes. He was aware of every carved scale, every shining facet. It was indeed a tuning fork, he realised, and it was just waiting for the right music to pass through its being and make it vibrate to life.

The symphony it needed was fire.

Feeling the power of the Shard of the Arcania thrumming up through both of his arms, Robin smiled to himself, invisible flames licking around ghostly horns that none could see, but that he could feel.

Make it sing, Puck, he told himself.

Power exploded from the Shard, funnelled away like flame along a lit fuse, directed and pouring through the very fabric of the Glassfire Serpent. It rocketed along the grooves of each glossy scale like a backdraught, filtered through the fabric of the structure as surely as Ffoulkes' fire had been by the grooved walls of the necessarium. Fiery power lit up the walls as the energy of the Shard roared along the great length, bringing the strange train to life. It glowed and hummed, vibrating around them and Robin's eyes shot open, bright green flecked with fiery gold, as the spiralling scales of the outer nose cone began to swiftly rotate a great diamond drill. Faster and faster it span in front of them, until each sharp, solid scale was a blur, and the serpent lurched forward in its entirely, a vast burrowing beast of scales and fire, which ate into the solid rock of the cave before them as easily as a hot knife through butter.

The Glassfire Serpent, alive with motion, fire and light, shot forward, burrowing into the darkness and uncertainty ahead with a deafening roar. Everyone but Robin lost their balance in the lurch and speed of the motion, falling to the floor in a yelping heap. Robin, however, couldn't help but laugh. The first real laugh he could remember in a long while, filled with joy and euphoria. He stood at the helm, his hands firmly on the Shard, filled with all the elation and music of fire, the dance of the great serpent, a blur of light, motion and power roaring through the black rock.

The journey through the darkness was strange and later on, Robin would remember it like something from a dream. He was not channelling the power source of the Shard of Fire to drive the serpent forward, tearing through solid rock at dizzying speeds. He *was* the power source. Plugged into the eldritch machinery of the workmanship of Lord Calescent like a great battery. His thoughts were as fast and fluid as flame itself, flickering wildly through his mind, in a body which felt as though it was formed of dark glass, superheated and bubbling over with light and fire. Around him, the vast train snaked through solid earth like an eel through water. He could feel the rocks shattering away from his long sides, the joyous motion of the speeding journey. It was every thrill ride in the world, rolled into one and plunged into darkness. Here, beneath the Netherworlde, Robin and the serpent – one and the same – plunged forwards, unstoppable and swift, a missile eating at the earth, and leaving only blackness in its empty wake as it blazed through the deep places of the world.

Robin felt connected to fire everywhere. He could feel candles burning in distant homes. He could sense far-off forest fires, and lightning strikes on distant mountains. And somewhere high above them, as the drill whirred and the train smashed forward, he felt the sun rise. The great, unimaginable large and distant ball of fire, roaring over the horizon and bringing the day of Pyrenight to the surface of the Netherworlde. Its energy and majesty flooded through him, burning under the earth. Its silent roar out in space was the ultimate song of fire.

In his flickering thoughts, piloting the Glassfire Serpent through the underworld, Robin considered the strangeness of the life of the Scion. A life where thought and will could meld you to majesty and power, a life where you might live to see the same eclipse twice. All the times when he had jealously wished for a normal life were gone. The freedom of fire and the speed and joy of the journey was something he would not have given up for anything.

"I think I'm going to pass out!" Henry yelled, barely audible over the roaring flames licking along the outside of the racing train. "Stop doing loops! You're doing loops on purpose!"

Woad, who was lying flat out on the floor, arms and legs outstretched as though he was pinned in place by G-forces, was laughing uncontrollably, and Karya clung to the angled walls as their transport dove through the blind darkness, looking queasy. The flashing light strobed across her face. She was watching the needle of the compass, flicking left, then right, then left. Each time, Robin adjusted the trajectory of the serpent, chasing after the elusive noon. It felt like being inside a space shuttle roaring up through the atmosphere.

"It's changed again!" she yelled. She grabbed Robin's arm to get his attention, immediately pulling her hand back with a pained hiss. The boy's skin was hot, as though she had just placed her hand on an iron. The toggles of his grey hoodie were smouldering slightly, as though they might burst into flame. "Scion, the compass … look."

The needle had indeed spun as they screamed along beneath the landscape, and now it pointed to a new tiny brass face. Karya tried to make it out in the flashing hull of their craft. The carved face looked thin and sour. Dark holes for eyes and a thin line of a mouth. It had hair slicked back from its head.

"Is it my imagination?" she asked, gripping the console edges to maintain her footing as the train lurched again, swooping downwards through the rock and sending her stomach up into the roof of her mouth. "Or does that look a bit like Mr Strife to everyone else?"

"It takes us where we need to go," Robin replied, without looking down. He still stood rooted in place. His hands fixed on the serpent, his flickering green and gold eyes staring out of the transparent nose cone, through the swirling motion of the drill. His voice sounded unearthly; flames caught in wind.

"We're close," he said, feeling it in every fibre of his being. "Dis!"

Through the monumental weight of the world above them, he could feel the city. It was like a bat using sonar. His mana flared up and out invisibly through the darkness above them, bouncing off the shapes above and sending back to him an echo of the great city. Writing in fire in his mind's eye. Dis, he saw, was built on a great hill, a towering encircling wall surrounding its base. Within, the city climbed this hill all around in a great spiral. Tall buildings crammed together cheek by jowl, districts of the city crawling up the wide hill in a suffocating wrap of stone. Buildings bare and brutalist, strong lines and sharp edges. Blank faced and stern. There were walls within walls, concentric circles slicing the city into different sectors, steeply walled and heavily guarded. And at the crest of Dis, a towering palace crowned the metropolis, watchful as a vulture as it loomed over all. Blank, dark walls and ugly battlements stabbing the air. The home of Eris. The workshop of Mr Nyx.

All of this flashed through Robin's mind. They felt as though they had been tunnelling in the dark for eternity and mere seconds, all at once.

"The city is immense," he breathed. The pull of the needle on his compass caused him to lean back, and the serpent lurched, tilting upwards as they began to tear up through the ground.

"We're surfacing?" Henry asked, gripping the walls as they thundered upwards.

"Inside the city," Robin said. "Somewhere in the lower tier. I can see it."

The others could see nothing but black rock and fire whipping by.

"Maybe we should slow it down a little then?" Henry hollered as casually as he could. "Or are we planning to burst out of the ground and send this thing right up into the air like one of those joke snakes hidden in a tube of Pringles?"

Karya nodded emphatically in agreement. Woad was still laughing, enjoying every second of their terrifying ride.

"Sneaky, remember, Scion," she yelled. "Henry's right. We're going for sneaky."

They felt the serpent lurch and slow – although that was a relative term. As far as Henry was concerned, they still felt like they were going as fast as a bullet train. Robin's eyes were narrowed as he channelled his mana, bringing the speed under control as their craft ascended, eating up rock.

"Maybe just a tad more?" Henry suggested lightly.

Robin, still filled with the high euphoria of the Shard, looked a little sulky. "Oh alright, fine," he muttered.

The ground shook around them as he reigned in the great snake and they all went flying again with inertia.

"This is your captain speaking," Robin said, unable to keep a straight face. "Please keep your arms and legs inside the serpent, and return your dinner trays to the upright position. We are coming in for landing."

"My ears just burst," Woad bellowed, as Henry and Karya were thrown around the cockpit. "Can we go again? Can we?"

The flames all around them suddenly dimmed, light and fire winking out all along the great length of the angular train. Solid darkness rushed up from the distant tail behind them towards the nose.

There was a tremendous crash and rocks fell away from the spinning nose as the Glassfire Serpent broke ground, finally free of the earth, and brought itself to a sudden and gut-wrenching stop.

Rubble cascaded over the transparent panes of the spinning drill, smashed to dust as rocks were caught in the rotating blades and flung away.

Robin, the only one still standing, stared out of their craft, his hands – both hissing and smoking with steam – still on the console. His fingertips were glowing like hot iron.

"Knock, knock," he said.

8

Enemies Close

As dust settled and the cloud around the front of the serpent began to
thin, they watched as the spinning drill of the obsidian nose cone slowed,
little by little, before finally coming to a full halt. The glowing lines of
power which had threaded through the length of the vehicle had dulled
and faded, until the train, the vast majority of it still deep beneath the
ground, slid into darkness, leaving only the nose cone glowing gently
from residual friction. The Shard of Fire popped from its moorings, like
a slice of bread from a toaster, falling into Robin's open hands, where
it hissed.

"We broke through something there, not sure if anyone else noticed,"
Henry observed, his voice shaking like a leaf. He pressed his face to the
fractured crystal walls of the snake, peering out at the clouds of dust. "Let's
just hope we've not surfaced in Eris' throne room or anything, eh?" He
chuckled. "How embarrassing would *that* be?"

"It looks like we're in some kind of cellar," Robin noted as the large
dust clouds finally began to settle around them. The stillness and silence
was unnerving after their adrenaline-fuelled rush through the dark. The
nose of the Glassfire Serpent had erupted through the floor like some
monstrous mole, and the space around them was large and dark, with
rough earthen floors and a vaulted ceiling above them in a series of
dark brick arches. Barrels lay all around; casks of wine or beer, perhaps.
The only illumination came from the still glowing drill of the serpent,
showing them that a short way off, a set of undecorated stone steps led
up and away, presumably to the upper levels of whatever building they
had burst into.

"You think we're really in Dis?" Woad sniffed deeply, testing the air. "It feels very Dis-like to me. Got that creepy lair-of-your-worst-enemy feeling about the place."

"We're definitely in Dis," Karya said. "I can feel it in my bones, although that could be just general ache, too." She patted the smooth angular interior walls of the now stationary craft. "I don't know what instructions Lord Oberon and Lady Titania gave when instructing the Fire Panthea to build this, but it's fast! Dis is over a hundred miles from the Black Hills where we boarded. We've only been riding this thing for maybe twenty minutes, through solid rock. You do the maths."

"I think all of my internal organs have been rearranged." Henry patted himself all over, still looking queasy. He looked at Robin, whose eyes seemed to have returned to normal, or as normal as they ever did. "How are you feeling there, Rob? That's the question. Come down off that classic ol' Arcania high yet? It's not that I don't appreciate being propelled through the underworld in a tube of glass and fire being driven by a laughing manic with flames in his eyes, it's the puns that sent me overboard."

Karya patted Henry comfortingly on the shoulder. "The real question is, how subtle was that entrance?" She glanced upwards. "I don't know if anyone's up there, but you'd have to be deaf not to hear us. I vote for us not hanging around here like a can of sardines waiting to be opened."

At Robin's touch, the scaled side of the serpent blossomed open once more in a dance of revolving scales, and the four of them clambered wearily out of the beast and into the dusty darkness of the room beyond. All of them wobbled a little, as if they had sea legs after a long voyage.

Robin had pictured their eventual arrival in Dis quite differently. It had seemed dramatic even to him, to have expected lava flowing down the walls and furniture made from human bones, perhaps the occasional skeleton rotting in a swinging cage hanging from the ceiling, all the trappings of "bad-guy" decoration. But the last thing he'd expected was beer kegs and wine butts. He had to constantly remind himself that the capital city of the Netherworlde was simply a *home* to many Panthea. A working city, full of real people, living as normal lives as they could, under Eris' stern reign and constant watchfulness – not some dystopian hell.

However, he reasoned, regardless of how oddly innocent their surroundings currently seemed, they still had to be cautious. They were still in the most dangerous place they could imagine.

"Someone's coming!" Woad hissed as the side of the Glassfire Serpent closed up again behind them.

Henry looked around. "I don't hear anything," He shrugged his bow off his shoulder, though.

"That's because you're not a faun," Woad hissed, exasperated. "You could be covered in ears – *made* of ears – and you'd still not have as good an ear as even one of mine." He narrowed his eyes. "Plus, you'd look totally gross."

A door burst open at the top of the stairs, swinging inwards with a bang, and several figures piled through it, making their way quickly down the steps. Peacekeepers. The shambling, soulless soldiers of Eris. Clearly, they had been stationed above and not entirely insensitive to the noise of a giant magical obsidian snake erupting into the room below them.

"Eight, no … ten!" Woad muttered, quickly counting the silent, scarecrow forms as they poured down the steps, flooding into the cellar to overwhelm them. Each was armed with a long and wicked-looking pike.

"We can't be taken here," Karya said, urgency in her voice. "Scion?"

There had been a time when the ghoulish sight of these animated puppets struck fear into Robin's heart. One of his first encounters with them had involved waking up in a cage on frozen tundra being guarded by one of the sackcloth horrors. But a lot had happened between then and now. A river never stops flowing forwards, and Robin was not the same boy he once was.

"Leave them to me."

As the last of the peacekeepers reached the bottom of the steps and they began to advance swiftly across the dark cellar towards the Erlkingers, Robin dropped to the floor, arms outstretched before him as he slapped the cold bare earth with the flats of both palms.

Mana rocked through him like a silent shockwave, and the floor of packed earth between them and the stairs rippled and shifted. In an instant, the solid ground was transformed into loose, fine sand, into which each of the peacekeepers sank swiftly, arms and legs flailing as they lost their footing. The sand shifted and whirled around them like waves, so they seemed adrift in a churning sea. Barrels and casks tumbled over, disappearing under the surface. The peacekeepers sank helplessly, tripping and stumbling, their pikes waving wildly and clattering against one another. Their wordlessness as they struggled only made them appear more alien and unsettling than ever.

Still with his hands on the ground, which was now soft and churning under his fingertips, Robin closed his eyes and bowed his head, concentrating. He thrust his fingers beneath the shifting sand, questing, and let all the emotion of the Tower of Water flow through him. The sand darkened, wetting and swiftly turning to sludge as the Scion pulled moisture from the earth and air, mixing liquid with the loose ground until it swiftly became a quagmire, the entire cellar floor a roiling mess of quicksand which sucked at the arms and legs of the stricken peacekeepers. The others stood behind Robin on the only solid part of the floor, while the swampy quicksand swallowed each of their puppet-adversaries hungrily, dragging them down with slurping and sucking noises as surely as a devouring bog.

When most of the creatures had disappeared beneath the bubbling, churning surface, and only one expressionless sackcloth head remained, Robin pulled his hands free and brought them down again with a hard slap. With an audible crack, the ground froze, turning in an instant from sloppy and boggy mud into solid and grey stone. The cellar was whole again.

Robin stood, a little unsteady, absently wiping a drop of blood from his nose with the back of his hand. He felt woozy, but he could still feel the powers of the Scion rolling around inside his ribcage like echoes.

"Well, Hawthorn would be proud of you," Henry said after a moment, looking impressed at the grave that had just swallowed their enemies. "That Earth magic …"

Karya nodded in approval, allowing Henry to take her arm for balance as they made their way across the newly-solid floor, now frozen in strange ripples and waves of solid stone. They dodged the odd pike-end, which stuck up here and there out of the rock like swords in the stone. "Calypso, too," she said.

One peacekeeper alone had not sunk entirely below the surface of the rock, its head from the neck up still protruding surreally from the very solid floor, as surely as if it had been buried in concrete. Its blank and ragged eyeholes regarded them with dumb malice as they passed it, the odd porcupine quills of its headdress quivering.

"Peacekeepers aren't alive," Woad said. "They're filthy puppets of Mr Ker's mana. But it's still satisfying to see them fall." He kicked at the scarecrow head with his bare foot as they passed, and it rolled away, torn from the buried body. It was nothing more than an empty sack, from which black and oily smoke momentarily spilled, dissipating before their eyes.

"We need to find out where we are," Karya said. "Dis is a large city, and we don't know where Jack and Ffoulkes are being kept."

They made for the cellar stairs, Robin nodding in agreement. He also had to find their hex messenger, the one who had led them to the Glassfire Serpent, and their way into Dis in the first place. He owed them a way out of the city – that had been the deal.

The door at the top of the stairs was still open, and they crept upwards, finding themselves in a hallway.

"We're in someone's house," Henry observed, as they looked around. To Robin it looked like an old townhouse. There was an open staircase along one wall, leading steeply to an upper floor. Doors of dark wood across from them, high baseboards and wainscoting, and to their left, what must have been the front door, leading out of the building. A faded, greyish hall carpet snaked away over polished floorboards. It might once have held a pattern, but it was worn and ghostly now.

There was a grandfather clock to their left, ticking loudly, slicing the silence into neat seconds. And halfway down the hallway, an old fashioned table held a dim lamp.

It all looked curiously normal. Robin felt they could have stepped into the house of Mr and Mrs Darling from Peter Pan – except there was something slightly *off* with the home. It was too quiet, for a start, and it didn't take him long to realise that it was the absence of any regular decoration that gave the place an unsettling air. It was the kind of house you might expect to see old, framed pictures on the wall. Dark old oil paintings of ships at sea, perhaps. Or framed photographs of family members parading up the staircases,

There was nothing of the sort, here.

"It feels like a stage set," he said to the others, keeping his voice quiet. "There's no … humanity."

There was one thing hanging framed on the wall, however. Across from the cellar door, beside the closed double-doors that presumably led further into the house. They approached and looked up at it.

Under glass was a sun-bleached ink print. It seemed to show a stylised illustration of the city; the wide hump of the hill, covered in streets and buildings. It looked like a mediaeval map of the city. Above the palace that sat atop the hill, there floated two watchful eyes, staring out at the world. Beneath, in highly decorated calligraphy, were the words: *Te Semper Vigilet*.

"Well, that's creepy," Henry commented. "Looks like some kind of propaganda poster. Like a 'Big Brother is Watching You' kind of thing. Am I close?"

"This hangs in every building in Dis," Karya explained. "It's a law. To remind the citizens to behave, to be patriotic, vigilant and obedient."

Robin tried the large doors. They slid open quietly.

"Where are you going?" Karya whispered.

"We can't just stroll out into the street," he reasoned. "You don't think we might stick out a little? We would be arrested on sight. We have to find out where the hex messenger is. All they said was 'down'. The lower portion of the city, perhaps? It's still morning. The eclipse isn't for an hour or two yet."

Off the hall corridor was a large sitting room. It was as stark and grey as everything else. Cold walls, grim dark floorboards. A sofa and two high-wingback chairs surrounded a thin fireplace, facing away from them. The surround to the fire was black stone, and the whole place looked funerary. Still and silent. Large windows to their left let in the morning light, but they seemed frosted, and gave no view of the city outside. Even the pale light flooding in through them seemed thin and cold.

"It's like stepping into Tim Burton's lounge," Robin muttered, looking around at marble-topped end tables with their unlit lamps. "If he had been a funeral director back in the 1800s, that is."

The fire was unlit, but they made their way over to it as it was the only focal point of the stark and unwelcoming room. This barely felt like a home at all. Were all places in Dis so devoid of warmth and light?

"I can smell dogs," Woad warned. "Whoever lives here might have guard dogs, so be alert."

"Whoever lives here is important enough to have a staff of peacekeepers, Woad," Karya pointed out. "And we managed to take them out okay." She leaned heavily on the back of a sofa, suddenly dizzy, and took a moment to collect herself. "Well, I'm using the royal 'we', of course. I'm in no fit state to do much. It's only Robin who was lucky enough to have the power of an Arcania Shard recharge him today."

"My mana is spent for now," Robin admitted, feeling his own stone cool and quiet on his chest. "The drive over here took it out of me. I understand jet-lag, now. That business downstairs just now was my last few drops of fuel. It will take me a while to get my breath back, so Woad is right. Let's be careful."

He stepped around the sofa and chairs, his eyes trained on the mantelpiece where there was an old carriage clock, a pair of thin candlesticks, and little else. He was searching for any personal item. Something that might help them get their bearings.

"There's nothing here," he said. "Nothing that might give us a clue where we are."

There was a creak from the deep shadows next to him. Something moving in the corner of Robin's vision. He turned, jumping as a figure leaned forward slowly in one of the high-wingback chairs. It had been sitting so deadly still in the darkness that he had not seen it as he passed.

"Where you are?" the figure said, in a voice that was cold as ice water and crisp as morning frost. "You are in a Grimm house. *My* house. And though I might have expected rats in my cellar from time to time, this, I must confess, is an unprecedented infestation."

The voice was horribly familiar. The crisp, sharp diction. The chilly tones. The figure Robin faced, still as a statue in his chair, was an old man, crisply dressed in a dark and old-fashioned suit, like some manner of ancient undertaker. His face was white as ash, eyes dark and black as space, and hair slicked back on his head a bright and ghoulish green, the only real colour in the room.

Mr Strife, chief amongst the Grimms, peered at them, one pale and spidery hand still resting gently on the arm of his old chair. His face was unsmiling and cold.

"Strife!" yelped Woad, and Robin automatically reached for his mana stone defensively, finding it still dead and dull after the exertions of the cellar.

Mr Strife eyed them all with cool interest, peering beyond them to the cellar floor.

"Bloody hell!" Henry leapt out of his skin. "Bloody, bloody hell, Rob!"

"There is no need for dramatics," Strife sneered at them. He turned his head to Robin. His black eyes flicked from the boy's face to his clutched mana stone and back. "You look close to collapse, little Fae. Do not do me the insult of attempting to suggest otherwise. I hear you have relieved me of my workforce, which is terribly bad manners."

The unexpected appearance of one of his oldest enemies shocked Robin. It seemed highly unlikely that they had just happened to enter Dis right beneath the feet of a Grimm – but the face that the compass had shown them certainly looked like Strife. It had brought them here deliberately.

"Were you waiting for us, Strife?" Robin demanded. He was eyeing the old man as one eyes a very still snake, knowing that at any moment it might strike. Even seated before him, the Grimm exuded malice and menace. "What is all this? Some kind of a trap?"

Strife's lip curled. "Such arrogance as always, Scion of the Arcania. The whole world revolves around you, does it?" He looked up at Robin with something like curiosity. "Believe me, boy. I am as surprised to see the rebellious brats of Erlking scurrying around my personal wine cellar as you are all, quite clearly, surprised to find yourselves before me." His eyes slid away from Robin, cool and narrow, to rest with interest on Karya, taking in her appearance. "Well, well, well," he said thoughtfully. "This leaf has withered and dried, has it not?"

"I would say the compliment is returned," Karya replied through gritted teeth. "But then, you've always looked this lovely, haven't you, Strife?" She stepped around to stand beside Robin. "Unless you want to join your peacekeepers under the floor in the cellar, I would consider getting out of our way."

Mr Strife didn't seem remotely threatened by the grey and wavering girl. He stood calmly from the armchair, springs creaking under his weight, unfolding long arms and legs like some hideous mantis until he towered above them all, causing Robin and Karya to take an involuntary step backwards, butting up against the dark and cold fireplace. The thin Grimm folded his arms, looking entirely unruffled.

"A cornered mouse does not command a cat, girl. You break into my home, trespass in the space of a Grimm … and expect *what*? My deference?" His eyes took them all in. "A spent Scion, a withered twig, a hapless human with a single arrow." He scoffed humourlessly. "The only one amongst you with any power right now is the tiresome blue imp, and even he could barely raise the hairs on my head with that crackling electric I can hear humming beneath his skin." Strife looked to Robin. "Have no illusions, Robin Fellows. Should I choose to, I can take you all down right here with a flick of my hand, and have you trussed and bound and delivered to the empress before lunch."

Robin didn't doubt it. Strife could see through any bluff. The main question was why he hadn't already attacked them. But the old man had a scheming and thoughtful look on his thin face.

From the doorway they had entered, two large shapes now slunk into the room. Large dogs, their forms shadowy and indistinct. Both were enormous, their eyes glowing and their claws clacking on the floorboards as they made their way into the room, heads low and hackles raised. Robin heard them growl deeply.

"Told you I could smell dogs," Woad muttered.

"You've met Spitak and Siaw before, of course," Strife said. His devil dogs began to circle the room, slowly, like hunting panthers. "I could have them tear out the throats of your friends here, one by one. Eris only wants you. And here you drop into my lap, right in my own home. I could bring you to the empress right now. Alone and defeated."

"If you were going to do that, you would have done it by now," Robin said, calling the Grimm's bluff in return. "If you really are surprised to see us, if this wasn't some kind of elaborate set up, then that means the reason we are here – specifically here, of all places in Dis – is because this is where the compass led us."

He could feel the confused frowns of his friends, but he didn't dare tear his eyes away from Strife's. Breaking eye contact with a creature like that would be like showing your throat to a lion.

"It's guided me where I needed to go, at each stage," Robin continued. "And it led the Glassfire Serpent here, to you of all people." It sounded incredible, even to him. "Which means that, as insane as it sounds, you, Mr Strife, must be where we need to be, in order to save Jack and Ffoulkes."

"Rob, have you lost your mind?" Henry spluttered. "Strife is not an *ally*. He's the worst of them!"

Robin knew this, but something definitely felt off, here. Strife could have attacked them as soon as they had entered the room. He could still overpower them now. His singular purpose in life was to serve the precious empress, to capture the Scion. The Scion had literally just dropped into his lap, and he hadn't attacked. Hadn't seized the opportunity. There had to be a reason for that. Something had changed.

"Oh, I don't doubt for a second that we're nothing like allies," he said to the Grimm. "You and me? We're never going to swap Christmas cards, are we? But there's a reason you're standing there instead of taking us down without a second thought."

The Grimm clicked his tongue, and on command, the two devil dogs came closer, weaving through the sparse furniture towards them.

"We've worked together before," Robin said, still watching the old man carefully. "At the labyrinth of the Minotaur. You got us inside the Hive. You did it for your own selfish reasons, simply to unseat Peryl from power, I know that, but still … war can make for strange bedfellows, right?"

"Are you forgetting the part where he totally double-crossed us and left us to be captured by Strigoi?" Henry argued. "If that compass of yours brought us here for a reason, maybe it was to put an end to this old bogeyman, not to try and make friendship bracelets with him. I think you're still high from the Shard."

"It's true," Strife mused, talking to Robin and completely ignoring his companions. "I will allow that, as odious as it was to me, a brief alliance with you served my purpose at the time, Scion. Things have changed since the Elderhart forest, however. I have regained my power, position and honour at court. So, if you think to bargain with me now, from where I stand you appear to be holding very few cards indeed."

One of the large shadowy dogs had sidled over to him, growling soft and deep in the back of its throat, and Mr Strife reached down to gently pet it, smoothing its hackles.

"You come all the way to Dis on some doomed and woeful rescue mission?" Strife almost seemed amused, although that very concept seemed utterly alien to him. "Pathetic. Your upbringing in the human world has made you soft and emotional, little Fae-spawn. Delivering yourself to me, whether by design or by accident. Have you any concept of the honours and power that would be bestowed upon me by the empress for capturing you?"

The clock on the mantle ticked quietly, counting off the seconds in the shadowy stillness. Robin swallowed. The part of him that was Puck was whispering in the back of his head.

"You're not going to do that, though," he said, trying to sound confident. "Someone has been speaking to us from inside the city for quite some time. Someone trapped here who wants out. And you, Mr Strife, are going to help us find them."

Strife raised his eyebrows. He seemed surprised by the audacity of the boy. "And why, in all the Netherworlde, would you believe *that*?"

"Because you hate her," Robin said quietly, holding Strife's eyes. "You *hate* Eris."

The absolute certainty of this had come into his mind. He felt it as soon as he realised they were in the Grimm's home. He caught a whisper of it when Strife didn't immediately attack them, but in truth, now he had finally said it out loud, he realised that he had known it to be true for some time. Ever since he had met Strife wandering around the great forest of the dryads, dressed in rags and stripped of grace and honour.

The old man had been cast aside by Eris then for his failure. He had been humiliated and abandoned. Stripped of his rank. And yes, he had regained them by betraying Peryl, had clawed his way single-mindedly back to his position of power and influence at court. But if there were two things about the cold and enigmatic Mr Strife of which Robin was absolutely certain, they were that Mr Strife did not forget. And Mr Strife did not forgive.

One only had to watch him showing affection to his dogs – made from his own mana, part of his own dark and twisted soul – to realise that such a gesture was the only singular act of affection Mr Strife had ever performed. A man preening, stroking his own ego. A creature who was truly loyal to no master, but only to himself.

Strife's eyes were dangerous. Glittering black beads. His face was a poker mask.

"Hate … the empress?" he whispered, like a promise or a curse. Clearly, even to voice such a thought aloud was a very dangerous thing to do in Dis.

"Scion," Karya stared at Robin as though he'd gone mad. "Strife is the most fanatical servant of the empress I've met! He hounded me all the way from Dis to Erlking on her orders."

"She tore you down and threw you away," Robin said to him. "We've seen it happen to others. But your sense of self-preservation is pretty strong, isn't it, Strife? You've crawled back into the palm of her hand, but not through love for her. Because that's the only place you have any power."

The two Skrikers growled low in their throats. Strife's hand hovered above their heads, fingers outstretched and steady.

"But you're wrong, Mr Strife. I *am* holding one card you need, after all."

Strife looked deeply offended at the thought that the Scion of the Arcania could have something he needed. "And what would that be, I wonder?" he asked, lip curling.

"I can give you back the only thing that, other than your pitiful self, you ever really cared about," Robin replied. He had produced his scrap of hex message parchment from his satchel. "My contact here in the city tells me they are being watched, all the time. They've had to write to me in blood. And they tell me they are 'down' in Dis." He waved the paper like an exhibit in court. "The deepest, most 'down' place I can imagine is Eris' prison, right? The Pits of Dis? A place she puts people to forget about them."

He met Strife's eyes defiantly.

"A place where your own dear brother has been held ever since your failure at the Isle of Winds. Poor, mad Mr Moros."

Moros was the first Grimm Robin had ever encountered, meeting him at the train station when he had arrived in Barrowood. Giddy and babbling and clearly not all there, even back then. The boy had come to know him intimately during the time the man masqueraded as his tutor, and Robin knew that Eris had kept him imprisoned ever since. Punishment for the initial failure to capture the Scion back on the Isle of Aeolus. A warning to the Grimms against failure. A bargaining chip to keep the others, especially Mr Strife, in line.

"I've wondered, you see," Robin said, "more than a few times, why you would never try to release him. In all this time. I saw strange things back in the labyrinth, when I looked at you through the Mask of Gaia."

Strife glared at him. No-one else spoke.

"The mask shows the wearer the truth of a thing," Robin said. "You remember that, don't you, Strife? I'll tell you what I saw. Two young boys sitting together on a narrow bed in a cold dormitory, very much alone. Very much unloved and forgotten by the world. Comforting one another. Brothers ... twins. There was care there, genuine affection." He folded and lowered the parchment in his hands, as Strife looked on, his face a pale mask. "But knowing what I do of you, Strife ..." Robin shook his head. "You would not risk putting your neck out. You are a calculating, self-serving creature, aren't you? You plot and you scheme, and you watch how every piece moves on the chessboard. There's no way for you to save your beloved Moros openly, not without rebelling against your cruel mistress. No way without endangering yourself?" Robin took a deep breath. "And if you do that, if *you* fall on Eris' bad side, you'd never be able get him out, would you? He'd be doomed. You'd end up in there with him, in the Pits of Dis, going as steadily mad as he is."

"This is … *all* … very touching," Strife drawled, his voice ice cold.

"You can't break into the pits of Dis and free prisoners," Robin pressed on. "You can't get past the gatekeeper, not without dooming yourself and your brother."

When they had first met on the steps of Erlking Hall, Robin was a scared child and Strife had been his worst nightmare, stalking out of the hall after a failed negotiation with Irene, a towering monster. That felt a long time ago. Now, Robin eyed the Grimm levelly.

"But *I* can," he said. "I'm the evil rebel, remember? I'm the terrible Scion. Practically *expected* to cause chaos. Eris will be furious when she learns the Scion was here, in Dis, under her very nose, and that he stole prisoners from her jail. But how could you have known I was even here?" Robin risked a smile, calculating. "When *you* never saw us, Mr Strife? When you were busy at the Pyrenight celebrations with the rest of her court? Doing your duty! And if, during this terrible act of criminality, *other* prisoners happen to escape and disappear in the confusion, including your brother … *you* are free from blame."

Strife did not answer for some time. His hand stroked the devil-dog absently. His face was an unreadable mask. Eventually, he lifted his chin.

"You are quite a dangerous one, Robin Fellows of Erlking," he said quietly. His voice was a low rasp, almost a whisper. "Have I underestimated you, I wonder? Persisted in perceiving you as a troublesome whelp, when you have grown into something more? Your eyes are more open than most, and you see much. *Too much* for my comfort. What you speak of is high treason." There was a hunger in his eyes. "You are correct in that I will not risk the displeasure of our glorious empress. I serve. I survive. Strife of Dis bides … his … time. Strife of Dis would not even speak of such betrayals."

"We speak of nothing," Robin said. "This conversation never took place. We were never here."

The Grimm eyed them all one by one, his eyes glistening slowly over them, like the careful judgement of some dark god of death who held life in the balance of its hands.

"You're the highest of the Grimms," Karya said quietly, daring to break the dangerous silence in this dark and quiet room, warming to Robin's perceptive play. "Although you'd *never* go against the empress and free her prisoners, of course. The very idea is laughable. They are, after all, rightly being punished for their disloyalty, their failures. But you certainly have the authority to *visit* the pits of Dis. A standard inspection." She shrugged. "Nothing more than that, of course. You must be able to bypass the jailer, the gatekeeper. And even you wouldn't know if you were followed, not by four shadows you never even noticed."

Robin's heart was in his mouth. This was a big gamble. If he was wrong about Strife and Moros, this bluff could doom them all.

"I am Strife of the Grimms," the old man said with an imperious air. His eyes were murderous and icy. "Know this, scheming rebels … and know it well. I have *no* allies. I have no … *conspirators*."

He spat the word. His eyes narrowed, and though there was nothing even close to pity in them, there was something else, something that for once was not cold spite. A faint echo that could have been curiosity or pride, but which, to Robin, looked more than anything like pain. Very quiet, and very deep. A slender muffled ghost of buried humanity.

"The Scion of the Arcania …" Strife said, dusting down his lapels with a sudden fussiness, "would never have the gall or the stupidity to come to Dis, of that I am quite convinced!"

With a wave of his hand he dismissed his Skrikers, the two hounds dissipating into thin air in drifts of smoke like exhaust.

"Nor would the Scion, were he foolish enough to step inside this great city, be idiotic enough to attempt to bargain with as loyal a subject of the crown as I, over such ridiculous and weak things as …" he scoffed to himself, "fraternal affections!"

"I have spent the morning alone….here with my thoughts…and I fancy I have dreamed of company. Though who, and of what we spoke, I cannot now recall. Such is the unreliability of dreams and all their insubstantial ways." He drew from the pocket of his frock-coat a pocket watch, set in silver with a small red gem, clicking it open and inspecting it. "The hour of the eclipse draws near. The Pyrenight celebrations begin shortly at the crest of Dis. An important event for all of us loyal and unwavering subjects."

He tutted to himself, fussily patting his pockets absently, as though distracted. "Everything must be in place for the empress. As head of the Grimms, I must ensure that there is nothing out of place…I shall take a circuit of the Pits, I think. Yes. Just to ensure that … all is well."

Henry and Woad exchanged confused looks. Robin didn't move at all. He watched Strife carefully, as if any sudden move might break this fragile affectation, might bring everything crashing down around them.

Strife walked to a dresser, set along one wall, where he lit an ornate lantern which sat atop with a long match, the flare briefly illuminating his pinched and sour visage, a mask in the darkness.

"I think I shall take the tunnels," he muttered to himself, turning away from them all and heading towards a closed door in the corner of the room. "The interior of the hill of Dis contains the Pits, of course. And there is no need for someone such as me to bypass any gatekeeper." There was a deep, resentful darkness in his face. "For I myself *am* the gatekeeper," he revealed. "In her infinite wisdom and judgement, our glorious empress saw fit to place me over the prison. To hold the keys."

Robin stared at the old man's back as he turned away.

"Some might think this to be a cruel turn," Strife said to himself bitterly. "Some might think it a torture to make one brother the keeper of the other. A punishment for them both, disguised as a responsibility of power. Those not inclined to understand true loyalty might wrongly assume this would make one … *hate* … her."

He slid open a door at the far end of the room. "But of course … not. The empress is always just, and correct, and unquestionable. And we are glad to serve. The streets outside will be busy now. The celebrations headed to the top of the city and so forth. The tunnels will be…quieter. And I of course…will not be…followed."

They watched the Grimm exit, descending a set of stairs in the darkness beyond. Mr Strife, so meticulous in all things, seemed to have forgotten to close the door behind him.

Robin breathed out shakily. "Come on," he said to the others.

Henry grabbed his arm. "Are you serious?" He looked flabbergasted. "You're really going to rescue Mr Moros? He's a Grimm. Like Strife, like Nyx! I don't care that he's a nutcase!"

159

"Our contact is down there in that pit, I know it." Robin said, shaking him off. "Trust me, Henry. Our contact is a prisoner and Strife is the warden. We find our hex messenger, we can find and save the others, Jack ... Ffoulkes. If that means releasing Moros from the clutches of Eris and doing Strife a service, at this point I really don't care."

"You *know* we can't trust Strife," Henry insisted. "He will turn on us the second we have served his purpose. The absolute second! He'll let us do his dirty work like he always does, get his mental brother out of the lock-up, and then he'll stab us in the back and give us to Eris. It's what Strife does ... It's ..." He waved his hands around in exasperation. "... It's what Strife *is*!"

"I know that," Robin said. "I'm not that bloody naïve. Just be ready for it."

9

Enemies Below

Robin and the others followed the Grimm through the door and into the tunnels below the house, down into darkness.

Dis is a spiral, Karya explained to the others as they walked. She sounded breathless all the time now. Her voice came like a fading ghost's in the dimly-lit pathways.

The stairs beneath Strife's charmless house had led them to a series of seemingly endless passages, pitch black and countless. The interior of the great hill of Dis was a honeycomb, the girl explained. Almost every building linking together beneath the street levels via countless twisting corridors in the darkness. The dark prison of Dis, known charmingly as the Pits, lay beneath the deepest of these subterranean paths, and they had been walking them now for quite some time in careful silence.

The only light at all down here in the quiet deep was the light of Mr Strife's lantern, bobbing some way ahead of them. Robin and the others had followed him at a distance ever since entering the underworld of the great city above. They dogged his steps and haunted his shadow around countless turns, left and right in the narrow spaces, and down a plethora of staircases here and there. Some straight, some wide or narrow, many spiral, but always downwards, deeper and deeper. The Grimm's lantern bobbed ghostlike ahead, a will o' the wisp in the shuffling blackness. The man had not looked back over his shoulder. Not even once, in all the time they traced after him. Why should he, after all? When he had no reason to believe he was not utterly alone in his dutiful service?

A spiral up, and a spiral down, Karya educated her friends as the damp dark bricks of the endless corridors slid by. The city outside was built on the slopes, the great river of the Dish curling around its base like a sleeping cat's tail, outside the city walls. Bloated and swollen since its long journey from the northern mountains, it thundered by, onwards towards the great delta skirting the borders of the Black Hills to the sea. Within the great outer walls, the city climbed the hill, its countless structures covering it like barnacles on the upturned hull of a ship. The main streets wound around and around the hill as it climbed, and a series of further inner walls separated the great capital into districts, distinct areas, circles within circles. At the lowest part of the hill, she told them were the slums, same as any great city, poor streets of packed earth and mud. Within the first wall, as the roads climbed higher, the second ward, a district of skilled artisans, trades-folk, Panthea of all walks of life. All trades and means. Further up the city hill, within the next wall of the third ward, the gentry resided. The buildings there were grander, though still stark and brutal in the style of Eris' reign. Functional and severe, but opulent nonetheless, with wider streets, cobbled paths, open squares and all the trappings and trimmings of luxury so necessary to the great and high society of Dis who resided there. Atop this hill, at the pinnacle of Dis and the heart of the noble ward, the palace of Eris topped the city like a crown. An imposing fortress. Thrusting tall fingers of stone high into the sky. The many towers of Eris' fortress were a cluster of spikes, looming over the city.

It was here, Karya told them, in the countless wings and halls that comprised the palace complex, that those held in the highest estimation by the empress lived and worked. Here the Grimms worked. Ker's war rooms, Strife's library. Here resided Strigoi and his battalion of ravens, those most elite of soldiers. The palace naturally contained the great hall of Eris herself, somewhere high, if rumours were believed, with a great balcony opening on to the world that was large enough to land a dragon on.

The tallest tower in the cluster of buildings, casting its shadow on the wards of the town below as the sun marched across the day, was Heaven's Lens. The workshop of Nyx, Eris' tinkerer.

Strife had momentarily gotten further ahead of them in the darkness, his light barely visible as he turned yet another corner, and they hurried forward in silence for a while, catching up with their stalking guide. Only when they had him back in sight, disappearing sleekly down a curve of steps and ducking beneath a damp-looking arch of brick, did the girl resume talking.

In that high place, Heaven's Lens, she told them, centaurs had been altered from the noble creatures they once had been to the mindless beasts they were now. In that high and lonely workshop, dryads had been twisted into the insect-like creatures known as the Swarm. Peacekeepers had been manufactured; vessels designed to hold the disjointed mana of Mr Ker. It was the birthplace of every dark dream the empress had, brought into being by her willing and faithful alchemist. And from Nyx's tower, Karya – now stumbling through the darkness of the earth, weak and shivering – had once escaped.

Strife had come to a large doorway of bolted iron and inserted a key into the lock, from a rattling ring produced from his pocket. The doors swung open, heavy and squealing, and as they passed inside behind him, they saw stencilled above the door frame in ugly block letters:

NULLA LIBERTAS

"As above, so below," Karya whispered as Strife led them deeper into the ground. They had reached and entered the prison. The Pits of Dis. The spiral outside the hill, she told her companions, was repeated within it too, only reversed. Spinning down into the burrowing darkness inside the hill, starting wide and coiling down tighter and tighter in a long airless corridor. A dark reflection of the outer world. Eris liked things like that, she explained. Such mirrors amused her. Here, in this hopeless oubliette, this honeycombed warren of faithless paths, Eris banished forever those no longer deemed fit to breathe the air above.

The worst offenders were at the base of this spiral, buried as far from the light and air as it was possible to get.

Even as they walked, spiralling downwards into the dark, the very floor beneath them now seemed to drag them onwards. The corridors were so narrow they were forced to walk single file, following Robin at the lead, who cradled in his hands the Shard of Fire, which was giving off a dull warmth at least, if not light. The light of Mr Strife ahead was cold, like blue fire, and it made the old man's shadow jump and dance on the close walls around him like demons in the dark.

"I don't know what we're going to find down here," Robin said. "But whatever it is, we need to find it quickly. I can feel the eclipse coming."

"Feel it?" Woad said in the darkness, walking along behind him, padding silently on his bare feet. His voice was quiet, as the smallest noise down here seemed to echo mockingly back and forth along the endless spiralling tunnel.

Robin nodded. Communing with the Shard of Fire, piloting the serpent and feeling its song singing through his veins, had attuned him to the element, and even now, as he slid the Shard into the deep pocket of his dusty hoodie, he still heard the humming of the distant sun in the sky. They needed to get to Jack and Ffoulkes – and quickly. The celebrations up on the surface had likely already begun.

"I don't know that I have much 'fast' left in me," Karya said. She sounded resigned.

Eventually, they began to pass doorways in the stone walls, placed at regular intervals well apart from one another. The doors were solid oblongs of metal, set recessed into the bricks. None had a handle. Each had only a small slit with a sliding panel which could be opened to view the room beyond. Prison doors.

All were closed and all were silent. Above each one they passed, on a looped thong of leather hanging from a rough nail, there hung a mana stone. Clearly, belonging to the person held imprisoned on the other side. Stripped of their power, their ability to conjure the Towers and escape, their mana had been hung on the outside of their cell – tantalisingly close, but forever and hopelessly out of reach.

"That's barbaric!" Woad was aghast. "Like separating someone's soul from their body and locking it away from them."

"That's Eris," Karya muttered. "The same twisted pleasure as making one of her subjects in charge of the prison where his brother was held. How fun for her to torment both allies and enemies alike. Only a mind like hers would design something like this."

Robin had expected wailing prisoners. Cups rattling on bars, gnashing of teeth, and cries and yells of protest from those held in the pits of Dis, demanding release or begging for mercy.

But as they continued down further and further, he came to realise that the place was silent. No one hidden behind these countless doors cried out or struggled, or made any noise at all. And Robin realised that it was simply because everyone here had long ago realised that to do so would be futile. No help was coming for them, buried here beneath the capital, no matter how much they might wail. They had not merely been imprisoned in these rooms for their crimes against the empress, supposed or real. They had been entombed. There was no one to hear their cries. No sound would reach the surface and no one would *ever* come to release them. Any cries or shouts there might have been, had been reduced to dust and dry throats long ago.

This was what it meant to be banished from the sight of the empress, Robin thought. To be forgotten forever, freedom and light nothing but a memory down here in the airless silence. He could almost understand Strife's dutiful show.

The Grimm had eventually stopped ahead of them, lantern held high, before a plain black door of rusty-looking stained steel. Robin had lost count of how many identical ones he had passed in their endless descent. It could have been a hundred. For a moment, Strife's white hand splayed on the surface, long fingers stroking the rough, cold metal. "Here," he whispered to himself, his voice coarse. "Here in the dark, the home of Grimms disgraced. Left to rot in blackness and sorrow."

He cleared his throat noisily. "And rightly so!" he added more stridently. "For none shall fail the Empress Eris."

"You really think whoever has been sending you messages is in this prison somewhere?" Henry whispered to Robin, who nodded.

"Answers are behind that door." He walked up to it as Strife moved aside, melting into the shadows like a bad dream.

Robin laid both hands on the door. It was enchanted, he felt immediately. Someone else's mana flowing through it – a wall of will, and powerful. He had expected as much. In a world where everyone who owned a mana stone could perform magic to at least some degree, a prison here would have more safeguards against escape than simply a thick iron door. Hung above the door on a looped nail were two mana stones, both blood-red rubies.

There was no keyhole through which he could cast a featherbreath to lift tumblers and unlock the cell. It was held fast only with this dark pulsing magic. With no better plan in mind, he closed his eyes, letting his forehead rest against the cold metal and concentrated. His strength had returned somewhat in the time they had travelled in the dark, and now he pushed outwards with his mind, sliding the invisible wash of his own potent mana over the door like poured gasoline. To the others watching, a shimmer appeared before Robin. He looked as though he stood in a mirage, a heat haze wavering as the door seemed to wobble in its deep and fixed moorings.

Robin allowed his mana to leach out, slowly covering the door, the frame, and the bricks around it. It felt shivery, this level of control directed into a cantrip he had not learned. One that he was designing for himself, feeling his way around it on the spot. It felt like bleeding out.

He felt his mana sink deep into the metal itself, as spilled wine sinks into cloth. The enchantment, the other power which was already set here, was strong, but it was old and remote. His was fresh and present. Frowning, he pushed it away, flooding the portal with his own will, letting the shadows and chill and pervasive hopeless darkness of the pits of Dis recede from around him, repelled by his determination.

The part of him that was Puck whispered through his lips,

"*Ex tenebris venit lux.*"

His eyes shot open, green and gold and glowing in the gloom, and their flash was a spark to the fuel of his mana. The invisible cloud of energy ignited, instantly engulfing him and the door in powerful white flame, which roared and echoed in the silence, blindingly bright. Bricks cracked in the heat like fireworks. The metal of the door twisted and screamed like a living thing as it melted away from his hands, glowing and licked clean with white flames and magic.

After seconds of noise and fury, of heat and light, the fire suddenly extinguished, flaring out of life with a *whoosh*. Henry, Woad and Karya, who had pressed themselves up against the narrow opposite wall, dropped their protective hands from their eyes to see Robin standing unharmed, glowing embers drifting down around his silhouetted form like petals. The door was gone, vaporised into a molten hole which was still glowing, bright and angry at its edges.

Flames licked up and down his arms, before flickering out. They had expected him to be immolated. A charred skeleton, but the Scion was unharmed. As Robin's eyesight returned, blinking away the after-images of the fire, he stared within.

* * *

The cell was small, windowless and bare. An oubliette of black brick. There were two occupants. One, huddled in the far corner wrapped in rags with his hands over his face, was a man, stick thin and white, with a dandelion puff of filthy hair the colour of tangerines. Mr Moros stared out at them with wide saucer eyes of shock and surprise through gaps in his fingers.

The other was a girl. Standing in the centre of the cell. Her weight was resting on one leg and she was hugging herself by the elbows. Her clothing was dirty and frayed, though it might at one time have been a smart charcoal suit. Her hair, loose around her head in long matted tresses, was as purple as plums, and she was staring at Robin with an expression of utter shell-shock.

Robin stuttered in surprise. "Peryl?" A small puff of smoke escaped his lips, remnants of the fire cantrip which had obliterated the door.

Miss Peryl, youngest of the Grimms, stared across the shadows at him for a few seconds. She looked harrowed. Traumatised and vulnerable. Too shocked at the sudden burst of activity to guard her expression, she stared at Robin with simple blank disbelief.

The others came forward, leaning around Robin to peer within the cell. Robin barely noticed them jostling at his sides. He stood, frozen, embers and ash dripping from his hands to the floor. "You're alive," he managed, eventually.

Miss Peryl blinked at the sound of his voice, seemed to realise he was staring at her across the cell, and quickly regained control of her face. She peered at the Scion and his companions, squinting in the light from Strife's lantern behind them. The girl looked strange without her habitual dark eye make-up and carefully painted lips. Much younger, more human somehow. But when she pouted and cocked her head to one side, arms still folded, the mannerisms were all familiar.

"Well," she croaked, clearing her throat, as though she had not spoken for quite some time. She took a deep breath and started again. "Well … you certainly took your sweet time, sweet cheeks. I was beginning to wonder if you'd stopped getting my messages."

"*Your* messages?" Woad piped up. He was looking from Mr Strife, to Moros, and then to Peryl. "There are a whole lot of Grimms here right now. Three too many!"

Peryl reached into her dirty suit pocket, pulling out a square of parchment folded over in half. She held it up to Robin across the cell with a smirk, grasped between her index and middle finger. Her expression was cocky, but her fingers were shaking slightly.

"My messages," she confirmed. "Be a dear heart and toss us our mana stones, will you? One does feel pretty funny without it. Not quite myself." She waved the hex paper at Robin, slipping it back into her pocket, and suddenly rushed up close to him, making him flinch instinctively. She reached up herself outside the door, grabbing the two rubies from where they were hung like mistletoe. Robin took a step back.

"On second thoughts, better not eh?" she said. "Terribly bad form, to touch another person's mana stone, you know. Would be like holding someone else's soul in your hands. How mortifying! What an unforgivable intrusion."

Despite her words, she juggled the two rubies casually in her hand, before carelessly tossing one to the crumpled and pitiful creature still squatting on the floor behind her.

"Here you go, Moros," she said, as his hand shot out and caught it in mid-air. "Present for you. Ought to cheer you up a bit if you can stop gibbering long enough to actually put it on." She glanced back to Robin, giving him a wink. "Between you, me and the completely molten doorpost …" she whispered secretively, "that one has *always* had bats in his belfry, but I think being here so long, the last one died a while back. They're just bat skeletons now, rattling around."

She glanced over Robin's shoulder, noticing the others. "Oh, look. You brought the three musketeers too."

"Wait … *You're* the one who's been sending me messages?" Robin stared at Peryl, as she fussily went about fixing her mana stone to her dusty and frayed jacket lapel with hands that were barely shaking now. Her eyes looked a little wet, though it could have been the effect of having been in darkness for so long.

"Mm-hmm," she replied distractedly. "You left that charmed little scrap of paper in the Hive. Remember? Back when you completely left me for dead?"

"You mean back when you last tried to kill us?" Robin replied.

She shrugged. "Oh po-tay-to po-tar-to. It's all bodies under the bridge now." Behind her, Mr Moros was standing, steadying himself on the wall as he got to his shaky legs. He was still staring around at them all with insanely wide eyes, as though he feared he was hallucinating.

"I did the writing, though brother Moros here supplied the blood, he's such a good sport. I was always a bit squeamish about my own blood, you know. It's a fact that surprises many."

Robin was rudely pushed to one side as Strife suddenly made his way into the cell, ignoring Peryl completely and crossing to Moros, whom he helped to stand.

"Brother," he said, as his orange-haired twin stared at him like a stranger. "You're still alive. Of course … Good … Listen well, you must flee. Get out of the city and disappear."

Miss Peryl made a face. "Ugh, family reunions? Really? I wasn't expecting dear old Mr Strife." She glanced at Robin. "You do associate with the absolute strangest people, Robin, you know that?"

Karya was standing in the doorway beside Robin. "And *you're* the strangest of them all," she said through gritted teeth. "The last time I saw you, Grimm, you threw a spear at me."

Peryl looked the girl over appraisingly, taking in her frail and drastically altered appearance. "Well," she clucked, her tongue in her cheek after a moment's thought and consideration. "For the record, I was deflecting a spear, not aiming it. I would love to say no harm done, but goodness …" She raised her eyebrows. "You *do* look a sorry state. And to think, you were his very best work once. Fat Old Nyx will be livid when he sees what you've been reduced to."

Robin was still baffled to find Peryl imprisoned with Moros. Was this the fate of any Grimm who crossed or displeased their mistress?

"Who put you down here, Peryl?" he asked.

She shot him a withering look. "*You did,*" she replied. "Back when I was riding high, finally doing well in the ranks. Got myself a nice gig running the Hive, the Earth Shard cosy in my grasp …" She threw her arms up. "I had Lady Eris practically *eating out of my hand*. And then you come along …" She pointed at him. "And tear down the Hive. Take the Shard. We lost every captive dryad, half the swarm and almost all the centaurs. Eris humiliated, the Elderheart Forest lost from our control, now in open rebellion. All on my watch, and all because of you." She snorted down her nose. "That was not a pleasant return to work interview, I can tell you that much."

"Own your own failures, girl," Strife spat in her direction without sympathy. "You were never destined to lead."

"No one asked you, spooky boomer," Peryl replied tartly.

She looked back to Robin. "Surprisingly, I found myself rather in the bad books for that little misadventure," she said lightly. "I was thrown in here with poor mad Moros to entertain the shidelings." She shuddered. "Could have been worse. Could have been a Travelodge."

She had clipped her mana stone in place, and gave a contented sigh. A change had come over her as she wore it. Her skin looked whiter and smoother, her hair regained its shine, and her eyes seemed clearer, a darker shade of black. She, and Moros too, were altogether more Grimm.

"Lucky I had your little novelty note to pass in class really. What other chance did I have of ever getting out of this place?"

"But how did you know how to get us into Dis?" Robin wanted to know.

Peryl shrugged. "One overhears things, especially around one's organisation. Everyone knows skin-crawly old Nyx has been tampering with that old snake forever, trying to get it to work to make up for his abject failure with *this* one." She flicked a hand dismissively at Karya. "Obviously it was *never* going to work without the Shard of Fire, and he only had half of that, with his little bootlicking lackey, the unbearably social-climbing Lord Flint."

She smiled at Robin. "It was quite funny, really. Knowing that he and Strigoi and the rest of them were out there, scouring the Netherworlde, scouring the human world, searching down the back of every sofa they could find for little lost Lady Tinda and her half of the Shard. And here I was! Sitting in the pitch dark playing I-don't-spy with gibbering Moros here, knowing all along where she, and presumably it, was."

"You knew Lady Tinda was in Barrowood the whole time," Henry said. "Robin told us. You were with him and Woad that day in the shop, though they didn't know who … what … you were at the time. You saw her give the bow to Robin there and then, and guessed who she was?"

Peryl didn't even look at Henry. Her eyes, filled with glittering amusement now that her mana stone was back where it belonged, were still fixed on Robin. "I recognised her, and yes, I guessed that one of the jewels in that bow might well be her half of the lost Shard."

"Then why didn't you take it from her, there and then?" Robin wanted to know. He pointed to Strife and Moros, standing together, odd reflections of one another, watching them from the corner of the cell. "Or why didn't you report it back to Strife, or to Eris herself? It makes no sense. You could have earned your desperately sought-after glory and position at court a heck of a lot sooner."

"More to the point," Karya folded her arms. "You've been locked up here ever since the Hive fell, with this information? You could have used it to bargain for your release."

Peryl's smile fell, and for a moment, her face looked very dark indeed. "But where would be the fun in that?" she said.

She shrugged lightly, shaking off her serious tone. "I was busy at the time, searching for the Water Shard with big noisy Ker. I was confident I could retrieve it." She gave a sly smile. "And I was half right. I thought it better to tuck away this information for later. Always useful to have an ace up your sleeve … for when you really need it."

"Our glorious Lady Eris will have you killed for withholding knowledge like this from her," Mr Strife sneered. "You thought your situation dire, locked up in here for your incompetence? You haven't begun to understand suffering, witless one."

Peryl rounded on him. "To hell with Eris!" she snapped. Strife visibly flinched back in surprise, and Moros clapped his hands over his mouth, looking scandalised and terrified.

Peryl tucked a stray lock of purple hair behind her ear, composing herself, though her face was pure white with controlled anger. "To absolute boiling hell," she said again, quietly, through gritted teeth.

"My loyalty …" She looked back to Robin and the others, "is now to no-one but myself. I have learned that to hanker after approval, to tug at the skirts and hope for attention, recognition …" She scoffed, a harsh and humourless laugh. "Praise? It's a fool's game. Eris can lift you to the highest pedestal, and one mistake …" She held up a wavering finger. "One! And you are cast into the Pits. Rejected, forgotten. Discarded like trash! I will not be thrown away!"

The girl walked towards the door, to Robin and the others. "There was a time, long ago," she said. "When I *was* indeed trash. Detritus floating helplessly on the surface of the world. Eris saved me from that. Or so I *thought*, at the time. But it was not salvation, it was *enslavement*, and I have had much time to think, here in the dark. Scribbling letters to you, trying to guide your clueless feet to this closed door." The girl swallowed hard.

"Peryl," she looked back at Strife and Moros, "no longer serves Dis."

"*All* serve Dis," the old man said, his withering stare boring into her. "All must."

"Oh really?" Peryl seemed amused, glaring back at him. "And I suppose *this* is your idea of loyally serving the empress, is it? Breaking out your beloved brother? Committing high treason against the law of Eris? At least *one* of the two of us has the mana stones to admit where we stand, Mr Strife."

Strife shook his head, a humourless smile passing across his face. He crossed the cell and pushed Peryl roughly aside, knocking her into the wall. Looming over Robin, still standing in the doorway, the old Grimm glared down at him with eyes as black and cold as deep water at midnight.

"The best place to hide is in the darkness at the base of the lamp," he said. "I am no romantic fool, willing to oppose the unopposable. *I* did not break open this cell. In fact …" He reached into his suit jacket and now slowly withdrew his dagger, a long slim blade, cruel and sharp, which Robin had not seen since their first encounter in the Forest of the Redcaps. "I arrived here in the prison only at the sound of chaos, to find this insurgent Scion trespassing." He raised his eyebrows. "Tragically, I was too late to stop the traitorous Mr Moros from escaping the prison. Goodness knows *where* he is now…somewhere far from Dis, no doubt… and *well hidden*." He glanced at his brother pointedly, before turning his attention back to Robin.

"But I *was* in time to capture the Scion and his crew of hapless idiots. To stop them, and to deliver them to the empress. What honours and powers to be bestowed? And when the Empress hears of the duplicitous Miss Peryl's disobedience, what fate awaits her? Eris rewards the loyal and punishes those who would dare stand against her."

Robin took a step backwards, his eyes fixed on Strife's knife. He had fully expected betrayal from the old man, but after tearing down the door of the cell, dispelling the powerful enchantment that had been laid on it, he found he had not a shred of mana left with which to fight back.

"Now would be a good time for you to disappear, brother," Strife said over his shoulder to Mr Moros. "I assure you, I am quite blind to your escape. I, on the other hand, will deliver this brat, who thinks to play Strife of Dis like a harp, to the empress. Whether whole, or in pieces!" A dangerous smile creased his thin face. "I've been looking forward to this for a *long* time, Robin Fellows. You think to pull my strings, but you are no strategist, not against Strife. Now…" He lifted the blade menacingly, its cruel edge glancing in the dim light. "Any last-"

There was a thud and Mr Strife's head wobbled, his eyes shooting wide with surprise. And then, slowly, they rolled back in his head. The knife fell from his hands, clattering to the damp stones below his feet, and with his long arms and legs folding like a collapsing spider, he crumpled to the floor.

Peryl stood behind him, still holding aloft a large brick that had been torn from the door frame in its destruction.

"Wow …" she said in a satisfied whisper. "I've wanted to do that for *ages*."

Mr Moros was at her shoulder, still looking scandalised. He nudged his brother gently with a toe. "Oh dear," he said in a high tone. He giggled nervously. "Oh dear, dear, dear. Now you've done it!"

"He's not dead," Peryl reassured him. "Just out cold."

She glanced at Robin and the others, who were all staring at her, wide-eyed. "That's the problem with you lot," she admonished them. "You're always 'magic trick this' and 'heroic sacrifice that', and none of you ever has the common sense to just think 'brick'."

She dropped the brick carelessly on the floor beside Strife's head.

"Shall we go?" she suggested. "You know, before he wakes up, perhaps?"

"Leave brother Strife?" Moros wondered. He was still peering down at the green-haired Grimm on the floor, a curiously vacant and wondering look on his face. Robin wondered if Mr Moros' mind truly was gone altogether.

"It's what he wanted you to do," Peryl told him. "Batty old beast risked a lot to get you free. Who knew, the old stain still has a beat in the shrivelled lump of coal he calls a heart. Wonders will never cease." She touched Moros lightly on the arm. "He would want you to flee. We have to leave him here. He's …"

"He's too scared to run himself," Moros said flatly. They all looked at him.

"He never was very brave. Always stays with power. Always. So he can protect us, keep us safe. Keep me safe. I don't remember much of anything, really." He giggled again. "But I remember us being powerless, long ago. And how he hated it. He needs power, craves it. Though I don't think he really remembers why, anymore."

Peryl led Moros out of the cell, stepping lightly over Strife's unconscious body.

"Well, look at it this way," she reasoned. "He'll be able to spin a heroic tale to Eris about how he tried to stop us escaping, won't he? She'll be happy with him, her most loyal and trustworthy one. He'll even have the head wound to prove it. It will keep him safe," she reassured him.

She looked to Robin and the others. "I said I'd get you *into* Dis, Scion. You promised to get me *out*. Where's this burrowing serpent of yours then?"

"Beneath Strife's house," Karya said. "And can I just mention that I'm still processing the fact that Grimms have houses. Like actual people."

"We are actual people," Peryl glared. "What, did you think we slept in coffins?"

Karya glared back. "It's in Strife's basement," she said. "But it won't move without the Fire Shard, and we have other things we need to do before we leave."

The Grimm girl gave her a look that was almost pitying. "From the look of you, sweetie, you don't have much of *anything* left to do, except maybe crumble into dust, but … whatever. Peachy keen for you. Enjoy your heroics. I'm not throwing my hat in with you lot and your suicide mission. Moros and I are gone."

"Wait, where will you go?" Robin asked, staring at her.

Her eyes looked around the close, bare walls of Eris' displeasure. "Anywhere," she said quietly. "Anywhere but here."

"The eclipse is soon," Woad reminded everyone. "Like, really *really* soon. The pyres will be being lit, right now."

"Best distraction ever." Peryl clapped her hands. "Easy to slip away amongst all the smoke and fireworks."

"Where are the bonfires?" Robin grabbed at Peryl's wrist as she skipped out of the cell and turned to set off along the dark corridor, his grip stopping her in her tracks. She glanced down at his hand around her arm, blinking, then looked up at him.

"Our friends are there," he told her. "None of us know our way around the city. There isn't time-"

"That's *really* not my problem," Peryl replied in a matter-of-fact way. "I mean … hooray for the rescue and all, Moros and I are super grateful, but that hardly makes us best friends, does it?" She raised her eyebrows. "Why do you think I didn't tell you who I was in the messages? Would you have been as likely to come if you'd known it was me?"

Robin peered unblinkingly at her, still holding her wrist. "Yes. Of course."

Peryl didn't reply for a moment. She simply stared back at him, and then she swallowed and shook her wrist free, as though he were being bothersome.

She stood, tapping her foot, considering things in the narrow corridor. "The Pyrenight celebrations take place in the large square right in front of Eris' palace," she sighed. "If your precious friends are being barbequed, that's where they will be."

"That couldn't be *further* from where we are right now." Karya sounded exhausted but exasperated. "Right at the top of the hill of Dis, and here we are right at the bottom of its innards."

"The eclipse is already beginning out there." Robin looked amongst his friends. "I can feel it. We don't have time to get out of here. To work our way through the city."

Peryl rolled her eyes and threw her hands heavenwards. "Oh, for the love of the fates, *okay*!" she groaned. "I will get you to the square fast, but then we're even, okay?" She narrowed her eyes at Robin. "Actually no, changed my mind. We're even already. You'll owe me one."

There was no time to argue, Robin nodded.

"Okay then," Peryl said, flapping her hands theatrically in the air to gather them all close together. Her mana stone had begun to glow like a small crimson furnace. "Gather round, children, and hold on to your hats."

Before anyone could speak, the corridor erupted with thousands of pitch-black moths, each as large as a hand span. Miss Peryl's mana made solid, fluttering and battering around the narrow cell and tunnel, solid shadow flapping and diving and making a mad flickering strobe of shadow and light in the glow of the pale lantern dropped by Mr Strife.

The gloomoths' beating wings rose from a rustle to a roar, like a hurricane in trees, and more and more passed between, through and around them, until all light was blocked out, and nothing was left but confusion and swirling chaos. And faintly, Robin heard the mad giggling of Mr Moros, filled with childish glee.

10

Betwixt and Bewitched

The corridor, the bowels of the prison, and all the claustrophobic despair of the Pits of Dis had fallen away. Robin could no longer feel the rock under his feet. He could barely tell which way he was facing. It was similar to travelling through a Janus Station, or when Karya tore a hole between the worlds. He understood instinctively that this place was an in-between space.

He couldn't hear, feel, or see any of his friends around him. Only moths, a vast glittering cloud of them, large and endless as a thunderhead, through which he drifted silently like a dust mote. It was oddly peaceful, though he was not entirely alone. Peryl was with him. He couldn't see her, or anything else, other than the flurry of dusty silk wings, black-tinged and edged with purple and gold, but they had both been touched by the Water Shard long ago, and he felt her smile somewhere in the darkness as surely as if it was his own expression.

"You'll never get out of Dis alive. You know that don't you?"

He wasn't sure if he had said this to her, or if she had said it to him.

"There's *always* a way out," the reply came from one of them. "No matter how deep into a bad thing you are. Something I learned."

He caught glimpses of her in the ever moving, near-silent maelstrom of gently shifting wings. The flash of an eye, the corner of a mouth.

"How do you stop being a Grimm?"

Again, he could not have said if this was his question or hers. Whoever asked it, the other wasn't sure there even *was* an answer.

"You're not the only changeling in the worlds, you know." This was Peryl. Her voice floated straight into his mind as they tumbled through the ceaseless rolling motion. "The only Fae hidden in the human world, yes. But these things flow both ways. Everyone knows Eris' tastes. She likes mirrors. It amuses her." She sounded teasing, poking fun at him.

"What do you mean?"

"The Grimms. Eris' only true creations," she replied. "All those old stories of the Fae folk who used to steal away human children, replacing them with a changeling, a mischievous spirit from the other world? Poppycock, of course, but clearly inspiration to your parents when they squirrelled you away out of the war." She sneered a little, unseen. He saw a flash of a hand in a break in the wings, like a sunbeam in cloud. There and then gone. "Of course, such ideas give rise to imitation," Peryl said. "Eris could not create. She could not surround herself with her own version of the Fae's noble Sidhe-Nobilitas. She hasn't the talent to make life, only to mimic it and warp it. But still ... she wanted her own Unseelie Court. The Grimms."

"You're not from the Netherworlde, are you?" Robin already knew. "Not originally. Any of you."

"Human once," she admitted. "Long time ago for some of us. Less for others. Lost boys and lost girls, spirited away to Never Never Land." Her voice sounded wistful. "And oh, we were all *so* lost."

"Strife and Moros too?" Robin remembered his vision through the Mask of Gaia. Young boys in old fashioned school uniforms. Long grey socks, T-bar shoes of polished leather. Sitting in a dormitory, engulfed by sadness. A school? An orphanage?

"Little lost boys for sure, those two," Peryl smirked invisibly. "All alone with each other in a cruel world that didn't want them. Moros as frail and delicate as a cracked egg. Strife with the responsibility of the world on his powerless shoulders."

Wings brushed endlessly across Robin's face and outstretched hands in the quiet maelstrom. It was not an unpleasant sensation.

"All of us, yes. Lost until found. Purposeless until given shape."

"What were their names? What was yours?"

"I don't remember," she replied simply, and he couldn't tell if it was a lie. "It hardly matters now. Me? I was homeless, a pickpocket. Starving to death in alleyways and dumpsters. Eris? She was a light to me, a burning sun ... to *all* of us. A new world, a new purpose. Safety, direction, meaning ... and something *none* of us had *ever* had ... power."

The moths seemed to increase in their speed and agitation, and though Robin was falling, moving through the strange non-space, it was like falling upwards, rising up from a deep ocean at a great and silent speed.

"The only cost for our deliverance from pain and suffering was our humanity," she told him, and there was a darkness behind her light and shrugging tone. "None of us had seen much of that anyway. Humanity, I mean. Hardly a loss. I was the last, you know? The others were already made. Some – Strife and Moros, Ker – they were tricked with lies … poison sweetened with honey … though they don't really remember that they were. Others … like Nyx, well … He's different." The air around the moths, in the tiny spaces between their millions of wings, seemed to cool. "That one came most willingly. Eyes wide open to what he would become. Eager to be what he could not be in the human world. Without censure or judgement from his fellow man. Nyx was hungry for it."

"Eris stole and used you," Robin told her, wishing he could find her in this great cloud.

"You don't understand. The empress gave us exactly what she promised to," Peryl argued, sounding rather petulant. "The removal of humanity is *glorious*, Robin Fellows. It's like shrugging off a suffocating coat that's too heavy. It's *your* fault I was reminded of its existence, no one else's."

"Peppercorn." Robin understood.

"Like a gadfly in the corner of my eye," she agreed, sounding sad and amused. "You're the stone in my shoe, Robin Fellows. Do you know what it is to be without conscience? Without uncertainty or care? Cruel and certain as a field of ice? It's a freedom. A lightness. A surety as pure and bright as a mountain stream. But then you come along…polluting dark perfection with messy human *feelings*."

"Come to Erlking," he offered. "Both of you."

Let me keep you safe, he added silently, in his own mind only. *Let me try to save you.*

Peryl actually laughed at this, and he felt her, surprisingly close to him in the blinding, ever-moving cloud. Her hand shot out and grabbed him by the wrist as they tumbled upwards. "That's your answer to everything, Scion of the Arcania. You can't save every lost puppy. Some of us are feral and will bite your hand off if you try. Besides …" Her hand was very cold on his arm, sending a shiver of goosebumps along his skin. "Erlking is going to burn. Ashes and ashes. And I'll be long gone before that. I can look after myself. Better than you can look after *your*self, that much is clear. I know how to disappear. A shadow in the shadows."

The moths parted a little and she was suddenly right in front of him, violet eyes piercing and filled with merry sadness. She grabbed the pockets of Robin's hoodie, drawing the two of them closer together, like swimmers floating in dark and turbulent water. Robin's heart pounded and he found his arms around her waist.

"I will miss part of you though," she admitted. "Not the Scion part, just the doomed and earnest ... other."

He hadn't been expecting to kiss her, but by the time it was happening it seemed like the most natural thing in the world – as though it had always been rolling towards him, unstoppable as fate, since their first meeting. A destiny cemented when the Shard of the Arcania had shattered in both of their hands, and a little of her darkness had rooted in him, giving him more strength and courage, and a speck of his light had buried deep in her, fracturing her simple and joyous Grimmness,

Hidden here between the worlds, under veils of black moth wings and shadow, Robin's first kiss was soft and perfect, and tinged with the salt of unseen tears and the whisper of words unsaid.

As they broke apart and Robin opened his eyes, feeling his cheeks redden, she gave him an odd look and a smile which was small, hidden in the corner of her mouth.

"Do your best not to die up there," she said. "You're the only interesting person I know. Later, Scion."

And the moths blinded him.

11

The Glory and the Fury

Cobblestones are never easy on the knees, especially if you hit them at speed, as Robin discovered when they flew up to meet him. He managed to break his fall at least a little by slapping out his hands as he fell onto all fours, and the cloud of moths dissipated from around him, drifting away into nothingness. He felt the sting of hard stone crack against his palms, pained sounds from all around told him that Henry, Woad and Karya were having similar encounters with the sudden floor.

The cloud of fluttering wings and confusion drifted away, disappearing like smoke and leaving the four of them to get unsteadily to their feet, Woad helping Karya to stand, with his head and shoulders under her unsteady arm as he hauled her up.

"Bloody ... bloody ... hellfire," Henry muttered queasily under his breath. "Just once – *once* – I'd like to get from A to B in the Netherworlde in some kind of *normal* way. You know, riding a horse, riding a bike? Dear God, I think I swallowed a moth." He coughed dramatically, making a retching noise.

Robin stared around. They were in a narrow alleyway, tall stone buildings on either side, grey as concrete and carved with angular stonework. They soared up on either side of them in the tiny street to the sky above, a narrow channel which was an odd colour looming over them, somewhere between bronze and blue.

"Where ... where are they?" Karya croaked, leaning unsteadily against a wall. She looked ready to collapse.

Peryl and Moros were gone. The four Erlkingers found themselves alone in the alleyway.

"Gone," Robin whispered, more to himself than the others. He could still feel heat in his cheeks and felt incredibly embarrassed that his friends would see it. He turned and looked about the narrow, cobbled street, making a show of looking for the two fugitive Grimms, when in truth he just didn't want the others to see him blushing. It took all his self-control not to raise fingers to his lips, where he could still feel the kiss.

"Long gone," he said, thinking: *Good. Run. Run and hide. Hide far from Eris, who does not forgive failure and does not forget betrayal.*

Somewhere far below the street where Robin now found himself standing, deep in the airless and merciless darkness of the Pits of Dis, Mr Strife would be blearily coming to. Knowing his brother had fled. Gone from Dis. Did Robin feel relief on behalf of Strife? Pity for him, even? It was hard to feel sympathy for a bitter old man who had just been holding a knife to your throat and willing to deliver you to the enemy. But all the same, Robin found himself picturing Strife down in the dark, sitting on the floor of the cell his brother had been freed from. The old man's mind full of distant memories. Grey socks, shiny shoes and quiet, terribly lonely rooms. And Robin found that he was glad that Moros was free.

"They can't get out of Dis," Woad said. "The Mad Hatter and the grinning Cheshire Cat. That's the thing about Dis, remember? It's hardly got an open-door policy. I'm not sure if you recall, but we had *quite a time* trying to get in here ourselves."

"They've taken the serpent," Robin said, looking at his friends as he realised this. They *must* have. Where else would they go? Peryl had kept her word, dropping them off above ground where they needed to be, at the very pinnacle of the city. But neither she nor Moros had any interest in hanging around to see how things played out. They had melted away. Shadows into shadows.

He could already see them in his mind's eye; traitors stealing swiftly through the cellar in the house of Strife, hand in hand, orange and purple, pale faces with black eyes and glittering red mana stones in the shadows. Lost ones fleeing forever their dark Neverland.

"But they won't be able to make the Glassfire Serpent work." Karya shook her head. "Not without the Shard of Fire,"

Robin's eyes flew wide, and a sense of dark foreboding settled in his stomach. He thrust his hands into the pockets of his hoodie. They were empty. Of *course* they were. The Shard was gone.

Peryl pulling him towards her in the cloud of moths, hands in his pockets.

"She was a pickpocket once, in another life," he said to himself.

Henry was looking at the slim sliver of sky they could see between the tall, close buildings, his face turned upwards towards the odd burning twilight.

"We don't have time to worry about deserter Grimms," he said. "We don't have time for anything. Look at the sky."

From the end of their narrow street, there was a din of noise. Shaking off the disorientation of their escape from the vile Pits, none of them had paid it much heed until now. It was the roar of a crowd, and now, beneath the noise, they heard the rolling, ceremonial beat of drums like a great heartbeat.

"Pyrenight." Robin dropped his hands from his pockets. He looked to Karya, concerned. "Can you walk?" She looked like a spectre, white-lipped and drawn, but she nodded.

With the others in tow, Robin cautiously approached the corner of their alleyway.

It opened up into a vast town square. All around on three sides, tall and impressive buildings rose, spiking the sky with spears of carved and decorated roofs. Dotted with many windows, their glass panes reflecting the odd colour of the sky above. Banners hung from the buildings, long crimson pennants flapping in the breeze like tongues of blood. Each was emblazoned with embroidered golden spheres. Suns, Robin thought at first, before realising they were fruit of some kind, apples perhaps. Twisting around these pictured and stylised fruits, commanding slogans of the rule of Eris cried out from the walls in decorative script.

Omnis Quae Videt Imperatrix! Cried one banner in huge letters.

De omnibus dubitandum! Another read.

Vigilate Hostem!

The fourth side of the huge town square was entirely taken up by the palace, a sheer wall of soaring stone, countless windows high above, thin and glowing with light. This stark and brutal edifice soared upwards, higher, *much* higher than every building facing it. Stern and bare-faced. Beyond the colossal and unyielding wall of the palace's face, it split into towers. Close together, these great cylinders of dark stone stabbed the sky like a cluster of vast industrial chimneys. A crazed latticework of gantries and bridges weaving suicidally amongst the spires.

Eris' palace, the dark beating heart of Dis, and of the Netherworlde, sat atop the hill-city. Heavy iron, cold stone, and looming violence.

The large square was packed to every edge with bodies. Panthea of every description were thronging the space in their hundreds. It was like Times Square in New York waiting for the new year countdown. Many of them had flags, and were waving them above their heads. Here and there, small firecrackers and bursts of light were already being set off as those skilled in mana began celebratory light shows. Robin saw plenty of peacekeepers threading through the crowds, a strong presence of threatening order.

But with all of this to see, Robin's attention was drawn not to the stunning and viciously stark buildings, nor to the banners and flags bellowing propaganda from every wall, or even the roaring festival crowd of Eris' most favoured nobility. What filled his vision were the two bonfires, large and unlit, which had been erected either side of the huge palace doors. A stage had been erected between them on which stood several peacekeepers in an orderly military line.

There was a figure lashed with heavy ropes to a pole atop each of the bonfires.

"Ffoulkes!" Henry almost yelled, clapping a hand over his own mouth just in time before he drew attention to them, hunkering down out of sight in the mouth of the alleyway.

The figure on the left was indeed Robin's tutor. Hanging limply and tied to a post like a witch in Salem, thick ropes around his waist and legs, his hands clearly bound behind his back. His bald head drooped and he looked in a terrible state, barely conscious, but there was no mistaking his fiery beard.

A huge surge of relief washed through Robin momentarily. Seeing his tutor here and in such a state was no good thing, but they were in time. Ffoulkes was *alive*.

Robin looked to the other bonfire, on the far side of the stage, and blinked in surprise. He had fully expected to see Jackalope tied to the other bonfire, awaiting ceremonial immolation in the same manner of his teacher. But the second figure was not the Fae boy.

It was a satyr.

"That's Swiftwings!" Woad frowned in confusion. "The old guy from the library. The satyr who helped us get back to the human world and to Lady Calescent."

The satyr, like Ffoulkes, seemed barely conscious. Delirious and roughed up pretty badly. Robin doubted either of the prisoners even knew where they were or what was going on.

"Where's Jack?" Karya asked, dumbfounded. The hornless Fae was nowhere to be seen. "He's not here!"

The sun in the sky above them was directly over the square, and the shadow of the moon had eaten a bite of it already. For the second time, Robin stared up at the same eclipse, watching the blazing disc of the sun slowly disappearing into a crescent. The light of the sky washing down over the festival square was odd and unreal, making the scene feel dreamlike, a stage set filled with actors, and the warm spring air, here at the very apex of Dis, had begun to cool as the unnatural midday twilight fell. Right now, Robin thought, somewhere in the past, this same sun was shining down on a lake at Erlking, at a boat and a faun and a cloud of angry pyreflies.

"First, we save them," Robin said, crouching low at the corner of the street behind the crowds. "Then we find Jack."

"Wait," Henry said, drawing their attention to the podium on the far side of the square.

A figure had appeared there on the long, raised stage set out before the palace of Eris, walking out from between the line of peacekeepers in slow and evenly measured strides. As it raised its hands, attentive silence fell across the crowds, rippling outwards from it in hushed obedience.

It was Strigoi.

His long, black-feathered cloak streamed out behind him as he made his way to the front of the stage like dark wings. The glimmering and fading sun above glowed in the polished metal of his armour, chasing deep shadows into the carved recesses of the grinning wolf face. His empty-eyed helmet looked out across the gathered citizens of Dis.

When all had fallen silent, the Wolf of Eris pointed upwards at the eclipse.

"People of Dis." His voice echoed around the buildings, low but resonant from within its metal cage. "People of the Netherworlde. Loyal and dutiful subjects of the great Empress Eris."

A dutiful cheer rose up amongst the crowds. People waved flags. Strigoi pointed upwards still, waiting for their fervour to settle before speaking again.

"Pyrenight is upon us!" he declared. "This day we remember our victory over the Fae! We stand and remember our liberation from tyranny, and the establishment of a new and glorious rule!"

More cheers, echoing off the walls all around. The sound of the crowd like thunder in the growing darkness.

"On this day, we remember a hard-fought war!" Strigoi continued. "We give thanks and honour to Eris, who led us from the darkness. Eris, who gave this land to us. Eris who drives the hateful and chaotic Fae before her like cockroaches under her righteous light! Who brings order and meaning to our world!" He spread out his arms, his armoured talons reaching for the bonfires laid out on either side of him. "With these offerings, we remember the fires of war! The lives lost to our great cause! And we remain *vigilant*! For even now, in the hour of our victory, there are those who would seek to undo all of our work. Even now, there are remnants of that old and broken world, still clinging uselessly to their dreams of power."

A few boos erupted from the crowd, and Strigoi nodded his head, the sunlight flashing on his tall horns. "A *rebellion,* they call themselves, these scattered few. A *resistance*!" He laughed, cold and utterly without humour, undiluted scorn flowing from him. "Pathetic, rag-clad Fae, hiding in hollowed trees and under leaf mulch, plotting and planning to cast us down! To level the great city of Dis itself! Their wish? To take from *you* that which we have fought so hard to give you!"

More angry and outraged jeers surrounded them. Robin could hear the hatred in the voices of the crowd as Strigoi whipped them up from his podium.

"These blasphemous outcasts, these … war criminals! Enemies of the peace!" Strigoi called out. "They scurry around in the ruins of our old enemy. They skulk in the shadows, and they hide in the wilds like the animals they are. They scheme against us, and in their ignorance, they believe that they, these ragged, pathetic few … can stand against one so great as *Eris*!"

This was met with laughter and applause from the crowd.

"Their poisoned words have even turned some good *Panthea*!" Strigoi sounded incredulous. "Made them *traitors* to their own kind! Satyrs, nymphs! Once noble and respected subjects of the empress, tricked and corrupted by the vile Fae spawn to turn brother against brother! Is this not shameful?"

Cries of passionate agreement rose from the crowds all around.

"Does Eris pardon these traitors any more than she pardons the Fae?" Strigoi did not wait to hear the anticipated cries of "'No", though they were deafening and certain when they came. "Does Eris forgive?"

The crowd roared again, louder still.

Robin exchanged looks with his companions. As the sky continued to darken and the twilight shadows of the eclipse spread long fingers of shadow across the square, their faces were becoming lost in darkness.

"Eris is *might*!" Strigoi played to the crowd, shouting now in his growl. "Eris is cold, hard *justice*! And *none* stand against her! These…deviants, these pathetic few. They scrabble in the dirt, searching for ancient weapons to undermine the world she has built for you. But today? Today is a great victory for us."

At his gesture, the line of peacekeepers stepped forward, each one of them holding aloft a different object, presented to the crowd. Robin strained to see.

"This satyr you see before you," Strigoi told the citizens of Dis. "This traitorous turncoat. Hiding in the mountains since the war, claims no allegiance to Eris, and no allegiance to the Fae. But his house is filled with wonders. Wonders from ancient times."

Robin recognised the odd assortment of objects now being held aloft. The mirror, the cloak, the spear. They were the relics from the Precipitous Library. The ancient and sacred leavings of the great Elementals which the library had kept safe and secret for so long, holding them in scholarly reverence. Until Robin had led Nyx and his forces right to their door.

He and the other Erlkingers had escaped the library, yes. But clearly Nyx had known the value of the artefacts left behind. He had ransacked the relics. Brought them here, to Eris.

Had the relics allowed themselves to fall into enemy hands? Robin couldn't comprehend it, and yet here they were, displayed like spoils of war.

What had happened to the other satyrs? Robin wondered in despair. Had they been captured? Imprisoned, punished? Were they even now languishing in one of Eris' camps in the Hills of Blood and Bone? Or had they all been cut down there and then, on that cold mountain? Their books, all that collected knowledge, had it been burned to the ground? While Swiftwings himself had been dragged back here with the relics, an example to be made to the citizens of the Netherworlde. A lesson in the punishments awaiting those who would choose disobedience.

"Our world is not a world of *no allegiance*," Strigoi was saying. "This is not a war anyone can choose to sit out. You are *with* the empress …"

Huge, emphatic cheers roared from the crowd.

"Or you are *against* her." He indicated Ffoulkes and Swiftwings again. The symbolism was clear – showing what inevitable fate awaited those Panthea who dared consider defying the empress.

"And with these hallowed and ancient artefacts, we will now have more power than ever before to crush our enemies beneath our feet. They are a gift! A sign from the Elementals themselves of Eris' rightful rule, that they should come to us in our time of need."

Robin was glaring at Strigoi across the square with pure hatred. At this monstrous figure, a literal bogeyman. The mouthpiece of the empress. This blunt instrument who long ago had been the one to lead the Grimms and all their forces to the hideout of the Sidhe-Nobilitas. Who had stolen hope from the Fae in the wake of the war. It took every inch of Robin's self-control not to leap up and declare his presence here. To stand and call Strigoi out, challenge and defeat him, here and now. To avenge every Fae who had fallen because of him.

But that would be foolish. Strigoi was strong. Too strong. And this was not the place. Right on the doorstep of Eris herself, with countless peacekeepers and loyal fanatics around them.

Right now, he had to focus on their mission. They had to rescue Ffoulkes, and Swiftwings too, now they saw he was here. They had to find Jack, whatever had happened to him, and they had to get inside the palace and up to the tower of Nyx. To Heaven's Lens, while Karya still had time.

"And this one?" Strigoi indicated Ffoulkes with a sweep of his arm, displaying to the crowd the man lashed to the other bonfire. "This Panthea, perhaps a servant to any one of you nobles of Dis. A *thief* of silverware, a *gossip* and trader of secrets. Many of you may have welcomed him into your house at some point. He may have served your food. He may have held the keys to your rooms. He may have held your trust! Your confidence!"

Murmurs of concerned disapproval rose from the crowd now, egged on by Strigoi's words.

"The enemy is not always out there," Strigoi stressed. "Horned Fae devils in the wild. The enemy also walks amongst our own kind. The enemy can wear the mask of our own servants. Our associates. Our own brothers and sisters. This loathsome creature fled the Netherworlde, deserted his people, a thief of his master's riches. Shamefully, he turned to Erlking. Unforgivably, he tutored the Scion himself! Is there any greater crime?"

Uproar in the crowd, deafening Robin with their outrage. "We captured this criminal again," Strigoi told them. "And *again* he escaped when the terrorist Fae attacked the Hive. When the so-called rebels broke our walls, and released countless dangerous criminals back into the free world. Will we allow this atrocity again? Will we find ourselves caught off guard again? Betrayed? Or will we be *vigilant*?"

"Burn him!" The cry came from the crowd, some furious noble shrieking from his throat. This drew cries of assent from all around.

"We will watch one another!" Strigoi told them. "We must! We will report *any* who seem suspicious! *Any* whose loyalty is doubted! We will lose no more honest and innocent Panthea to the forked-tongue promises and lies of Erlking! Here, today, we celebrate Pyrenight! And we offer punishment to these lost and fallen souls! Here, beneath the shadow on the sun, we send their betrayal to the skies in embers and in ashes! For Eris!"

"For Eris!" the crowd chanted, whipped into zealous frenzy, whether genuine fervour or fear of being deemed suspicious themselves, every person present was baying for blood, eager to prove their loyalty to the empress. Their shouts echoed from the walls of the large square.

"*Vivat Imperatrix!*" shouted Strigoi, and the crowd shouted it back at him, many throats roaring at once. In the unnaturally dark space, the freakish line of peacekeepers flanking the man on the raised platform shook their stolen ancient artefacts in the air like rattled sabres. Spoils of war and shows of power.

The eclipse overhead reached totality, the orb of the sun flashing into blackness, a perfect dark circle, and the blazing corona shot out arcs of silent, shimmering flame across a suddenly dark sky. An all-seeing eye peering down upon the shadowy crowds below in arcane judgement.

The two bonfires burst into flame with a *whoosh*, bright orange flames erupting all around their bases, bright and sudden in the darkness.

The crowd cheered, stamping their feet and waving their flags, countless faceless silhouetted in the blackness of noon. Above and all around them, in the skies above the capital, there was the crackle, hiss and bang of fireworks, lighting up the stark stern face of the palace, exploding in great joyous flowers of crackling light high above the rooftops.

"Now!" Robin yelled to the others over the cacophony.

They didn't have a plan. There hadn't been any time to form one, but the twin pyres were burning, flames climbing their rough pyramids of stacked wood with alarming speed and hunger, closer every second to the two prisoners tied atop them. They had to act now.

Strigoi stood on the platform in the distance like a hellish evangelist. He had turned away from the crowds to face the palace, and the reflected light of the twin bonfires glittered across the glossy black of his feathered cape, painting his metal horns in fire.

"I'll hide us!" Robin cried, shoving himself roughly into the dark crowd. "You free them. And then inside, all of us together!"

The crowds of Panthea nobles jostled and stumbled around him as he shoved his way forward in the darkness, elbowing people aside roughly, pushing bodies away, stepping on feet to cries of outrage and confusion in the firework-flickering shadows. Woad, Henry and Karya were right behind him, plunging headlong into the darkness and confusion as the sky lit up above them, flash after flash of bright crackling blooms filling the darkness around the black sun.

"Inside?" he heard Woad's incredulous cry, but Robin was already concentrating, his mind whirring as they ploughed forward, shouldering through the crowds. They needed a distraction, a smokescreen, or the next best thing.

When he had first begun to learn the Towers of the Arcania, he had stood on a hill in the grounds of Erlking, trying to knock his tutor off balance with a simple cantrip. It had taken all of his will and concentration, standing stock still and pulling at every reserve he had to form even the simplest manifestation of mana. Since then, he had communed with four of the Shards of the Arcania. Air, Water, Earth, and now Fire. He found himself changed by them, as surely as he changed his relationship with the very idea of magic itself.

As the Scion, fully accepting of himself and his role here in the Netherworlde, the skinny blond-haired boy now barrelling determinedly through the crowds of the square was unrecognisable as the lost and uncertain child he once had been. His eyes blazed with determination and, neither breaking stride nor pausing to allow himself a moment of doubt, he reached deep within and called on his mana, knowing with every fibre the certainty that it would answer and obey.

"*Occultatum*," he breathed, and outwards from him in all directions flew a shockwave, carrying with it a swiftly forming mist. Robin threw his mana out around himself like a cloak, pulling the moisture from every inch of air in the vast town square and bending it to his will, making it dense, making it low. His alone to command and direct.

The square filled quickly with a thick and freezing fog, blinding all in attendance as it poured over the crowd in a soupy grey and silver wave. The fog was shot throughout with glittering suspended ice crystals, and the blazing corona of the dark sun overhead caught every mote, making the cloud dance and sparkle like embers. The fog reached the edges of the square and flowed up against the sides of the buildings, a dense rolling wave hiding everything. It threaded around the bonfires, its thick, damp tendrils pushing back the flames, starving them of oxygen and making them splutter and roar. It made ghosts of the peacekeepers, and chaos erupted in the square all around them.

Pushing forward, Robin reached the platform as many of the people in the crowds panicked. Disoriented, blurred shadows were shouting and falling over one another in the blinding mist, people stumbled and stampeded, tripping over one another and grabbing out for balance. The nobles of Dis dragging each other down in their efforts to steady themselves. A tangle of flailing and stumbling limbs.

To the sound of their cries and shouts of alarm and confusion, oddly muffled by the fog, Robin clambered up onto the great platform before the palace, scrabbling desperately to his feet like a rabid concert goer dragging himself up onto the stage.

Amidst the cries from the crowd – their shifting forms glimpsed in bright supernova bursts as the fireworks continued to explode high overhead, lighting the cloud of fog in hazy and diffused flashes – he saw the shadows of the peacekeepers turning blindly to him in silent confusion.

Galestrikes loosed from his palms sent them flying, one by one, down into the unseen crowd below. Strong javelins of air cutting clear paths through the heavy, glittering fog as scarecrow bodies were sent somersaulting bonelessly from the platform, Robin spinning and dodging between them, lashing out again and again, taking them down one by one. From the corner of his eye, he glimpsed the shadowy forms of Henry and Karya, scrambling up the sputtering stacked wood of the bonfires in the flashing darkness of the eclipse, heading towards the prisoners.

Momentarily distracted, Robin turned to the other bonfire, trying to get his bearings in the mist. He was panting hard, his mana roaring in his veins, deafening in his ears.

And something blocked his view. Strigoi, looming suddenly out of the mist, a demon out of the gloom, took him by surprise. The man's gauntleted hand shot out and caught Robin across the cheek; a hard and flashing backhand that landed with a metallic crack so hard it sent a white flash across Robin's vision.

The blow was vicious, knocking the boy from his feet. Robin fell hard, slamming onto his shoulder against the rough boards of the platform and cracking his head hard. Woozy and shocked, he spat, tasting blood on his lip. His cheek and jaw felt like they were on fire.

"Scion!" Strigoi's hiss cut through the fog. The horned man loomed over Robin where he lay prone, still smarting and trying to stop the ringing in his ears. A heavy boot clanked down onto the boards either side of the boy's fallen body. He stared down, like dark judgement, the carved and angry face of his wolf-helmet seeming to sneer as it glared at him from above. "You should never have come to Dis!"

Robin rolled onto his back, shaking his head clear. The crowd, unseen in the fog, were still roaring in confusion, stampeding in panic, but he could barely hear them. Somewhere in the mist, peacekeepers ran and leapt through the crowds, spectres in the fog, and Karya and Henry struggled to free their friends. But here on this platform, Robin was alone beneath the black sky with the Wolf.

He tried to scurry backwards, to get away and put a little distance between himself and Strigoi, but the man stepped down hard, placing a booted foot on Robin's chest and holding him in place like a trapped animal. Robin struggled to breathe, feeling his ribs grind. His face burned as he stared upwards to see the tall horns of Strigoi silhouetted against the dark sky above, through the fog. Beyond them, high above the soaring walls of the palace, the black disc of the sun blazed. A ring of fire in the darkness.

"You are an arrogant fool, Robin Fellows," Strigoi spat. His long black sword dangled loosely from his hand, scraping the boards and Robin saw his armoured fingers flex against the hilt. "Where is the Shard of Fire?"

Robin blinked up at the man, unable to stop a grin that was half grimace spread defiantly across his face, aware that his teeth were bloody. "Gone," he wheezed, struggling to draw breath under the crushing weight of Strigoi's boot. "Gone from Dis, and from you."

Strigoi tilted his inscrutable head in the mist, but before he could say or do anything further, he suddenly stiffened, standing bolt upright. The man shook and quivered. His foot flew off Robin as he staggered and his fingers spasmed, dancing helplessly, causing him to drop his sword to the boards with a clatter. The fallen blade missed Robin's face by inches.

The boy scuttled backwards. Strigoi shook and jumped, thrashing in the mist that coiled around him. There was a series of loud crackling noises rolling through the air, and Robin stared in alarm and confusion as countless tiny worms of blue electricity threaded across the creature's armour. Lightning flashed across his metal muzzle in small arcs. It leapt from one horn of his helmet to the other in a bright arc. Robin's gaze lowered as he sat up, and he saw a hand wrapped tightly around the man's ankle. A small blue hand. Woad was behind him in the mist, having leapt up onto the platform unseen, thrown himself on his belly and slid across the boards, grabbing Strigoi's ankle. The boy was glowing like a gas lamp, his skin flickering, pouring pulses of Skyfire into their enemy.

Shocked and electrified, trapped within his skin of metal, Strigoi stumbled off balance, and Robin kicked out at him hard with all his fury, knocking the large man off his feet. Released by Woad, he fell away sideways, tangled up in his own cloak like a black shroud as he tumbled headlong from the platform and down into the mist and the chaos of the crowd in the town square below them.

Woad grinned, jumping from his prone state into a catlike crouch as the glow faded from his skin.

"Bet that attack came as a bit of a shock," the faun quipped, smiling from ear to ear.

He sprang forward, his hand immediately on Robin's jaw, the smile on his face replaced immediately with a look of angry concern.

"Did he break your jaw, Pinky? Your face looks swollen like a pumpkin!"

Robin instinctively flinched, half expecting to be electrocuted by the faun's fingers, but the small – yet clearly capable – boy had managed to rein in his energy. Only a small crackle erupted from his fingers, like static pulsing into Robin's jaw, which had the odd effect of quite effectively numbing the pain.

"I'm fine," Robin insisted, still wheezing from having his chest crushed. "Just…sore. Thank you, Woad." He took the other's hand, allowing himself to be pulled clumsily to his feet, and gratefully dragging in large lungfuls of air.

"You're going to have one heck of a bruise," the faun said with an air of excited interest. "Don't worry, I'll tell the others that you got it in noble battle. Buckling swashes! Not … you know … squirming helplessly like a trapped worm on a hook." He gave Robin an encouraging thumbs up.

"Thanks … I think." Robin rubbed at his jaw, looking around. He was scanning the confusion in the mist. Strigoi wouldn't be down for long. And he was going to be *incensed*. "Where are the others?"

"We're here!" Henry's voice came from behind him. Robin and Woad span. Henry was stumbling along the platform towards them, his arm around a freed Ffoulkes, who stumbled blearily but was at least awake and walking. Karya and Swiftwings materialised out of the fog behind them. It seemed the satyr was holding up the girl more than the other way around.

"Master Robin!" Ffoulkes spluttered, his eyes wide and shocked as they approached. "Why, never in a million eclipses did I expect to see *you* again!"

"We cannot stay here," Swiftwings told them all. The old faun looked weak but steady on his feet. He seemed more concerned for Karya than he was for himself. "We must flee, Scion of the Arcania. Leave Dis while confusion holds sway."

Robin considered telling them that there was no way to flee. There was no way out of Dis. Their only method of escape, the Glassfire Serpent, along with the Shard of Fire, had been taken by Peryl and Moros. Likely by now they were halfway across the Netherworlde.

There was no going back from here.

"This way," Karya commanded, stumbling off towards the great palace doors, tripping unsteadily with Swiftwings supporting her. Robin, Henry and Woad followed her, trailing Ffoulkes.

"Wait!" Ffoulkes cried. "We're going *into* the palace of Eris? Ahahaha, are you *mad*? We need to run! Make good our escape!"

Karya ignored him completely, reaching the doors and slapping her hands against them, finding them barred shut. "I am *done* running," she said, without turning around. "I came here for answers." She took a deep and shuddering breath which rattled alarmingly in her chest. "I have no running left in me ... no time."

"Where is Jack? Why wasn't he with you?" Robin asked Ffoulkes, grabbing the man by the arm to steady him as they quickly approached the doors. The Fire Panthea looked weak and disoriented. Robin shook his arm. "We have to find him."

Ffoulkes shook his head. "I don't know," he said. "That Grimm ... the fat smiling creature. Lord of the spiders, he took him away." He pointed upwards beyond the towering face of the palace and the great chimneys and towers rearing above. "He took him upwards. Other plans for this one, he said. Replacements."

"Heaven's Lens." Karya span at the doors, issuing commands. "Robin, the doors."

Robin urged them all to move aside and placed his hands on the doors. They were stone. Deep, closed fast and very heavy.

He had never felt so tired. His energy was spent. His mana was already spread out all across the square, filling it with fog. In truth, Robin didn't know if there was anything left inside him to draw on, his legendarily abundant mana felt dried up at last. But then he saw Karya looking at him earnestly through the glittering mist. She looked shockingly old in her young face. Thin, and brittle, and so very tired. Like one ravaged by a terrible wasting illness, robbing her of light and vitality. But her eyes were still gold, and she stared at him with demand and expectation. With the same unshakable belief in his capabilities she had always had. The same faith.

There is always more to draw on, he told himself. *When you think there isn't, there is. Always.*

He threw every inch of the Tower of Earth out of his body in a shuddering breath. The stone rang like a struck gong, and with every gasp of will straining, he forced them open. The great doors of the palace of Eris swung before them, grinding and creaking, until there was a gap wide enough for the four children, Ffoulkes and Swiftwings to squeeze through.

Dizzy and nauseous with the effort of it, Robin turned once they were

195

all inside, and with a simple bunching of his fists, caused the great doors to slam closed again with his mind.

"Rob?" Henry sounded worried. He was suddenly at Robin's side, helping to hold him up as the boy stumbled a little. "Are you okay, mate? You look like you're going to pass out."

Robin's legs felt like water. Sweat had broken out on his forehead, cold and ticklish. "I'm fine. I will be. Just … let me get my breath back," he insisted, shaking off a high ringing in his ears.

"Where now?" Woad's voice echoed strangely in the dark interior. The huge thick doors had effectively cut off the noises and shouts, the fireworks and fury, the confusion and mist. All the chaos of the eclipse and Pyrenight. They had locked it all outside for now. Everything around them was quiet and still, other than their own ragged breathing.

"We keep moving," Karya answered the faun, leaning heavily against the doors and looking as though she would like to slide down them and sleep. Her golden eyes were turned upwards into the interior of the palace. "Up, of course. To Heaven's Lens."

12

Reflections in Heaven's Lens

The Erlkingers and their rescued allies stepped away from the doorway, walking slowly into the vast room they found themselves in. It was deathly still and quiet as a tomb.

"So, this is the home of Eris," Robin said, getting his breath back. He wiped sweat from his brow with a still-shaking hand. His jaw felt sore, but he was alive. They were all alive. For now.

They looked around at the great space. Only the odd echo of Robin's words gave any idea of its immensity. The floor and walls were relentlessly dark, the light-devouring void of Vantablack. Harsh geometric lines of shining inlaid gold ran away, threaded across the surfaces in odd angular patterns, like some cubist nightmare. But far from relieving the suffocating depth of the room, they seemed designed to emphasise it. A brain-twisting illusion of infinite chasm. The hall yawned around and above them, and silence, thick and heavy, hung in the dark air. Long blunt stairs led up and away in every direction, glimmering and free-standing, with no signs of handrails or supports. Merging seamlessly with the inlaid designs of the floor, these blocky and harsh-edged golden slabs seemed to stretch away to vanishing points. Aligning with one another at impossible angles as they shone in the dark. It made Robin's head hurt to try and follow their paths.

The disorienting nature of the palace was not relieved by the many long firepits which threaded through the space, infernal glowing canals. They widened and narrowed in their lengths, toying with the depth of field and creating lies of illusion which made every step taken a gamble.

Reflecting this pervasive fiery glow, thousands of mirrored orbs cut across the patterns. Polished golden bubbles catching the scant light in the deep blackness and holding it jealously. With no clear point of reference in the flickers of gold, Robin could not have said if these globular mirrors were embedded in the floors and walls, suspended from some high ceiling on unseen chains, or merely free-floating. They could have been metres away and as large as houses, or inches from his face, small as a marble. Even if he reached out, it was impossible to tell, as his hand was lost in the flat and hungry dark.

It was like being on Escher's staircase suspended in a cosmic nebula, a galactic furnace of richness and deceit.

"That's … a lot of gold," Henry observed, a little cross-eyed.

They had not seen much of the outside city of Dis, but what they had seemed utilitarian. Sheer flat walls, functional and plain, almost as though such things were an affront to the new order. To the controlled and obedient world of the empress' rule. Within the palace was a jarring juxtaposition. It felt like cracking open a dull grey rock and finding inside a glittering geode.

They took some tentative steps. The patterns of gold shifted as they did, revealing more that had been hidden only a moment ago. Great thick pillars of squared black marble strode away along the hall, punctuating the bold space like silent exclamation marks. These standing sentinels soared up into the unseen heights above, seeming to pass around and sometimes through the golden landings and galleries.

All was gold and black and glittering silence.

"I'll say it, seeing as no one else seems to want to," Woad said. "Do you think *she's*, you know, at home?'

Robin had no idea if Eris herself was here, somewhere in this vast linear opulence, hidden in this great labyrinth of silence like a sleeping dragon guarding its gold. He found, to his surprise, that he didn't care. They were not here for her, not now. The palace complex was obviously enormous and their goal today was rescue, not confrontation. They were here for Karya and Jack.

"A fly trapped in a web would be wise *not* to seek out the spider," Swiftwings muttered in warning. "The palace of the empress is city within a city. If we are here for the lair of Nyx, we should concentrate on that. One demon at a time."

"Those doors behind us won't hold forever," Henry pointed out. "They must know we came in here. Strigoi will be blasting through them any minute with who knows how many peacekeepers behind him. We need to get a move on."

Karya made to take a step towards one of the shimmering staircases but stumbled and fell to her knees. The noise echoed oddly, receding away beyond the void and coming back to them from somewhere above, in the dizzying heights of the twining bridges spanning the darkness. The others rushed to help her.

"Damnit!" Karya hissed, frustrated at herself. Her hands were shaking. Robin could see every vein through the back of them. Her skin looked paper thin. "Stupid body, I think I'm one fallen leaf away from a full winter here," she wheezed, shuddering a little.

"It's okay, boss," Woad said quietly, kneeling on the floor next to her. He gave her a bright reassuring smile and patted his own shoulder emphatically. The girl looked at him through narrowed eyes, then nodded, and the faun hauled her weak frame up onto his back, putting her arms around his neck as he stood again, hoisting her up like a backpack, her heavy animal-skin coat trailing out behind her.

"Can you carry her?" Robin asked, as Woad steadied his footing.

"I could carry all of you, pterosaur." Woad winked at him. The faun's eyes were bright and yellow as always but, twinkling as they were, Robin saw a worry in them that Woad was trying very hard to hide. Robin refused to acknowledge his concern out loud. He felt superstitious, as though to do so at this point would bring some immediate calamity, would cause Karya to crumble away like chalk and blow away through their fingers and into the wind. Away from all of them, forever.

Woad made a show of huffing and puffing, but Robin guessed that the girl's ghostly frame hardly weighed a thing – and this was the most horrifying thing of all.

"Nyx's lair is the tallest tower," the girl said quietly, sounding as though she were talking in her sleep. "Closest to the sky. Closest to the night."

"Let's go," Henry insisted, leading the way towards the stairs, his shoes squeaking on the black and gold floor, his mirror image reflected underneath him as though he crossed a black and frozen lake. He had unslung his bow, his one remaining arrow lonely in its quiver. Like thieves, the others followed, quiet and careful as they stole through the glittering wealth of Eris' bastion.

The stairs led upwards for a great height, changing directions frequently and alarmingly. They tripped often on the uneven step height, and at times, the whole staircase seemed as though it were tilted to one side or the other. The gold-black void yawned nauseatingly at the edges of their untrustworthy paths of gold. Between this and the vertigo-inducing patterns carved and flickering all around them, it was all they could do to stay upright and continue putting one foot in front of the other. They felt great relief when their staircases left the mathematical nightmare hall far below, moving ever on and skyward as they following what seemed an endless procession of glassy golden paths. Stairs led up to other landings, other floors and other stairs. The spaces they passed through were always golden, always dark and always silent – save for their echoing steps, the soft clack of Swiftwings' hooves and their increasingly laboured breathing as they ascended, in a twisting and criss-cross fashion, the vertiginous heights.

They met no resistance along the way. There seemed to be no guards, no staff, no life at all.

But unlike the emptiness of Glassfire Manor, this place did not feel abandoned. Everything gleamed, dark and soft. There was no dust, no mess, and for all of their lonely and unimpeded progress upwards, it felt filled with a presence. Very much occupied.

Robin couldn't shake the feeling, as they climbed and threaded their way along corridors and landings, that they were creeping through the shining lair of some enormous sleeping dragon. A beast of ancient and unknowable power and rage, slumbering alone and silent, surrounded by a maze of rich and empty shadows.

Time passed and they didn't dare to stop, listening always for the sounds, somewhere far below them, that the doors had been breached, that Strigoi and his peacekeepers were inside, pursuing. They padded quietly, climbing onwards and upwards. Turning this way and that along great corridors where the smooth and polished walls were inlaid with the same eye-bending geometric designs of gold, or filled with a parade of closed doors, each edged in shimmering metals. At Karya's direction, they made their way out along wide and glassy balconies offering dizzying views down to glittering expanses below them.

The great palace here was lit everywhere with unnaturally still candles, like constellations in the dark. It must be mana that kept them burning,

Robin reasoned. It would take an army of servants to light these spaces every day. And servants were conspicuously absent.

None of them spoke as the walkways and corridors of the palace stretched ever higher. Woad was silent in his concentration, carrying his burden and friend. Henry was alert, watching the shadows like a scout, often casting furtive, worried glances at the slumped and silent girl being ferried through the darkness. Robin hadn't noticed until now, but in the dim and glimmering light of the palace, he saw that the skin of Henry's forearms looked red and sore. Had he suffered burns freeing Ffoulkes and Swiftwings from their funeral pyres? If so, Henry had made no mention of it at all.

The satyr Swiftwings walked behind him, as enigmatic and inscrutable as all his kind. He clicked along smartly on his hooves, sly and watchful eyes scanning the darkness of every empty staircase and every deserted gallery through which they passed. Robin wondered if he was listening for echoes as he would have back at his home, the great library. He wondered if the satyr was aware that the remaining relics had been taken by force and brought here to Dis. And he wondered if the library still stood. Something in him doubted that Nyx had the power to do any great harm to that building. It was a construct of the Elementals themselves, after all. It had resisted moving long ago, when the rest of the satyrs' town had torn from the earth and been moved away. Swiftwings had clearly been brought here as a punishment for helping the Scion. Robin wondered if the other satyrs, scholars of the library, had survived – or did that great storehouse of knowledge now stand silent?

Even Robin's tutor, Ffoulkes, was uncharacteristically silent as they walked on in their exhausting ascent. He was wringing his hands, clad in tattered lace cuffs, in worry. He bit his lip frequently, scurrying after the others. One of his eyes was badly swollen, and he clearly would rather have been anywhere else but here. But to his credit, for all his many faults and shortcomings, the man was still Robin's tutor, and whenever Robin caught his eye, the Fire Panthea made a show of ensuring there was a defiant tilt to his chin, sticking out his forked beard. Robin hadn't abandoned him to Eris, had not left him to burn, and he in turn, he indicated with a respectful nod, wasn't about to abandon his student, even walking into the belly of the beast.

Onward they quested, into the cavernous heights. Endless stairs, spanning great drops into darkness. Twisting snake-like along sloping corridors. Steps of gold and black that flowed upwards in spirals around immense, thick marble columns. Robin's ears popped with the height. Dwelling on the satyrs of the library as they forged ahead led Robin to think of the other people he had met. He thought of Luna, the curious, veiled soothsayer, and the lamia sisters who served her. Of the simple farmer whose cart of pigs they had ridden. Of the terrified pawnbroker pushed back into the shadows of his shop at Titania's Tears by Strigoi and Nyx. The chatty old shopkeeper who had pointed their way through the streets, and the flustered woman who had suggested he sell Woad for a good price.

They were Netherworlders, all of them. Subjects of Eris' rule. But how many of them, he wondered, were aligned with her views? From Strigoi's speech earlier and the responding roars of the crowds of Dis nobles, the rich and the powerful, it would seem that obedience and loyalty were not only valued in this iron-clad world, but expected as a natural and unquestioning state of mind. Robin wondered if perhaps this were not the case. If it was not just the openly stated 'rebels of Erlking' who stood opposed to Eris, but perhaps *many* of the inhabitants of this strange place. Simple people, caring not for politics or power, for crusades or causes. Just people, wanting only to live their quiet and unassuming lives in peace.

Wars, Robin thought, are fought between the few, but they affect the many. So many lives dragged into the gravity of a conflict, whether they want to be or not.

But surely, he thought, no matter how much the average person might want a simple and undisturbed life, when it came down to Good and Evil, it was not enough to say, 'this does not concern me'. Surely it was not sufficient to ever claim, 'this is not my fight'.

Not when camps in the Hills of Blood and Bone overflowed with prisoners, punished only for their species. Not when an entire people were being systematically demonised and driven to the very edge of their existence. But when any who would dare speak out against this horror risked finding themselves punished also … good people silenced into fear for their own friends and family, for their own skins … was that understandable? Perhaps, in principle. But was it *acceptable*?

No, he thought. There is no room for neutrality. He was aware that he sounded like Strigoi in his own head. "You are with the empress, or you are against her,' the wolf had shouted to the baying crowd. Robin found he couldn't agree more. You either embrace evil, or you make a stand against it.

He chose to stand against the darkness, to shout and struggle, even if it might be the end of him. Because to not do so, to remain silent in the face of such oppression, such crimes – that would be worse than being swallowed by the darkness. That would be becoming the darkness itself, in which such evil deeds could go unchallenged and unchecked. Everyone at Erlking was *far* from silent. Calypso, Ffoulkes, Irene, Hestia, Lady Tinda… They had chosen to stand and risk everything to do so. Hawthorn too, and many others he had met along his path. Some, like Phorbas, had died for their defiance. But he had died in defiance of this glittering gold darkness. This elegant and beautiful lie of silence.

Even Eris' closest court plotted against her, Robin reasoned. Moros and Peryl had both turned away. Strife himself, a mean and bitter shell of ambition, remained with Eris not through belief in her cause, but fear of it. Calculating survival and chance. Determined to play the odds in his own favour.

"B*ut some had come willingly,"* Peryl had said to him. *"Like Nyx."*

Nyx was the vilest Grimm Robin had met; of this he was sure. The world of Eris, the dream of her ordered and breathless world, where silence was the only safety from death, where one is always watched and controlled. A world with no way but her way, no thoughts but her thoughts, and no dreams other than power, always more power. These are things which would appeal to a man like Nyx. A man with dark appetites. A person with interests for which in the human world he would be shunned and reviled.

But when you sit at the right hand of the most powerful person in the world, there is no one else to stop you. And a dark freedom to experiment without censure. It made Robin's skin crawl.

To think of Lord Flint, worn away, chewed up and spat out by Nyx. Cast aside when he was no longer of any use, leaving Nyx to search for a new toy to spoil. This is the wages of Eris. To drink up the world and leave it in dust and ruin outside … while within, her palace glows and glows with gold and adoration.

"Up here," Karya's voice was barely a whisper, drifting in and out, but she patted Woad on the back, indicating that he should put her down.

She slid from his back with some difficulty, leaning against the wall for balance, looking like an ancient thing. They had reached a long corridor, at the end of which stood a curved archway wherein a very wide spiral staircase led away.

"Oh, wonderful," Henry said, as they all wheezed quietly. "More stairs. I hope Eris owns a slinky. She'd never be bored in this place."

"Here is Nyx's realm." Karya closed her eyes, opening them again only with effort. "His tower. Heaven's Lens. From here I fled. And to here, at last, I return."

Robin went to take her arm, to help his friend up the steps, but she shook her head, giving him a patient look.

"I have to walk in here myself," she told him. "I will meet my truths on my own two feet."

He nodded. Far below them, somewhere deep in the seductively glittering shadows filling the labyrinth of the endless palace, there had been a distant noise. Swiftwings tilted his head, listening with his keen satyr senses.

"The dark wolf comes," he said quietly. "He is inside. He is coming for us all."

Karya nodded and set off up the stairs, slowly and laboriously, and the other followed her, spiralling up towards a dark heaven.

At the top of the tower, Karya pushed open large double doors, leading them into what was clearly the laboratory of Mr Nyx, the Alchemist of Eris. It was a large, circular room with a ring of slender arrow-slit windows on the far walls of dark stone. Across from them, another great archway, mirroring their entrance, but open and without doors of any kind, led outside where it seemed they could glimpse a large balcony, a pathway leading away to what looked like some kind of enclosed roof garden. Even here in the blackness of the eclipse, the first sky they had seen since entering the palace, they could make out the silhouetted trees and the improbable glint of water. The motion of the moon in the heavens had finally cleared the totality, and the thin edge of the sun in the sky was finally reappearing, a shard of crescent fire, cold as mercury and impossibly distant in the inky heights.

Between where they stood at the doors and the archway leading outside, the laboratory itself was full. Curved tables everywhere, following the roll of the tower walls, carried the countless paraphernalia of dark alchemy and science. Tubes and beakers, small scientific cauldrons burning under low flames, letting off noxious fumes. Piles of scrolls and tattered-looking books with yellowing pages everywhere, many of them open to reveal odd, blotted handwriting in unknown languages, strange symbols and diagrams. Charts covered much of the laboratory walls, detailed constellations, dissections of animals and depictions of creatures so strange and fearful that even here, in the Netherworlde, with all its multitudes of natural wonders, they seemed to depict otherworldly demons. The most striking feature, as they stepped within – an odd and acrid chemical smells assailing their noses – were five large tubes of thick green glass. These odd containers lined the walls in the spaces between the narrow windows, topped with complicated brass lids, domed and covered in dials, cogs and snaking tubing. They were each filled with a dark greenish liquid, milky and softly glowing. They seemed to Robin to have been placed reverently, like standing statues of saints decorating the alcoves of the room. They reminded him of the specimen jars one saw in old horror movies, in which you might see a brain floating, or a pair of severed hands. The collected wonders of a mad scientist. Only these green and humming glass canisters were each taller than he was, and they were attached to all manner of hissing and clicking machinery, rendered in smudged bronze and covered in dials and levers. Thick rubber tubes and twisting copper pipes snaked between them, connecting each unearthly tank to the next one along like twisting vines.

There were two people in the room, tending the machines and the other bubbling and unfathomable instruments covering the various tables. A boy and a girl. They were standing together as Karya and her companions burst in, apparently going over some schematics. As the children entered the laboratory of Heaven's Lens, these two figures turned, and the sight of them stopped Robin and the others in their tracks.

One was Jackalope. The boy had bruises around his mouth and dark circles beneath his eyes. His grey hair was dishevelled, but although he seemed slightly disoriented, he looked otherwise remarkably unharmed. The hornless Fae stared at them with only the barest flicker of recognition. But it was the other occupant that Robin could not draw his eyes from. The other was person was Karya.

Or very *nearly* Karya. The real Karya, frozen at his side, was a grey and failing shell, but the girl before them, working in Heaven's Lens, looked exactly how Karya *had* looked before she began to unravel. How they all remembered her. Long copper hair in a wild tangle falling down her back. The same face, the same golden eyes. Whole and undamaged. The girl blinked at them, taking in the appearance of these interlopers with the same distracted lack of interest as Jackalope had. Her oddly emotionless eyes alighted finally on the girl by Robin's side; her mirror image, only with white hair and sunken cheekbones and a face as faded as an old photograph left too many years in bright sunlight.

Robin had seen this girl before. This doppelganger of Karya.

He had seen her in London at the National Gallery when he and Jackalope hid behind the door in Mr Knight's office. He recognised at once not only her striking resemblance to his friend, but more her strange, *empty* way of moving. She exuded no sense of self, no spark of life. She seemed like a waxwork or mannequin brought to motion.

"What are you doing here? Why have you come?" Jackalope asked them. He was peering at them all with a frown, as though they had rudely interrupted him in the middle of something important. An unwanted nuisance. Robin noticed his eyes seemed bloodshot. Something was very wrong.

"What do you mean, what are we doing here?!" Henry said, aghast. "We're here to rescue you, you moron!" He swept his arms around the strange laboratory. "What in God's name are you doing? What's going on here?"

Jackalope blinked a few times as though trying to bring them all into focus before shaking his head. "No, no," he said dismissively. "No, that's all wrong. You shouldn't be here. You're all troublemakers. You act like family …" He waved a finger at them, turning away and back to the worktable as though he had lost interest in them completely. "But you're not. It's a *lie*. You're rebels. I have work … Important work. I have to do a good job."

Robin took a cautious step into the workroom, looking warily between the two occupants. Everything was wrong here. Something in Jackalope's manner was too familiar. He had seen the same movements from someone else, recently. In the Black Hills

"Jack, do you know who we are?" he asked carefully. A sense of foreboding was settling in his stomach.

The older boy ignored him completely as they all made their way into the room.

"He knows you don't belong here," the girl who looked like Karya told them. There was nothing familiar in her voice. She had no inflection. The girl spoke as though reading lines plainly from a sheet. It didn't sound like real speech, more like something that had been carefully trained to mimic human noises.

"But this one does." She pointed listlessly at Karya, who seemed to be in a state of shock, and had grabbed Robin's arm for support. "This one belongs here. Welcome home, sister."

Karya was shaking her head in horror, her eyes roaming around the room, at the girl, at the large fluid-filled tanks of glass around the walls.

"Jack, snap out of it! Why are you here in Nyx's den? Did he bring you here?" Robin demanded. He pointed to Ffoulkes behind him. "Ffoulkes just nearly got put to death downstairs, are you even aware of that?"

Jackalope glanced over at both Ffoulkes and the satyr beside him, but seemed to consider them both strangers. He looked very distant. "Who?" he murmured. Then he looked away "No...you mustn't distract me. I have work to do. He promised. He can do *miracles*, you see? I wouldn't have believed it, but he can. And he promised."

He scratched at his head again, as though irritated by a deep headache. "He needed a new assistant. Last one was ... lacking. If I work hard ... if we ... if we can find another...there *has to be* another out there, just one more ..." He leaned against the table over which he stood, swaying a little. His fingers bunched in a sheaf of scattered notes. He turned again and looked directly at Robin, who was taken aback at the look in Jackalope's eyes. They were shining suddenly. It looked for all the world like hope. Some kind of desperate, cold hope.

"You'd never understand," he said. "If we can find another feather, we can *bring him back*, you see? He will bring him back ... for me. Nyx can do that." He nodded as though convincing himself. "He says Eris wants it ... That all that was done to us ... She wants to make it right. She will allow it. Nyx will bring him back." The Fae blinked at Robin and the others, flinching a little under their stares. "That's more important. It's more important than *anything* else. I won't get another chance. Family is the most important."

Swiftwings lay a hand on Robin's shoulder. "Nyx has polluted your ally, Scion," he said quietly. "He has placed his spiders in him. Deep into his mind. Just as he did with Lord Flint. That much is clear to see. You cannot reason with him now."

Robin shook his head. "No, that's nonsense. Jack, snap out of it will you?" he insisted. "You *can't* be working with Eris' people. Have you forgotten everything they did to you? To your brother?"

Jack's eyes lit up at this last word, coming fully into focus for the first time. "Yes! Brother! That's the one. I had … I had forgotten the word. He can … I keep forgetting words for things … it feels like something is crawling in my head … like a … so many shadows." He shook his head, frustrated with himself. "I miss music," he said randomly.

"But yes, brother." He waved a hand at Robin. "See, he promised. If I can find one for him, for Nyx, he *can* bring him back to me. He used the last one, you see. And there aren't any more now. All the birds are dead. Plucked and burned." He pointed carelessly at Karya. "Used the very last one on *her*, and now they're all gone."

"Silver Top," Woad said, his hands on his hips. "You can't trust a *word* Spider-breath says. Have you forgotten that he wrapped you up in webs like a Christmas present and kidnapped you? It's horrible, I know. Your brother died. A *long* time ago. But he *did* die. He's gone. No-one can change that. Nyx can't bring him back. He's just using you for labour like he used Lord Flint."

Jackalope glared at the faun. "Shut up!" he snapped. "You don't know anything! Yes, he can. He can do wonders."

He turned away from them all again, crossing his hand over his eyes and rubbing the bridge of his nose with shaking fingers, clearly in pain. "I'm so tired," he said. "Of being afraid and hiding all the time. I'm tired of being lonely, even in a crowd of people like you lot. I'm still alone. I've been alone since he died." He dropped his hand and looked around the Grimm laboratory with something close to reverence. "But I'm safe here. I have a purpose. I finally have a purpose. And Nyx *can* bring him back." He pointed at Karya. "With the right ingredients. He brought *her* back. If he can do that, he can do anything."

Robin was struck with the memory of Peryl's words. *This is what Eris does.* She finds the lost and alone. Those without purpose. She finds their deepest wish, their most desperate desire and promises it to them.

208

"Who are you?" Karya asked her strange twin, her voice rattling. "I don't remember you, or this place." She shook her head, looking close to collapse. "No, that's not true. I remember, but it's fragments. Shards."

The other Karya stared back at her blankly, an expressionless doll, her eyes like polished glass. Clear and unseeing. "Who am I?" she said. "One of seven sisters. Although you're not *really* talking to me."

A voice spoke from the doorway behind them.

"You are, in fact, speaking to *me*."

Robin and the others whirled. Standing in the doorway behind them was Mr Nyx, filling the space with his ample frame and luxurious suit. His usual wide and warm smile was spread across his face, as though welcoming old friends into his home, but his dark eyes were colder than the grave as he surveyed them all. The Grimm looked terrible. Sickly and somehow diminished. Less human than ever.

Before anyone could speak, the man lashed out, flicking a hand either side of him with a striking speed that belied his size. Black whips of shadowy mana flew out and thrashed at Ffoulkes and Swiftwings at either side of him, sending them both flying off through the air like thrown dolls. They crashed and clattered against the walls, both crumpling unconscious to the floor in a heap.

"There." Nyx smiled, sounding satisfied. "No more ... interruptions." He raised a hand to Robin as though in surrender, as he saw the boy reach for his mana stone. "Now, now, young Lord of the Rebels. Let's have none of that now. You look as though one more featherbreath could cause a bleed on the brain, and we wouldn't want that now, would we? Let's simply ... talk."

Robin wondered if the Grimm looked so sickly due to the destruction of the giant spider back at Glassfire Manor. It had been formed from him, after all. The ease though, with which he had taken Ffoulkes and Swiftwings out of the picture, suggested that even in a weakened state, Nyx was dangerous. In the way of a wounded animal.

"What have you done to Jack?" Robin demanded.

Mr Nyx stroked his own eyebrow, still smiling, as though Robin had just made a comment admiring his artistry, not throwing an accusation. "Done to him? Why, I merely appealed to his nature," he said. "Opened the doors of his desires. My spiders can do that you see. What greater work is there, than the unlocking of the ambitions of the mind? For Lord

Flint Calescent, it was power, status, ambition." The large man sneered a little, looming over them in the doorway and blowing air down his nose as though these were the most lowly desires possible. "But with this young, beautifully *broken* boy ..." There was admiration in his voice, as though he were back in the gallery in London, admiring a work of art. "Loneliness, inferiority, suspicion, guilt, and my personal favourite flavour of all – *intoxicating* loss."

He looked over to Karya. His deep-set eyes were glistening, wet black stones. "It's good of you to finally come home," he said to her approvingly. "Even in such a ... sorry state. You were, after all, my one true success. The zenith of all my achievements."

Karya pointed to her odd, zombie-like clone. "One of seven sisters," she said, forcing herself to meet the monstrous man's piercing eyes. "That's what she said. What did she mean? I came here for answers. I don't have long left. Give me that."

Nyx rolled his eyes, as though Karya was incredibly dense. He seemed utterly unmoved by her condition. "I have already told you," he said. "*She* has said nothing. When you are speaking to her, you are ..."

"Speaking to *me*," finished the disturbing girl in Mr Nyx's voice.

"This one, number six," the man explained, waggling a finger at her, "was *almost* a success. Physically manifest, certainly." He shrugged his large round shoulders and sighed. "But *empty*. As much of a soulless puppet as one of Ker's peacekeepers. A hollow sack of manufactured flesh and bone. A doll, a totem. The only thing making it walk and talk at all ... is me."

He held out a hand, and across the room, the Karya-thing opened her mouth wide and a large black spider scuttled from it, dropped to the floor, swiftly crossed the room, and was snatched up by Mr Nyx, who closed his wide palm around it. It disappeared in a puff of smoke, and at the same time, the girl standing in the middle of the room dropped lifelessly to the floor, like a puppet whose strings had been cut.

Mt Nyx sighed as they all stared in horror. "I only kept that one around for company, I suppose," Nyx said. "Pardon my sentimentality." His smile was wide and cold. "After losing the *real* you. The *success*! The only recreation I managed to perfect, my seventh attempt. And you had to slip through my fingers and escape. *Such* betrayal."

Karya stared at the empty doll version of herself on the floor, shaking. Then, her eyes roamed around the tall specimen tanks lining the walls, glowing with their green and sickly light. Leaving Robin's side slowly, she walked over to them on unsteady feet, counting. There were five of them. Five hissing, mechanical tanks in the laboratory. The hideous empty doll on the floor, and herself ... seven.

"What are these?" she whispered, her voice shaking. She couldn't tear her eyes from the deep green liquid roiling in the large tubes.

"Failures," Mr Nyx said, dispassionately. And then, seeing the ghastly horror on the girl's face as her realisation dawned, his smile widened horribly at her discomfort. "*Sisters*."

There were *things* suspended inside each of the tubes. Things like her, but not like her. Some of them had hair, floating like drowned things, perhaps mercifully only just visible in the cloudy water. Some of them had faces of a sort, rudimentary – monsters drawn in the dark by children. Simple, horrific, unfinished things. Others bore little resemblance to anything she knew. Strange arrangements of parts. Mistakes that should have been destroyed. Not kept. Not displayed here like trophies.

"Karya?" Robin said, his voice quiet. He watched the white-haired girl raise a trembling hand to the glass of one of the tubes.

She ignored him, turning back to Nyx, staring at him across the room. Her face was wild, eyes wide with the horror of seeing herself reflected, distorted in the bottled monstrosities. "What *are* they? What am I?"

She shot a glance to Jackalope, who was still standing off to one side, watching proceedings with a jittery, detached look. "He said you brought me *back*. From where?"

Nyx stepped further into the room, letting the doors to the laboratory close behind him, shutting all of them in with an air of terrible finality. A spider settling comfortably into its web.

"Does it really matter to you anymore?" he mused. "I wonder. You've been wounded, I can see that. An odd side effect to the damage ... you have begun to unmake yourself, and I'm not sure if even my considerable skills could bring you back now. I don't have the tools I once had. There are no feathers left. The Calescents' bird is long used up."

Karya slammed her fist against the huge jar, making it wobble.

"What am I?" she yelled, her voice a rasp.

"You dare to look on my with such pious judgement, all of you? I am a restorer of broken things!" Nyx snapped. He indicated the workshop around them. "An *improver* on the natural order! An alchemist! An artist!"

He swept a hand across a table, proudly displaying a sheaf of yellowed diagrams. "The centaurs, the Swarm, the shidelings ... *all* my creations. Taking things that are broken or flawed, forgotten, or weak, and making them *better*." He indicated Jackalope, who was standing by his odd work-station shivering and looking sickly. "Bringing back things long *lost*. It is not impossible. Not for me." He chuckled a little to himself, shaking his head. "Although I must admit, my skills were tested to the limit. The empress had rather more *ambitious* tastes than the simple resurrection of a dead brother." His dark eyes flicked to Robin.

"The war was won. The Fae, your people, were defeated," he said. "The so-called king and queen, gone! Eris ruled. *We* ruled. The Netherworlde was *ours*. Every inch, except for the blasted ruins of Erlking, which even the great empress could not enter. But that was a small detail. *We had won.*"

Nyx took a step towards Karya, still looking sickly, sweat beading on his brow. He walked carelessly past the unconscious forms of Ffoulkes and Swiftwings, paying them no heed.

"But an idle victor soon finds himself unseated," he said. "Eris is not one to rest on her laurels. To abandon vigilance. To leave things to chance." He shook his head. "Oh no, we had fought hard to win, and we were not going to lower our guard and allow anything to take that from us, you see."

His head turned to Robin as he crossed the room. "Long had there been rumours, whispered on the wind by the Oracle, that one would come to unseat her. One who could end her rule. One who would be able to find and reunite the shattered Shards of the Arcania itself."

Robin bristled, hearing the dripping scorn in Nyx's voice.

"The great and legendary Scion of the Arcania," the Grimm said, making a sarcastic display with his hands. "A myth, a whisper, a prophecy. Likely nonsense, but Eris does not ignore whispers. And so we scoured the Netherworlde. The Grimms, Strigoi and his Ravens. Every force of Eris was bent on locating this *legendary warrior*, this ... terrible doom to our order. We would find it, and we would eliminate it before it could pose a true threat."

"You were all looking in the wrong world, you morons," Woad said witheringly, rolling his eyes. Nyx shot him a black look.

"Quite true, little beast," Nyx allowed. "We were empty handed. We found nothing. We needed guidance." He smiled proudly. "I was tasked by the empress herself with a great responsibility. An undertaking none could imagine possible. The great source of magic, the Arcania itself, was shattered of course. Our own magics were many and varied, but prophecy? Sight beyond?" He made a derisive noise. "That is no domain of the Grimms. And the many gifts of the Fae were barred to us." He rapped a large finger on a tabletop for emphasis. "We needed to tap into something *more* than the Panthea, *more* than the Fae. Something … *older*."

He looked back to Karya, his white face a shining mask.

"Something *Elemental*."

Everyone's eyes fell on the girl standing shivering by the wall, her hand still resting on one of the monstrous cylinders of vile liquid. She stared back at Nyx, seeming barely there. A light sketch of a person.

"Lost for words, are we?" Nyx asked, lacing his hands across his stomach in a show of pride. "I suppose I should be accustomed by now to the genius of my work rendering those around me speechless."

The Grimm turned to Robin. "The great Elementals, who were here before any of us. The great Elementals, who shaped this land, who first gave the gift of the Arcania itself to Lord Oberon and Lady Titania, before …" He flapped his hands theatrically, mimicking birds' wings, "fading away, out of reality and into legend. Surely you've heard of them? Seen their relics? Witnessed their gifts? Ah, the legendary ones."

Nyx grinned at Karya. "One stands before you now. Or at least, my own personal homage to them. A replica, a copy, a shadow of nature's former glory. My best work."

The relics of the Elementals were scattered throughout the Netherworlde, Robin knew. Many, once held in reverence at the Precipitous Library, were now in Strigoi's keeping. One, the Mask of Gaia, was in the Elderheart. He glanced towards Henry, at the arrow sitting in the quiver on his back. And one of them was right here in this room.

But … an actual *being*?

"I'm an … *Elemental*?" Karya breathed. She sounded shell-shocked. Disbelieving.

"After *several* extremely failed attempts, I might add," Nyx said testily, sweeping a hand at the morbid experiments held under glass and liquid around them. "You cannot imagine the amount of time it takes, the amount of skill. The amount of pain and dark and intricate magic needed to pull the essence of one of *your* kind back from the beyond. To summon your energy back into actual being." He sighed deeply and theatrically, with the put-upon air of a misunderstood genius. "Five times I failed, five feathers I wasted from that moulting bird. Creating useless monsters each time! Creatures whose very existence, every second, is an unnatural, unfathomable agony."

"*Is?*" Karya looked like she was going to throw up. The thing in the tube beside her moved softly and slowly, rolling over, half glimpsed in the dark liquid. "These … they're still alive?" Her voice cracked with horror.

"The sixth time," Nyx continued, as though his monstrosity was a mere footnote, "I was almost there, so very close!" He looked sadly at the doll-like version of Karya lying empty on the floor. "The *vessel* worked, yes, but I could not hold *you* inside it. Your Elemental nature, it's very hard to control, even for me. Like trying to bottle lightning. And let me tell you something, you valuable, expensive thing." He glared at her, as though she had been a deliberate bother to him. "It took … everything! One cannot resurrect without a phoenix feather. Everyone knows this. *Everyone*. And as we all know, that pitiful bird was hunted to near extinction long ago. Only one remained, and I used every quill of that blasted animal. Every … last … one."

He smiled. "But the fates blessed me. The last feather in existence went into *your* making. It was meant to be. It was my destiny to succeed. For science! For alchemy! For the glory of the empress." The Grimm laced his hands together, reverently, as though in prayer. "And then … there you were. Complete and whole."

He paused, as though expecting a round of applause from the room, clearly breathless with his own unmatched genius.

"I told you," Jackalope said quietly from his place at the worktable. "He *can* bring them back. He just needs the feathers, that's all."

"There *are* no more feathers, Jack," Robin breathed. He couldn't tear his eyes off Karya.

An Elemental. Torn from the void beyond the worlds and forced back into a physical vessel. A timeless, eternal creature of raw power, unknowable forces existing beyond the two worlds, beyond time itself. Nyx had made such a thing manifest. He had captured his lightning in a bottle.

Unbelievable as it was, so much suddenly made sense to Robin. Why the dryads at Rowandeepling had treated Karya like royalty. Why the Undine in the hidden valley of the frozen Gravis Glaciem had seemed to recognise Karya from long ago, but remarked how different she now seemed. Both peoples perhaps sensing the true nature of the girl. Her primal force, hidden in such an unassuming form, had echoed out to them.

The fact that Karya could remember things from long ago, before her own lifespan, before the arrival of the Panthea, from before the rise of the Fae, even. Why she was able to see into the future, or at least possible futures. Elementals exist *outside* the frame of time. Beyond it. Elemental energy is past, present and future all at once, a constant force.

"Is this why Karya doesn't need to use Janus Stations?" Henry realised all at once. He was staring at the tired girl with sheer disbelief. Nyx barely looked at him.

Of course, Robin thought. Space and distance was nothing to an Elemental. They are not tied to one world or the other. Even trapped in a physical form, imprisoned in a body, Karya had retained the ability to punch her way between one world and the next. Her unique skills, her visions, her memories, all made sense at last.

"Why?" Karya whispered, her voice quiet but furious. "What did you want with me?" She spoke to Nyx through gritted teeth. Her white hand was still on the green tube, her eyes still roaming the other versions of herself, unnatural, failed, in constant pain, any one of these could have been her own fate. "A toy for your empress?"

"No, no, little one," Nyx said, tutting, as though he thought Karya was being unnecessarily modest. "Not a toy … a *tool*."

The Grimm strode to the great stone archway, the doorless portal which looked out over the strange high roof garden beyond. "A circle of trees, a central pool." He turned back to face them. "Do you know what this place was? Before it was the great city of Dis?"

He grinned, not waiting for a response from any of them. "It was a holy site. Sacred to the Elementals. A garden of scrying, used by the Oracle herself, they say. Our glorious empress Eris built her palace, and Dis, around it. The Oracle fled north, the coward," he scoffed. "But the garden remains, although we used some skill to relocate it up here of course, out of the way of the common folk."

"You wanted my knowledge," Karya realised.

Nyx nodded. "Now, at last, you understand your purpose!" he said. "We couldn't find this threatening spectre. This elusive and dangerous 'Scion' who was rumoured to be fated to unseat us all. But we know the Elementals see forward and back. We needed *you* to scry. We had failed to locate where in the Netherworlde this looming threat might be." He bowed, almost respectfully, to the frozen girl. "You are the Elemental of Earth, child. *Wherever* the Scion of the Arcania may be standing, he could not hide from *you*. We knew you would be able to find him."

"I've seen this garden," Robin said to Nyx. "In my vision; when I held the phoenix quill, your final one, that burned out tool. I saw these trees covered in your webs. How you and your dark mana had *corrupted* this place."

Nyx's beetling eyes were still trained on Karya, ignoring all else.

"You found the Scion!" Nyx said, rumbling with pride. "Your mind was shattered, broken and confused. New-born. You barely knew who or what you were, only that you were a possession of the empress, and you had been given a task to complete." He gritted his teeth. "Find the enemy, so we can eliminate the future threat!"

"I scried …" Karya remembered, staring out into the garden. "I found the changeling." She looked across the room to Robin, her eyes suddenly full of tears.

"Robin, I'm so sorry," she said. "It's true. I remember now. I found you. They were expecting some kind of great warrior. But I learned you were in the human world. Defenceless, ignorant, just a child." She looked down at her own frail white hands. They were shaking. "That's when everything began. You should have stayed safe. Hidden. Your grandmother is dead because of me."

Robin shook his head, staring back at her, lost in her guilt and revelations. "You didn't know what they would do," he said to her.

"Oh, but we got *so much more* than we expected from you, didn't we, little Elemental?" Nyx interrupted, grinning hungrily. "You exceeded all of our expectations at the scrying pool. You didn't *just* find the Scion for us. Your trance was deep, and it revealed much more than a helpless, clueless boy squirrelled away in another world."

Robin tore his eyes away from his friend, glaring at Nyx, standing framed in the archway.

"You uncovered a great secret of the king and queen," the loathsome Grimm whispered. "You saw further and deeper, into something they didn't want *anyone* to know about. A book. The deepest hidden secret. The cubiculu-argentum."

Karya shook her head in confusion. "I don't remember. I saw…a lot of things. Pasts, futures." She looked to Robin; her golden eyes wild. "I saw a vision of you in the future, Robin. In that vision I saw *hope* for the Netherworlde. They brought me into being to ensure their *victory*, and in my scrying, I saw the key to their *defeat* ... in you."

She stared out of the loathsome laboratory, at the circle of trees in the roof garden beyond, dark and shadowy beneath the night-time sky of Pyrenight. The sun was still a crescent, hanging above the pool

"I remember that much." She looked back to Robin. "It's why I ran. It's why I fled this vile place," she said. "To find you before they did. Strife and his dogs had already been set to hunting you. I *had* to find you first. I had to get you to Erlking, to *safety*. I had revealed your existence to Eris. Put you in danger ... put the only hope for the future of the Netherworlde at risk. I barely knew what I was, but I knew I had to undo my mistake. I had to get to you before they snuffed you out." She ran her fingers through her brittle white hair. "I forgot ... a lot of this ... after that. The further from the pool I got, the less clear everything became."

"Well, this has all been a *very* touching reunion," Nyx said, snapping their attention back to him. "But because of your sudden disappearance, your utter *betrayal* of your purpose and your empress, I suffered great losses." His lip curled, baring his teeth. "We had lost our greatest tool. You can have little understanding of what it means to be on the receiving end of the empress' displeasure for such a failure."

Robin thought of the other Grimms and figured he had a reasonably good impression.

"To redeem myself, I have been heading the search for this fabled lost book ever since," Nyx said. "Even scouring the vile human world, walking amongst those pathetic creatures in the guise of Mr Knight. A pale imitation of my true self, I'm sure you'll agree."

He regarded Karya with something that was a twisted parody of affection. There was no humanity in his stare. He looked over her as one might a great work of art, not a person.

"But I could never recreate you, my dear. Not without another phoenix feather or the power of ultimate resurrection, ultimate fire."

"You'll *never* get your vile hands on the Shard of Fire," Robin said, his voice shaking. "Or a phoenix feather."

"Considering how much time I have devoted to scouring both worlds looking for the lost halves of the Shard of Fire, I think I deserve both!"

Nyx snapped, suddenly vicious. He took a deep breath, regaining his composure.

"Presenting the Glassfire Serpent to the empress was to be my *redemption*!" he said dangerously. "To earn back my honour after the betrayals of this little one quivering here. And you … you have *taken* that from me."

Behind his friendly smile, Mr Nyx was grinding his teeth and these final words came out with strained venom.

"You are a creature utterly *without* honour," Robin said. He looked around the room, at the hateful and horror-filled vials of wasted life and eternal pain. At the girl he knew, faded to a dying ember and lost in revelation. He looked at Jackalope, mind scrambled by Nyx's venomous lies and promises.

And this old man talked proudly of these nightmares. He dared to speak of honour and glory.

Robin stood with fists clenched, knuckles white, at the vile injustice of Nyx. His mana stone was indeed cold and dead, as empty on his chest as an abandoned shell washed up on a beach. But it didn't matter. A fury was in him. He wanted to cry and rage. He wanted to destroy this place, destroy this man, and all the damage he had done. For Jack, for Karya, for Gran.

The song of fire was in his veins, roaring through him without help from his mana stone. It was no sweet symphony but a deafening cacophony in his mind. His hands, still clenched, burst suddenly into flame, cold and blue, the tongues of fire roaring quietly over his untouched skin, coiling around his knuckles and between his fingers, flickering as though fuelled by a high wind.

Outside, the sun had slid silently further from behind the moon as the eclipse waned, the sky was flooding into crimson, making the boy a silhouette.

"Make … her … whole," he demanded. His voice flickered and growled, and he felt heat and fire in his mouth.

Nyx stared at him, still smiling, although for the smallest moment, it seemed to falter on his face, a sliver of uncertainty. But his eyes grew thin, black slits in a white and crumpled brow. If anything, he looked faintly impressed.

"I *cannot*," he replied slowly, with clear and obvious relish.

Robin was faintly aware of Henry and Woad moving behind Nyx.

Henry had his bow drawn and Woad was crouched, ready to pounce. Both boys were staring at Robin in wonder. Atop his head, he could feel the flurries of heat around invisible horns, making them the wavering image of a mirage on a baking road.

"There is no way to save your friend, Robin Fellows of Erlking," Nyx said, and his horrible grin spread impossibly further across his face. "She is doomed."

The man spread his hands wide. "The *means* to do so are gone, long gone. She is nothing but a failed experiment. The age of the phoenix has passed from this world, little Scion." He glanced at Robin's burning hands. "You can burn me to ashes. You can tear this tower to glowing embers, and all the righteous rage and indignation in the world will not … change … that."

Robin felt Jackalope move behind him, stumbling forward. "Wait … there is one. There is one feather somewhere, though," he said, stammering. "You said … you promised me. If I helped you." His eyes were wide and desperate. "We just have to find one … for my brother."

Nyx threw back his head and laughed. To Robin's appalled ears, the noise was horrendous. The Grimm took genuine pleasure in poisoning the Fae's mind. He had devised a fate worse for the boy than simply burning him at the stake with the others. He had filled Jackalope's mind with dark hope. Had clouded thoughts and reason, and promised the impossible. The most tempting lie. That he could take away the pain and guilt.

That for only the price of obedience, a heart could be made whole.

"Hope is a weapon," Nyx told Robin, not answering Jackalope directly. He seemed not to consider the other Fae worthy of his attention. "Serving the empress has taught me this much. If you wish to destroy your enemy, give them hope, let them believe, and then take it from them. Watch as they fall into a deeper darkness. Knowing they have betrayed everything they believed they stood for, for nothing but an empty and selfish dream."

Robin raised his hands, arms shaking as he held back his anger with all his might. Nyx looked at him pityingly, clearly calling his bluff.

"Oh dear, sweet fool," he goaded. "You are not going to kill me. You are *good*. Good to the core. It flows from you in nauseating waves. You don't have the darkness. You are no murderer." He spat the words, revolted by the Scion before him.

"No," Jackalope cried, his head was in his hands, shaking. "Not him. But *I* can be!"

The boy sprang forward with a cry, something bestial tearing from his throat, the pained scream of a grievously wounded animal. He rammed past Robin, sending him clattering sideways into one of the many cluttered work tables. As Robin fell, the pent-up mana loosed. Fire shot from his hands, two great balls of flame flying wildly across the room. They hit the roof and wall, shattering them in a deafening explosion of stone which blew a great and gaping hole in the solid flank of the tower, shattering the balcony outside. Bricks and stone and scattered masonry exploded out into the bloody sky, wrapped in a burst of flame. From the corner of his eye, Robin saw Jackalope leap through the air at Mr Nyx, who threw his hands up in shock to defend himself. Something silver flashed in Jack's hand, amidst the flames and smoke of the explosion, catching the arcane sunlight and flashing it back into Robin's eyes.

Phorbas.

The boy, the Grimm and the knife fell backwards and away, in a tumble of confusion and fury, stumbling against one of the great green vials, which toppled and shattered, collapsing around them with a flood of thick liquid and a great hiss of acrid steam which rose up thickly and engulfed them both. He heard Jackalope roar over the splintering and crumbling sounds of the tower collapsing, over the roar of the flames and Nyx's screams, but only briefly. The noise cut off horribly in the unseen struggle within the spilled cloud of alchemy.

Across the room, as the floor shook from the destruction and everywhere tables fell, their contents smashing onto the flagstones, Karya collapsed, falling into a crumpled heap, her eyes rolling back in her head. She seemed to fall in slow motion, a last skeletal leaf drifting from a dying tree. Robin, scrabbling to his knees, was aware of Woad, suddenly leaping across the room, a blue smear through the debris and smoke, to catch her, his eyes wild and shining. And behind, Henry crouching protectively over the unconscious bodies of Ffoulkes and Swiftwings, sheltering them as best he could from the dust and plaster raining down from above. Then the doors of the laboratory through which they had first entered burst open.

From the darkness of the stair beyond, figures began to pour in. Peacekeepers. A dozen of them. And striding roughly through their midst, tall and dark, Strigoi emerged from the rolling smoke and steam.

The Wolf of Eris surveyed the room. The settling dust, the huge gaping hole where the wall had been, through which the high winds at this altitude was already streaming, whipping the smoke and dust away and out into the dizzying sky, bleeding at last from crimson to gold as the last of the eclipse passed.

Strigoi watched Robin getting to his feet, unsteadily, over by the ruined wall. Woad standing, dragging Karya up, his hands under her arms, and the girl hanging as limp and empty as her doppelganger doll on the floor.

With an attitude of disgust, Strigoi flicked his hand. A wave of sheer spirit mana rolled out from him, lifting the bodies of Ffoulkes and the satyr like rags and sending them scooting across the floor to land at Robin's feet, almost knocking him out of the ragged hole in the tower wall to his death far below.

"Get your trash from beneath my feet, Scion," the wolf hissed. He motioned behind him and the squadron of peacekeepers fanned out to block the exit back into the palace.

Strigoi was breathing hard, rasping through his helmet following his chase up through the great heights and corridors of the palace. His stance was victorious. The chase was up, and here, finally, he had his quarry cornered.

"Give me the Shard. Now!" he commanded.

Robin stared in disbelief. His mind refused to think of Karya. She looked dead. She couldn't be dead. If his friends hadn't been in mortal danger all around him, he would have laughed. "The *Shard*?" he croaked.

"The Shard of the Arcania!" Strigoi growled impatiently. "Now! The Shard of Fire!"

"We don't *have* it, you stupid metal idiot!" Woad shouted defiantly, still holding up Karya, whose head lolled back. The faun looked murderous. Tears were standing in his eyes. "It isn't here!"

"Lies!" Strigoi snapped angrily. His head tilted towards the cloud of hissing steam and shattered machinery from which neither Jackalope nor Mr Nyx had yet emerged. He looked to the girl and the faun, taking in the devastation around him with cool interest.

Woad looked to Robin desperately. "Pinky. She's not moving." His voice was shaky. "Boss isn't breathing."

Henry had taken a faltering step away from Strigoi and the peacekeepers, paying them no heed at all. They may as well have been mannequins.

All of Henry's attention was trained on Karya's limp body. His face was a grey mask of shock.

Robin slipped his pack from his shoulders. "You want the Shard, Strigoi?" He reached inside, fumbling around until his fingers closed around what he was looking for.

He withdrew a red gem, casting his pack aside and holding it triumphantly above his head. The multifaceted sides of the stone glittered against the golden backdrop of the sky.

"It's yours!" Robin shouted. "Burn with it!"

He threw the gem across the room at Strigoi. The cubic cornucopia flew through the air, across the still settling dust of Nyx's laboratory, glinting and shining as it tumbled over and over, again and again through the air. Robin remembered the fire roaring at Erlking. Lady Tinda's pain fuelling the fire grate into an inferno as she told her tale. She had plucked the fire-storing gem from the hearth, drawing all of that rage, pain and fury into its crystal depths. Sealing it in, before she had passed it back to Robin.

Instinctively, the Wolf of Eris held out his hands to catch the gem. The second it touched his gauntleted claw, it activated, releasing all the fire trapped within. A great burst of flame roared over him, spreading out to the peacekeepers standing behind and engulfing them all in its fury.

The fire hit the walls, shaking them terribly, and it climbed upwards like a wave, flowing and licking hungrily over the laboratory like lava, tumbling bright and hot across the ruins of the ceiling. Strigoi was thrown backwards with the force of the blast, his armour shining in the blinding flash. His cloak singed and tattered in billows of smoke as the many feathers curled and burned.

Robin took a staggering step backwards, gripping the wall of the great ruined hole out to the sky for balance. Several loose bricks dislodged, tumbling away out into space, cast down through the sky to the city far below.

In the wall of flame released from the cubic cornucopia, the peacekeepers writhed and flailed, trapped against the burning wall. Their sackcloth bodies caught alight, dry straw. The fire was eating hungrily into them, until they resembled souls trapped writhing in the fiery lakes of hell, their empty shells casting leaping, dancing shadows on the wall behind them.

Robin turned away from the blaze, shielding himself from the heat with a raised arm as he pushed himself away from the stones. He rushed towards Karya and Woad, vaulting the shadowy bodies of the unconscious Ffoulkes and Swiftwings.

"Robin." It was Henry who spoke. He stood across the laboratory from the others, the blaze with its trapped demons at his back, the heat of the fire raising his hair. Henry was staring at Woad and Karya. He was holding his bow in his hands. The tall boy looked harrowed. Tears had cut clean tracks in the dust and grime on his face, but there was something in his voice and expression that made Robin pause, turning to him.

"I think I know what to do," Henry said, barely audible over the roar of the burning tower.

In the rising heat of the fire, the other large vials were exploding along the walls, the green tanks erupting like gunshots. A sudden movement caught their eyes, and they all looked to see Jackalope. The boy was struggling to his feet, emerging from the cloud of greenish alchemy smoke which had been whipped away in the heat.

Presumably, somewhere in the tangled wreckage of apparatus behind him, Mr Nyx lay, though none could see him. Jackalope's face looked blank. Empty and hopeless. His expression was broken, traumatised. He still held Phorbas loosely in his hand.

"You!" he croaked, his voice rasping through a dry throat. He was pointing the knife at Henry. "Stop!"

Henry ignored him. He had drawn his last arrow and was staring at it. The relic of the Elementals that he had taken from the library. The arrow that sang out to him in that strange place. The relic of Fire.

"Remember what Swiftwings said to me?" Henry said to Robin. "Back in the library? He said I would enter a heart."

Jackalope was waving the knife wildly at Henry as he tried to pick his way through the mess towards him, stumbling unsteadily over fallen rocks and timbers, flinching from the roaring fire consuming the peacekeepers and walls. The grey haired Fae had a wild light in his eyes, the spiders of Nyx still rolling in his mind. "That arrow!" he croaked, desperation in his voice. "That feather! That's a phoenix feather! Stop! I *need* that!"

Robin and Woad held Karya's wasted form up between them. The girl weighed nothing. She was still and grey as dust on a tomb. They looked across the room from Henry to Jackalope.

With steady fingers, Henry nocked the white arrow with its red and gold fletching to his bow.

"Jack," he said, shaking his head. "I'm sorry."

Jackalope stared over at Robin, Woad and Karya, his eyes wild, shaking his head. "No! No! I need it! It's my only chance to get him back! Please!"

"This is Karya," Woad yelled, his lip quivering. "Karya! She's *ours*. She's one of *us*. Your brother is gone."

"You can't choose a dream over saving a life, Jack," Robin pleaded, trying to appeal to the other Fae through his confusion and hysteria. "It's *Karya*. She kissed you, remember? She understood you. We *all* did. We all *do*."

The grey haired Fae looked more feral than when first they had met. His head was still full of Grimm spiders, Robin knew. They had made a nest in his grief. He was, perhaps more than anyone else, a lost boy.

Henry drew his bow, his eyes never once leaving Karya. Behind him, flames roared, the peacekeepers' shadows of fire and fury falling down in the inferno, toppling one by one, unwatched and unheeded.

"Come back to us, Jack," Robin asked desperately. "Don't fall into darkness. *Please*. Don't let Eris take you."

Jack seemed to struggle. He stared down at his shaking fist holding Phorbas, gleaming and sharp. He swayed back and forth unsteadily, then looked back up at Robin.

"No!" he shouted. "I *need* that arrow. She's not *real*! She's a made up thing! *You* are the ones choosing a dream!" He flung himself towards Henry, raising his knife.

Woad yelled, and Robin threw out his hand, casting a galestrike.

It hit Jackalope hard, sending the blade spinning from his hand and throwing the boy high in the air with a whoomph. His body spun up and over the flames of the cubic cornucopia to fall in the shadow and darkness by the doorway, a crumpled heap that moved no more. The flames leapt higher, obliterating him from their view.

Henry held his breath. He muttered something no one else could hear over the crackle of the fire and loosed the arrow. It sailed swiftly across the laboratory, hissing in the air. Mid-flight, it shone, bursting into white flame.

The bolt hit Karya directly in the chest with a blinding flash, knocking her out of Robin and Woad's grip and sending all three of them flying as it buried into her, disappearing with a glowing scream.

Robin and Woad scrambled quickly back to their feet as Henry sprinted across the room towards them, dropping to their knees beside the fallen girl lying on her back.

On the edge of the broken floor of Heaven's Lens, a wound of brick and stone open to a golden sky was filling with blazing sunshine. Fire licked at the walls, cleansing and purifying the dark horrors that had been held here so long. The many parchments and scribbled sins of Mr Nyx littering the room were singed and burned, pages catching and curling in the heat and being lifted away, drifting way into the sky, like disintegrating black birds.

And Karya opened her eyes.

They shone gold. All of her shone gold.

"Boss?" Woad whispered.

The glow around Karya slowly faded. She sat up. The girl's skin was flushed with health. Her hair had returned to its usual tangle of golden-brown curls. Gone were her hollow cheeks. Gone were her sunken eyes. Karya slowly stood, swaying slightly on her feet, flexing her hands, and holding them before her as though she had never seen them before. Health, vitality and power, raw and pure, seemed to flow through her, exuding from her in palpable waves. She had never looked more present. She seemed the most real thing in the room. And her mouth was set in a thin line of determination.

"It would be nice," Karya said, in a slightly wobbly voice, as she took a deep breath which was wonderfully, joyously free of rattle, "to get through one expedition, just *one*, without me being stabbed or run through in any way."

To her great surprise, she found herself immediately besieged with arms. Henry, Woad and Robin had all flung themselves around her, almost choking her in a tight hug.

"Boss, you're back. You're alive! You're okay!" Woad yelped with pure, undiluted joy. "Remade!"

"Elemental, my dear Watson," Karya smirked. "Ugh, get...off, will you? You're all going to choke me to death, which, let's be honest, would be ironic after all this."

They released her, all still staring in disbelief at her restored state. She looked a little uncomfortable and embarrassed under their scrutiny.

"What's the matter with you all?" she said. "Haven't you ever seen an immortal ancient spirit trapped in a body constructed by dark magic raised back to life by a magic arrow before? Honestly."

"It's good to have you back," Robin said, unable to stop staring at her.

The ground shook dangerously under them. The fire still raging around the ruins of Heaven's Lens was working deeply at the very structure they stood in.

"Nyx?" Karya asked.

"Dead," Robin replied.

"Good." Her eyes flashed.

"We have to get out of here," Henry said, looking around at the workshop being consumed by fire, crumbling walls and creaking roof. "This whole place is going to come down around us, and it's a hell of a long way down to the ground floor."

"We can't leave without Jack," Robin said, as they all got to their feet around the girl.

Henry glared at him, aghast and furious. "You're not *serious*?" he spat. "He made his choice!"

"We have to *go*, Pinky!" Woad said. "Eris *must* know we are here, with all this noise and fire. It's not like we've been sneaky creeping around. If the empress is in residence, she'll be coming. She won't be best pleased that we've destroyed this place, and you're in no fit state to fight her."

"I'm *not* leaving him!" Robin insisted. "I wouldn't leave *any* of you."

"Rob! He was happy for Karya to *die*!" Henry said. "He chose himself over her. He's not an Erlkinger! He never was!"

The fire had grown fiercer, pushing them back towards the lip of the open wound of stone as it gobbled the oxygen up here, high in the atmosphere.

"I don't think we could get to him, even if we wanted to," Karya said. Her hair whipped out behind her in the wind, and it was such a strange sight, seeing her strong and whole. She seemed like a small fierce goddess standing against the blazing sky. "Woad is right in his assumption. Eris *is* coming, Scion. I know the feel of her. I've been in her presence far too often in the past not to recognise it."

"We can't run!" Robin insisted.

"Rob, we *have* to," Henry pleaded. "We got what we came for. We got Karya back. We saved Ffoulkes. We stopped Nyx and we freed Lady Tinda. There's no time. You can't save everyone all the time!" He stared into the flames. "Some people can't be saved."

Something was moving in the glare of the flames. A large shape was advancing unsteadily through them. Robin caught the flash of tall horns.

"But, where can we go?" Robin wondered. He looked out of the broken wall of Heaven's Lens. The great roofs of the Eris' palace lay far below them, and dizzyingly further still – the height making his stomach flip – the great city of Dis lay beyond, the vast metropolis spread out distantly like a model. There was nowhere to escape.

"You're clearly forgetting my talents," Karya said. She rolled her eyes in an attempt at dark humour. "Honestly, you lot are hopeless. You would be lost without me."

Robin looked at her levelly. "We would," he said.

She looked away, embarrassed. "I can open a tear between the worlds," she said. "Right now, the way I feel, I can open a *thousand* tears. A thousand thousand. I can get us down to the ground, leap by leap. From this world to the other and back again. Putting miles and miles between us with each leap, you'll see." She turned back to them, grinning. "It will be fun!"

Henry stared at her incredulously, beaming and shaking his head.

"Who are you, and what did you do with Karya?" he said.

"Someone who has had *enough* of darkness. And enough of Dis." As the others watched in shock, she put her boot to the prone bodies of Ffoulkes and Swiftwings, lying tangled in a heap, and with a grunt, kicked them through the hole in the wall and out into space. Turning back and grinning, she grabbed Henry's hand, lacing her fingers through his and, with twinkling gold in her eyes, she stepped backwards off the edge, into fresh air and oblivion. Henry, yelling obscenities, grabbed Woad's hand as he followed her out of the hole in the wall, and the faun, cackling with high merriment, reached in turn for Robin.

The children of Erlking leapt from the tower of Heaven's Lens into the open golden sky beyond.

Robin heard the tear as Karya opened a path between the worlds, a shimmer in the atmosphere just below them. He closed his eyes as they tumbled out and away from the smoke and burning horrors of Nyx's workshop, a line of rebels, joined hand to hand passing down and out and between the worlds.

And something caught his other hand.

Something hot and hard, grabbing him as he fell. Robin was brought up with a jolt, his shoulder almost dislocating with the jarring grip. Woad was yanked from his other hand, and Robin's eyes shot open as he yelled in surprise and pain. Looking down, he saw Woad, Henry and Karya, falling away below him, the city of Dis a distant backdrop. He saw their shocked faces staring up at him helplessly as the three of them fell into the wavering mirage of the tear between worlds. They shimmered and disappeared, out of the Netherworlde, leaving Robin dangling by his other hand, caught like a fish on a hook.

Looking up, he saw it was Strigoi who had thrown himself out of the flames and across the floor. The Wolf of Eris was lying prone on his front, half hanging out of the broken wall of the great tower. His outstretched arm had reached down and grabbed Robin around the wrist at the last second.

Robin reached up, grunting and trying to pull free, struggling against his captor. He stared up into the grinning teeth of the carved metal face, blackened by fire. The furious muzzle glaring hungrily down at him.

"Let go!" he yelled, swaying in mid-air, his body dangling out helplessly in space. "Get off me!"

Strigoi grunted, reaching down with his other hand, trying to get a better grip on Robin. The boy was filled with such a wave of hatred for this man, such a deep loathing, he screamed and swung his free hand up, managing to grab hold of one of the dark metal horns of his helmet and started yanking.

"Where is it?!" Strigoi yelled, his hissing voice raw through his muffled armour. "Where is the Shard?!"

"I'll kill you!" Robin twisted his other hand, desperate to be free, feeling the bones of his wrist grinding against each other. The tear between the worlds still shimmered beneath him. Escape. Hope. But the Wolf held him fast in his iron claw, trying to haul the boy back up into his clutches, to drag him back into the burning tower, into the grip of Eris, to reel him back into that place of despair and hopelessness that had claimed Jackalope.

"I hate you!" Robin roared through gritted teeth. "You murderer! You killed my parents! Let go of me! I don't have your Shard! Take that news to your precious empress!"

Strigoi's head bent this way and that, twisting as Robin wrestled with his horns, dragging at his enemy. It was rage flooding through him, not fear. He wanted to tear the man's head off. All the injustice he had seen in the Netherworlde. In the Black Hills, in the Pits of Dis, here at Heaven's

Lens. This nightmare looming above him embodied all of it, and he didn't even have the guts to show his face.

"Where, boy?! Who has it? You *will* tell me, brat! The empress approaches!"

Robin almost laughed, dangling there helplessly and furiously. "Is that supposed to scare me?" he shouted up. "*You're* the ones afraid of her, all of you! Not me!"

"Witless child!" the wolf hissed. "You ignorant, arrogant saviour of the world! Tell me! Now!"

"Your own has it!" Robin spat. "How's that for love of your empress? One of your own! *None* of you are loyal! You're all a nest of vipers!" He grinned up at the wolf, furiously. "Eris will *never* have the Shard, she will *never* have the Glassfire Serpent!"

Strigoi released Robin suddenly, making to drop him, but Robin still held on tightly to the helmet, swinging back and forth as though he hung from the horns of an angry bull.

"No!" he shouted, now gripping on determinedly. "You think you got the information you want and now you just throw me away? Well, I've changed my mind. I *want* to stay! I want to see Eris! I want to see what she *does* to you, knowing you have failed! Are you afraid, Strigoi?"

Strigoi batted at Robin, trying to shake him loose, but Robin gripped the twisted metal horn tightly, swinging his other hand up and managing to grab at the collar of the man's chest plate.

"You really are a fool. Defiant child. You think your anger is stronger than Eris? Stay here now and you *will* die," Strigoi hissed. Below them, the tear in the world wavered and shimmered, still hanging in the air. Was Karya somewhere on the other side, holding it open? Waiting for Robin to come through … hoping?

"You can't threaten me. Eris will kill you before she kills me!" Robin shouted defiantly. He grappled at the helmet, pulling at the frozen wolf maw. "What kind of monster fears monsters? What are you under there?!" Robin wanted to know. He needed to know. He needed to stare into the face of Strigoi. He had seen the darkness in Strife's eyes. He had seen the madness in Moros, and the evil joy in the wide grin of Nyx. No monster deserved to hide from him. Robin would allow no more shadows.

"You do not decide when you die!" Strigoi roared. "You may wield the Arcania, boy, but know this! Your death and your life belong to me!"

The wolf twisted, trying to wrench free, and with a squeal, his helmet came apart. The faceplate fell, a separate piece, and the horned surround slipped from his head, loose in Robin's hands as, wide-eyed, losing his grip, he fell.

Strigoi's hand shot out and caught him by the wrist as Robin lost his desperate struggling hold, the separated pieces of his headgear tumbling away and into the air, flashes of metal, and for a moment, he held him there swaying, as layers of armour fell from his head.

Robin hadn't known what darkness lay within the wolf. Fur or teeth, scales or shadow, but now he stared up in disbelief.

A man stared down at him. Face pale, jaw strong and clean shaven. Hazel eyes furrowed under thick black eyebrows. A thin silver scar traced a line diagonally from the bridge of his nose, across his eyebrow to his forehead, a lightning trail. In a thick mane of curled hair, black as coal, there were ram's horns, twining close to the man's head.

The two stared at one another in shock for a moment. Caught between fire and shadow above, and golden light below. The Scion and the Wolf, suspended between the worlds.

"You ..." Robin stuttered, breathless with shock. "*You're a Fae.*"

Strigoi opened his hand, releasing the boy, and Robin fell, unable to stop himself, grabbing at nothing as he plummeted helplessly through the air, watching the pale and shocked face stare down at him from the ruins of the tower.

Robin fell through the tear, its golden mists rushing up to envelop him in a soft and silent cloud, and the Netherworlde was swallowed away.

Robin fell from

World

to

World

230

The golden sky of the Netherworlde was gone, replaced suddenly with another, this one tumultuous with snowy clouds and icy air.

There was another tear in this world, just below. He fell into this one too, leaving as soon as he had entered.

Another sky. The Netherworlde again. But not Dis. Somewhere else, scattered clouds, blue sky. And Robin tumbled through them, misty and cold, and into another tear below.

The human world now. Bright blue sky, a white trail, the jet-stream of an aeroplane briefly glimpsed high above, and another tear below, carrying him away again.

Karya had not been merely boasting about her restored talents. Back and forth Robin fell, layers upon layers of gaps between the worlds, through which he plummeted, tumbling over and over until he no longer knew which way he faced, or through which world he was falling. Each tear was not only taking him lower, but also travelling in distance, miles and miles each time away from Dis, crossing back and forth between the geography of the worlds in a series of blips. Morse code writ large in magic and the fabric of reality, etched across two skies.

Karya had laid out a pathway for them, stitching the two worlds together, back and forth and back again. Robin fell through skies of gold and grey and blue. Through cloud and ice and sun and snow. And in his mind he heard Woad's imagined voice: *She's just showing off now.*

And he thought: *I'm going to throw up, or pass out, or both.*

The worlds passed back and forth before his vision, faster and faster in a strobe, until they were a blur, and in every world, in every sky, Robin saw Strigoi's face.

He hit the ground, not nearly as hard as he'd expected to. Landing in a deep flurry of cold snow, somewhere in the dark. The wind was whipping around him.

"He's here! He's here! He made it!"

That was Woad, he thought, his eyes still closed, as he waited for the world around him to stop spinning. He felt like it might never. Robin wondered, vaguely and distantly, where they were. He opened his eyes and looked upwards. A field, somewhere high and hilly. Stars shone down on him. The sky was clear and icy cold. He could hear distant muffled traffic. A motorway perhaps, somewhere nearby.

The human world, then, he thought absently.

"I think we're near Glasgow," he heard Karya's voice. Even after everything they had been through, or perhaps because of it, the sound of her healthy and hale was wonderful to him. Like song. "I mean, I can't be absolutely certain, but we're at a lot higher elevation than we were in Dis. Honestly, I've never done that before. Do you have any idea of the calculations I had to do to move us far enough and fast enough and high enough so that the drop from Heaven's Lens was actually only about fifteen feet or so?"

From somewhere nearby came the less song-like sound of Henry being violently sick.

"Can we *please* go home now?" the boy complained.

Robin closed his eyes again and lay in the snow, shivering slightly, and exhausted, but content to wait for his friends to find him in the dark.

13

Found and Lost

A week later, after an initial day of moving across the country, with much less haste, through Karya's rips in reality, followed by time spent resting and healing back home, Robin was standing alone in the quiet chimney of the necessarium at Erlking Hall.

When Henry entered, his arms still bandaged from the elbows to the wrists, Robin didn't hear him approach. He had headphones on, listening to music and lost in his own company, looking up around the twisting funnel of stone at the bright sky peering down through the oculus.

Henry tapped him on the shoulder, making him jump.

"Sorry to interrupt, mate," he said, as Robin removed his old fashioned headphones and clicked the machine he held in his hand to stop the noise. "I mean, I know you like your lonesome Gatsby moments lately, here in this …" He looked around at the carved and fluted chimney where they stood. "Charming space," he finished, lamely.

"What is it, Henry?" Robin asked. "Is Karya …"

"Karya is *fine*." Henry held his bandaged hands up. "For the millionth time this week. She's fine. Better than ever." He smiled. "Wow, I thought *I* was the worry-wart. You've become worse than me since we all got back."

He shook his head. "Our resident unstoppable force of potentially limitless Elemental power is absolutely thriving, don't worry. She's currently helping Calypso make a list of allies, as it happens."

Karya had been very focussed in the days following their return to the hall. Renewed with life, she had made it her mission to ascertain what forces they could muster to defend Erlking against Eris. Now that the empress had her hands on many of the powerful relics of the

Elementals themselves. 'We need to be ready for full-on war,' she told them all frequently.

She had not mentioned the nature of her origin once. She had not discussed her Elemental nature, and taking their lead from her, nor had anyone else.

As far as Robin and the others were concerned, she was just Karya. And they were all grateful for her.

"It's your aunt," Henry said. "Lady Irene is back from her adventures."

Robin nodded. When they had returned to Erlking, Calypso had been waiting for them, but Lady Irene had not. She still had business abroad with Hawthorn, she had told the nymph, sending Robin's tutor home ahead of her. She would return when she had set up what she aimed to do.

Robin swallowed, fiddling with the old-fashioned Walkman. He knew he was going to have to have a long conversation with his aunt. He was going to have to tell her about the Fire Shard, and how it had been lost, and to whom.

He thought of Peryl often. Very often. He wondered where she was now, her and strange, mad Mr Moros. Somewhere far from Dis, he hoped. Somewhere safe and out of sight of the forces of Eris. He had received no messages from her. The scrap of hex message parchment remained blank and quiet. He wondered what her plan was for the Shard of Fire. She was a calculating and shrewd girl, resourceful and determined, and a Shard of the Arcania was one hell of an ace up the sleeve.

He was also going to need to talk to his aunt about Strigoi. He had told the others of course, Woad, Henry and Karya, the truth that he had discovered. That Strigoi, the Wolf of Eris, the dark creature responsible for his parents' death and the enslavement of the Fae, was one of his own kind.

Robin hadn't thought he could hate the man more than he already had, but this made things worse. Strigoi was a traitor to his own kind. A turncoat and betrayer to his fellow Fae. It was no wonder that Robin had seen how much Hawthorn had despised him when they had met at Briar Hill, calling him the worst of all monsters. It made Robin sick to his stomach.

But most of all, he was going to have to talk to her about Jackalope. About terrible choices made, about corruption, temptation, and about failure. Robin's failure, although the others had tried over and over to convince him the fault did not lie with him.

What had Swiftwings said to him, back in the library? *'The road you tread is littered with sacrifices, not all of them yours.'*

"Your aunt isn't alone," Henry told Robin. "Everyone's there." He patted Robin's shoulder. "Come on, Scion of the Arcania. Mope later. Put your Puck head on. Duty calls."

Henry left, and after a moment, Robin followed, glancing down only once at the ancient cassette tape he had been playing. In scratchy biro: *To the least of my enemies.*

Aunt Irene was waiting for him in the entrance hall and Robin was delighted to see Hawthorn at her side, looking healthier and better fed than he had seen the old Fae before.

They exchanged greetings, hugging awkwardly, and Hawthorn exclaimed he had heard that his former Earth student had taken to the study of the Tower of Fire like a duck to water.

"Indeed he has!" Ffoulkes answered for Robin. He was also in the entrance hall, dressed in his usual finery and sitting nonchalantly posed on a small sofa, reading. He pointed his pipe at Robin. "But then … ahaha … he does have a most excellent teacher."

Calypso was also present, standing with Karya, both of them holding armfuls of rolled scrolls. Woad squatted at Hestia's feet in the doorway to the parlour.

"It's good to see you home, Aunt," Robin told Irene. The old woman looked at him carefully with her piercing eyes, still standing in the doorway.

"It is good to be home," she said after a moment's consideration. "And it is terribly good to see everyone here *whole.*" She nodded approvingly at Karya, before looking back to Robin. "Although it is not terribly good not to see *everyone* here."

Robin nodded to her, his face serious.

The old woman turned briefly to Calypso. "The satyr, Swiftwings, was it? He has returned to his library safely?"

The nymph nodded. "He wished for us to extend his apologies that he could not remain longer here at Erlking," she said. "But he and his people have much restoration to do. The library still stands, after all."

Irene nodded, shrugging out of her heavy coat, which Mr Drover took from her.

"You went to Dis after all," she said, turning her attention back to her nephew. There was no accusation in her voice, only a statement of fact.

"Yes."

"And did you gain more than you lost?" She now slipped off her pale wool gloves, one finger at a time.

As with most things Irene Fellows said to him, Robin considered his answer carefully for a moment.

"I don't know yet," he answered.

She nodded, seeming satisfied with this answer. "Yes," she replied. "Such is the way of life after all."

She crossed the hall to him and laid a gentle hand on his face for a moment, tilting it so she could inspect his jaw with a frown. His ugly bruise had faded now to a dull yellow. It barely hurt. "When we pass through shadows, Robin, we can emerge with them etched on our faces. You look older." She narrowed her eyes behind her glasses. "Older in the eyes, and the soul."

She dropped her gloves onto a small silver tray on an end table, as though that was that.

"But shadows pass," she said, in a much lighter tone. "What do eclipses show us, if not that? Even when the sun itself seems to abandon us, and we are plunged into darkness and cold, it is only a temporary state. The sun passes back into light, a cloud…a dream only of darkness. And that is nothing to fear, dreams."

She beckoned Robin to follow her into the parlour.

"But now is no time to rest, my young ward," she said. "Hawthorn and I have been very busy indeed. Much has been learned about the workings of Sire Holdings in your absence, and you are soon to go on a trip."

"A trip?" Henry interrupted. His father, now sitting in the parlour, tutted at his manners.

Irene regarded Henry, then looked to Karya and Woad. She sighed, looking a little amused. "Well, I *was* speaking to my nephew, but I have come to peace with the fact that the Scion of the Arcania most definitely has more than one shadow. Perhaps you should *all* come through and discuss this journey."

"A trip to where?" Robin wanted to know, perplexed as they all followed his aunt into the room.

"A journey to meet my master," Hawthorn told him. "Your admirable aunt and I have been very involved setting up a parley, tracking down various parties, and arranging a safe meeting place." He scratched at his horns. "It has taken *quite* some organising, but you, Robin Fellows, are requested for an audience with the leader of the Fae resistance himself." Hawthorn smiled, his eyes crinkling reassuringly, although Robin caught something hidden behind it. He had come to notice these small expressions which people tried to hide. It looked to him almost like concern.

"We are sending you to the underground Fae resistance, Robin," Aunt Irene said, her tone business-like. "You are going to speak with the greatest of the living Sidhe-Nobilitas ... Peaseblossom."

She turned to face him, as he, Woad, Henry and Karya all filed into the parlour after her.

Something about her posture seemed stiffer than usual, and wary.

"And, Scion of the Arcania," she added in measured tones, looking directly at him. "You are going to be very, very *careful*..."

Epilogue

In the ruined, dust-choked embers of a broken tower high in the sky, a figure lay still amongst the rubble.

The fires had long since died away. They had gutted the tower and licked away to nothingness. Night had come eventually, then day, then eventually night again. Jackalope lay still, content to despair. He watched the sky and stars wheel overhead through the broken roof and did not move.

When, after an eternity of stillness, he heard footsteps approaching softly on the stairs, he did not rouse. He did not look. There were shadows in his mind and he could barely think. Something dark, like a spider, had been inside him, but it was dying, leaching away like smoke, like a terrible dream. In its wake, there was only sorrow, and he found it difficult to bring himself to form thoughts.

When he found he could, all he saw were faces. Faces of people he might once have called friends, standing facing him across this ruined space, their expressions horror and disbelief. He couldn't bear to look at them, even in his mind. It was easier in the shadows. Quieter.

So he paid no attention when the doors of the room opened. He lay there, sprawled in rubble on his back, wishing simply not to be.

The girl who picked her way through the ruined room seemed slight. Not much older than he was himself. She wore a long dress, bright crimson edged with swirls of gold, with wide sleeves. It looked like something a princess would wear in an old fairy tale, perhaps. From the corner of his eye, trying to ignore her, he saw the girl stoop, delicately and carefully, nearby. She bent over another figure in the rubble. This other figure did not move either.

"Oh. My dear Nyx."

Her voice was a whisper. Sorrow and regret. A sigh. He watched her remove something from the figure's fallen body. It was a brooch. Her slender fingers were careful, respectful and reverent almost, as she unclipped it and slowly stood again, an elegant, willowy thing.

The brooch glittered in her hands under the moonlight, ruby red.

The girl seemed to peer down at it a while. Her long hair was loose down her back, thick and wavy, like spun gold. He heard her sigh, tucking a long lock absently behind one ear.

And then, slowly and carefully, mindful of the rubble and debris, she picked her way through the darkness towards him.

Please go away, Jackalope thought. He was exhausted. Empty. He didn't want to move, but he wasn't sure he could have, anyway. Something felt broken.

But the girl didn't go away. She knelt gracefully by him in the dirt, seemingly unconcerned about the charred debris marring the expensive crimson of her elegant dress. Her slim hand, fingernails perfectly shaped and painted a pale coral, reached out and gently brushed his hair back from his face.

"Oh, you poor broken thing," she said quietly in her soft voice. "What have they done to you?"

Jackalope swallowed. It had been a while since he made a noise, and he barely knew what to say.

"I did ... a terrible thing," he whispered. "An unforgivable thing."

"You're in such pain," she said. Her face came into view above him. He didn't want to look, he wanted anything except to look, but he had to, and she was beautiful. Young and clear and fair, like fresh water on a hot day. Her face was like the gentle light of the sun, and she smiled down at him, open and warm. Jackalope stared up into eyes which were golden, like amber. They warmed him, chasing away the chill night of the ruined tower.

"Hush now," she said, comforting him. "You've known enough pain. You reek of it." She shook her head, a tiny crease appearing in her perfect brow as she looked over the fallen boy. "I can take it away."

He blinked at her, unable to speak. His throat had closed up and he wanted to cry.

"No more of this fear," she promised him, stroking his cheek. "No more pain. No more loneliness." She smiled at him, as though he was the most perfect thing she had ever seen in her life. "No more lost."

"I don't want it anymore," he croaked. "I can't live with it." He wanted to cry, but his eyes felt dry as stones.

She nodded. She understood. "Let me take it away. All of it. Let me make you whole and strong and free. Will you let me do that?"

Jackalope nodded. He was terrified. He felt that he was lying on soft sunlit grass beneath a gentle summer sky, warm sunshine playing on his face and chasing away any darkness. And he could stay here, forever, safe. For just the price of his soul.

"My name is Eris," the girl said, lifting her hand gently away from his face. She smiled down at him once more, and then carefully, with some ceremony, she clipped the red brooch she carried to his shirt.

"There," she said, sounding quietly pleased, as though she had just sewn on a difficult button. "Now this is yours, and you are mine."

Under the moonlight, Jackalope's pale skin paled further, until it was as white as milk and he almost shone in the darkness. The grey of his hair faded, bleaching out to a white as soft as snow, and he closed his eyes, feeling a shudder run through him. The warmth had gone, the spring grass and the summer sun, and now he was cold, so endlessly, sharply cold that it numbed him. And he welcomed it. Numbness was good.

He could feel nothing.

"Open your eyes, Mr Nyx," Eris whispered softly to him. "We have so much work to do, you and I."

The hornless Fae on the floor of the ruined room opened his Grimm eyes.

They were as black as a starless sky.

CPSIA information can be obtained
at www.ICGtesting.com
Printed in the USA
LVHW030601230122
709011LV00003B/144